PENGUIN BOOKS

BRAVING *the* STORM

Elliott Rose is a bestselling author of romantasy, dark paranormal, and contemporary cowboy romances, including the Crimson Ridge, Port Macabre, and Nocturnal Hearts series. She lives with her partner and rescue dogs in a tiny beachside community in the south of New Zealand and can be found online at ElliottRoseAuthor.com or on social media @elliottroseauthor.

ALSO BY ELLIOTT ROSE

Crimson Ridge
Chasing the Wild
Braving the Storm
Taming the Heart
Saving the Rain
Bouquets & Buckles (Novella)

Port Macabre
Vengeful Gods
Fox, Thorne, Ky, Ven (HEA Novella)
Noire Moon
Macabre Gods

Nocturnal Hearts
Sweet Inferno
In Darkness Waits Desire
The Queen's Temptation
Vicious Cravings
Brutal Birthright

BRAVING *the* STORM

ELLIOTT ROSE

PENGUIN BOOKS

For a full list of content warnings, visit:
www.elliottroseauthor.com/braving-the-storm-content-and-trigger-warnings

PENGUIN BOOKS

UK | USA | Canada | Ireland | Australia
India | New Zealand | South Africa

Penguin Books is part of the Penguin Random House group of companies
whose addresses can be found at global.penguinrandomhouse.com

Penguin Random House UK,
One Embassy Gardens, 8 Viaduct Gardens, London SW11 7BW

penguin.co.uk

Penguin
Random House
UK

First published in the United States of America by Kensington Books 2026
First published in Great Britain by Penguin Books 2026
002

Copyright © Elliott Rose, 2025

Interior design by Kelsy Thompson
Images courtesy of Adobe Stock

Printed and bound in Great Britain by Clays Ltd, Elcograf S.p.A.

The authorized representative in the EEA is Penguin Random House Ireland,
Morrison Chambers, 32 Nassau Street, Dublin D02 YH68

A CIP catalogue record for this book is available from the British Library

ISBN: 978-1-405-98644-1

Penguin Random House is committed to a sustainable future
for our business, our readers and our planet. This book is made from
Forest Stewardship Council® certified paper.

*For the readers ready to wear the cuff
and get on their knees . . .
Uncle Storm will take good care of you.
If you beg nicely, that is.*

CHAPTER 1

Storm

Fucking snow.

Living in this part of the mountains is pretty goddamn awesome if you hate people, but it means putting up with being entombed in a grave of white powder and ice for what feels like half the year.

Tires crunch. Gravel sprays. Heavy metal pulses through the speakers. My truck rounds the final bend, and the A-frame peak of my roof comes into view.

How long has it been since I was last here? With one hand on the wheel, I reach up with my other hand to rub the back of my neck as I try to think.

A little too long.

Although, that transient shit was my entire life before I settled in this place. Plus, I don't mind helping a guy like Colton Wilder out.

He's about the only person in Crimson Ridge who doesn't listen to gossip or rumor.

But fuck me, after weeks of taking care of his ranch while he's been away and helping his son out as he prepares for his next rodeo event . . . I am more than ready to collapse in my own bed.

As I pull up outside the cabin, conifers stand like proud,

ominous sentinels around this place. Keeping watch over the only location I've ever felt like I can truly rest. Even if there's no guarantee that will always be the case for a guy like me.

The sky above is mostly clouded over, only partially allowing a faint glow of stars and moonlight to peer down on Crimson Ridge tonight. Drifts of snow are clumped around here and there, glowing an eerie shade of white even through the darkness. I already know that after not being here to see to things, I'll need to do a thorough check around the property throughout the depths of winter.

All of that can wait for the morning.

Right now, I just want a hot fucking shower and a stiff drink.

Grabbing my duffel from the passenger end of the bench seat, I sling it over one shoulder and heave myself out of my truck. It's only a few strides to cross the gravel and make it up the couple of steps to my front porch. As I shove the key in the lock and step inside, the warm scent of cedarwood floats up to greet me.

Fuck. Can I even be bothered with lighting the fire? Suppose I should, before I throw myself in the shower, at least. The old girl needs time to get some heat into her bones, and right now, it's as frigid as a nun's cunt in here.

When I go to kick each boot off, my hearing catches on a noise. The hairs on the back of my neck rise, and my skin prickles. Something moves deep inside the house, and I'm immediately on edge.

Not something . . . *someone.*

The distinct sound of shuffling, moving, is human. Not an animal who managed to find its way inside, seeking shelter from the tail end of winter.

Setting my bag down softly, so as not to make a sound, I know exactly where my hunting knife is, but that's back in the glove compartment of my truck. I also know where my rifle is stashed in my bedroom, but that's down the hall in the direction of the noise.

Not that I need either of those things to defend myself against some fucking idiot who thought they could break in to my place. People don't scare me. I've got a body built off the back of willingly tangling with nearly-two-thousand-pound, angry-as-fuck creatures. When you've sat on the back of a bull that wants nothing more than to toss you and stomp your ribs into the dirt, that shit fundamentally changes your perspective on life.

With a shrug to get rid of my jacket and free up my arms, I roll my shoulders inside my shirt and flex my knuckles. Tattoos and the flash of silver from my rings peer back at me in the gloom. Fitting, really—whoever this is can wear a face full of my ink and take an imprint in the shape of my metal bands as a gift when they run their sorry asses back down the mountain.

It'll be some hillbilly dipshit who married their cousin creeping up here. Fancying that they can poke around my property and find the stacks of gold they all think I'm sitting on after a pro career. Acting like I'm rich or some shit. It won't be anyone who lives out in these parts. While I might not be friendly with every single person who lives on this mountain, no one from the Peak is dumb enough to pull a stunt like this.

The short hall leading down to the bedroom is almost pitch black, but I see where whoever this is straight away. Soft light and shadows move on the other side of the open bathroom door, and I slow my progress when I realize there's music drifting softly from within.

Music?

That makes me pause. I crept this far on silent steps, and now my mind is turning the situation over, trying to make sense of whatever is going on.

I hear a feminine sound, a hum, and my eyes squeeze shut. Dragging a hand through my hair, I tilt my head back.

Goddamn, it wouldn't be the first time a fucking buckle bunny has let themselves in up here.

3

Even though I'm mildly hacked off that whoever this is turned up unannounced and uninvited, my dick stirs. The thought of a quick fuck before I kick them out and send them packing back down to Crimson Ridge sounds pretty damn appealing.

Being stuck up at the ranch and buried in the snow on top of Devil's Peak for the winter has had my balls on ice. Literally.

The blackened, twisted part of me wants to make this a game. This cunt thinks they can slip into my house and make themselves at home? Well, this is my arena, my rules.

Silently, I inch toward the open entry, keeping myself hidden in the heavy shadow, as I make my plan to find out who the fuck is in my bathroom and exactly what sweet flavor of pussy is going to be on the menu tonight.

As I get to the doorway, I watch with hungry eyes and a rapidly hardening cock to see a girl inside with her back turned. She has only the small lamp above the mirror switched on to see by. It's dimly lit in here, like the rest of the house, everything shrouded in shades of black and gray.

With her back still turned to me, she hums along with whatever folky, girly shit plays through the speaker on her phone.

Then she starts to get naked.

This girl is entirely unaware that I'm here, and fuck . . . it's the hottest thing.

She isn't doing a strip tease to try to seduce a pro bull rider. She's not a girl on a pole shoving her fake tits in my face. She's not a buckle bunny offering to get on her knees in a filthy back alley at three a.m. to suck my cock till I blow all over her face.

No. This is someone who is sexy and curvy, slowly removing each item of clothing at her own leisure. Like she's enjoying all this for no one but herself.

Jesus. My cock is begging to get in there and make a reacquaintance with whoever the fuck this girl is. I've fucked my way through life, never having repeat hookups—even during a regrettable goddamn catastrophe of a time better left forgotten—but I certainly don't remember *her*.

If I'm really honest with myself, there's no way I would.

I don't remember them.

I don't remember their faces or their names, and I certainly never kept their numbers that they sneaked into my phone's contacts when they thought I wasn't looking.

Her arms tug the cropped sweater she's wearing over her head, revealing a pair of high-waisted leggings. Fuck. No bra. Just an expanse of smooth bronzed skin and a flare at her hips. There's the tiniest roll over the top of her waistband, and that softness makes my mouth water.

Having a handful of pliant flesh to squeeze and dig my fingers into, leaving a bruise or five in the shape of my grip, is my favorite type of fuck.

The long, dark curls hanging midway down her back swish over her skin as she moves. Dragging my gaze down . . . down to an ass that is absolutely begging to be palmed and spanked and pounded into while I fill this girl's cunt from behind.

My breathing grows more ragged as I lurk in the shadowed hallway, continuing to devour the sight of the feast preparing herself for me. Because there's only one reason this girl is in my house, in search of my dick, then I'm going to enjoy every second of playing with my meal.

She strips off the rest of her clothes. Sliding those skintight leggings down, panties gone at the same time, revealing even more to me. Humming along to the music, this girl is entirely lost in what she's doing. Oblivious to her surroundings.

I'm fully hard and have to quietly, carefully readjust myself. The head of my dick has already started leaking because of how fucking hot this girl is. Her arm lifts, and I can't help but notice a small tattoo with fine-line text curving around the outer side of her breast. Tits that even from here, from a barely there glance side-on, I can see are heavy and full and just made to be tortured.

She bends over to fully tug those sinful, fitted leggings off, and that's what breaks me. I catch a glimpse of her from behind. Soft and dusky rose–colored pussy lips peek out at me.

Just at the moment she's fully naked, still halfway bent over, I strike.

My long stride closes the gap between us in a second. Wrapping one hand around her throat to lock her against my front, my other hand fumbles with my button and fly. As I do so, my knuckles graze against the bare skin at the top of her ass, brushing her lower back. Maybe I'll paint that part of her later with my cum.

"Darlin' . . . that's no way to go about begging for my cock. Kinda rude to be letting yourself in without asking," I growl, my lips pressed against her ear. "But you're lucky tonight. I'm feeling generous. So much so, after watching that little performance, I might even let you come."

She's rigid as a board beneath me. I feel her throat working frantically below my tattooed fingers. Pulse fluttering in the side of her neck. This girl is short compared to me, barely reaching my chest. Her head tucks perfectly against my torso, and my filthy thoughts are already running wild at the prospect.

"Now, I'm gonna bend you over that counter so I can fuck you into next week . . . then you're gonna get the hell off my property."

She yelps as I relent a little pressure on her throat, easing off her windpipe ever so slightly. As I do, her hands fly up to pry my fingers away, but I'm not in the mood for anything that isn't my version of this game. I spin us toward the vanity so that we're both facing the mirror.

Catching sight of her front on for the first time, I have to stifle a feral noise.

Fuck, she's got amazing tits. Hard nipples stare back at me in the reflection and the soft glow of the lamplight. Maybe because I've been stuck with nothing but cattle and horses for company this winter, I decide right then and there that there's going to be a second round to this game. I'm not going to pass up an opportunity to come all over them. Mark her the fuck up and enjoy sliding my dick between that soft valley . . . then I'll let her go.

I mean, she is naked and waiting for me in my house, after all.

She really should count herself lucky I'm interested in fucking her more than once to begin with.

As I position her body exactly where I want her, keeping a tight hold over her neck, my other hand shoves my briefs down. Freeing my aching cock, I give it a couple of firm strokes, swiping the precum off the tip. Goddamn, her cunt is right there, and the heat flowing between our bodies makes my head spin in anticipation.

Her hands fly out to brace against the counter as I tighten my hold on her throat, using the leverage to bend her forward. The action makes those perfect tits hang a little lower, full and soft.

But it's her eyes.

Eyes that stare back at me, wide like a doe's in the mirror.

Dark eyes that seem somehow familiar. More than familiar.

I was sure I didn't recognize this girl, but now I ransack my mind, trying to place her.

"What the fuck?" she croaks, sounding panicked and strained. Her voice finally breaks free as she braces herself against the sink with one hand and tries to claw my fingers away from her neck with the other.

"Uncle Stôrmand?"

I go still.

Jesus.

Fuck. *Fuck my life.*

My hand is on my rigid, leaking cock, and I'm staring at my niece's nipples.

CHAPTER 2

Briar

I'm trembling like a fragile leaf about to blow away in the wind. With wobbly fingers, I make several clumsy attempts to knot the sash around the waist of my silk robe. One that is far too thin, too short, too slinky, and made for LA temperatures.

In fact, my entire hastily packed suitcase is stuffed full of expensive clothes suited to a blue-skied day in the mid-eighties.

Clothes that he bought, because they were the type of thing I should be seen in whenever I was on his arm.

Not because I actually liked them.

Certainly not the kind of wardrobe suited to mountain survival in some back-of-beyond, snow-covered, frozen cabin. I'm almost positive there are rats in the walls, based on the scurrying I heard when I first stepped foot inside.

Yanking the pink sash to make sure it's secure, I quickly tie my hair up in a bun and do a final check to ensure I'm approaching halfway decent before venturing into the living area.

Before I figure out what the fuck is going on.

In my twenty-six years, I've always assumed I'd be at the greatest risk of a home invasion while living in the Palisades. Not barely half an hour after arriving in bum-fuck-nowhere Crimson Ridge, and not at the hands of the giant, tattooed man who nearly left a hole in the wall trying to get out of this bathroom as fast as humanly possible.

My uncle.

Technically, adopted uncle. My father's estranged adopted brother from when they were fostered together. But still . . . Uncle Stôrmand is the last person I expected to ever see again.

And now? Now I know. I know what it feels like to have his hands on my naked body. Shame coats me in a rapid, clammy sweep down to my cold, bare toes . . . because I froze.

When he grabbed me, I froze.

When he growled in my ear, I froze.

And up until the moment I finally recognized the man I hadn't seen in over ten years, I liked what I saw.

Jesus, the fucking mess made by my exploding life over the past forty-eight hours must have taken more of a toll than I realized.

For the briefest moment, with this man, all I felt was relief and anticipation colliding with an addictive hit of adrenaline. A temporary moment of insanity fisted my every last brain cell, just like his hands had grabbed hold and taken command of my body.

Guaranteed, a man like *that* would know exactly how to fuck a woman.

Relief that even if a purely carnal experience came at the hands of a stranger, I might know what it would feel like to give my body what she craved . . . something I've desired for so long, and yet I've never had a clue how, or what, that might even feel like.

Oh god, if I'm even *close* to allowing those sorts of deranged thoughts to grow roots, then I am most definitely a sleep-deprived, strung-out head case.

My feet carry me on cautious tiptoes, drawing closer to where I can hear my uncle crashing around. He sounds like a wild beast who was set loose indoors. A fearsome creature who's escaped from his enclosure.

Wrapping my arms around me, I clutch my wafer-thin robe as if I'm at risk of revealing every exposed inch of my flesh to him all over again.

The lighting in here is soft, warm, forgiving on my heartsore, weary eyes. A couple of bare bulbs are illuminated. One hangs over the tiny kitchen space and basin set beneath a narrow window. The other dangles on a wire above the weathered L-shaped sectional positioned in front of a fire.

In LA, they'd call this look rustic-chic.

Here, I suspect it's less intentional and just the interior of an old, uncared-for cabin.

Uncle Stôrmand crouches in front of the now-crackling flames, methodically feeding in small pieces of wood one after another. He doesn't look my way.

Does he come here often?

I still don't understand why he's here.

This week has been a mess, and I'm too tired after a full day of traveling, that floaty, neither-here-nor-there sensation clinging to my limbs. My eyes are scratchy. My head fucking aches.

Earlier, when I eventually located this address, found the hide-a-key, and let myself in, I took one look at that lifeless, charred fireplace and nearly cried.

I don't know how to do any of this. I don't know fires or snow or how to get by without cell phone reception.

This escape plan sounded really cute and perfect, until I arrived, shivering in the dark, and figured out pretty quickly that I was so far out of my depth it wasn't funny.

Am I a little relieved he's here to prevent me from drowning in my own inadequacy or, more specifically, freezing to death?

Maybe.

Do I need to stop staring at my uncle's ass in those jeans?

Absolutely.

I swallow hard and avert my eyes. This is so fucked up.

The man practically forced himself on me without consent ten minutes ago.

He's my father's brother.

Adopted, is all my stupid, scrambled brain seems to want to gleefully fixate on.

God. I need a drink. There better be something to drink in this place.

"Cupboard to the right of the sink. Glasses live beside the stove." Rich, gritty words drift up from the man intently focused on the fire. It's the kind of voice I'm so unaccustomed to. Weathered and gruff.

He rests on one knee, with jeans stretched tight over his backside and thighs—a place where my eyes keep wandering back to because I am so much more fucked in the head than I ever realized—while he continues to load kindling into the growing flames.

I turn in place, taking in my surroundings. There's barely four feet to this entire quaint kitchenette, laughable in comparison to the ostentatious expanse of shiny white marble I ran out of two days ago.

Hooking open the slightly crooked cupboard reveals a few different bottles of liquor with time-worn labels. Whiskey? Yes. Whiskey is the choice my fingers settle on because I am in cowboy country, after all, and I follow that by plucking a glass off the shelf beside the stove.

Do I pour one for him, too?

I'm fucking freezing. I need to dig more clothes out of my suitcase. I need to charge my phone. I need to figure out what the hell I'm doing with my life.

My uncle doesn't say anything else. Doesn't try to start a conversation or apologize or do anything remotely normal for whatever just happened back there. And I don't exactly know what to say either.

It's nice of him to light the fire for me, I guess, but I also am entirely confused as to why he's here in the first place.

This is—was—my dad's cabin. He left it to me. Before Dad's death, he hadn't spoken to his brother in ten years, not since *her* funeral.

"Do you want one?" I concentrate on pouring myself two fingers, then decide to fuck it and slosh more in the glass. Hopefully, it'll burn away the memories of the piece of shit I left behind and knock me out so I can get some sleep.

My uncle remains silent. Arms folded over one bended knee as he studies the flames.

Over the top of my glass, as I take a sip, I allow my eyes to roam freely for a second. Dancing streaks of orange and gold lick his rugged face, revealing every sinfully attractive line of ink up the side of his neck, the silver ring in the side of his nose, and flickering shadows that highlight his dirty-blond hair. Unruly, almost-curls sit tousled, as if he's been running his hands through those wild strands.

He's got a long-sleeved top on. Charcoal colored. A little threadbare, worn, rugged, just like the broody energy he emits. It stretches tight across his broad shoulders, and my mind is going to bad, bad places, seeing how big this man is. Sleeves pushed up his forearms reveal a leather cuff on his right wrist and two thick concentric rings of ink on his left. As he tosses a slightly bigger piece of wood into the flames, silver flashes on his forefinger and thumb.

That glint drags my focus to those veined, powerful hands. A grip that minutes ago was fixed around my neck, removing all capacity to form words because the feel of him commanding my body like that did things to me it definitely should not have.

Those hands decorated with inked lettering I can't quite make out from here match his throat, and as the burn descends low in my belly from the whiskey I hastily gulped down, mixed with another sensation that has absolutely no business being there, I wonder just how much of this man's skin is tattooed below those clothes.

Briar Indigo Lane, you need to pull yourself together right fucking now.

Uncle. Remember?

He's your uncle.

How pathetic and touch-starved must I be if the sight of any man, especially my own uncle, makes me feel some kind of way?

I fight back a teeth-chattering shiver—wanting some privacy in order to tear open my suitcase and find warmer clothes. Socks are a priority, at the very least. While shifting in place, I sip—or more aptly, gulp down—more whiskey.

However, I'm also hyperaware of the fact that my uncle doesn't appear to be in a hurry to leave, and this silence between us is so awkward that I don't know where to even begin.

Part of me is hoping he'll finish building up that fire and then vanish.

Surely he won't stick around . . . Will he?

An entirely inappropriate spark flares deep in the recesses of my brain. Something dangerously alluring that whispers all too eagerly, hoping this man might remain here with me in the deepening shadows of the night and the lateness of the hour.

I don't trust that bitch at all. She's the queen of poor decisions.

As I knock back another sip, feeling the glow of warmth hit my chest and start to spread through my veins, he heaves himself up.

Eyes widening, I watch him stand tall, then cross the room, and his icy-blue eyes flick up to connect with mine as I stare over the rim of my glass.

My uncle doesn't stop his advance on me. Glaring. Menacing. Each stride forward is hypnotic and dangerous, and—oh, sweet Jesus—makes my body react in a way I don't want to dare acknowledge. All I can do is flatten myself against the cracked

Formica counter, allowing him to do whatever the hell it is he desires at this moment.

When he's so close, his scent of smoke and citrus and spices rushes over me. My fingers tighten around the glass now clutched against my chest.

I'm wholly trapped in the surge of black coming off him. It feels predatory. Thrilling. *Wild.*

Tattooed fingers reach past me. The front of his shirt brushes up against my knuckles, and the heavily inked rose covering the side of his neck detailed in black and gray is so close I see the stubble coming through along the underside of his jaw.

Then, as quickly as he invaded my sanity, he straightens up again and steps back. This time, he's got the whole bottle wrapped in his fist.

"Bedroom's all yours," he grunts. Swigging straight from the neck. Adam's apple bobbing as he swallows heavily.

He turns, long strides carrying him across the room in a blink. One of those tattooed hands collects his jacket before he stoops to pick up a set of black combat boots, then slams the door as he goes out into the night.

Leaving me breathing hard and wondering what the fuck any of that was about.

CHAPTER 3

Briar

I crack one eye open. My nose feels like it's about to fall off. Coming to this place is like moving to Alaska, not Montana. I had to get up three times during the night to keep adding more clothes.

Feeling a lot like a marshmallow of a woman, I've got the covers tucked firmly under my chin and have no desire to drag myself out of this warm cocoon.

Dread fills me at the thought of having to try to figure out how to light that stupid fireplace on my own. I'm also going to have to get myself back down the mountain to Crimson Ridge without plunging over the edge of the ravine and dying in a fiery crash in the process.

I think the only reason I survived getting here last night was a cocktail of anger, desperation, and exhaustion.

My tiny rental car was supposedly fitted with winter tires, but even I know it's not suited to a remote, mountainous location like this.

Driving in nose-to-tail traffic on highways and crawling through suburban rush hour did not equip me for gravel or ice or the constant terror that a wild creature might bound out onto the road in front of me at any moment.

At least for now, I'm safely hidden here amongst the pines and the snow. I left without telling a soul where I was going, and fortunately for me, I've got a credit card in my name that none of them can trace. Maybe someone might eventually connect the contents of the will with my disappearance, but in all honesty, they only want me back for one reason.

And fuck them—I'm done being someone's pet.

I'm done living a lie and being kept inside a glass cage.

They can go screw themselves and take their little power games and corporate empires and shove them.

No wonder my uncle cut ties and didn't look back.

Perhaps there was a reason he chose never to reunite with my father after their rift. I know I certainly have no intention of ever speaking to my family again, if I can help it.

Stôrmand Lane is so completely unlike any of them. He's different, in so many ways . . .

No.

No, Briar. You need to shut that shit down. There is nothing your silly little brain needs to start fixating on or obsess over in this set of unusual circumstances.

What happened last night was clearly a misunderstanding of planetary proportions on his part, and what happened, what he did, was an accident. As soon as he recognized who I was, he nearly broke his neck to get out of there. While I have no idea why he turned up in the first place, the only explanation I came up with as I lay in bed wide awake at three a.m., compulsively overthinking everything, was that maybe he used this cabin for his hookups. Had he been expecting to find some other woman awaiting him in the dark?

God, I need to stop thinking about his hands being on me. How a split second of him being rough and demanding turned my insides molten with desire.

It's wrong. Immensely so.

Maybe I can find a cute cafe in this one-horse town and hope there is cell phone reception or Wi-Fi, and I'll get myself on one of those dating apps. I've never used one, but now is absolutely the time to learn.

I'm not heartbroken—I'm pissed off, and my pussy deserves some attention. It's been a long, long time with only my vibrator for company.

Which, of course, explains why I reacted the way I did last night. Nothing more.

I scrunch my fingers in the thick blanket. The room is barely big enough to fit a double bed, which is entirely unlike the California King I'm used to sprawling on all by myself. If two people were to sleep on this mattress, they'd practically be on top of each other.

Maybe that's the point.

Casting my gaze around the gray morning haze, I take in the room. Simple, functional finishes. A tall dresser and a freestanding wardrobe both in wood. A mirror facing the end of the bed is the only thing approaching decoration. Total log-cabin vibes.

Nothing here suggests who might have last used the place; it certainly wasn't my father. Erik Lane's taste was much more Malibu waterfront and Michelin Star restaurants where he could shake hands with self-important people. I doubt he ever set foot here, but for whatever reason, this property wound up in our family, and he left it to me. At least, he left it solely under a trust listed in my name in the will. If that was the only good thing he did for me, it gave me a place to escape and hide out when my whole world imploded.

Turns out once I knew what I was looking for, it only took me about ten minutes to uncover just how much of a cheating douchebag Antoine was. He also had the absolute audacity to make no attempt to hide what he was doing.

God. I can still see the sight of her neon-purple satin underwear stuffed in his suit pocket burned into my retinas.

My skin crawls.

Did he want to get caught? Or did he just think I was so pathetic I would never find out, or that I would be too much of a wet blanket to confront him if I did?

Did he just expect me to roll over and look the other way?

Ugh. I can't believe I ended up being someone who was cheated on.

Even worse is that I allowed myself to be in a relationship with a guy who, now that I look at it, was always going to be *that asshole*.

I'm so disappointed in myself.

Huffing out a breath, I decide to face the day.

Wallowing is not going to solve the problem that I allowed myself to be involved with a guy named Antoine Montgomery III. Or, more to the point, that I allowed my asshole family to push me into a relationship with someone on the pretense of connections and business. The Montgomerys are the type of people my father loved to golf with and name-drop into conversation. Somewhere amongst it all, Antoine was someone I tried to convince myself I could grow fond of. I was gaslit enough times into believing there's no such thing as *love* or *soulmates*, that it's only business and connections and the passing on of a legacy built on generational empires. You start to sip the Kool-Aid when you've been worn down for long enough.

My sister is the one who typically loves to hit the emotional wounds and really drive the knife home at every opportunity. *It's a small sacrifice after what you did.*

Meanwhile, my father only ever saw dollar signs in the Montgomery media empire, and Antoine's family saw power in being aligned with Lane Enterprises.

A shudder passes through me at how I managed to go through three years of being under the same roof as that prick. Of pretending to be the perfect ornament to complement his life. Even his name is enough to make me gag now.

As I swing my feet out from under the covers, the chilly air feels less than welcoming. I've got double leggings tucked into three pairs of socks and more layers than I can count on my top half.

Blowing on my fingers, I open the bedroom door, and a wall of warm air stuns me, as if I just walked into the path of a hair dryer.

At my back, the bedroom feels like the interior of a walk-in chiller in a restaurant kitchen. Whereas, in front of me, on the other side of my previously closed door, the rest of the cabin is toasty warm.

Dishes clink in that watery way they do while being hand-washed, and a sizzling sound comes from the kitchen.

Confused as fuck, I tread lightly down the short hallway—if I can even call it a hallway, since it's barely more than the length of a couple of short paces—and realize my uncle's presence fills the kitchen.

"Uhh. Hi?" Reaching up, I quickly run my fingers over my hair, tucking a few loose strands behind my ears. Do I have sleep drool on my face? I hastily swipe the corners of my mouth with my sleeve. My eyes are trying hard to look anywhere *but* in the direction of the broad planes of his shoulders.

He's dressed in a blood-red and charcoal checkered flannel shirt pushed to his elbows. From this angle, where he stands over the sink, all I can see is the outline of his muscles rippling below the faded fabric.

"Coffee's there, if you want it," he grunts. Not turning around.

Do I ever. My stomach immediately growls as the smell of whatever he's cooking fully hits my nose. It's fatty and delicious, and I secretly hope there might be some leftovers that I can steal once he's done.

I vaguely remember eating a granola bar sometime yesterday afternoon, but I didn't even stop to buy myself any groceries on my way here; being in such a state of nausea and self-disgust, nothing mattered more to me than arriving at my final mountainside destination.

A mug with a chipped rim is already sitting on the bench, and I grab the pot, sloshing some desperately needed coffee into it. As I do so, my brain starts functioning properly.

Why is he here, in my cabin, cooking?

Why is he even here at all?

"Thank you." I take a gulp. Black coffee, bitter, definitely not what my taste buds would prefer, but it's coffee, and all things considered, I'm grateful for its warmth at the very least.

He continues rinsing off dishes in the sink, placing a few on the tired, worn draining rack. Stony silence is all I get in response.

The fire cracks loudly, and I slip onto a seat tucked under the small wooden table. It's a nook that is hardly big enough for two people but offers a breathtaking view of the world that's waiting for me in the glimmers of morning sunlight.

From the looks of it, I've woken up inside a fairy tale, or a snow globe. I'm almost expecting a winter queen to pull up in a chariot pulled by reindeer at any moment to offer me Turkish delight. Dizzyingly tall trees are coated in dustings of white on all the pine needles. Piled snow is heaped around the outside of the cabin. Off in the distance, I can see a long spine of reddish-looking rock rising into the sky.

Crimson Ridge.

"It's beautiful here," I find myself murmuring out loud, clutching the mug between my fingers. "Do you live nearby?"

When I turn my eyes back toward the man mountain filling the kitchenette, my smile falls. His arms are folded over his chest, piercing blues locked on me, a snarl pulling at his upper lip.

"Are you shitting me right now?"

I blanch a little at the force of his bark. "What?"

"I said. Are. You. Shitting. Me."

Shifting in my seat, my eyes flicker around. What does this man want me to say? "Sorry, I don't mean to be rude or anything . . . I'm just curious. I mean, I've never been here before and don't want to come across as ungrateful. Thank you for lighting the fire . . ." I gesture in the direction of the flames and dare a glance back his way.

"Didn't do that for you, darlin'." His voice is mocking.

In my life, I've had very few encounters with my uncle. He was always traveling, living the high life of the rodeo star, and my dad wasn't exactly close with his adopted brother. Then things went from bad to worse between them for whatever reason when I was about sixteen, and Dad told us to never have anything to do with Uncle Stôrmand ever again.

"Utter his name into this house, ever, and I'll disown you." I still remember how terrifyingly mad he was. Spit flecking at the corners of his lips. Flush reddening his cheeks. It was a formidable sight as a young girl. Certainly enough to make me wonder, more than once, what my uncle could have done that was so unforgivable.

And now here we are, alone together on the side of this mountain, and he looks ready to snap my neck.

Oh god. Should I be worried about being here alone with him? Is he violent? A criminal?

Suddenly, the memory of his fingers around my throat flies back in, and my body heats involuntarily.

This is so fucked up. So. Fucked. Up.

"I just . . . I don't know why you're here," I mumble. Running my touch over the chipped rim of the brown mug, I kind of like the way the sharp edge of the ceramic digs into my skin beneath the pad of my forefinger. It's broken and yet somehow resilient, stubbornly still intact, looking like a relic from the eighties.

"Why I'm here?" he repeats my question, narrowing those impossibly blue eyes on me and tilting his head to one side.

"Yes. I mean . . . you didn't know I was arriving . . . I only made the decision to come here myself at the spur of the moment." With a shrug, my cheeks continue heating the longer he keeps glaring at me.

"I'm no fucking gentleman, but even I know it's not exactly polite to throw someone out on their ass when we're barely beyond the depths of winter."

My mouth opens and closes. "What?"

"I don't really give a fuck that you're my niece, or family, or whatever, but I'm in no mood for this bullshit you're selling . . . so I'll let you get a coffee and some food in your belly, then I'm taking you back down to Crimson Ridge."

He turns and begins shunting the contents of the pan onto plates and aggressively opens a drawer with a loud *thunk*. Cutlery clatters as he digs some knives and forks out.

All the while, my head is spinning.

Instinct has me moving before necessarily thinking. I'm up out of my seat and crossing the few feet back to the kitchenette without paying any heed to, or forming a proper plan of, how I wish to respond.

"Excuse me? I'm not going anywhere. Thank you for your help, Uncle . . ." Inwardly, I wince, hearing myself say the word out loud, especially considering the very *unfamilial* places my mind has drifted to since last night. "But I'm going to have to ask you to leave."

"Leave?" That drags a menacing bark of a laugh out of him. It's a cold sound, one that echoes around this small space. "You lot really are a piece of work. I bet Erik put you up to this, didn't he?"

"Pretty hard for a dead man to put me up to anything." I grit my teeth. I didn't know if my uncle knew. He wasn't invited to the funeral, and considering my father had cut him off from the family so ruthlessly, I assumed he probably wouldn't have known or, if he did, simply didn't care.

His broad shoulder lifts in a shrug. Is that his way of sympathizing? Apologizing? I don't know that I exactly loved my dad, but he was my parent all the same, and with that comes a fuck-load of complicated emotions when they're no longer around.

No matter how much they hurt you while they were still alive.

My uncle turns and shoves a plate into my hands before pushing past me. A couple of bits of extra crispy bacon. Scrambled eggs. Toast cut in triangles.

Do I want to laugh? Cry? For years, the only thing I've been permitted for breakfast is a green smoothie.

I don't remember the last time I ate bread.

Such is the vanity of LA life in the glare of the Lane Enterprises empire. Life under the fishbowl scrutiny of a million eyes and a hundred shutters clicking at every turn. I had it drilled into me as soon as I could walk that someone is *always* watching.

Hence, I've spent my entire adult life armed with nutritionists, private chefs, and wellness specialists, who have all been neatly packaged cult leaders bowing at the altar of *skinny*. All hail the latest trend, and thou shalt let nothing pass thy lips deemed to be "unhealthy."

God forbid I might be naturally curvy, no matter how many hours I spend in the gym or carbs I avoid.

My mama's genes came through strong with me, and I adore that aspect of myself. It's always been others who've seemed to scrunch their face while looking at my hips and thighs and boobs as if they were a complex calculus problem to be solved. Whereas my sister was graced with the gazelle-like bone structure passed down by my dad's unknown lineage prior to being adopted. The two of us couldn't be less alike if we tried.

I realize my uncle seated himself at the tiny table over by the window, and if I'm going to cling to any hope of making sense of this, it looks like I'll need to follow after him.

"Are you going to at least answer me?" I place my plate down and fold my arms over my chest. If I remain standing, I feel like I've got some tenuous thread of power in this conversation.

Stôrmand Lane is damn imposing.

He dwarfs the little breakfast nook and yet somehow looks perfectly suited to where he's seated all the same.

It's confusing. Perplexing. I don't like it.

Nor do I like how my skin prickles beneath the surface when I'm this close to him. As I stand here, my eyes have absolutely no business continuing to trace over the tattoos lining his forearms and hands. The veins and corded muscles revealed by his shirt rolled to his elbows are far too alluring for my health.

Yet my gaze flickers to the ink adorning his right knuckles. Letters that spell *STORM* span across each individual digit from little finger to thumb.

"My niece wants to know why I'm here?" he says through a mouthful. Mocking me again.

"Yes." I shift my weight.

"This is my house, darlin' . . . my home." He leans back in his chair and studies me with fierce, ice-cold eyes as he washes his food down with a slurp of coffee.

"So, the real question I'm needing to hear your excuse for, is why the hell *you* are trespassing here."

CHAPTER 4

Storm

"Trespassing?" Her voice comes out high-pitched.

My niece's eyes go wide. Lips parting in a way that makes my jaw tighten, because it's impossible to look at her mouth and not think about other parts of her body. Forbidden parts that have that same dusky-rose color that I should never have seen, and now . . . *I know*.

I know what Briar Lane's cunt looks like. I know how heavy and full her tits are beneath that thick sweater she's wearing. I know too much about the girl sitting in my house, drinking my coffee, eating my food, talking at me like I don't fucking belong here.

My back damn well aches after getting exactly zero sleep on the couch last night. My head pounds like a hammer on an anvil after finishing off that bottle of whiskey while sitting outside in my truck.

What in Christ's name was I supposed to do?

I'd stayed out there, hidden with only my depraved thoughts for company, until I figured she'd gone to bed and it was safe enough to come back inside.

God fucking dammit.

"You're the one creeping around in the dark, accosting me in the bathroom," she splutters, flush painting her cheeks.

"Says the girl breaking and entering in the first place. Count yourself lucky I wasn't in a worse mood."

I'm not thinking about her naked and bent over in front of me. I am not.

"That wasn't breaking and entering. I have a key."

"Stealing the hide-a-key doesn't equal permission to enter a man's house."

"Oh my god, you can't be serious." She sits down with a heavy exhale and rubs her temples. "This is my cabin. My property . . . or whatever the hell you call someplace like this. What part of that aren't you understanding?"

"Sorry, but I think you're mistaken," I drawl. Taking another big sip of my coffee, I push my now-empty plate away, noting as I do so that she still hasn't touched her food. "Been living here for ten years."

Her eyes snap up to mine. "A decade? Then why . . . why did Dad leave me the deed to this property in his will?"

My gut twists. Fuck, Erik is such an asshole. Even in death he's still interested in tipping gasoline all over my life, then lighting the match.

I shrug. Playing it off as nonchalantly as possible. "Beats me. But I can tell you right now, I ain't moving. My life is here. My business." I tap my finger against the wood surface, staring her down.

Briar looks like she's about to crumble.

I know it isn't for show. I've seen the way girls with fake tans and even faker tits pretend to cry and clutch at you to get what they want. Jesus, I've had enough run-ins with manipulative cunts to know one when I see one.

My niece is nothing but genuine in her body language right now. She's about one more piece of bad news away from

26

dissolving like the snow outside when that sun finally gets its ass out of bed.

"Eat." My jaw works as I try to settle on words that won't make me sound like the world's biggest asshole. But it is what it is really, and she needs to know that about me. "That plate is already cold, I bet, but you can shove some of it in your mouth to keep that tongue busy instead of yelping at me. I'm not interested in wasting good food on prissy little city princesses."

That seems to stir a little life back into her, and she lets out a snarl, but at least begins to eat.

She starts off slow, pecking at her plate like a sparrow. I watch on as Briar cuts herself polite, dainty bites and diabolically small pieces before giving in to the hunger as she ends up inhaling her breakfast. The entire time, making tiny noises of pleasure that screw with my already messed-up head.

As she eats, I try to remember the last time I saw my niece, who is looking decidedly un-niece-like. Instead, she is a whole lot like the type of woman I would be content to explore with my tongue until she screams my name.

I readjust myself in my seat. Fuck. This girl is young. Much younger than me, at any rate. Much younger than a forty-year-old has any business looking at.

I hate that I'm fucking forty. Also, very surprised that I'm still here to see that number.

There were plenty of days when I'd convinced myself I'd never make it past my twenties.

Turns out the pro circuit, sponsors, and endorsements don't want anything to do with a bull rider surrounded by certain kinds of rumors.

They dropped me like a cold cup of sick, leaving me with nothing.

One day, I was winning buckles and being begged for my autograph every five seconds—the next, my phone stopped ringing and my name was quietly removed from every competition event in the country.

Fuck all of them.

I survived on my own.

And now, what do I have to show for my sins? A girl sitting at my table, sleeping in my bed, bearing my last name—even if it's not by blood—and a head full of extremely impure thoughts.

Goddamn filthy thoughts I gotta figure the fuck out how to tame. I can't go walking around with a permanent hard-on in front of my own niece. Or, so much fucking worse, *because* of my own niece.

Jesus.

She scrapes her plate clean, then sits for a moment, chewing thoughtfully.

"I needed that. Thank you," she says, quietly. Almost to herself.

Something glows inside my chest as she says those words, and I quickly tell it to shut the fuck up.

Niece.

She's your *niece*.

Erik's daughter.

Yeah, that'll do it. The mere thought of my brother's name is a surefire way to replace any misguided notions I might be experiencing with pure anger.

"Can I make some more coffee before we have this conversation?" Briar asks.

I nod. "Do what you want. I gotta get some more firewood anyway."

A little time spent outside in the crunching ice and crisp first days of spring does wonders to clear my foggy head. I split a bit more kindling and take my time loading up the firewood supply both inside the cabin and on the wraparound porch.

By the time I've done all that and clomped my way back inside, kicking off my boots at the door, I find Briar on tiptoes, leaning over the benchtop, exploring the pantry cupboards. Only problem is she's gotten changed in the time I've been outdoors.

Now she's wearing pale jeans and an expensive-looking, camel-colored jersey, probably cashmere or some shit. And fuck me, this girl has got a body to worship. Curvy and sexy and a whole lot of other descriptive words I evidently need to scrub from my brain.

None of which are appropriate for the cold, hard fact this girl is not supposed to even be on my radar.

Christ, I must need to get laid worse than I thought if I can't go five minutes without imagining what her ass would feel like under my palm.

I cough into my fist to give her a little warning I'm here.

To get her to try to please stop being so fucking tempting for five minutes.

She doesn't exactly smile but ducks her head and pours two coffees before handing me one.

"Thanks." The word barely makes it past my clenched teeth. Except, that's when her fingers brush mine. As I take the mug from her, my rough touch grazes hers, and there's a crackle. A spark feels like it flows from the point of contact, and she must feel it too because those brown eyes jump up to snag on my own.

Her brow furrows, and she quickly steps back, hastily puts distance between us, and leans up against the bench, cradling her own coffee between two hands.

"So . . ." she says, carefully, before taking a sip. I see the way her nose scrunches, and have to hide a smirk in my own cup, because I'd wager everything I own this girl has never voluntarily drank black coffee in her life.

"So," I echo.

"How do we resolve this? I've poked around, and there's obviously only one bedroom in this place. So, as gracious as it was for you to give me what I'm assuming is your bed, I can't expect you to do that every single night."

"Couch is fine." No, it's not. It's fucking uncomfortable and way too small for me, but I don't want her knowing that.

"Oh my god. You slept on the couch?" She looks horrified.

"Well, where else did you think I slept, darlin'?" As I take another sip, I see her cheeks go pink again.

Interesting.

"I just thought . . ." Briar is suddenly very concerned with examining the contents of her mug.

"Go on, I'm all ears. Where'd you think your uncle slept?" Something tells me I already know what her assumption is going to be. Probably half the time, she'd be right. But certainly not last night. I had no intention of finding another bed to sleep in.

Why am I enjoying this so much? Watching her squirm every time the word *uncle* gets uttered between us. A dangerous thought flickers in my head like a neon bulb. Maybe she liked what she saw in the bathroom before we recognized each other, too.

Nope.

Stôrmand fucking Lane. Straight to hell. You are going to burn for an eternity thinking like that.

The asshole joy-rider devil who lives on my other shoulder pipes up and tells me I'm already going there, so might as well have a little fun while I'm at it.

"Just assumed you had plenty of other options for where to park your truck at night." She composes herself and juts out her jaw. "Not my place to judge."

Oh, so Briar Lane has got a bit of fire sparking away beneath that timid exterior after all.

I narrow my eyes. "Well, happy to report I was parked here all night long." What do I fucking care what this girl thinks about my life? I've been accused of far worse than being a play-boy pro bull rider with a different buckle bunny riding my cock every night.

"So, in that case, I should probably find myself somewhere to stay in town until I can book a flight, and then . . ." She trails off. I don't miss the way her voice cracks.

As I chew on the events of the past twelve hours or so, it suddenly becomes very clear. I already know this girl came here on a whim. She doesn't appear to have anything with her except for hand luggage and the piece-of-shit rental car I discovered parked around the back of the cabin.

If I had to throw a dart at why she's here, I bet the bullseye I'd land on would be that she's run away from something, or some-one, back home on the coast.

"No." The word comes out more forcefully than I intend it to. "I mean, evidently, the cabin is legally your property, and it would hardly be me doing very good job of being your uncle by shipping you off to some shitty accommodation in town."

She looks at me with . . . relief?

"Are you sure?"

"Of course." No, I'm not sure. In fact, I'm certain it's a terrible idea, but I can keep myself busy and bury myself in work and whatever pussy I can find come Saturday night.

"Roomies, then, Uncle Stôrmand?" This time, a ghost of a smile lights up her face as she sticks out a hand.

I reach out to take it. Her soft palm fits perfectly inside my calloused, rough grip, and another of those tingling sparks shoots up my arm as our hands make skin-on-skin connection.

"Just call me Storm."

There's a glint in her eye. "Okay . . . Uncle Storm."

Fuck my fucking life.

CHAPTER 5

Briar

After settling on our roommate truce, Uncle Storm—or do I call him *Storm*? I still don't know—announces that he needs to head out to the ranch where he has work booked for the day. Which makes me realize, with a jarring thud, I don't know anything about this man's life, other than having heard glimpses of his past as a professional rodeo star. A world champion at one time, no less, from what I remember people mentioning when I was young.

There were times he visited the house and met with my father in the years they were still talking, and I remember overhearing snippets of conversation. Snatches of words the two of them exchanged about things like winning buckles, and prize money, and usually what sounded like my father trying to shove business advice down his brother's throat.

I know nothing about ranches or rodeos. I also don't know anything about surviving how cold it is here. Never in my life have I lived somewhere with seasons, not even for a brief vacation. Our family trips were always the same. Tropical destinations, calculated to perfection, where my dad could spend his entire time on golf courses rubbing shoulders with wealthy and powerful boys' clubs.

"Could I come with you today?" I dry my hands on a tea towel with frayed edges and at least five holes in it. After he cooked breakfast, the minimum I could do was wash the dishes.

Steely-blue eyes meet mine from where my uncle is busy collecting his phone and keys before lifting his coat by the fleece collar.

"Out to the ranch?" He furrows his brow.

"Uhh. Well, sure . . . But also, if it's at all possible, could we maybe go into town on the way there or back? I arrived in the dark, and I think I'm going to need some groceries and things . . ." I trail off once more. God, I seem to be unable to finish a sentence around this man. As I hear myself say the words out loud I feel a little foolish—because I've got a perfectly good rental car, don't I? Which means I'm independent. An adult capable of getting myself around. For fuck's sake, I even made it here in the first place, despite all the odds and ice-bound elements stacked against me.

Except, in the cold light of day, I now feel extremely nervous about driving, especially when I've never faced snow or frozen roads from behind the wheel before.

My uncle, however, seems like he'd handle it as easily as breathing.

I bite down on the inside of my cheek before my brain can start commenting on how easily he handled *other* things, too . . .

"Sure. Might as well show you where to find everything in Crimson Ridge." He shrugs, then in a soul-stealing moment, his eyes drop down my figure.

Heat floods my pussy, lavishing me with a traitorous sweep of tingling sensations between my thighs.

"Is that what you're planning on wearing?"

I open and close my mouth, glancing down at myself, confused and determined to ignore the visceral reaction my body just had to his eyes being on me.

"Yes?" It comes out as a question.

"Nope. Absolutely not." He grunts and stomps past in the direction of the bedroom, crashing around in there for a minute before returning with a thick flannel shirt and heavy coat. Dropping both items on the counter beside me, he carries on toward the door and picks up a tan-colored cowboy hat—one I didn't even notice hanging on a hook behind the door before now—and shoves it on his head.

Do not stare. Briar, don't you dare. Do not let yourself be swept away by how unbelievably hot your *uncle* looks covered in tattoos and with his sexy leather cuff on his wrist and wearing too-tight for my sanity Wranglers. Ignore, with every ounce of self-restraint you possess, the fact he's now gone and added a motherfucking cowboy hat into the mix.

Screw my miserable life.

"Put those on. And for the love of god, I hope you've got something less flimsy to wear on your feet because I ain't dealing with you losing toes to frostbite on day fucking one out here." Then he's out the door, taking his perfectly fitted jeans with him, calling over his shoulder before the door slams, "I'll be waiting in the truck."

I've had the grand tour of Crimson Ridge.

It took all of five minutes.

This place is reminiscent of a quaint Hallmark-y setting. I'm sure there are a hundred movies where the city girl goes to a town like this and gets swept off her feet by a volunteer firefighter, his eight-pack abs, and a golden retriever named Pumpkin Spice.

Folks wave for no apparent reason. Even people passing each other on the road driving in the opposite direction of one another. What the fuck? I genuinely didn't think people did that kind of thing.

Back home, the unspoken rule is to avoid eye contact and look the other way. Strangers are exactly that: strangers.

I picked up groceries, winter-appropriate layers, and two different kinds of boots—one pair in a chunky work style, and the others are some proper black cowboy boots because my uncle looked like he was about to burst a blood vessel when he saw my white sneakers. And the whole time I had to do so while drowning in his masculinity.

His shirt and jacket are a potent scent of *man* that I'm entirely unprepared or ill-equipped to deal with. My body took one deep inhale of the collar and promptly turned into a purring feline ready to rub and twine around his ankles, drunk on a heady blend of woodiness, spices, and leather. There's a smokiness there, too. Faint and subtle, but it keeps tempting me to bury my nose in the fleece lining, chasing that charred scent.

Wearing his clothes makes me drift off into reveries of nights in these mountains, beneath the stars, curled in front of a bonfire, being held in strong arms.

An embrace that I could only ever hope, in my furthest-away fantasies, might end in heated kisses and perfectly rough touches.

"Devil's Peak Ranch is at the top of the mountain access road. Colt is who you might call a neighbor out here, except you'd be trekking a hell of a long way to borrow a cup of sugar."

Uncle Storm's words jolt me out of my daydream. How badly my cheeks flame doesn't bear thinking about. It feels like I've been caught red-handed in the act of something *very* wicked . . . namely that the stranger I was picturing was tattooed and broad-shouldered and far too similar to the man filling the opposite end of this long seat.

The truck tires bump over the gritty, rough road beneath us, and I realize we've passed the turnoff to get to the cabin.

Our cabin? My cabin? I don't even know what to call it.

Ours feels too much like we're a couple, and with my current predicament of how badly my body is behaving all because he insisted on my wearing his clothes, I'm not certain it's a good idea to entertain thoughts of anything along those lines.

Maybe I need to name the cabin. Like how people give a sailboat a name?

We carry on higher up the mountain, passing more and more snow as we do so. It's obvious, even to my inexperienced eye, that wherever we are headed, this ranch would get snowed in much more frequently.

"Do you work up here a lot?" My eyes track the scenery. There's a steep ravine on one side of the road—terrifying, thank you very much—on the other are sturdy pine trees and rock faces. Everything appears frozen in crisp shades of white and pale blue.

"When the horses need shoeing. Or when Colt needs help getting shit done around the ranch."

"Shoeing?" I give him a look, but he's concentrating on the road, and that sets my pulse a little more at ease. Not that I've been white-knuckling the seat this entire ride, but I might have been as we traversed some of the narrow bends and blind corners.

"You'll see." He doesn't give me any more than that. Around us, the truck speakers thud with a whole lot of angry-sounding drumming and aggressive lyrics. My uncle's choice in music is . . . a lot.

But he drums his fingers in time, seeming to enjoy his taste in death metal.

The din is not doing anything to calm my jangled nerves, but I'm hardly in a position to take control of the playlist.

Sucking in a breath, I focus on the winter wonderland outside, which is utterly breathtaking, prompting me to dig out my phone—which has been intentionally left on airplane mode ever since I boarded my flight—and film a little of the snowy vista as we drive.

"It's so pretty," I murmur.

And that's when we crest the final ridge, and Devil's Peak makes her dramatic appearance on the horizon.

"Stôrmand Lane's niece has never ridden a horse before?" A sapphire-eyed cowboy with an impeccable jawline leans on the side of our vehicle. Kayce Wilder was all beaming smiles and seemed friendly enough when he came out of the barn to greet us as we arrived and first hopped out of the truck.

Uncle Storm grunted something before striding away, leaving me unsure whether to follow after him, or stay put.

So I've ended up standing around in the gravel parking area outside an incredible-looking mountain homestead, trying not to openly drool over how gorgeous this ranch is.

Not that I have any experience in visiting other ranches before, but this one seems picturesque and has an energy about it I can't help myself from immediately being drawn to.

"You're for real?" Kayce looks me up and down with a bemused expression.

"Nope. I can't even remember the last time I saw a horse in person, either." I grimace and cover my face with my hands. "Annnnd now you probably think I'm some sort of city-girl-idiot admitting that out loud."

Kayce laughs, a deep, genuine chuckle that lights up his eyes. "Nah. Don't sweat it. If you're Storm's niece, you'll do just fine around 'em. That man is like the fucking horse whisperer, I swear."

I have to bite my tongue in about five ways as the immediate urge bubbles up to shout and dramatically wave my arms in an effort to emphasize that Storm and I are not related by blood in any way, shape, or form.

Except, I realize how utterly absurd that would be . . . and not suspiciously odd behavior at all.

God, I really am the queen of overthinking.

"Can we go see them?" Deflecting to something other than talking about uncles and nieces, I give Kayce a hesitant smile.

I mean, it's the truth. I am genuinely curious. Although part of me spent half the truck ride up this mountain imagining how my own uncle's stubble would feel brushing over my lips, and that hussy has an ulterior motive.

Something about the prospect of seeing that tattooed, giant of a man around animals is doing things it shouldn't inside my stomach.

Fluttery, swoony things.

"Yeah. Come on, Briar. He's only checking them out for who needs what for their shoes. Now that the snow's thawed and the forecast is good, Storm's gonna come up and get them all done."

I feel like this man could be speaking a foreign language, but I trot behind him to keep up with his long strides. With every muddy patch I navigate, I'm ever more grateful for my new boots that are keeping my toes warm and dry.

"Is this your ranch?" As we walk into the barn, I take a couple more photos and videos on my phone. This feels magical. A picture-book level of unreal. Am I romanticizing this entire moment, or does the air even feel lighter up here?

After being trapped for so long, this mountain is absolutely the place my tattered heart needs to be in order to find some solace.

"Ah, you won't get much use out of that thing up here. There's no cell coverage up on the Peak." Kayce jerks his chin towards my phone. "Reception down in Crimson Ridge can even drop in and out when the weather gets hectic. We've got patchy internet up here inside the house, at least. Drives me nuts, being so isolated, but it is what it is. Come to think of it, Storm might have only just managed to get Wi-Fi at his place. Pretty sure he lived all hermit-style without it for years."

"You know, I actually could use some digital detox time

while I'm here, so that doesn't worry me in the slightest." Hopefully, I sound breezy as I say the words. Inwardly, I'm dreading what will be waiting for me on my phone when I do eventually check my messages.

Kayce stops beside a wooden partition, and a horse's head immediately pops over with a loud snort.

The size and suddenness of the movement makes me jump and stifle a squeak. This horse is taller than Kayce is, even with his cream-colored cowboy hat on, which means they both tower over me.

"Hey Winnie-Win, meet your boyfriend Storm's niece . . . This is Briar."

My cheeks go a little pink at the introduction, but I quickly shake it off.

"Can I take a photo of her? She's beautiful."

"Of course. Winnie's a total slut for the camera. But come give her a pat and say hello first, city girl." Kayce chuckles and shows me how to do a proper horse greeting.

I'm in love within seconds.

Not with the charming cowboy—I mean, he's nice to look at, and I'd be blind not to appreciate that golden, athletic all-American glow. I'm in love with the horse. Actually, all the horses.

We work our way around the barn, and Kayce is the perfect tour guide. Which I discover is actually what he does here at the ranch during the warmer months. Visitors come and do activities like trail riding, and some even stay over at the property while they still operate a herd of cattle and run a relatively small ranch operation.

Or, at least, Kayce's dad does, and Kayce helps out, from what I can gather.

"You'll vibe with Layla when you get to meet her. She and Colt will be back any day now . . . They took off for the winter, and last I heard, they were in Ireland somewhere but getting ready to fly out."

Half my attention is on the man beside me, and the other half is on the prickling sensation that dances along the back of my neck. I still haven't seen sight nor sound of my uncle, and feel a little disappointed that I didn't catch a glimpse of him around the horses.

They're such gentle giants. Old souls speaking through big, liquidy eyes as they peer at me and nibble on my hair. Their whiskery muzzles and velvety lips explore my pockets, searching for treats, which leaves me giggling each time at the tickling sensation.

I'm aware that my curiosity is worrying, as I very much want to see what he's like around these creatures. It's barely been a day and I have an unhealthy amount of interest in the man I'm going to be leaving here with—going home in the company of after we're done here. *Alone.*

The man I should not be thinking about at all.

Kayce ushers me down past the rows of stalls filled with shavings and hay, surrounded by an earthy smell that hits my nose, and we head in the direction of a room found at the far end of the building. It smells rich and leathery inside the cramped space, and I see all sorts of riding-related equipment. Saddles and halters and stirrups, or at least, that's what I think these things are called.

Then, my eyes fall on the figure I've been secretly hoping and sneaking sidelong glances to watch out for. He's leaning over a table along one wall, flipping through a notebook, and when we walk in, he straightens up, letting the pages fall shut with a thud.

His blue eyes flicker to me, and then to Kayce. It's quick as lightning, but I see the way his eyes tick down ever so slightly.

That's the moment I register that Kayce's hand is settled on the small of my back. It's not anything more than a guiding touch, a polite motion to show me through the doorway before him, and there definitely hasn't been anything more than friendly chat between the two of us.

I feel awkward all the same.

Does Storm think I've been out here flirting and throwing myself at a man after the first sign of attention?

Would he care if I did attempt to date someone, anyone, while I'm here in Crimson Ridge?

Do I care if he cares? Do I want him to care?

Oh my fucking god. If I'm even thinking about this for two milliseconds, then that is certainly my sign that I need to try to find myself a date.

"You two all done?"

"Yup. Catch you tomorrow, old man." Kayce steps back, and I can hear the smirk in his voice.

"Meet you at the truck." A wall of muscle pushes straight past me. He does that thing again, where he's out the door without a second's hesitation, muttering over his shoulder as if I'm a giant inconvenience.

While I've been stuck in my little internal battle, the other two have been talking, and I've been completely zoned out. So now I'm scurrying to catch up with my uncle, while behind me, I hear Kayce call out.

"See you tomorrow, city girl. Wear something for riding. We'll have you up on a horse in no time."

CHAPTER 6

Briar

My boots crunch across the loose gravel as the cool early morning air whips against my cheeks. With fingers clutching my coffee thermos tight, I make my way over to the cowboy perched, waiting for my arrival, on the tailgate of his truck.

Kayce gives me a lopsided grin before jumping down. He's dressed in faded denim, a worn hoodie with a logo featuring a bucking horse, and a cream-colored cowboy hat.

This man also looks far too cheery for this time of the morning.

"Good morning, Stôrmand. Lovely to see you . . . Looking handsome as always," Kayce calls out, saluting the man who is currently making his way to the barn.

All he gets in reply is a middle finger raised in the air and the man's back.

"Come on," Kayce says to me. "You can come feed the hungry fuckers with me, and then we'll saddle you up." Kayce shakes his head, a smug expression on his face, and slams the back of the truck shut.

My scrunched eyebrows give away the fact I didn't understand a word of what he just said.

"Hop in. Come meet the cows."

"Oh, right." I slide in the passenger's seat. There are assortments of food wrappers lying around and empty coffee cups in the holders. My lips quirk. "Looks like a teenage boy stole your vehicle when you weren't paying attention."

"Don't you start . . . You sound too much like my dad spouting that kinda nonsense."

I nudge the graveyard of candy wrappers and crumpled brown takeout bag to one side with my boot. "What exactly are we doing? And please don't expect me to be anything but a hindrance."

"This time of year, we're still feeding out the cattle. If the snow's thick, we bring the horses whenever we need to get down to these parts of the ranch, but right now, the track's good enough we can sit pretty in the truck." He starts the engine, and we idle and bounce our way down a muddy, rutted path leading away from the big house and the barn. In the distance, Devil's Peak watches over the ranch. Pine trees rise up some rocky outcrops to our right, and on the left, grazing land stretches out as far as I can see.

It's rugged out here, but beautifully so.

"How do they survive the cold?" Considering I'm busy wriggling my fingers in front of the heating vent, I'm already feeling sorry for these cows being out here through the depths of winter.

"They're built for this. We run an Angus breed that can handle the ice and the snow. Even when the weather is ugly as shit up here, they can hack it. The snow packs into thick layers on their coat and acts like an extra layer of insulation."

"Like wearing a jacket?"

Kayce chuckles. "Yup, keeps 'em real toasty warm."

"But you still have to feed them every day?"

"While the snow's here, and until the pasture really starts to come away again with spring growth, we feed out."

As Kayce explains things to me, we draw up to a line of

black snouts and fluffy-tipped ears peering over the fence at us. Some hang back, a little uneasy of the approaching vehicle, while others are practically hanging over the gate, waving with eagerness.

"They knew you were coming." I can't help but smile.

"Like I said . . . hungry fuckers. They can tell time better than you or I can."

"Is that what they're waiting for?" I point toward large round bales, much taller than me, that are arranged in a long row near the fence. There's a tractor already down here, with two long, forklike prongs attached to the front. If that machinery were in the wrong hands, surely it could be lethal.

"We cut and bale in summer, then store it for winter. Keeps things simple so we don't gotta bring in feed from elsewhere."

"And you use the tractor to roll it out there or something?" I'm quickly presuming that must be the way to skewer and actually shift one of those monstrous-looking rounds.

"Sure do. I mean, ranching on horseback is good and all, but some things just need a bit of modern machinery thrown in the mix to make life a bit easier. Lets me get a good look at 'em all, keeping an eye out for injuries or lameness while I'm at it." Kayce drums his fingers on the steering wheel, not in an impatient way, but like he's got energy to burn at all times. He's so patient with explaining everything. I feel like I'm lobbing fifty questions across the net in his direction, yet he volleys them back without seeming overly concerned that I'm being a nuisance.

It's refreshing not to have curiosity used against me as if I'm stupid for a change.

"How do you manage this all? Or manage that many cows all at once?" There seems like so much work needing to be done—I wonder when he ever sleeps.

"Oh, we bring in some extra help when we need to round the

herd up. That's when Storm comes in extra useful. That bastard can rope 'em with the best."

At the mere mention of Storm's name, I immediately picture my uncle on horseback . . . the whole cowboy package, with chaps, a tan-colored hat settled on his head, guiding his horse with complete confidence. Heat flushes through my traitorous body, and it has nothing to do with the warmth from the air vent.

"You wanna drive the tractor?" Kayce interrupts my thoughts.

I look aghast and hide behind my thermos mug. "No thanks. I'd be terrified I might crash it or run one of the poor cows over." My gaze drifts over to where the line of bellowing, impatient cattle are waiting, probably wondering what's taking so long for their breakfast to be delivered.

Kayce snorts. "Fine. Stay in here and keep warm. It won't take me long." After he slides out the driver's side, he ducks his head back in and taps the center console on the dashboard, dragging my eyes to what looks like a handset and a speaker unit. "If that radio starts blowing up, just answer for me, would ya?"

I give him a look. "What do I say?" Surely, if the radio starts going off, it's going to be important, and I have no idea what to do.

"Just start yapping. It'll most likely be Sheriff Hayes checking in, and he won't bite." With that nonreassuring statement and a wink, Kayce jogs off toward the tractor. Leaving me to settle back in the front seat and watch on, feeling like my entire world has transformed beyond anything I could have ever fathomed before arriving here in Crimson Ridge.

Fuck you, LA.

I'll happily sit here and listen to cattle making their sweet noises and watch the steam rise off their black coats.

Maybe, just maybe, this is the place I'm meant to be to mend all the broken pieces inside, after all.

I've had my first official lesson in fitting a saddle, and Ollie, the horse I'm going to be riding today, has me wrapped around her hoof already.

No need to attempt hopping up onto her back, I'll just stand here stroking her mane and cooing at her. She's beautiful. A pale golden color, like froth on top of a latte, with milky-blue eyes.

Kayce hands me the reins and gestures with his chin to follow him outside, leading Ollie through the space between the stalls lining either side of the barn.

He clicks his tongue; I'm not sure if it's meant for me or the horse. "Come on, you girls."

Ollie rumbles and clops forward. She knows much better than I do how this is supposed to go down.

This horse could probably take *me* for a walk outside, rather than the other way around.

"So, Briar Lane. Tell me where you've drifted in from?"

A snort escapes me. "Is this your patter with the tourists? Are you gonna give me the *Devil's Peak Ranch Handbook*?" I shoot Kayce a raised eyebrow, feeling a little hesitant to go near this line of conversation.

"Nah, man, just color me curious." He strolls on the other side of Ollie's bobbing neck while we walk toward a fenced area next to the barn.

"Have you heard of Lane Enterprises?"

"Nope."

"Good."

Kayce doesn't speak for a moment. "Not your kind of people?"

We reach what looks like a small arena designed for the horses. As we stop beside the wooden railing, Kayce leans an elbow on the highest rung and waits for me to answer. He's easy to talk to, in a way I don't know that I've experienced before, and I find myself with words bubbling up that I usually would never even consider uttering to someone I'd only met a day ago. "Did you ever feel like you were born in the wrong place? Like everywhere you looked around, you just felt wrong? As if you were wearing a shirt three sizes too small, and it's itchy as hell, and you couldn't ever figure out how to get out of it?"

My hand rubs Ollie's neck. I'm talking more to the horse than Kayce, yet both of them stand there and listen to my nonsense.

"Weirdly specific, city girl." He narrows his eyes at me. "Are we talking itchy like sheep's wool, or itchy like hay getting stuck down your jocks?"

I roll my eyes at him in return. "You know what I mean."

It's Kayce's turn to run his hands over the horse now. Stepping in front of Ollie's nose, he glides both palms up and down her face as though they're having a silent little conversation.

He gives her a crooked smile as her lips pucker and roll. Ollie grins back at him, and it's such an endearing little gesture between them. Their bond is evident with each secret glance they exchange.

Kayce readjusts one of the straps on the halter before speaking. "I didn't get the opportunity to grow up here. My dad gave me up because he was seventeen and thought it was the right thing to do for me at the time. Except it turned out he couldn't have picked a worse person than my mom to leave me with." He methodically strokes and scratches around Ollie's ears. "So yeah, I get it. My life might've been a hell of a lot better if I'd been able to stay here with him, but either way, I'll never know. All I've got is the opportunity to start over and take each day as a fresh opportunity to make better choices."

"I'm sorry things weren't good with your mom."

"Take it you know a thing or two about shitty parents?"

That makes me laugh. "What gave it away?"

"Other than the fact you've landed in Crimson Ridge . . . the fact you're willing to put up with Stôrmand Lane as opposed to whoever you're leaving behind."

I feel my heart kick up, thudding a little harder at the mention of his name.

"Is that what brought *you* here? Running away?" I ask.

"Something like that . . . Maybe more like trying to outsprint my own bullshit and demons."

"Are you getting back on the rodeo circuit soon?"

"Hopefully." He flashes a wide grin, an immediate lightness filling his eyes at the mention of what he obviously loves so dearly. "I put in a fuckload of work last summer, and then Storm's given me hell all winter to keep my head in the game. I'll be back training now that it's spring—gotta get my ass ready for when the circuit kicks off."

"Does it scare you at all? The competing side of it, I mean." While I know next to nothing about rodeo, the concept of what he willingly does by getting on the back of an animal determined to throw him off seems like it should, by all rights, be terrifying.

"Nah . . . horses? They're easy. They speak a language that's simple . . . Respect is all they want. Knowing the true things to be scared of in life, being in the saddle is the only place I wanna be most days."

Hell, with the people I've had the misfortune to be surrounded by my whole life, don't I know exactly what he means.

CHAPTER 7

Storm

"Be a good girl for me. Nice and easy." My voice drops low. "Just like that."

The mare at my back huffs before obliging my instruction.

Wrapping my hand around Peaches's leg just above her hoof, I settle her between my thighs, resting over my chaps, and get to it.

There's always been something about farrier work that has appealed to me. It's methodical. Tough. Physical. Quiets my mind, being around horses for hour upon hour.

Give me a barn full of chuffs and snorts, sounds of munching hay, and rumbles of contentment—I'll take that shit over interacting with people any day.

But Christ, this is a job that's hard on my back at the best of times. Being bent over for hours on end, removing shoes, cleaning and checking hooves, heating and forming metal, and then fitting new ones . . . Well, after a couple of nights on a far-too-small couch staring at the wooden beams of the ceiling until dawn . . . I feel four hundred years old.

My body aches in places I only ever used to know about after the toughest bulls did their worst. Those hellish days in the arena when my glove would get jammed in the rope, or my shoulder would damn near dislocate during a ride, or my leap to the ground as soon as that buzzer went off would jar my whole spine wrong.

Right now I feel just as sore and mentally exhausted as in the height of my pro days.

And as much as I keep cursing myself for it, the reality I can't ignore is that I'm distracted as fuck.

Kayce goddamn Wilder, and his pretty-boy charm, has been all over Briar like a rash since we arrived. She offered to help out with shoeing, without knowing a single thing of what the process involves, but I didn't feel particularly well equipped to handle being in close quarters with her all day long.

Not after grinding my teeth all night, getting exactly zero sleep, with a half-hard cock I couldn't will away, knowing she was in my bed on the other side of the fucking wall.

While I don't want to think about it more than I have to, Kayce is the perfect guy to teach her how to handle herself on a horse.

He's a professional. Up and coming on the bareback bronc circuit. Kid's been riding horses and around the rodeo scene since he could barely walk.

So, then, why am I fighting the urge to go out there and be the one to show my pretty little niece a thing or two?

Why did the sight of his hand on her yesterday make my fists ball up and my jaw clench so hard my molars almost cracked?

Why can't I find it in myself to put Briar Lane out of my mind and back in the box labeled "family" where she fucking belongs?

I rub my damp brow with my sleeve, then tug my hat back down. It takes everything to stifle the groan that wants to burst out of me as I roll my shoulders and straighten up.

The sound of clopping hooves draws my attention, and coming in through the doors at the far end of the barn is Kayce. He's all toothy grin, bright blue eyes, and twenty-something swagger as he leads one of the trail horses.

Ollie is a gentle soul. One of the most chilled-out mares here. Nothing makes her bat an eyelid.

The perfect horse for Briar to learn the basics on.

And when my eyes lift to the girl seated on Ollie's back, I'm left forgetting what the fuck I was even doing.

Briar's cheeks are pink with the cold and the thrill of riding. That mane of long, dark hair is pulled back, with stray curls falling loose around her jaw. But it's her energy that really grabs me in a pincer hold and refuses to let go. Excitement, satisfaction, and thrill radiate off her, vibrating like a tuning fork. You can't help but be in the vicinity of someone who has done something for the very first time and loved every moment and not feel that same level of emotion.

That shit is addicting.

I want to drag my eyes off her, I really fucking do, and I know I shouldn't be watching her so openly. But goddamn.

I've seen a thousand women on the back of a horse before. Professional riders, racers, amateurs, you name it.

Never have I been so captivated by the sight of someone like Briar, the way she glows in the saddle. I'm glad I've been busy in here all day. Yet, I'm also pissed off as all hell that Kayce has been the one to catch all her smiles and laughter.

She already seems to have changed; one day out here on the ranch will do that to a person. It's like injecting pure bliss, a concoction of fresh air and vast skies, shot straight into your bloodstream.

Either way, I'm fucked. Because I want to see her looking like this all the time, and yet I have absolutely no right to be the man wanting to help bring that side out of her.

No right at all.

Other than being her goddamn uncle.

So maybe that's what has me walking toward them, closing the distance, despite everything I know I should be doing to the contrary.

Before Kayce can get his hands all over her again, I step up beside Ollie's shoulder and give her long neck a pat. Gliding my palm over her glossy cremello coat.

"Look at you. One day on the ranch and you're riding in like you own the place."

Briar looks down at me and wrestles her grin into an effort at a playful scowl. Dammit, why does this girl have to be cute *and* hot as fuck?

For the sake of my crumbling sanity, couldn't she have at least been boring and stuffy and entirely uninteresting.

"Kayce is an incredible teacher." She turns to look at him standing on the other side of the horse, all blond messy hair and perfect white teeth, reminding me of my own reflection a lifetime ago. "God, you were so unbelievably patient with me. Thank you."

"She's a natural, Storm. City girl here nailed everything the first time."

Fuck off. He's not giving my niece cutesy nicknames. There are plenty of other skirts in Crimson Ridge he can chase.

"Kayce, you good to check the shoe I just fitted for Winnie? Front left. Want to make sure you're happy with how it's looking, since we know Colt's a fussy bastard and all." I settle on the first excuse that comes to mind to get him to piss off. It's a complete lie. Those shoes are perfect, but Winnie's housed the furthest away, down at the opposite end of the barn.

"Sure, man. Though you know these horses just about better than I do by now." He hands me the reins, shakes his head, and then heads off, whistling in the direction of Winnie's stall.

"Let's get you down. You've done the fun part. Now you can do the real work. Help sort out Ollie's tack and get her fed and watered before we go." I tap Briar's knee, indicating for her to swing her other leg around.

As I do so, she stiffens ever so slightly. Dark eyes flicker over the hovering position of my hand, quickly up to meet my gaze, and then back to the horse beneath her.

"Don't drop me," she mutters.

"Would your uncle do that?" I raise an eyebrow, studying her from beneath the brim of my hat. Why? Maybe I'm testing her, pushing the limits on purpose like this because it's just how I'm wired.

I'm curious, and I absolutely have to be certifiable that I'm watching for her reaction this closely. To see how she responds when I float that word between us.

"I don't know if I trust you."

"Good. So you *are* a quick learner."

"Ugh." She rolls her eyes but then does as I asked. Twisting her body in the saddle, she swings her leg behind her while holding the pommel.

"That's it. I've got you." As she slides down, I grab hold of her waist, supporting the long drop to the ground.

Fuck, she feels . . . There's something so goddamn wrong with me that the minute I close my fingers over her jacket—my jacket, that she's still wearing since I told her to yesterday, and I'm not ready to face the reason why I like the sight of her dwarfed inside it so damn much—I'm itching to drag her against my chest.

"Thanks." She sounds a little breathless, and for a long moment, we linger much closer than necessary. Briar's head is turned ever so slightly to the side, near enough I can see her long eyelashes, near enough that my mouth could very easily brush against her ear if I bent closer.

The things I could whisper to this girl if she were someone, anyone, else.

What devilish promises I would make to lure a gorgeous

young woman into doing very improper things with me on the other side of the wooden door to the nearest stall.

Dirty thoughts about her on her knees, giving me those shimmering chestnut eyes. What her pretty pink tongue would look like presented for me, willingly, between lush, parted lips.

As it is, her scent of vanilla and peach rushes through my nose, and my thumbs graze up and down the spot above her waist.

Briar's shoulders rise and fall, and the seconds drag out. The air filling the space between her spine, mere inches from my chest, and where her ponytail runs down between her shoulder blades is electrified. Each invisible molecule almost crackles.

Or maybe that's the blood rushing in my goddamn ears.

Long curls hang down the back of her neck, and I'm sick and twisted enough to be itching to wrap that ponytail around my fist. Wanting to hear exactly what her breathy gasp might sound like if I tugged hard. Just the way I bet this girl likes to be treated.

Well, shit. I've officially crossed another depraved line I didn't know was there until I ignored everything and sailed right past it. Now I know exactly what is going to preoccupy my perverted goddamn mind all night as I toss and turn on that fucking unbearable couch.

The scuff of boots and Kayce humming to himself jerks me out of whatever trance I was just caught in. I cough into my fist to clear the rock lodged in my throat, stepping back to put a healthy—you know, appropriately uncle- and niece-sized—distance between us, and Briar ducks her head.

She reaches out to pat Ollie's neck, splaying her pastel-pink-painted fingernails wide, but speaks softly enough that only I can hear. I don't know whether it's on purpose or just my imagination, but it seems like she doesn't want Kayce overhearing her words.

"I'd love to see you in the saddle sometime."

CHAPTER 8

Briar

It has been a week since I uprooted my life, flew halfway across the country on a whim, and arrived in Crimson Ridge.

One week.

Seven days since that night, when my uncle not only wrapped his tattooed hand around my neck but, I'm certain, also reached inside my brain and did something to alter the cogs and inner workings of my mind while he was at it.

I haven't been the same since.

Ever since that encounter, I've been craving the glimpse of the sensation he gave me . . . and infuriatingly, I can't grasp what that might be, what my body needs, on my own.

I'm also far too conscious of how small this damn cabin is, so I haven't been able to do anything about the ever-intensifying ache swirling and building and presenting itself.

I'm beginning to think I really need to get over these nerves and find myself a Crimson Ridge cowboy to fool around with, even if only for one night. Someone who hopefully doesn't need a map and step-by-step instructions on how to find their way to a woman's clit.

What does it say about me that I'm a twenty-six-year-old

who has already had to endure being with someone entirely un-interested in having sex . . . with me, at any rate. I'm not exactly inexperienced, but I'm not exactly experienced either. Falling somewhere in the middle of knowing what I want to have with a sexual partner, while also not having the first clue of how to actually ask for what I want. I'm too timid. Too caught in my own head.

But maybe in a new town, with a total stranger, the stars might align for me to finally enjoy sex that can be a little dirty and a whole lot of hot. While a one-night stand doesn't hold a lot of appeal right now, I'm prepared to set aside any thoughts of being fussy. So what if I never see the guy again? At least I will have started giving myself a glimmer of pleasure and a way to actually start enjoying having sex.

Antoine sure knew how to get what he needed, without a second thought for anyone but himself.

Nothing like a man rolling out of bed straight away. I didn't exactly want him to stick around, but it doesn't excuse how dis-interested he was after filling his condom and patting himself on the back. The asshole had an unenviable talent for making me feel like it was my fault I never orgasmed.

God. It's no big surprise I'm messed up in the head where sex and my body's neglected desires are concerned.

What I do know is that I need someone to fuck me and erase the constant insanity of inappropriate thoughts I keep struggling to navigate in regard to my uncle.

I might be finding my feet here now that it's been a few days, going with him to the ranch, helping a little with his farrier work, and having more riding lessons with Kayce. But, Jesus, nothing could have prepared me for how challenging it is to be around Stôrmand Lane constantly.

Every time I turn around, he's there, and my ovaries start squealing like they're the presidents of his own personal fan club. Each holds up scorecards showing perfect tens, judging him as sheer perfection, the best in his field.

Meanwhile, the cabin that still requires a name is so tiny that we're on top of each other at every turn. To make matters more complicated for my unruly hormones, if we're not tripping over each other while making coffee in the morning or cooking a quick meal at the end of the day up at the ranch, we're cocooned together in the cab of his truck.

The bench seat stretches between us. Calling my name with a smooth, supple invitation to slide closer, feeling far too tempting.

I'm sure whoever designed that particular feature had only *one* kind of activity in mind.

And it certainly wasn't driving.

Another thing about all this time in close quarters with each other is that I've come to realize my uncle is the definition of stubborn. Tell him not to do something, and he'll do it twice and send you the pictures with him pulling the middle finger. Tell him to do something, and he'll be the classic donkey at a gate.

It's no wonder he allowed himself to be flung around like a ragdoll atop deadly-looking muscled bulls for years. The man is determined, to a fault.

Yes, I've developed more than a little obsession with sneaking any opportunity I can to watch old clips of him from his pro days. Kayce showed me a few videos up at the ranch the other day after I admitted I knew nothing about rodeo or my uncle's professional career.

The look on Kayce's face was the cowboy equivalent of clutching his pearls; the way he gasped and staggered, I expected him to reach for his smelling salts.

So, riding lessons morphed into rodeo lessons. Blame Kayce all I like, there's no avoiding the truth—that seemingly innocent little exposure to watching rapid-fire eight-second clips and slow-motion montages of "Stôrmand 'Storm' Lane" evolved into me stalking his infrequently updated social media later that night, and now here we are.

I officially have a dirty little secret.

One where I lie in bed in the dark with my headphones in and the volume turned down as low as possible because, even though I'm plugged in, there's still a hint of paranoia he might have developed supersonic hearing. And I would simply combust into an inferno of embarrassment if that man could hear what I'm watching.

Or, more to the point, *who* I'm watching.

It's a sensation I can't quite describe, sharing this tiny space with an almost stranger, yet his likeness graces my phone screen.

Thanks to the old bones of the cabin, I've discovered since my first night waking up nearly frozen in my bed that to survive this mountain, I need to sleep with the bedroom door wide open to allow the warmth from the fire in. So, while I tuck myself away at night, only a few feet away, the man occupying my phone screen—the veritable god of bull riding himself from when he was in his prime competition years—lies sprawled on the couch.

A couch that he really shouldn't continue to sleep on, considering the unending pressure his body is under all day.

From what I can see, being a farrier is grueling on the body. There's a lot of yanking at metal to remove the shoe the horse has outgrown because who would have known horses need regular mani-pedis? Then, he does things with tools that look like torture implements and I was sure must hurt the animals, but each that I've seen has stood there seemingly docile and content while he firmly handles them.

I've never wished to be a horse more than in the past couple of days.

There are lots of other complicated tasks involving fire and heating metal until it glows bright orange, then more hammering as he forms it into the required shape.

The whole process is fascinating. I got to stand and hold one of the horses, stroking her long nose and mane as he went through the entire rigmarole. Apparently, some of them get a little nervous when it comes time to have their hooves attended to and need a friend to hold their hand . . . so to speak. Some have their own little quirks, a special spot to scratch behind the ear in this particular case, which helps them stay distracted. This horse had themselves a little bag of feed to munch on, and my job was to hang out, dragging my fingers through her mane, petting, and stroking and reassuring her that despite how it might look to the contrary—with all the bashing and filing and hammering going on—she was in the best of hands.

It seemed hard to believe that, for the most part, the horses don't mind literal nails being driven through the horseshoes and their hooves.

For my uncle, the work amounts to hours upon hours bent double between the hammering and the metalwork and the filing. There are no shortcuts, and it's even more obvious now why his body is so well defined. This man doesn't need a gym when this kind of physically demanding, rigorous workout is on offer.

Add in the fact it involves horses and a picturesque ranch backdrop? I mean, a girl could become weak-kneed extremely easily seeing that kind of show on repeat.

We're not going to mention the hat, either.

Nope.

We're resolutely ignoring what the sight of my uncle in a cowboy hat does to stir up butterflies in my stomach.

The image paused on the screen shows him mid-ride from one of his early career championship runs. One arm is flung high in the air, and the fringe of his chaps mimics the action.

His chin is tucked, and that hat fixed on his head looks so damn good, along with the rest of him on top of that bull, the tattoo reaching up his neck. It makes my thighs squeeze involuntarily.

Later in his glittering pro life, he switched to a helmet, which is only mildly less terrifying. Lord knows that tiny bit of rigid plastic would do next to nothing to prevent possibly fatal injuries if things went wrong inside the ring.

He's fearless in a way that makes my insides melt.

Not for the first time this week, I find myself drifting toward dangerous thoughts. Wondering what it might be like for a man like him, one who isn't my uncle of course, to look my way.

A man who is rugged, wild, and chaotic but exudes charm and charisma in a gruff and silent manner.

His stubbornness just adds to the layers of this man. There's something about it that I find infuriating but also deeply captivating.

Bull-headed fool that he is, he has refused my offers—of which there have been many—to swap places. Even if only for one night, which I damn near pleaded with him about during dinner. I'm more than happy to take the couch, but my uncle keeps insisting that he's fine, when he's clearly not.

I see the dark circles under his impossibly blue eyes.

Those weren't there a week ago.

As the truck headlights swing over the front porch of the cabin—should I call her something old-fashioned? Clarabelle, perhaps? Or something named after the mountain forest, like Cedarwood Acres?—I'm beyond ready for a hot shower, food, and to crawl under a fluffy blanket.

I helped around the barn as much as possible today. Mucking stalls, dealing with literal piles of horse shit, basically being a ranch hand, the absolute definition of someone who has no idea what she's doing but is just happy to be here.

I've also now met Layla and Colt, who just arrived back after they've both been away traveling. I think I might have developed more than a bit of a girl crush on the gorgeous babe who must be the same age, or thereabouts, as me. The girl with coppery curls, green eyes, and energy that made me want to traipse around as her shadow all day as she showed me what to do with the horses.

My crush was totally at its peak when Layla looked at me and announced, "Thank fuck there's another woman living on this mountain. Pinky-promise you'll come to the bonfire next winter, if you're still here?"

I don't know what this bonfire is or what it entails, but I enthusiastically nodded. And I can see why her rugged-looking cowboy, Colton Wilder, was hardly able to take his eyes off her wherever she went. Totally, one hundred percent in agreement with that. Facts are Layla is a babe and she's so fucking nice; I wanted to hug her when we left this evening. Is that weird? Maybe, but whatever.

There have been so few times in my life when I've met other women who didn't have an agenda, or only wanted a fake friendship because of my family, or, even worse, only wanted to hang out with me in order to try to get to Antoine.

Fake fucking bitches, the lot of them.

I'm so relieved to be out of that toxic fishbowl.

After showering and changing into clothes that don't smell like a horse's ass, I make my way into the kitchen, half expecting to find it empty. Much to my surprise, there's a mountain of a man already seated with a heaping portion of steaming food in front of him and a similarly overloaded plate on the opposite side of the table waiting for me.

It looks like meat, mashed potatoes, and a whole lot of gravy and smells heaven sent after a day working outside and in the barn. Cold weather does something different to my taste buds, I swear, because I'm the girl who has been on-again, off-again vegan, and never once in my life have I craved something that looks and smells like this. Yet, I'm ready to fall upon it, inhale that entire plate, and go in search of more.

"You didn't have to do all this." I slide into the seat at the opposite end of the table. My uncle already damn near finished his meal in the time it took for me to get cleaned up. He already went through and showered first; somehow, I scored a win on that front. Him going first was something I absolutely refused to budge on since the first day I joined at the ranch. He's the one manhandling horses and putting his body through a punishing day's work.

Insisting that he should have the first shower seemed only reasonable. Although I've found attempts to negotiate with this man are more often than not futile.

"God, this smells delicious. Honestly, thank you."

"It's nothing." He shrugs.

We descend into the usual silence that comes with finishing our meals. Sitting here at night, like this, we don't exactly talk a lot, I've come to realize. Which honestly suits me, and I can understand. Here I am, treading all over this man's peaceful, reclusive existence, and I'm still not quite sure how to resolve the issue. I usually scroll on my phone and he does the same, and then I disappear off to the bedroom while he watches something on the small television in the corner of the living room.

For now, I'm ignoring the elephant in the room—you know, the whole part where I come to my senses and figure out what I want to do with my life. Truth be told, I don't even know how long I'll stay here in Crimson Ridge, so I don't want him to feel like he needs to leave or move or something stupid like that.

Maybe I'll just use this cabin as a place to come once in a while for a vacation? I've got more than enough of my own money to look after myself for the immediate future. One of the upsides of working in the Lane family business since I was sixteen was that I've carefully squirreled away those paychecks year after year.

How glad am I that my gut told me never to trust a man, so right now, even though I hate the fact that it's *Lane money*, there is a decade's worth of savings at my fingertips, allowing me freedom to find my feet and a job.

Until I make some decisions, however, I wouldn't mind making the place feel more . . . I don't even know the word for it. Homey? Less austere?

Which is why I blurt out my question after hastily swallowing a mouthful of mashed potato, without thinking. "Where's all your stuff?"

Piercing blue eyes tick up to meet mine across the table. It feels as though the room shrinks by about five feet whenever he studies me like this. As if I'm a puzzle, and not the kind that is a welcome challenge, more like a burden to be undertaken under pain of life or death.

These sorts of moments feel like I'm some riddle he's been presented with in order to save himself from the gallows.

"Stuff?" His brow creases. Every part of his face is a temptation. It's so strong and angular, like a craggy statue. I want to drag my fingertips over to appreciate how finely it has been crafted over time.

"You know . . . things . . . possessions. Haven't you been here ten years, you said?" Waving my fork at the bare room, I gesture vaguely at its barren appearance. Tumbleweeds wouldn't look out of place inside these walls.

"Why would I need a whole lot of crap?"

"But . . . surely you would want it to feel like a home?"

"Briar." He sighs heavily and pushes his empty plate away, leaning back in his chair. "I lived on the road for most of my life. It's an unusual existence, but you get used to living out of a duffel bag and not needing to clutter your world with useless shit. It just is what it is, and I don't expect you to understand it if you've never lived that life. Most people can't get their head around it."

He shoves both hands through his hair. Making the dirty-blond strands curl in an unruly, tangled mess, sticking up at odd angles. God, he looks good no matter what, and I have to duck my eyes in an effort to stop my body from reacting to how hot this man is.

Especially when he's in that drowsy evening state, matching the heavy weight of darkness that has blanketed the cabin.

"Besides. You can hardly talk, little thorn. Turning up here with a single piece of hand luggage." His lips tip up on one side when I dare glance back at him. Teasing me in that way that makes my body tingle.

I'm also refusing to acknowledge how my heart starts thudding a little harder.

Did he just give me a nickname? He just did it so casually, without breaking stride, and, oh god, I like that he just called me that. Far too much for my own health.

"Well, do you mind if I make the place feel a little . . . cozier?" I have to pinch my thigh below the table to stop myself from fluttering out of this chair.

"You planning to build a nest in here or some shit?"

"No." I shift my weight in the seat, and shoot him a small scowl. "Just . . . maybe some extra throw blankets for the couch. Some cushions. I saw a cute art gallery in town; I'd love to grab a few things from there and put them up."

He shakes his head with a wry smile, getting up to clear our plates now that he sees I've finished eating. I notice he seems to do that a lot. Waits for me to finish before he moves.

I've been so used to being ignored most of the time, I'm certain my family, and even the man I lived with, didn't ever actually eat a meal at the table with me.

When he returns a moment later, he's got a beer in each hand and offers me one.

"Oh. Thanks." Again, I have to duck my head after reaching out to take it because there's something twisting low in my stomach at the sight of his tattooed knuckles wrapped around the slender neck of the bottle.

It reminds me of having his fingers around the column of my throat. The gentle slope of the amber glass caressed beneath his fingertips is causing embers to flare and heat to pool low in my core.

Look at me. Managing to make the act of my *uncle* offering me a drink all sexual.

That's gotta be my last straw. There are no two ways about it, and no more putting it off. I'm getting myself on a dating app tomorrow.

Surely, I can find a cowboy somewhere around here who is interested in no-strings-attached sex. Guys are into that, right?

He settles himself back down in his seat, spreading his legs wide and looking too fine for his own good. A fact that does nothing to calm the steadily building inferno between my thighs.

"Is that why we've got fucking twigs in a cup sitting on the table?"

I've barely managed to raise the bottle to my lips and end up producing an awkward little spluttering noise. "They're not twigs. It's . . . It's . . ."

Blue eyes twinkle at me over the top of his beer as he tips his bottle up, watching me intensely the whole time.

"You wouldn't understand," I mutter and gulp back a sip. Something else that I can't remember the last time I had. Beer. The slightly sour, hoppy flavor settles nicely over my tongue.

Yesterday, I went out and foraged around the property for something resembling flowers, but in the midst of early spring, there wasn't exactly much to choose from. So I had to settle for some fronds of a plant that had buds on the tips. Eventually, they'll blossom, but I guess in their current state, they do look more like a collection of brown twigs neatly arranged inside a water glass.

Silence stretches out between us as we both nurse our drinks.

"Of course you can decorate the place," he says, softer this time. "It is yours, after all."

"I don't want to impose. This is your home." I chew on my bottom lip. Holy shit, between the delicious meal and the alcohol and hearing his voice turn a honeyed shade when it drops into that lower octave, my cheeks flame.

The light has drained out of the room while we've been sitting here, and now there's mostly just a warm orange glow flickering over our skin. It's the kind of setting that feels deeply intimate, and I see the moment his expression changes.

Those bright blue eyes harden. His jaw tightens.

It's as if I've said, or done, the wrong thing.

Pushing to his feet all of a sudden, he leaves the half-finished beer on the table. "Don't wait up. I've gotta go out for a while . . . to meet a friend."

And with that, my uncle vanishes like a whisper into the dark. His jacket and boots are barely on before he heads out the door with such abruptness I'm left clutching my beer, feeling like a fool. The rumble of his truck purring to life outside stabs a painful reminder square in my chest.

Of course, he has somewhere to be.

Of course, he has someone else he wants to spend an evening with.

And that woman certainly isn't me.

CHAPTER 9

Storm

Driving around Crimson Ridge, after nightfall when it's fucking freezing out, isn't ideal.

Snow is the worst, too. Sure, it's all pretty when it's flaky and puffy in the sky, but then that shit sticks to the ground and melts and turns to ice . . . and, well, this place has got snow on fucking bulk order, shipped in for months at a time.

However, being out here, piles of snow on the sides of the roads and all, sure as hell is a better option than remaining trapped in that cabin. I'm damn near crawling out of my skin, my blood racing and itching beneath the surface, longing to reach out for the girl I am supposed to be about as interested in as a shovel.

Maybe I need to find myself one and just dig myself a goddamn hole, bury my black soul in there, and be done with it.

Half of this town already believes the worst of me. The other half is morbidly curious.

I certainly deserve to bury myself in the pit of shame at the dirty fucking thoughts I keep having about my own damn niece. What the hell is wrong with me? It's like someone flipped a switch and glitched the universe, and I've gone from enjoying the idea of a little fun with anyone, any warm and willing hole, to now having an unhealthy obsession with knowing what Briar looks like naked.

With one hand, I grip the steering wheel harder, while the other scrubs over my mouth.

Fuck. My. Rotten. Life.

How long she's staying is another giant goddamn issue. I don't know and, quite frankly, have been too shit scared to ask because I'm terrified of the possibility she might fix those glittering eyes on mine and part those pouty lips and tell me in her breathy little voice that she isn't going anywhere.

That she intends to stay, permanently.

If so, what the hell am I going to do? I can't spend my life sleeping on the couch fantasizing about how experienced my niece is at sucking cock. Whether she likes her ass being played with at the same time as feeling a tongue run over her clit. And I certainly can't spend all day wondering how her nipples might taste if I were to pinch a hard little bud between my teeth.

Christ, I need to stop thinking about her tits.

It's become an occupational hazard by this point. I nearly drove a nail through my thumb earlier today because I was too distracted by the sight of her helping out in the barn.

Once she started talking about decorating and buying shit for the cabin . . . it stirred something up inside me, and I'm too much of an asshole to stop and look properly at what that might be.

Getting my ass the hell out of there was the only option.

My phone buzzes where I've set it in my cup holder next to the pair of pliers I always have floating around in here. Tapping the screen, I can see it's a text from Beau.

I pull over, turning down the music, so I can reply now while I still have reception. At least that's one benefit of being in Crimson Ridge at this hour: my phone can regularly pick up texts. Even if it's just a rodeo buddy wanting to shoot the shit, it'll take my mind off Briar temporarily.

Beau:
Wild one, where are we at with getting you out to the ranch to help me out with some renovations?

You know me. That sexy fucking mustache of yours gets my engine going every time.

Name a date and I'll be there.

How does next week sound?

Got some final paperwork crap and lawyer bullshit to deal with first. Then, the ink will be dry on the deal.

Oh, poor Beau Heartford.

Too much money and porn-stache for your own good.

We can't all be Sasquatches hiding in the mountains when we retire.

Some of us have real-life responsibilities.

Oh yeah, sucks to be you. I bet you cry into those wads of Benjamin's.

How's Mandy handling the idea of settling into ranch life retirement?

Dots bounce on the screen, then pause.

Don't fucking breathe a word, or I'll castrate you in your sleep

. . . but, it's over.

Media doesn't know shit. Her team wants it all hushed up till after the opening.

Fuck. Sorry man. Or congratulations?

You know I'm here. Whatever you need.

You good?

Yeah. Been a long time coming.

Can't wait to be away from this goddamn circus. Just gotta push through a few more months, and then we'll do the usual PR spin bullshit.

You know how it goes.

Yeah, I do. Beau has it even worse, considering he's been married to country music's golden girl and in the spotlight for as long as I've known him. The world has been hanging on to every possible crumb of a sign pointing to when and where they might finally get to the point of popping out a few kids.

Hell, even I initially thought the fact Beau purchased his ranch out here was them finally taking the plunge and doing the big ol' happily-married-with-a-white-picket-fence bullshit.

Some might even say his pro career only happened the way it did because of the impact her superstardom brought his way. Sponsors and opportunities that mere mortals could only dream of landed in his lap, people fawning over his every move once they caught sight of the two of them holding hands one time.

That shit went viral overnight.

Doesn't take away from the fact he's a fucking outstanding athlete and rider. But he's had more than the rub of the green being hitched to her star.

Even if it's secretly been hell for more years than not.

So, next week?

You bring that big talent, head over there, and the place is all yours. Stay however long you need.

Just promise me, no buckle bunnies, wild one. Can't have any shit like that following me to Crimson Ridge.

I'm gonna have enough of a PR headache to deal with as it is over the next few months.

What about convincing you to hop on your private jet and bring that sexy as hell 'stache out here?

I promise I'll purr real nice for you, sugar.

Fuck off, you're such a slut.

For a tickle of your magnificent facial hair, I'll do anything.

Smartass.

Don't you have hillbilly happy hour to get to? Or are you sitting in your truck parked up some chick's driveway, trying to figure out if you've already fucked this one and need to dip?

Surely you've worked your way through the entire population of Crimson Ridge by now?

> Damn, Heartford. You wanna come here, and I'll show you how to put that mouth to use?

You couldn't afford me.

Gotta run, man. Pick the key up from my realtor in town, and charge whatever you need to at the hardware store. We can video chat or some shit, and I'll give you the rundown, but it's pretty straightforward. Sand and paint. I know you know the drill.

> Got it. Dream of me.

Fuck off.

> *kiss emoji*

I toss my phone back in the holder. It's late now, after my evening of aimlessly driving and driving and driving.

While I don't know if I'm ready to head back up the mountain, I'm also itching to get back. What the fuck is the deal with this permanent carousel of conflicting emotions? It's like I can't shrug off the weird set of feelings that have landed and claimed their territory and now refuse to leave.

So, I guess that's why I find myself making a direct line back to the cabin. By the time I haul myself out of the cab and drag my heels to head inside, my neck is killing me, my spine feels like it's been put through a meat grinder, and I've got the hips of an eighty-year-old.

With the best will in the world, there's no way I'd be fucking anyone tonight; they'd be having to do all the work riding me while I starfished on my back the whole time.

Fortunately for my sanity, and my perverted goddamn brain, the cabin is quiet as I slip past the threshold, shedding my hat and jacket, and dropping my boots beside the door. When I take a glance down the hallway, there's no light coming from the bedroom. Hopefully, she's long gone to sleep.

I didn't miss the hurt look that slid across her face when I ran out earlier. But I'd rather she's pissed with me than deal with the other problem—that I was way too fucking close to doing something even more regrettable than spying on her while getting naked.

I roll my shoulders, feeling every crunch and knot, then stretch my neck side to side. My mind runs through the few things I need to handle before another sleepless torture session on the couch. Stoking the fire back up and tossing some fresh logs into the flames only reminds me of precisely how sore and exhausted I am.

Nothing some pills and a little muscle rub won't fix.

Reaching behind my head, I tug my shirt off and wander down to the bathroom in the dark, mentally preparing myself, playing that old familiar game—the one where I grit my teeth and try to convince myself that my back isn't killing me. Used to play that one a lot after particularly gnarly bull rides. It's real fun.

I flip on the lamp over the mirror and open the medicine cabinet, rummaging around looking for painkillers I know I've got stashed and some rub I'm sure was in here last time I checked.

"Oh, shit . . . sorry." A raspy, sleepy voice comes from behind me. When I spin around, Briar hovers in the doorframe. And, oh fuck, she's in only a baggy hoodie and skimpy sleep shorts, rubbing her brow with bleary eyes squinting at the light. "I woke up and thought I must have left the light on by accident."

She starts to back away, then as her hand drops from her eyes, they go wide, obviously waking up really quickly as she notices the half-dressed state we're both in. Maybe it's just my filthy imagination, but it's far too easy to imagine a much better version of this scene.

I'd much prefer to have her ass perched beside the handbasin, knees spread, those tiny shorts tugged to one side while I'm knuckles deep inside her pussy as she moans against my neck.

My fist tightens around the tube of cream and packet of pills, making the foil crinkle. I figure the only way out of this is to shrug her off and sulk away in the direction of the living room with a boner I can't do anything about and feel guilty as hell if I dare touch.

Because that asshole shouldn't be perking up at the sight of my niece. Yet, here I am, already thinking about her completely naked, bent over this very counter, with her heavy tits, and—oh my fucking god, the situation in my jeans is not being helped the longer I stand here.

"Bathroom's all yours. Night." Grunting, full caveman style, I set my jaw and prepare to squeeze past her.

Keep your eyes to yourself. Do not look at her tits, or ass, or bare thighs. Jesus.

"Wait, what have you done to yourself? Are you injured?" She shoots out a hand in the direction of my shoulder, then stops, fingers hovering in midair before dropping back down to her side.

"It's nothing."

Her eyes scan over the items clenched in my fist. "Oh my god. I *knew* it."

My neck prickles. I can't stay here with her. Not this close. Not this late at night.

"Just leave it, Briar."

"You're in pain, aren't you? Every time I ask, you keep brushing it off. Stop being an idiot about this and let me help."

Maybe I'm too tired, or maybe I'm just a bad, bad man, but I hesitate. And in that moment, she turns into the world's most tempting nurse.

Fuck a slutty Halloween costume where a chick has her

tits and ass hanging out in a miniature white dress with a fake stethoscope dangling around her neck.

This is more dangerous . . . a thousand times more alluring.

"Sit." She jabs a finger in the direction of the bedroom, herding me in there like I'm an unruly calf.

"You're mighty bossy for this time of night, little thorn." A wince shoots across my face before I can disguise it as I lower down and perch on the edge of the bed. My own fucking bed. One that is currently rumpled with the covers thrown back because she's been sleeping in here.

Her scent drifts up, gently, subtly coiling through my awareness as soon as I'm seated.

"Well, you're getting me at my optimal social powers. The middle of the night is when I'm known to be the most tolerant of idiot uncles crashing around in the dark."

That draws a chuckle out of me. "Can I give your bedside manner a rating? I'm already sensing there might be room for improvement."

"No. But you can take those pills and hand me that muscle rub and do as you're told."

"What's your preferred place for review? Is there a website that I can log in to?"

Briar swipes everything out of my hands, rolling her eyes at me. While I've been teasing her, she moved close enough to be standing almost between my knees. She pops two painkillers out of their casing, drops them into my hand, and presses a pastel-pink water bottle into my other. It matches the shade painted on her nails. There are stickers and shit on the outside of the bottle, but I'm too distracted by the girl caged in by my legs. I didn't even notice her collect it off the nightstand, too preoccupied with this unguarded version of the girl in front of me.

"Cute," I murmur. Eyeing her as I chuck the pills back and let the cold water chase them down. Hopefully, she thinks I'm talking about the water bottle. I *should* be talking about the water bottle.

"What part hurts most?" She watches me swallow the painkillers, keeping her eyes firmly on my face.

My niece is trying very, very hard not to look at my naked chest. And I'm that much of a prick that I'm soaking up every second of her squirming in place.

"Told you, I'm fine." I set the bottle at my feet. As I lean forward, a sharp, searing pain rockets through the fleshy part between my shoulder and neck, like I've been stuck with a cattle brand.

"*Anghhh.* Fuckkk." I don't even get to fully register that she's touching my bare skin because this girl just savagely digs her knuckle into the knot that's been building all week.

"Oh, good. You're absolutely right. Completely fine," Briar huffs. "Jesus, you're as bullheaded as those creatures you used to climb on. Sit still."

The cap on the tube clicks, and the bed dips, and that's when my mind blanks.

Briar's soft hands are on me. They're covering my muscles and my aches, and she's kneeling on the bed behind my back, so close her hoodie brushes up against my spine over and over. "Tell me if there's a spot in particular you want me to work on."

I bite my tongue so hard there's surely going to be blood coating my teeth after this is all done. Maybe I'll have bitten the damn thing clean in two.

She methodically works over the tension in my shoulder until I wince again.

"Sorry," she murmurs. "But you kind of deserve it after refusing to admit this was causing you pain."

Yeah, the kind of tormented agony caused by my back, the shitty couch, and the pretty young niece sleeping in my bed.

"Does that feel any better?" She gentles over the particularly sore knot, working it, easing it, deftly kneading and rubbing, and driving me insane with how good it feels to have her hands on me.

Thousands of sparks ripple along my nerves. Every place she glides her palms and fingertips over hums with deep satisfaction.

I squeeze my eyes shut. "*Mmhm.*" It's official. Briar has rendered me incapable of logic or speech. All that keeps thundering around inside my brain is an awareness that, goddamn, *this* feels amazing.

I can't think of the last time someone touched me like . . . this, and please don't let her stop anytime soon. I don't want her to stop. I've had women's hands cover every inch of flesh on my body, yet it's always been with a singular goal in mind. Sex.

But this . . . this is veering into an unfamiliar realm. A place where reality has warped, distorting like ancient glass. For whatever reason, the stunning girl who I shouldn't be noticing, let alone craving, has willingly entered into this momentary blurring of lines between us.

Maybe this is the price I'd be prepared to pay. Torture my body on the daily if it gets me the ultimate prize, or goddamn punishment, of my niece's hands all over my naked back and shoulders.

Because it's a kind gesture, but also an incredibly fucking intimate one. It allows a tiny spark to rekindle and begin glowing around the idea that Briar might be a whole lot more interested in her *uncle* than she should be.

Shit. Even to myself, I sound drunk thinking like that. I must be drugged by her closeness, the attention I've never received without something expected in return. While the black humor and dripping irony is that I've lost track of the number of times in my life that a set of false eyelashes fluttered my way with a not-so-subtle offer to come back to my hotel room and give me a massage, or the times that a nameless buckle bunny offered to give me a rubdown after an event. I'd trade any of those moments for the guarantee it could be the gorgeous girl at my back with her hands on me.

A girl who is entirely off-limits.

Feeling like a horse getting a thorough grooming, I feel my muscles dip into that drowsy state . . . relaxed and heavy. I'm in some sort of trance, bespelled by her deft touch and ability to ease the tension and aggressive ache that I've been carrying around.

"Better, Uncle Storm?" Her voice is throatier than before. Jesus, is that what she sounds like when she's turned on? I'm such a sick fuck, because hearing her call me uncle in *that* voice makes my cock jerk.

My blood quickens as she slides off the bed and comes to stand in front of me.

Christ. Why does my throat feel dry, and what happened to my ability to form words? Every single letter of the alphabet has flown out of my brain. I have to squeeze my fists against the temptation to reach for the backs of her thighs. She's right fucking there. Within arm's reach and close enough that the material of my jeans brushes up against her soft skin.

My niece stands close enough for me to say a *proper* thank you.

One that involves no words being spoken, but I certainly would put my mouth and tongue to good use.

"Need something else?" I swear she nearly whispers the words.

Goddamn, is she fucking with me?

"No, thanks. That's much better," I croak out. Holy shit. The air swirls heavy and potent between us, and Briar isn't moving away.

I stare up at her. Dark eyes framed beneath a thick curtain of lashes. Her cheeks are dusted with a tinge of pink. Full mouth hangs open ever so slightly.

"Good," she breathes, teeth catching her bottom lip for just a second. The flicker of her eyes is so quick I could almost convince myself it didn't happen. But it did. It does. She lets her eyes drop to my mouth before bouncing, startled, back up to hold my gaze. "Sleep well. Good night."

She's gone before I can say anything. Disappearing into the living room, leaving me there, on my own bed, with a raging hard-on, the ghost of her touch lingering on my skin, and surrounded by her intoxicating scent.

CHAPTER 10

Briar

There are seventy-eight planks in the ceiling above this couch. One piece of the amber-colored wood has a sequence of dark knots that look like a dog's face. Long snout. Eyes. The whole effect is rather surreal. Like one of those visual tricks—once you see it, you can't unsee it.

I spent the night lying wide awake. My body tingled with forbidden temptation and sulked with shame, twisting all the way the fuck up on the inside as I replayed the events from the bathroom and the bedroom.

Holy fucking shit.

One glance at my uncle's bare chest, his expanse of tattoos . . . my pussy just about climbed onto his lap to start grinding on him of her own volition.

Little slut.

Why he was half-naked in the bathroom at god-knows-what-hour is a mystery for another day.

What is now going to lurk in my mind, dangerously peeking around the corner on the regular to remind me with flashes and glimpses of memory imprinted upon my brain, is how his body is so fucking hot. He's hot. Hotter than a man who is my uncle should have the audacity to be.

It's obvious he's muscled, defined, broad through his chest and arms. I mean, a girl can see that without any need to strip his clothes off. But his torso is sculpted, impossibly honed from the time spent on the rodeo circuit during his professional years and, nowadays, through the back-breaking hours of labor he puts in working on ranches like Devil's Peak.

Those indents leading into a dusting of dark hair and a V pointing straight below his belt—well, shit. I was blissfully unaware of how erotic a man's hard-worn body could look.

Especially more so when covered in ink.

Now, most likely I'm going to be walking around in a daze, itching to run my fingers across that stretch of skin and firm muscle.

That compulsion I fight all night long is heightened and brightened up to *absolutely goddamn blinding* on the scale because I know exactly what the man's back muscles feel like.

There is a snapshot in my mind of every indent, dip, and ripple falling below the slope of his neck. Everything extending from his mussed hair down has been cataloged by my fingertips. Where his shoulder blades moved, the fleshy part across the top of his spine flexed, the indentation running the long length to the waistband of his pants.

My throat bobs a heavy swallow of guilt.

Didn't think clearly last night before climbing on that bed and massaging him without warning, obviously.

Although . . . I regret nothing.

Was I also a teeny tiny bit spurred on to do what I did because I'd convinced myself he'd gone off to slide into some girl's bed last night?

Hell yes, I was. Pettiness and horniness teamed up to make an insane decision. Before I knew what was happening, I had my hands all over him.

I don't want to admit how much it stung when he disappeared abruptly without warning. Just when it felt like we'd settled into something comfortable, an ease flowing between us, a familiarity I've been craving, he upped and headed out the door.

Leaving me alone, but mostly confused and swimming in a sea of heightened emotions at the thought he had someplace better to be.

Someone he'd much rather be with.

It dredged up all my memories of nights on my own. *Sorry, honey, I've got to work late. You know what these client deadlines are like.*

When the reality was much more willing to be a convenient fuck in the meeting room.

Ugh. I want to bleach my memory of that man and his terrible dick and how pathetic I was to not see the signs. Nausea rolls through me whenever I stop and think, even for one second, how many people knew and didn't say anything.

How many people back there—not that I want to call that hellhole home anymore, because it's not—were laughing at me on the daily? Did they have group chats gossiping about my failure to keep a man faithful? Did the running joke center around how easy it was to manipulate poor, pathetic Briar Lane?

The urge to hurl up my bacon and eggs comes on strong.

I spin the handle on my coffee mug back and forth, letting it rotate on the wooden table, the coffee and creamer swirling inside as I do so.

It's how I imagine the contents of my brain are sloshing around, encased by skull and cerebral fluid.

The man who is partially responsible for the chaos unfolding within me took off already this morning. He huffed something at me about needing to go to Crimson Ridge to see about an upcoming job, but that he wouldn't be long.

I got the impression he didn't want me tagging along, so I've sat here in the breakfast nook, watching the pine trees glisten with melted ice and early-morning sun.

Spring is deciding to put in an appearance, and while the night was icy with temperatures below freezing, there isn't any fresh snow to be seen.

I wonder what it's like up here when it truly snows during the winter. Layla mentioned that this mountain up at Devil's Peak Ranch often goes through long periods, weeks at a time, where the roads are closed due to heavy snowfall.

My utterly dysfunctional mind instantly conjures up a scene of being curled up in front of the fire, with nowhere to go and nothing but a rugged, muscled man all to myself.

We'd be here all alone. Cut off from the rest of the world. There would be no way for anyone to know . . .

A ping comes through on my phone that makes me jump. I'd been so caught in my little forbidden fantasy that I forgot I had connected to Wi-Fi earlier and made a brave attempt at opening my emails and messages.

I have absolutely no intention of replying to anything or anyone, but it felt somewhat cathartic to bulk delete everything with the name Antoine Montgomery in the sender's name.

Then I blocked him, everywhere.

But this ping is followed by a new-message tone. My heart immediately leaps into my throat as the name appears on my screen.

Crispin Lane.

No one holds a grudge longer, or could detest me more passionately, than my older sister.

Seeing that she has not only emailed but also sent a follow-up message to my Instagram makes my stomach knot. The woman never speaks to me. We've been strangers for years now, but that has never stopped Cris from enjoying a front-row seat to my humiliation.

I bet she knew about Antoine; that bitch is a savage. I'm sure she keeps a jar of souls stashed in her office somewhere, along with her wheatgrass shots and cayenne-pepper cleanses. All the people she's screwed over, done dirty, then profited off because that's what it takes to make it inside the Lane empire.

Dear old Dad would be so proud.

I catch sight of the first couple of lines: "This isn't humorous, Briar. You need to start replying to Antoine's messages and come back. The man is worried sick." I know there will be more emotional manipulation throughout the rest of her message.

Delete.

I don't want anything to do with them. As far as I'm concerned, that part of my life is over, and whatever new horizon I'm headed for is going to be entirely focused on what makes me happy.

No longer am I going to settle for being trodden on, or simply enduring the act of going through the motions with a fake smile, doing what is expected of me. Not carrying the burden of guilt for something I don't have any memory of being responsible for. Not dressing perfectly and posing for the photo opportunity in order to be a dutiful Lane heiress.

Another ping, and I glance down. I already know it'll be my sister, but while I had no issue blocking Antoine's ass, I can't bring myself to do the same to her contact details.

God, I really was expertly trained in the act of loyalty to her and my father. They did a stellar job there. Ten out of ten for manipulating me into feeling guilty for wanting better for myself.

"Briar. You are being selfish and childish, as usual. I cannot believe this is how you choose to behave. You know it would have been her birthday next week, but thanks to you, we won't get to celebrate it. And now with Dad gone, too . . ."

My fingers clench so tightly my nails embed themselves in my skin. Rage pours through me, and hot tears prick the backs of my eyes like a thousand tiny needles.

I delete the message without opening it.

How fucking dare she.

Always, without fail, she turns everything into a boiling vat of oil to throw over me, scalding me alive with shame for even existing.

My blood feels trapped inside my body, like I need to release the toxins somehow, like that black gunk my sister brings with her everywhere she goes seeps beneath my skin, and now I can't breathe.

I'm on my feet, heading for the door. It feels like a thousand degrees in here. Cold air. Fresh air. That's what I need: to fill my lungs with icy mountain oxygen and do something productive. Something physical.

I've watched how my uncle splits kindling wood with an ax. I know we need to restock wood regularly at the cabin.

That's something I can do.

That's what I need to do. Right now, I need to be away from my phone, outside of these four walls.

Shoving into my boots, I grab the jacket I've been wearing since the first day he gave it to me and yank open the door much harder than I need to.

I want to scream into the void.

Can I do that here?

There's no one around to hear me.

I spot the ax handle sticking upright in the large chopping base and make a beeline for it. It takes two hands and a sharp tug to get it loose, but once I hold it, it feels weighty and deadly in my hand.

For a moment, I pause—there are about a thousand things that could go wrong trying to split wood. Top of that list would be potentially chopping off my own damn foot if I'm not careful. Except I'm in a savage-enough mood that I really don't give a fuck.

My rage is at its boiling point, and I want to slam this sharp metal head into wood and hear the satisfying *thunk* and splintering of fibers giving way.

So that's exactly what I do.

I set the wood before me and swing the ax up, feeling the weight distribution and flexing my hands over the smooth grip on the handle.

Then, I let it sail down, allowing the momentum and swing and blunt force to do the damage.

The log cracks but doesn't give way fully, so I tug the ax head out and repeat the process. Second time, it splits with a cathartic, tearing, splintering noise.

God, that felt good. Like a tiny fraction of the emotion I've been carrying around and repressing constantly for years could finally be flung into the universe. My pent-up anger has transformed into something useful and split that log that can be used in the fire at some future point in time.

I morph into the picture of a woman possessed. Starting small. Some of my attempts are weak, but with each blow, I let the rage eke out gradually, becoming a torrent, finally evolving into a full-on downpour. Giving my best warrior cry, I swing and land blows, all while salty tears stream down my cheeks.

Cheater.

Liar.

Asshole.

Well, shit. Turns out if I'm handed an ax and some firewood to chop, that shit is more fucking cathartic than any overpriced LA therapist.

Time disappears on me, and when I finally stop, sweat beading on my lower back and dampening my forehead, I pause to breathe heavily, and as I take a look around, it's obvious I've chopped far more than I originally intended to. A much bigger pile exists than we potentially needed, but oh well.

Chalk that up to feminine rage.

I wedge the ax back in the block where I found it and gather up an armful of wood to carry around to the pile on the porch. I'll start there and then finish up by stacking whatever we need inside afterward.

With the few chunky pieces bundled in my arms, I head for the front of the cabin, feeling incredibly self-satisfied. Down this side is still shaded between the cabin and tall pines, and there's a bit of a concrete pad outside what looks like a small workshop.

Just as I'm looking around, taking in the quiet beauty out here, everything turns on me without warning.

My boot hits the concrete and instantly gives way. With my arms full, there's no possible way to break my fall. Both legs flip up, and I cartwheel backward.

My breath leaves my lungs in a crunching rush, a heavy blow to my spine.

The last thing I remember is the dull thud ricocheting through my brain as the back of my head collides with the ground.

The trees towering over me, peering down like curious statues, are swallowed up in a misty black void.

CHAPTER 11

Storm

Eight seconds.

For so many years of my life, that was the measure by which everything was counted. The adrenaline of busting out of that chute, gripping tight to the heaving, snorting beast beneath me.

The entirety of my world would narrow down, zeroing in on an infinitely small circle of focus. Posture. Core. Arm. Grip. Chin. Ultimately, a trivial assortment of shit that was entirely irrelevant in regular life.

No one willingly gets on the back of an angry bull. You've gotta have a certain type of fucked-up motivation, be it the money or the glory or the infamy or an unhealthy relationship with the meaning of life.

But then again, I've never been one to do what others expect or want from me.

So I'm intimately familiar with the way eight seconds can feel like an eternity when, to most people, it's hardly the blink of an eye. A meaningless pause between breaths.

Right now, I'm back in that arena, heart pounding, brain zeroed in on a sight that makes my blood turn cold. My legs carry me the short distance between the truck and the hopelessly small, terrifyingly still body lying flat on the ground, and each second turns to molasses.

Each tick of the clock seems to pass in a thick and sticky and terrifyingly slow pattern. It feels like an eternity from the moment I fling myself out of the driver's side to when I reach her fragile figure.

"Briar. Fuck. Can you hear me?" I fall on my knees beside her and nearly slide off balance myself on the black ice. Her face is so goddamn pale; there's wood everywhere, tumbled on the ground in a haphazard arc.

"Briar?" Repeating her name louder, more panicked, I desperately search her face for a flicker of recognition. There's no blood on the ice that I can see, but I'm reluctant to shift her head in case something happened to her spine as she fell. Straight onto concrete. Fucking fuck.

It's like every nightmare I used to have about not making it to safety and ending up trampled. Not that those dreams were frequent occurrences, but when they happened, I'd wake up with soaked sheets and a throat raw from hollering with no one to hear me.

Which is how I feel now.

No cell coverage.

Miles away from medical care.

My radio unit is inside the cabin. I could contact mountain rescue and Sheriff Hayes. Fuck, I could easily radio Colt to get his ass down here. But I don't want to leave her side, and I'm terrified of hurting her more, of making an injury worse if I try to move her myself.

Could I live with the guilt of doing more harm if there is spinal damage? A busted disc or vertebrae? Nerves that could so easily be severed if I shift her even an inch?

"Fuck. Briar. Please wake up for me." I gently brush her hair back off her forehead, and just as I'm steeling myself to check for a pulse, her eyelashes twitch.

Thank fuck.

My heart is in my mouth as I brush one thumb over her soft cheek. Seeing her so ghostly, with all the life drained from her features, I don't know if I've ever felt this nauseous before.

"Can you hear me?" God, every instinct I have is to scoop her up, and it's killing me not to. But the pure terror of causing more harm is what holds me back. Barely.

She lets out a croaky sound, groggy, followed by a slow groan. Her eyes flutter open with a struggle.

"Take it easy." I'm still stroking her cheek, but at least she's conscious and breathing, and there's a torrent of relief flooding my veins at those two little details.

"I'm sorry. The wood." She winces, as if talking out loud is an effort.

"Fuck the wood. I'm going to move you inside, out of the cold, okay?"

"I wanted to help."

"Well, let me help you right now."

"Everyone hates me." Her nose scrunches while those brown eyes of hers shift around, a little unfocused.

Hearing that, how forlorn she sounds, makes me stiffen. But I guess since she must have cracked her head pretty hard, things might not make a whole lot of sense for her right now.

"Can you sit up for me, darlin'?" Sliding a hand beneath her head to cradle it, I half expect to come into contact with wetness or sticky evidence of blood, but as I very carefully help her into a sitting position, I don't feel anything.

"It hurts."

"I know. Let's get you inside so I can take a proper look at you. I think you still have a brain, but we'll need to make sure."

"Not funny."

"I'm very funny. Ask around."

She closes her eyes and grips the sleeve of my jacket. "I want to say something witty but my head is too sore, so you'll have to imagine it instead."

"If it's anything like your glittering sense of humor in the middle of the night, I can only imagine." I watch her breathe a little harder through her nose as she adjusts to sitting upright. "Ready to try standing up for me?"

She makes a little noise of agreement. "Sorry for ruining your day. I'm sure you've got better things to do than deal with this."

"Briar. You don't have to apologize for needing help."

She digs her fingers into my arm a little tighter. "Well, thank you, anyway. You don't have to."

Jesus. I knew Erik had a fucked-up relationship with his daughters, hardly being around as a parent, but the fact this girl feels guilty for getting hurt and needing help has got me wanting to go dig the motherfucker up from his grave just so I can punch him in the jaw all over again.

I help Briar to her feet, and we slowly make our way inside, carefully steering our path to avoid any other patches of ice. I've got half a mind to just say fuck it and carry this girl, but even while shaken up, she seems determined to walk, even if it does require using me as a crutch to steady herself a little.

"I might shower to warm up, if that's okay?" she says as we get inside.

"Door open."

She turns on her heel to look at me, her brows drawn together.

"Can't have you passing out on me in there."

Briar tucks some hair behind one ear. "I think I'm good. It just took me a moment to get my feet back under me."

I know exactly what she's doing, and trying to brush this off as unimportant ain't gonna work with me.

"Door. Open. You answer me if I call out so I know you're al-right." I cross my arms and look down at her. "Don't think I won't hesitate to come in there, either, if I think something is wrong."

"Okay." She gives me an odd look, then takes off. The water starts running and I hear the slide of the shower curtain over the rail after a few moments.

The painkillers from last night are still sitting on the bench, glaring back at me reproachfully, because as much as I meant that in a protective "I'm here to take care of you" kind of way, there is also a very large part of me that wants to ignore our circumstances, and the difference in age between us, and go in there anyway.

I brace both hands on the kitchen bench and drop my head.

Is there a hell reserved for men like me? A man who spent a lifetime not wanting anything meaningful with anyone, only to find the person I'm drawn to in ways I cannot fucking fathom or explain is someone who I'm sure there are laws in certain states prohibiting me from going anywhere near.

"*Hiiii.* Still alive," Briar calls out. Interrupting my sudden compulsion to start trawling through online search results and the legal quagmire of relations between adopted family members.

Jesus fucking Christ.

"Don't use all the fucking hot water," I shout back with my eyes squeezed shut.

After a couple more minutes, the shower turns off, and I can hear her moving around. With a mug in hand, I stand and stare at the three different types of fruity teas Briar bought the other day in town, lined up on the shelf.

How the hell am I supposed to know which one she'll want? Coffee has been my go-to for years; I've never voluntarily drank hot fruit-flavored water. The concept is fucking weird. After sniffing each of them, I settle on lemon and ginger. I'm sure that's supposed to be good with nausea, and there's every chance she might feel pretty rough later on.

Christ, I didn't fall off a bull during my pro years, but I certainly hit my head enough times doing dumb shit when I was young and too much of an idiot for my own good. Personal experience and being around enough rodeo injuries taught me how damaging that lingering impact can be on the brain.

Briar emerges, smelling like soap and flushed with steam, and there's a now-familiar tug of a hook in my gut that makes me want to hold her.

Wanting to hug my niece isn't the weird part; the messed-up bit is that after I hug her, I want to be able to duck my head and wrap my palm around her jaw as I brush our lips together. And within those illicit acts lies my giant goddamn problem.

"Sit down. Chill. Put a movie on or something." Jerking my head, I gesture in the direction of the sectional couch. "Don't touch that phone of yours." I place the tea on the coffee table beside her before handing over a couple of painkillers and a glass of water. This is the world's weirdest UNO Reverse from the events of last night.

She downs the pills, but I see the tightness in her face at the mention of her phone. "No need to worry about that."

My mind is still chewing over what she said outside. Turning over how secretive this girl has been about the entire reason she's landed here in Crimson Ridge in the first place.

Everyone hates me.

"I'll be right here while I get some paperwork done. Just let me know if your head starts to feel worse, or if you feel like you're gonna hurl." I rub a hand over the back of my neck, hovering as she settles herself with feet tucked under her. "Have you eaten? Are you hungry?" Realizing I left pretty abruptly earlier, I don't actually know if she ate after I took off to town to sort out the shit I'm going to need for Beau's ranch job.

After I ran out that door, because last night was . . . well . . . too close.

Not to mention, I actually slept for the first time since she arrived, and getting such a good stretch of uninterrupted sleep reminded me of all the issues around our complicated goddamn set of current living arrangements.

Briar hits me with a smile that doesn't quite reach her eyes. "I'm fine. Thanks all the same . . . and I promise to say if I need anything."

"You don't have to treat me like I'm made of porcelain." The girl with the potentially bruised brain follows me into the kitchenette, huffing at my back as if doing the basics like feeding her dinner and then collecting her dishes is some sort of above and beyond feat I'm performing.

Christ. I hate anyone and everyone who was in her life before she came here.

"Sit your ass back down. You nearly cracked your skull open today," I grumble.

"But I didn't. So, at least let me do the washing up." This space is too cramped for both of us to be in front of the sink at the same time, but she tries to squeeze past me all the same.

That puts us in very, very close quarters.

Her soft, little body is pressed up against my hip and my thigh, making it all too easy, when I look down and see the tangle of dark hair bundled on top of her head, for my mind to begin wandering into territory I should steer well clear of. Picturing exactly how we would fit together in *other* ways.

"Fine. Have at it." At this point, I'm surviving on sheer will-power alone to not start getting hard every time she's within breathing distance. So I flick the soap bubbles and hot water off my hands and grab the dishcloth. Propping my ass against the kitchen bench, I stand there and wait for the clean dishes to emerge from the suds.

We work in tandem to clean up in a comfortable sort of silence. That's one thing I've noticed about having her in this cabin—Briar seems happy with the long stretches of quiet. The quiet is not intentional on my part, but after living on my own for so long, the prospect of having someone chatty in my space would be a living nightmare. No matter how hot they are.

I crave my peace. I enjoy the quiet. I don't exactly feel like talking much before about ten in the morning, and after a long fucking day of shoeing horses, my brain and my body are exhausted.

Somehow, Briar molds neatly around all of that, and I don't entirely know what to do with that golden nugget of information that is incessantly, triumphantly, presenting itself inside my mind.

When we chat, it's easy. She's got this dry sense of humor hidden away, and I love seeing it rise to the surface every now and then when she doesn't notice she's let her guard down. Like she did last night when she played nurse and helped my stiff muscles and wrecked back more than she knows.

Thanks to her impromptu massage, coupled with sleeping properly, I've been able to move around freely today, so I'm back to almost feeling brand-new again.

Which is possibly why I'm drying each item coming out of that sink with extremely thorough precision. There's a conversation I need to have with Briar, and I'm not entirely sure how it'll go.

It's been kicking around my brain all afternoon, while I should have been focusing on accounts and invoices and paying bills and shit. Instead, I was yet again distracted as fuck by the gorgeous girl curled up on my couch, directly in my line of sight from where I sat over at the table.

The final piece of cutlery emerges, sparkling clean and covered in a sheen of water, and I damn near bend the thing in half as I wrap it in the towel and dry the spoon with far more force than is necessary.

Briar lets the plug out of the sink, and the only sounds then filling the space are the draining of used water and crackling of logs burning low in the fire.

"I'll need to take a proper look at your head." My throat is thick, voice gritty. "You know, see if your brain has leaked out."

What the hell is wrong with me? Evidently, I'm trying to make jokes, while the situation we're gonna have to discuss is anything but a laughing matter.

In fact, this entire prospect might go up in flames.

Dark eyes bounce to mine, her hand flying up to the back of her skull. "I'm pretty sure it's fine." She says the words slowly, her features tightening as her fingers make contact, which immediately makes me narrow my focus on that spot she just touched.

"Up there. Let me look." Dropping the towel like a hot coal, I advance. No pausing or asking for permission—I just hoist Briar by the waist and deposit her ass on the benchtop.

She makes a squeak of protest, her tiny fists pressing into the front of my shirt.

Reminding me all over again, with that small act of connection, just how fucking good it felt to have her hands on me.

But, no. Goddamn it. This is me being a caring and responsible person, for once in my life. I can't in good conscience let this girl go to sleep tonight without knowing . . . without being certain.

Pushing against me with fists clenched, Briar holds her body stiff as I stand my ground. We're back in that place where we're both much closer than we need to be, but I'm feeling all kinds of protective over this girl, and she won't tell me the truth about shit from her past or how she's feeling after her fall earlier.

So she's just going to have to suck it up and deal with the way I do things.

"Turn your head for me, darlin.'" My thighs are wedged between her knees so I can remain close. There's a moment when I weigh the consequences, when I hesitate for all of the length of time it takes her to suck in a sharp inhale. I'm caught up in a place where *should* has become a weighted word.

Should I be touching this girl?

Should I be so worryingly attracted to her?

If anything, I *should* be thinking about stepping back or putting an appropriate distance between us, but then concerns about whether or not she has a bleeding brain take precedence.

"I'm going to check the place where you cracked your head, okay?"

Briar huffs out another soft noise but obliges and turns her neck to the side, keeping her eyes low, focus dipped toward the floor.

"Tell me if there's pain." I swallow heavily and slide my fingertips gingerly up from the base of her hair. The soft strands are slightly curled around her nape from the steam of the shower earlier, and loose tendrils framing her face shift beneath my breath as I lean forward. Just like on the day in the barn when I helped her off that damn horse, my mouth is so close to the shell of her ear that it wouldn't take anything to close those frighteningly small series of inches and make contact with her bare skin.

Oh, how simple it would be to eat up that whisper of distance and feel the shudder run through her beneath my lips.

What I really want to do is thread my fingers into her hair. To see the way her dark curls look wrapped in my fist, intertwined with the ink of my name across my knuckles. Holy shit, the image sends something streaking like a comet straight through my bloodstream.

Purely possessive, maddening thoughts about how this girl

should be mine burst through my veins, feeling like the first explosive fraction of a second after being released from a bucking chute into the arena.

Drawing in a steadying breath through my nose, I try to calm my racing pulse. This is something I gotta focus on and not lose my shit, or my mind, down a gutter of filthy goddamn fantasies.

If I'm ever going to earn this girl's trust, this is one step in that direction.

"No pain yet." Briar's voice is quiet. A whisper.

"How about now?" I murmur as my fingers glide up higher, tracing the slope of her nape up towards the base of her skull.

She shivers when the heel of my palm grazes her jaw. Tilting her head further to the side, Briar gives me greater access.

Goddamn. It's the smallest gesture, but there's so much submission in it, and a look of ease softens her face. It's as if she's soaking up every moment and actually enjoying this. Seeing that wash of relief is what makes me linger, drawing this moment out. Rather than being brisk or functional when I should be entirely focused on the task at hand—the one where I'm checking her head for a sign of swelling or excessive bruising—instead, I'm allowing her the sensation of touch that it's obvious she's gone without for far too long.

This is all it takes to have her melting in the palm of my hand? Christ. The shit that stirs up behind my ribs, squeezing hard inside my chest . . . There's a feral beast wanting to leap out and devour the pretty little thing seated before me.

Her eyelashes rest on her cheeks, her pouty little lips parted on a shaky exhale, and her pink tongue swipes over her bottom lip, leaving a glossy, wet line.

As I study her up close like this, my mind descends to the most depraved of places. There's surely a hell reserved for uncles who can't keep their hands to themselves. Right now, I am tumbling headfirst down the rabbit hole with no hope of emerging unscathed from this misadventure.

I'm essentially cupping my niece's face, standing between her legs. If this were any other woman in my kitchen positioned at my mercy like this long after dark, we'd be about twenty seconds away from fucking.

But this moment, right here, sucks the air from the tiny distance between us. Time gets hung on a hook, calling a truce, while allowing us to explore an intimate moment that we both realize shouldn't be indulged.

My fingers walk their way higher. Tracing the spot where the top of her spine meets her skull. Then higher still. Coming to tentatively rest on the back of her head.

"There's a bump there," I say, stating the goddamn obvious. My tongue feels heavy and awkward in my mouth as I gingerly draw the pad of my fingertip over the raised welt at the back of her head.

"It's a little sore," she admits.

"Worse than earlier?" I gently brush over the bump, not pressing hard, but wanting to make sure there's not something more concerning going on.

Briar makes a humming noise. "No. About the same."

In no universe do I need to be touching her still, to be lingering in such an intimate way, but Briar leans ever so subtly against my palm, so I choose to leave my hand there.

Christ, she's so beautiful, and I don't know how the fuck I'm going to get through this next part.

"You have to promise me something," I say.

"Not to rage chop a mountain of wood?" Her eyes stay closed, but her lips tug into a wry smile.

I swallow down the avalanche of inappropriate sensations vying to occupy my chest. Batting back all thoughts of how this girl is funny, and sweet, and sinfully gorgeous. As much as I'm supposed to, I can't deny the reality to myself anymore, even though I can't and *shouldn't* acknowledge the truth.

She's every inch my dream fucking girl.

"What I'm about to suggest. You have to promise you'll be reasonable."

"You're the stubborn bull around here. I'm the most reasonable person you'll ever meet."

"I'm serious, Briar."

The heaviness in my tone makes her lashes flutter, her dark eyes tilting toward me.

"You aren't allowed to fight me on this."

"Okay . . ." She wets her lips once more and gives me a highly suspicious glance.

"I can't leave you on your own tonight." Swallowing the rock determined to occupy my throat, I let my hand drop away. "Not while we need to be sure you're in the clear after taking such a heavy knock to the head."

Briar's chest rises and falls a little faster.

My pulse races loudly in my ears.

"You're saying . . ."

"I'm saying that you need someone to be there for you—in case something happens during the night, you know—and both of us ain't gonna fit on that couch."

Her throat bobs. "Sure."

The air damn near vibrates with the words I haven't yet said but that we both know are coming.

"It's fine," she adds quickly. Removing the need for me to actually say it out loud and risk confessing to every depraved second I've imagined saying fuck it and following her in there at night.

Briar shifts her weight and slides off the counter. "We're both adults. We can share a bed. Besides, you'll sleep better than you do torturing yourself on that couch."

And that's precisely the problem.

As I step back and watch her walk away, I know it.

As I build up the fire for the night, I know it.

As I hear her rustling around in the bedroom, I know it.

And when I make my way down the half a dozen short, familiar paces in the dark, drawn like a moth to the soft spill of light coming through the open bedroom doorway, my pulse jackhammers in my throat.

While that couch might have been physical torture to endure, as I ease myself into the other side of the bed, with every dip of the mattress beneath my bulk, I'm certain of one thing.

This . . . this is going to be a brutal punishment of an entirely different kind.

CHAPTER 12

Briar

This morning feels extra cozy.

The weight of my blanket feels like utter perfection, as if I'm safely cocooned. Warmth seeps through every part of me, radiating down to my toes.

Last night, I slept better than I have in . . . well . . . ever?

My eyes are still scratchy, and my head kinda throbs a little in a way that I'm not sure whether I should be concerned and start researching how far away the nearest medical center is, or if it's nothing to worry about.

Honestly, one positive I can glean from recent events is that after dropping into such a deep sleep, I feel a whole lot less like someone who is running from her past and more like a brand-new woman.

Yet, when I go to adjust my weight and stretch, I realize it isn't the heaviness of the blanket that feels so damn exquisite.

That pressure is coming from another body.

An extremely large body.

Oh my god.

My eyes pop open and that's when it all rushes back in. Vivid Technicolor replays of everything that happened on the kitchen counter last night begin sizzling through my brain.

How I practically nuzzled my uncle's hand in desperate search of a morsel of attention.

Then, what came immediately after.

Sharing a bed.

Sharing. A. Bed.

Now? Well, now . . . I've woken up somehow tangled with his figure, spooning him on this minuscule mattress, and the giant tattooed arm belonging to a man I shouldn't be in bed with at all is draped over my waist, securing my back against his chest.

What's worse is that my body already *knows*.

I have to squeeze my eyes shut and suppress a moan. Even though my brain might be lagging behind, struggling to catch up on events, my pussy is alert and awake and begging for attention. She has a megaphone in hand and zero intention of paying heed when told to politely sit down and shut up.

The intense ache between my thighs is unbearable.

As is the location of my uncle's hand. Because I don't want to dare lift the blanket to confirm what the lusty bitch occupying my brain has already gleefully discovered.

His forearm bands across my waist, and as I follow the sensation of every point of contact, I follow that heavy weight to where his hand rests over the top of my sleep shorts.

At first, I refuse to believe the facts as they are excruciatingly presented. The reality currently pressed hot and seductive over thin cotton.

However, a single, tiny shift of my hips confirms everything I'm unwilling to admit to myself.

The feeling of him cupping my sex, while asleep, sends sparks and shivers racing beneath my skin. Two minutes ago, I was asleep and blissfully unaware of what was happening here. Now I'm awake, and my body is already coiled tight, begging for release, all thanks to the fact he's holding me.

I mean, he's holding a very fucking intimate part of my body, but as far as I can tell, it isn't a conscious decision on his part.

He's dead asleep behind me. The steady rise and fall of his chest, the reverberations of his deep breathing flow through me from my spine to my chest, and it's hypnotic.

God, I need to move. I need to very quietly and carefully escape from this clusterfuck because my ovaries feel like they're about to start whining out loud if this unintentional teasing continues a moment longer.

As I try to plan my extraction from beneath his impossibly strong hold on me, that's when I feel it. There is absolutely no ignoring the sizable truth.

The impressive length of him digs into my lower back, and this time I genuinely have to bite down on my bottom lip to suppress the horny gasp that threatens to escape.

Holy shit. He's fully hard. His hands are all over me. I'm almost panting with need and utterly confused because there is no way a man like him could be attracted to a girl like me. Even in his sleep.

This is a level-ten alert. DEFCON One. Sound the emergency warning system. Shit is about to detonate. Every inch of my skin tingles with static and desire, and my thighs squeeze together. His fingers are right there, resting on top of the scorched material covering my pussy.

My plan yesterday had been to get on a dating app, but after everything that happened with those messages and my fall, I now don't want to go near my phone. Besides, I'm sure I remember hearing something at one time about limiting screen time if you're concussed.

Oh god, but I'm so unbelievably horny.

As I make another tiny shift, clenching and squeezing in my futile effort to ease that unbearable ache, I wince, not because of my head but rather because that small movement just revealed the truth of exactly how slick my pussy and upper thighs are.

Well, shit. My body has been on a sexual starvation diet for so long—it only takes a second to confirm exactly how soaked I am.

Clearly, with my banged-up head and all, while I've been sleeping, my body has responded to his touch, and I'm left battling the urge to bite down on my pillow and scream.

I have to fight about a thousand other urges floating to the surface like champagne bubbles. Namely, ones that involve straddling my insanely hot uncle and waking him up by demanding that he fucks me so hard I see stars.

If our situation were different . . . would he be interested in me? If he were awake, would his body respond in this same way?

Other than his mistaking me for someone else that first night and his looking out for me, there have been a few moments where I've wondered. But then he's been impossible to read. Brooding and quiet, yet charming as sin when he fixes me with those bright blue eyes I could drown under the weight of.

God. *He's big.* The size of him pressing insistently against my spine is enough to leave me breathless. And I'm so unbelievably morally fucked up because even though I should be moving away, I'm still lying here, stealing the touches and warmth of him pressed along the length of my back and ass and thighs, touching almost every part of my body with his. Stealing all of that touch I've grown so desperate for over the years.

Even if he's giving it to me unknowingly.

Nope. No. Briar, you need to get yourself out of this disaster right now. You're tired, you're needy, and this man has been good to you.

Don't go spinning this into a golden thread of meaning when there is absolutely nothing to whatever happened during the night.

He's obviously accustomed to having women in his bed, and I'm sure that this is just a reflex for him. After years of entertaining his bed buddies.

Ugh. Why does that thought—even just the droplet of an idea forming of him being with someone like that, of being with a woman—make me want to growl?

Then, a more serious thought douses cold water all over the flames that have been licking at my core beneath his hot palm.

How many women has he fucked in this very bed?

How many others have been tangled with him in these sheets as they've cried his name into the wilderness while he's fucked their brains out?

That sends a chill trickling ice straight to my toes. Galvanizing me into action.

Fuck this. I need to get myself away from whatever devilish little twisted-up monster has taken hold of my thoughts.

Slipping out from under his arm with all the skills of a ninja, I slide as gently as possible from the bed, and tiptoe my way to the bathroom in the filtered gray murkiness of predawn. I don't know if I hear him stirring in the bedroom behind me, but I've never been more grateful for a lack of creaky floorboards or squeaking door hinges.

At least I've extracted myself from what could have been an extremely awkward situation. If he wakes up in bed alone with morning wood, there's nothing unusual about that, right? Happens to guys all the time.

My fingers grip the edge of the bathroom door as I hover in a state of indecision. Should I leave it open or closed? Last night, he insisted on me keeping it open while I showered, and right now, I don't know what would be worse—leaving it open when I really, really need to take care of the situation between my thighs, or closing the door and risking that he'll barge through like a snorting bull.

Weighing my options rapidly, I figure it is much more likely that my attempts to quietly get myself off in the shower would be rudely interrupted if I close this door. So I suck in a breath and step toward the shower. As I flip the water on and begin to quickly ditch the hoodie and sleep shorts I'm wearing, my mind drifts back to being in that bed and the sensation of being wrapped in those strong arms. The heat and forceful weight of him still lingers on my skin.

Surrounded by all of that sensory overload, I had a fragmented glimpse at what it must feel like to have someone love and care for you. Despite being so unfamiliar to me, is that what it's like when a person can't go a night without touching you?

God. I spent too long trapped in that house, sleeping on my own.

It's better if we have our own rooms, babe. I work late and can't sleep unless I've got my own space. I know you'll understand.

Ugh, it was such a classic line—why the hell I let myself fall for it is a nightmare I don't intend to revisit.

Stepping into the tub beneath the stream of hot water, I can't help myself from wondering if the man who had my body wrapped tight in his grasp this morning . . . was there any chance he thought about me at all through those hours of sleep? Did his subconscious know it was *me*, or was it another woman he dreamt of taking up that spot in his bed?

I'm so tightly wound, just the lightest, briefest brush of my fingertips over my hard nipples sends a swirl of pleasure blossoming in my core. The water drums a steady beat onto the bottom of the tub, sluicing across my skin. Even though that door is wide open, even though I wish I could use my vibrator carefully hidden inside my bag, I have no other choice.

This is something my body needs. I can be quiet and quick about it. All I need to do right now is take the edge off this insanity.

Bracing one hand against the wall, I shift my weight so that one foot rests on the ledge. My fingers slide down through my slit, and the slippery wetness waiting there for me tells me everything I need to know about how desperate my body has been.

With that hand, I part my pussy lips and glide a finger over my swollen clit. Holy shit, the relief that floods through my veins is a powerful, heady feeling when I finally make contact with that part of me that has been in need of attention.

Pleasure bursts through me beneath my circling motions; it's not going to take me long to shatter into a thousand pieces. Between the heat of the water and the desire running like liquid fire through every inch of my skin, I can feel the heat flush my cheeks and my chest, building and intensifying with each rub over the bundle of nerves.

My eyes squeeze shut as my fingers claw against the tiled wall. Everything glows and tingles, and that coil winds tighter. The same sensation as last night when I had a rugged cowboy standing between my knees. He loomed over me as I sat there unmoving, tall, and imposing, like the pine trees surrounding this cabin. The press of his fingertips against my nape damn near had me whimpering, just like I'm at risk of doing right now.

I can't make a sound . . . I can't—

"Briar, are you okay in there?"

Oh, fuck. Oh god. My fingers jerk away from my clit. Embarrassment flushes straight up my chest. He couldn't see me, couldn't hear anything . . . There was no way, surely?

"Briar?" That deep, familiar voice is closer now. Too close. He's inside the bathroom, and I see the faint shadowy outline of his presence on the other side of this flimsy shower curtain.

"Umm. Yep. Just needed a quick shower," I stammer out. As my hand drags up over my hip, I wince, realizing the slick trail of my arousal coating my fingers has left a residue behind.

"Are you sure you're okay in there?"

Something akin to a strangled noise comes out of me instead of words.

That, unfortunately, draws him closer. I'm nearly convulsing with embarrassment and panic. "Do you need some help in there, darlin'?" His voice is raspy with sleep and doing that deep, sensuous thing that tempts me to fling this curtain aside and launch at him.

"Need a hand?" He's so close I see the shadow of his hand when he yawns and reaches up to roughly thread his hair.

Oh my fucking god. I want to dissolve down this drain right this second.

"No—No, I'm fine." Stammering, I can only hope to all things holy that the pounding shower spray on the base of the tub disguises my strained tone.

"You hungry?" Even over the drumming water and hammering of my pulse, a heavy rasp of sleep coats his voice, and my mind immediately wanders to illicit places. I'm making everything so goddamn sexual, and I need him to go the fuck away so I can get myself off. I need to successfully get rid of this tornado of lust flying around, trapped beneath my skin, and him standing over me in the bathroom is not helping any of this highly inappropriate confusion I've been experiencing.

"Thanks, some breakfast would be great." Do I sound like I'm falling apart in here? Because I'm about one second away from combusting.

He doesn't answer for what feels like an eternity. "Okay." Then, his footsteps retreat.

Relief interlocks with a torrential downpour of self-judgment as my fingers seek out my clit. This time I make desperate, hard, fast circles when I reach out for that precipice I had been so close to before.

Sparks begin to creep up from my toes. God, all I can see behind my eyelids as they fall shut again and my head drops forward is *him*.

I try my hardest to picture someone, anyone else. But I'm evidently a slut for the man only a few feet away.

I shouldn't picture him like this, but he invades my lust-soaked brain.

His strong arms.

Tattoos filling my vision as he snakes his hold around me from behind.

His rough hands seek out my breasts, my stomach. His hard planes of muscle cover my back, and that sensation of his arousal digs into my spine.

The rumbling sound of pleasure fills my ears as he feels just how slick and slippery I am. How swollen my clit is, just for him.

Deftly nudging my hand out of the way, he takes over.

Let me take care of you, darlin'. Let me show you what you need.

Holy shit, my body ignites.

There's a ringing in my ears, and my knees almost buckle as the wave crashes immediately. Driving fast and hard through me as soon as I picture the man who I shouldn't be thinking about *at all* touching me.

With fumbling hands and my heart galloping like the wind, I turn the water off—because I've definitely been in this shower too long—feeling the intense sting of disappointment as silence envelops me.

The man I can't bring myself to stop craving, who is just down the hall, is one I cannot ever have.

And more than anything, I have to admit the glaringly obvious reality.

I might have wanted him to go away before.

Yet the truth is I wish he had joined me.

CHAPTER 13

Briar

"Wait here, I've gotta fetch some sandpaper, then the last stop is to grab the paint."

Sneaking a look at my uncle as he disappears off down the aisle of the hardware store, I do my utmost not to stare at his ass inside those perfectly fitted Wranglers.

I fail miserably.

This store seems to be relatively deserted at this time of the afternoon, so I don't think anyone saw my eyes linger enjoying the sight of him walking away. But even so, I've got to quit this unhealthy obsession with a man who is entirely off-limits.

Ignoring our complicated family dynamic, he's fourteen years older than me. Not that I'm counting or fixating on tiny details like that or anything. Why am I even spending time working that kind of thing out in my head? What does our difference in age matter when the man is my *uncle*? He's someone who I absolutely cannot, and should not, desire.

Yet, here I am. Far too enamored with this muscular, tattooed, farrier-come-ranch handyman, who wears a pair of chaps like God hand-selected them just for him.

I bend over and rest my forehead against the handle of the cart, barely restraining myself from letting out a wail of frustration. What is this hellscape of temptation I've wandered into? Standing in the middle of aisle five, surrounded by nails and screws, meanwhile, I can't stop thinking about the man who I now share an impossibly small bed with.

Even though we shared a bed that first time to make sure my concussion didn't worsen, it naturally evolved into an unspoken agreement that he needed to keep an eye on me the next night, so we carried on sharing the bedroom. Then, the night after that.

His room.

His bed.

Now, I'm right in the thick of a nightly cycle with a cowboy who invariably finds his way to be wrapped around me. When I wake up, I'm encased in his arms. No matter how hard I try to escape to the very edge of the mattress in a half-hearted attempt to put distance between us, both nights now, it's happened without any say on my part.

The budding secret I'm harboring is that I eat up every single occasion, even though so far it's only been two additional nights. I'm more than addicted to opening my eyes before dawn and feeling the delicious weight of his forearm banded around my waist, along my body, both times cupping over my shorts again like that first night.

He seems to sleep so heavily—probably making up for that weeklong agony of being on the couch—that I don't know if he even realizes what has been happening while he slumbers. I've long disappeared from the bed before there's ever any sign of him stirring.

I know it can't go on, but I'm also too greedy for whatever this is to put any effort into coming up with an alternative solution to our sleeping arrangement.

Because you're being a needy, touch-starved little slut for your uncle.

Scrunching my eyes shut, I clench my fingers tighter around the handle of the cart.

As I'm busy judging myself for all my messed-up daydreams, my bag slung across my body vibrates with an incoming call. It startles me out of my haze. I've gotten so used to being either at the cabin or Devil's Peak Ranch, blissfully without cell reception; I had completely forgotten that down here in town, we would be somewhat reconnected with the outside world.

The vibrations stop, but I know that won't be the end of it. On cue, they start up again, the buzzing drone vibrating through my cross-body purse.

Letting out a frustrated huff, I dig out my phone—sure enough, "Crispin" flashes across my screen. My grip tightens as I stare at the phone ringing until she eventually gets the hint and hangs up.

I'm just about to put it back in my bag, when it starts vibrating again in my hand. This time, "Unknown" shows on the display.

While I've blocked my ex on everything, I could put money on this being him trying to call.

"You gonna answer that or just stare at it?" My uncle's voice cuts through my blank state, and I quickly hit Decline with my thumb.

"Unknown number." I shrug, but before I can stuff my phone away, it starts up again with another attempted call.

"Looks like someone's mighty interested in getting ahold of you." He tosses the sheets of sandpaper into the cart.

"It's not important." Declining the call again, I plaster on a smile. "What did you say we needed to pick up next? Paint?" I go to push the cart forward, then wince as my phone starts vibrating, this time even louder because it's still clutched in my hand and pressed against the hard plastic handle of the cart.

"Sounds like it might be important." The wall of man at my side flicks his eyes between my phone and me. His steely blue gaze is unreadable. "There something going on that you need to talk about?"

I shake my head, trying to figure out the best course of action to get him off my back. I'm far too embarrassed about the reasons I ran to Crimson Ridge, and I'd rather eat a frog than tell my uncle anything about why my asshole ex is trying to harass me over the phone.

"Briar." His jaw flexes.

"It's just Crispin being her usual self." I figure a fragmented truth will be better than nothing. He knows exactly the type of person my sister is, and while I feel uncomfortable lying to him, at least what I said is partly true.

I've allowed myself to be treated so badly by all of them for so long, it's humiliating. And I can't bear the thought of him thinking less of me.

"You want me to sort her out for you?"

God. I find myself staring at him open-mouthed. Just like that, without question, this man would be prepared to willingly tangle with the source of pure misery herself, would be willing to go into battle against the human equivalent of a toxic, twelve-headed Hydra . . . on my behalf.

"Uh, no. It's fine. She and I had a disagreement before I left. Don't really feel like taking her calls just yet." Which is a very polite way to summarize how my own sister told me I should count myself lucky a man like Antoine would tolerate me and that it was perfectly normal for him to get his dick wet somewhere else.

Jesus. I'd gladly never see that woman's face again as long as I live.

"She always was a piece of work," he mutters, then strides ahead in the direction of the paint aisle. As I trundle after his broad shoulders, I feel like I can somewhat breathe again.

By the time we finish getting everything required for the ranch fix-up job my uncle is going to be working on—something about an old rodeo friend with a new dude-ranch venture he's preparing to open for business—we're both starved.

The prospect of neither of us having to cook tonight is what lures us to a bar—one, I assume, must be the only place in Crimson Ridge to get a drink or a meal after dark.

A cowboy joint, aptly named the Loaded Hog, is lit up with a warm glow and a country-bar feel when we get inside. There are booths along one wall, a lengthy wooden bar, and leaners scattered around a space that looks like it becomes a dance floor when the place gets busy.

I feel a tad self-conscious in jeans, a cropped sweater, and boots. Not that I don't like how I look, but I've had it drummed into me for so long that my appearance had to be *perfect* at all times. God forbid I potentially bring the Lane or Montgomery family names into disrepute if I was "papped" in public portraying anything less than a perfectly curated appearance. Before coming to these mountains, I would never have been allowed to wear something so casual out for dinner, but then again, I decide as I glance around that what I'm wearing is far more the style of everyone else in here tonight.

Plus, I love the hell out of these jeans. They work magic on my ass, so I'm quietly pleased to have more opportunities to wear them around Crimson Ridge.

"Oh hey, Storm."

I've barely slid into the booth when we hear a sultry voice at the end of our table, arriving within seconds as if by magic. The waitress, who just performed a miracle and formed out of thin air, is fixated on the man seated across from me and cocks her head to one side while loudly chomping gum. Eyes bouncing across every muscle in his body, she practically drools all over our table.

This girl is pretty, damn her. Glossy chestnut hair tied in a ponytail. Blue-eyed. A walking showcase for whatever flawless skincare regime she abides by. To top it all off, she's got the kind of effortlessly perfect makeup worthy of a centerfold spread. She's a walking, talking, perfect country-princess package.

My hackles are up within half a second.

"Briar, this is, uhh—" He readjusts himself in the booth and scowls at the menu already on the table.

"Luce . . ." She flashes me eyes that have unmistakable, thinly veiled daggers where her pupils should be. "Cute sweater, Briar."

Her eyes take in my appearance and then bounce back up with a half-hearted, fake-ass smile. Those eyeballs of hers nearly rolled straight out of her head as she drawled my name. This bitch doesn't think my sweater is cute at all. Her claws are unsheathed and ready to shred me for daring to sit in the same booth as Stôrmand Lane.

God, could she cock a leg and piss all over the place more?

"You want to order?" The man across from me doesn't seem to be taking any more notice of this girl, who probably is younger than me, and while that should make me feel better . . . somehow it doesn't.

"Uh, yeah, I'll have the grilled chicken."

"You want the usual, Storm?"

Yeah, the message is loud and clear. Our waitress is pretty much ready to pop her shirt buttons to prove there's some sort of history between the two of them.

I busy myself pouring some water from the carafe already on the table.

"Just a burger will do, thanks."

"You want to order anything to drink with your meal, Storm?"

"Briar?" He deflects the question to me.

My eyes meet the fierce blue gaze directly across from me. "No, I'm fine with water, thanks."

He shakes his head and slides the menu toward her. I do the same.

"No problem." She scoops up both menus, cradling them against her chest, starts to walk away, then turns back. "Oh, so, it's silly, but you never texted me back, and I wasn't sure if I left my lip gloss in your truck . . . I mean, it might have slipped out of my pocket that night."

Fuck my entire life. Try as I might, I can't sit here and listen to this girl start reminiscing about her activities involving my uncle that may or may not have led to her misplacing a tube of lip gloss.

"I'm just gonna use the bathroom," I mutter, sliding out of the booth without looking at either of them.

Behind me, I can hear Luce continue to chatter away, not like she's got other customers or anything better to do than hit on the man who possibly, maybe, most definitely fucked her in his truck.

When I find the bathroom, I'm glad to shut the door and let the air rush out of my lungs. God, I'm such a jumbled-up mess of emotions. There is absolutely no reason for him not to be with someone. I mean, for god's sake, that girl could have been who he rushed off to see the other night for all I know.

Ugh. Yuck. It was her, wasn't it?

Rubbing my temples, I take some deep inhales, then flip on the faucet to run some cold water over my wrists. My body feels hot and prickly, and I'm suddenly imagining exactly how well Luce and her shiny chestnut hair, which looks like she came to work straight from the salon, attend to my uncle when she's not waitressing.

I have no right to feel any sort of way about them. None at all.

Drying my hands and smoothing down the front of my jeans, I take a final glance in the mirror. All I need to do is go sit through a meal. I've sat through plenty of awful dinners and galas and stupid high-society events with miserable, vain people in my life.

I can handle an irritating waitress, even one who intends on shoving her tongue down my uncle's throat before I've managed a bite of my meal.

As I emerge from the bathroom and make my way back down the hallway to the main bar, I change my mind. A drink sounds like a fucking outstanding idea, after all.

I have no idea what to order without sounding like a total "city girl," as everyone up at Devil's Peak Ranch has grown fond of calling me, now including both Colt and Layla. So I join the line of bodies standing and leaning around the bar and order myself a beer. Seems like the easiest option.

A sweet-looking older lady serves me, who I give my thanks to. Based on the twinkle in her eye, there's no doubt she could wrangle any rowdy asshole in here with ease. Grabbing my drink, I turn and immediately bump into a broad chest.

"Oh, shit. I'm so sorry." It's damn lucky I didn't spill my entire drink over this guy's shirt.

"Nothing to apologize for, ma'am. It's me being clumsy over here and getting in your way." He flashes me a smile that is utterly charming. Of course, this is cowboy territory, after all.

Looks like I might not have to brave the terrifying jungle of dating apps, since the universe has literally dropped a dream candidate right in my path.

This guy is probably in his late thirties from the look of him, with a little rugged stubble going on and tousled dark hair. Total lady killer with a smile like that, and the tall, dark, and tempting look is absolutely working for him.

This.

This is exactly what I need.

I swiftly boot aside my pouting bitch of a heart, who loudly protests that this isn't the cowboy I *want*. Clearly, my own sense of judgment has been entirely misplaced, and I cannot have what I want, so please, god, let this man smiling down at me be single and have a nice-looking dick he knows how to put to use.

"No ma'ams here, just Briar."

"Pleasure to meet you, just Briar." He extends a hand to wrap around mine, and he's got that calloused, warm sort of touch that should be making my heart flutter. But instead, I'm more fixated than I should be on the fact there was no jolt of a spark like those times when I first brushed fingertips with . . . No, pump the brakes. Stop it right now. I am not thinking about him or late nights in that cabin alone or waking up with his torso, and other large appendages, pressed against the length of my spine.

Do not for one goddamn second think about Stôrmand Lane's cock.

Do. Not.

I force a smile and bat my eyelashes at the charming cowboy. Crap, did he say his name, and I totally missed it?

"I'm Westin. Or, just Wes will do just fine."

He squeezes my palm, and there's enough of a little hit of nervous excitement at the closeness and charm of him. Okay. Mr. Cowboy is certainly promising. That right there, I can work with.

"Pardon me for being forward, but I gotta ask one question, and that's gonna decide what happens next."

I twist my lips into a smile. "Oh, is it now?" He's still holding my hand, and his eyes have crinkled around the edges from that sexy kind of smile guys like him can totally manage to pull off without even trying.

"Stôrmand over there . . ." He gestures with his chin in the direction of the booths. "Are you here with him tonight?" It's a genuine question; he's not being pushy or demanding. But I can tell straight away he knows exactly who my uncle is and isn't keen to tread on any cowboy boots.

However, none of that helps me where my awkward search for an answer is concerned. When I take a fraction too long to answer, I already see him start to withdraw.

"Oh, no." I laugh. Do I sound carefree? Like it's the most preposterous thing I've ever heard? "That's my uncle." I sure as shit hope that came out sounding natural, because, to my own ears, saying that word out loud feels like dragging fingernails down a chalkboard.

Westin—Wes's smile brightens. "Uncle? Shit, okay, wasn't expecting that." He shakes his head and blows out a breath.

"So, what happens next, now that I've answered your question . . . ?" With my free hand, I take a swig of my beer.

From across the room, I swear I can feel eyes on me, but I refuse to look in the direction of that booth or the waitress who might be straddling his lap by now for all I know.

"I don't want to disrupt your family dinner plans, but is there any hope a beautiful girl like yourself could put up with a rough-around-the-edges cowboy over coffee?"

Do not cringe at being referred to as family.

"Are you asking me out on a date, just Wes?" I allow a smile to creep over my lips. Please and thank you. I mean, coffee is a good-enough start, and from the look of him, this man could show me a good time around Crimson Ridge, I'm sure of it.

"You name the time and place." He's still got my hand wrapped in his, and as he says the words, his thumb slides over mine, and while it doesn't exactly shoot sparks through my blood, it feels nice.

"Tomorrow? I've got some things I gotta do around town, so I could use a coffee, even some lunch if you cowboys eat?"

"Oh, we know how to enjoy a meal, don't you worry about that." His eyes stay firmly fixed on my face, but my body flushes all the same at the cheeky insinuation hidden behind his polite mountain charm.

Yup. Cowboy here can absolutely sweep me off my feet and show me a good time. All my prayers have been answered.

We quickly exchange numbers and make plans for our coffee and lunch date tomorrow, which sounds entirely wholesome, but I'm secretly hoping it will lead to some very unwholesome behavior in the not-too-distant future.

As I float away, feeling a little more confident in the new Briar Lane who is determined to find her feet in Crimson Ridge, I look up to see the waitress with perfect hair, whom I never want to see again in my life, placing our meals down on the table.

Sliding back into the booth, I attack my plate in an attempt to fill the awkward silence stretching across the table. All while the most ferocious yet stunning set of blue eyes opposite me remain cold.

And the entire time, they're brutally fixed on me.

CHAPTER 14

Storm

Fuck this shit.

Fuck having to endure watching a bar full of assholes stare at my niece like she's a slab of meat all night. Now I'm the lucky guy who gets to take her home, take her to my bed, and for all my sins, I can't do anything more than wish like hell our circumstances were different.

"Didn't know you were an uncle there, Storm. At least you're not her dad or some shit, but either way, hope you don't mind. Briar and I got chatting over at the bar before, and we're gonna meet up to grab a coffee in town tomorrow."

I've known Wes for a long time. He's helped at a few of the same ranches as I have and is decent enough, and on the face of it, he's the perfect kind of guy to treat Briar the way she deserves to be treated.

But goddamn, if I didn't want to slam his mile-wide smile into the bar top when he came up to me as I paid the check. Chatting away all sparkly-eyed because the prettiest girl in this whole godforsaken town simply looked his way twice. Screw him and his perfect country-boy bullshit. I already had to damn well sit there watching as she smiled and flirted and gave Westin Hayes her number within all of two seconds. Then, to top it off,

I had to put up with the prick coming to regale me with all the details of the scene I just witnessed.

She even told the asshole that I'm her uncle. For fuck's sake.

Why that pissed me off so much is a question that doesn't bear answering.

I can't have this girl, yet I want her so fucking badly, and I'm about one more interaction like the one tonight away from threatening every male with a pulse in this entire goddamn state to stay the hell away from her.

Thank fuck she and Kayce seem to get along just as friends because I'm not sure how I would have explained to Colt that I'd reversed my truck over his son and dumped that blond idiot's body over the ravine if he'd shown even the slightest hint of interest in Briar.

He can give her horse riding lessons, and that's about as much as I'm willing to tolerate.

The truck bumps over the shingle as we draw up to the cabin. We've both been silent through finishing our meals and for the duration of the drive back up the mountain. There are a thousand things I want to say to Briar, but none of them are appropriate, and certainly the things I don't want to say but want to *do* are even less appropriate.

So silence has seemed like the safest refuge.

Cutting the engine, the quiet is oppressive. Deafening in contrast to the hum of the motor and my usual roster of metal blasting through the speakers. I flick the headlights off, and darkness seeps in, wrapping around us. Only the glow of the porch light left on outside the cabin spills out a warm patch of yellow, reflected off the faded reddish paintwork on the hood of my truck.

Neither of us moves.

"Your car's a piece of shit, by the way. Total death trap." I tighten both hands around the wheel, staring straight ahead while painfully aware of the small space filled by the two of us.

Briar seems a little surprised that I've finally said something. As if she'd been caught out while somewhere far away from this mountain, lost in thought herself. "Oh . . . it is?"

"Don't go driving anywhere in it." And by anywhere, I mean the date she's got coming up tomorrow. I'd prefer she never leave this mountain unless it was under my supervision, but it's hardly likely she'd be happy to tag along with me for the rest of her time in Crimson Ridge.

Suddenly, I'm seeing images flash in front of my eyes of Westin fucking Hayes pulling up this very drive, in his truck that looks identical to mine, with Briar cozied up next to him, tucked under his arm.

"If you ever need to get into town, especially if it's icy, take my truck, not that heap of junk, okay?"

Briar twists her body to face me and laughs softly. It's a sound that makes my gut twist because I want to be the only man she laughs freely like that around. I want to be the one she exclusively rolls her eyes at and graces with disapproving huffs and gives her smart-mouthed side to.

"I'm serious." My knuckles are white, gripping the steering wheel like I'm intending to rip it out.

"Well, I have no idea how to drive a stick." Briar rolls her lips together. "So, in that case, it looks like I'm going to be stuck up here."

The temperature in this truck skyrockets as she says those words. She's got that raspy edge to her voice as she says out loud what shouldn't sound so alluring but does.

Is Briar content to be stuck up here . . . with me?

Fuck. Maybe it's the late hour or the tension of seeing her with another guy, one who was busy stealing her smiles, but something breaks inside my brain.

"Do you want to learn?" The words are out of my mouth, and I can't take them back. Either Briar is going to vanish out that door, slamming it in my face, or she's going to step across this line with me. Embers build low in my stomach as soon as she locks her dark eyes with mine.

Her tongue darts out to wet her lips, and she slowly nods her head.

"Slide over here then, darlin'." There is absolutely no doubt that I'm going to hell, but fuck it.

She hesitates for a moment, then inches closer. Her jeans crease around the tops of her thighs, and it reminds me just how difficult it has been today not to stare at the way they suction perfectly around her ass. This girl has a body designed to bring a man like me to his knees.

"You're not gonna learn from all the way over there." I ease myself further back in the seat to create more room between my thighs and the wheel. Yup. Straight to hell.

Widening my legs, I reach one hand to settle on the headrest, opening my lap in invitation.

"Come here."

Her eyes widen slightly, and goddamn, do I eat up every second of her starting to squirm at the prospect of what shouldn't exist between us. Of the two of us dancing around this closeness that we've both tried our hardest to ignore.

But like the good girl she is, Briar slides over onto my lap, and I have to stifle a groan at how fucking perfect it feels to have her back tucked against me, her hips fitted to mine, our bodies lining up in the most sinfully, temptingly, perfect way.

"Now what?" She tilts her head to one side, voice barely a whisper, just like the night in the kitchen.

"You have to use the clutch to change gears." I show her with my feet on the pedals. "When you want to shift up or down, you gotta use this guy right here. It's like a dance. If you ease this one down, you let up on the accelerator. And then do it all in reverse." My voice is low, my chin just about resting on her shoulder as I talk through the motions.

"I can't reach the pedals," she protests.

"Just put your feet on top of mine. I'll guide you through it."

Briar's steady breathing picks up a little as I shift my arms, caging her in to demonstrate shifting in and out of gear.

"Seems complicated." Her fists are balled on top of her thighs. With the way my head is spinning with her scent and the heat between our bodies, I'm not entirely sure whether she's talking about driving a stick or something else.

"Nothing you can't learn if you give it a try." I wrap my palms over her fists, and she hitches in a breath, that preciously soft body jerks slightly when I make direct contact to lift her hands.

"I—I haven't had much experience."

Jesus. My cock jerks hearing those words, that admission. It sends a surge of something primal right through me. All my blood is running south at a rapid rate.

"One hand here . . ." Placing her fingers on the steering wheel, I guide her other to the shifter. "Use the other, like this, see." Closing my hand over hers to hold the top, I'm acutely aware of how many lines we're crossing right now.

But she isn't running from me. This girl could have fled this truck and left me sitting here in the dark the moment we arrived. Yet, she stayed.

She's just as drawn into the depths of this illicit thing as I am, and maybe we can't cross every line, but right now, trapped up here alone, in the dark and the silent chill of the night air, maybe we can blur those lines and pretend for a little while.

"Try the pedals." My lips are so close to her ear that I see the way she shivers as my breath glides over her skin. Fuck, all I want to do is suck down on that pulse point fluttering in her neck. I just know that spot would have her arching her back and grinding her ass into me, but I'm exercising a saintly level of restraint by maintaining a fraction of distance between my teeth and her throat.

Trying to completely ignore the fact my niece is sitting in my lap and that there is no doubt she absolutely feels how hard I am beneath her ass, even through both of our layers of jeans.

"That's it. Push down on me." My Adam's apple bobs as I swallow heavily.

Briar does as I showed her, guiding my feet to depress the clutch and shift into gear, then switching her weight to ease back on one side and press down on the other, where the accelerator is wedged beneath my boot. We're parked and the engine is off, so there's only the quiet clunk of the pedals moving around to act as a soundtrack to this moment.

With each shift of her legs and feet and hand, our bodies rub against one another in a way that has me damn near groaning.

"A little slower, darlin'," I murmur. Bringing my hands to her thighs, I slide my hot palms across the tight denim and guide her movements into a smoother transition between the clutch and the accelerator.

As my fingers hook the inside of her knees, squeezing a little, Briar's head drops back against my shoulder. I hear the air leave her lungs, and the tiniest sound of need slips past her lips.

If I wasn't already fully gone and ready to risk it all, that tiny act of submitting beneath my touch would have just unraveled the last thread I was clinging to.

"Good girl. That was perfect for your first time." I let my fingers stroke over the inside of her knees a little more, brushing and exploring a little higher, and she melts against my chest the longer I keep holding her like this.

Her hands slide down the steering wheel, coming to rest at the base.

"What else did you never get taught?" Holy shit. My mind had already conjured up far too many filthy scenarios with this girl, but now I'm hungry to hear what she might admit to me out loud.

She lets out the softest whimper as my palms glide along the inner swell of her thighs. "Lots of things."

"How long has it been since someone taught you something new?"

"Are you offering?" She drags her teeth over her bottom lip, and I'm damn near feral for this girl.

"I could show you a lot more than any of those assholes back at that bar could." The growl that comes out of me is low and possessive. At this stage, I don't fucking care anymore. She might as well know that anything she does with anyone else around here is going to drive me insane.

She drives me insane.

My hands squeeze her thighs harder, and this time, Briar makes the sweetest little noise of need. "It's been a long time . . . since anyone showed me . . . anything."

Fucking idiots, whoever wasted their chance with Briar Lane deserves a shotgun to their balls. But it somehow led her to me, hidden away up this mountain, so I'm more pleased than I have any right to be about the circumstances that have led to us being up here like this.

"How long?" I exhale heavily.

"A very long time." Her voice hitches as I gently slide her knees wider. We're both fully clothed, but fuck me, this is possibly one of the hottest things I've ever experienced.

"You must be pretty good at taking care of yourself, darlin'."

Briar hums and presses her ass back against me, and I nearly fucking blow in my jeans. "I'm a quick learner."

The air crackles as my breath fans across the side of her cheek, my fingers tracing up and down, running along the inner seam of her thighs.

"Do you want your uncle to take care of you tonight?" My lips finally make contact, brushing over the soft, delicate shell of her ear. I whisper words that we both know shouldn't be allowed between us, but here we both are, and nothing about this feels wrong.

The faint touch draws out one of those little noises I'm

growing addicted to. I want to see just how loud my niece can be when she's lost to the rolling waves of pleasure.

The girl perched in my lap feels like she was goddamn made to fit against me, to draw out something in me that has lain dormant until she came along. It would take nothing at all to draw her earlobe between my teeth and suck. To explore one of those gold hoops she wears with my tongue.

"Teach me something, Uncle Storm." She arches her neck, exposing that curve of flesh, while keeping her head tucked against my shoulder. Oh, she wants to play this game? *Uncle.* I hear the hint of not-so-innocent Briar in the way she floats that word. Hanging it tempting and seductive in the air. I see the moment her eyelashes flutter closed, and it stokes the flames riding hot and wild through my veins.

But I can't touch her. If I do, there is absolutely no way I'll be able to stop, and I suspect that come tomorrow, things are going to have to go back to how they need to be between us. As much as that fucking kills me to admit.

"Have you ever touched yourself while someone watched?"

Her lips hang open. A quick shake of her head comes in silent reply.

"Then go ahead and unbutton those jeans, little thorn."

"You . . . you want me to do it?" She sounds breathless.

"Do you trust me to tell you what to do? To teach you what your body needs?"

"I've never . . ." Her fingers are a little shaky as she pops open the button.

My mouth keeps brushing against the edge of her ear. "I know you haven't. But I know this is what your body craves. Having someone who will watch you, pay attention to you, to see exactly how perfect you look when you fall apart."

Briar sucks in a ragged breath, her fingers pausing on the loosened material at her waist. Goddamn, the way she's eager to wait for my next instruction.

"That's perfect. Now, lower that zipper, nice and slow."

Another one of those delicious noises escapes past her lips, accompanying the glide of her zipper, filling the truck with an unmistakable sound. One confirming we've gone far, far beyond the lines that should divide the two of us.

"Good. Now slip that hand inside your panties for me—that's it. Lift your hips if you need to." I talk Briar through her next moves as she eases below her waistband. Soaking up the sight of the shudder that rolls through her body as she makes contact with her pussy. Her delicate fingers are wedged in tight, thanks to her jeans and the position our bodies are in.

"Oh god." A moaned whisper fills the darkened cab. "This is so wrong."

"Darlin', you can stop this anytime you like. You've got all the power here." Skating my palms across the denim covering her perfect thighs, I keep my touch feather-soft. Reminding her that she can leave anytime she likes, even though I know she won't.

Turns out my niece is just as turned on playing this wicked game as I am.

If I have it my way, she'll go on that date tomorrow and spend the whole time thinking about this forbidden moment right here with me in the dark. Because I'm a selfish fucking asshole like that.

"I know you're soaked. So slide that finger through the mess you've made in your panties while you've been sitting in my lap, and then I want you to pull that hand out and show me."

"Holy shit. That's so dirty." She exhales shakily but does as I say. Tugging her hand out and holding her fingers up for me to see the slick sheen coating them.

A rumbled noise brews in my chest. "Mmm. Now taste yourself."

She sucks in a sharp breath.

"That's it." I devour the way she obediently raises that hand to her mouth, those pretty pink fingernails brush over her plump lips, and they close around her middle and forefinger. "Right up to the knuckle, then slide in and out for me, stroke your tongue, press down, and enjoy how good that feels."

Goddamn. I'm unable to keep my hips still as I watch her follow my instructions. All I can see is her unraveling perfectly, with the way her loose sweater has slid off one side of her shoulder, showing off rounded and full cleavage. An expanse of bronzed skin I so desperately want to run my tongue across and slide my cock between—fuck, she'd feel like heaven.

Breathing harder, I shift beneath her ass and eat up every tiny whimpering noise Briar makes as she fucks her mouth with her fingers and tastes her own arousal.

"Now you're gonna touch that needy little clit. Get your fingers nice and sloppy first. Good girl." She's desperate now, dragging her fingers out of her mouth with a wet noise. As she wedges her hand back down the front of her panties, her lips are parted, and a small whine accompanies the moment her fingers brush over her sensitive bud. Briar's so lost in this that she's not self-conscious or questioning what we're doing anymore. She's desperate to come, and I'm hungry to witness how beautifully this girl shatters.

"Just like that, hard and fast for me, darlin'."

Briar is panting and writhing in my lap as she chases her climax. My eyes are fixed on the spot where her hand disappears below the waistband of her lacy black panties. Frantic movements of her fingers, circling, seeking out her climax, are the most illicit thing, hidden away from sight beneath the silky material.

"I'm so—I'm nearly—" she gasps, and moans—that seductive sound has my hips shifting against her ass even harder. My fingers dig into the fleshy part of her thighs, and I wish we could say, fuck it, and do so much more, right here, right now.

"You look so pretty touching yourself in my truck." I lower my lips dangerously close to her ear. "If I were any of those men, those men tonight who *all* wanted to take you home, this is exactly what I would give you, because I know this is how your body would want to be played with."

My niece is panting, whimpering, almost there, but needs that final push to tumble over the edge.

"I know your sweet little pussy needs to be licked and sucked and stretched full . . and I know you want someone to give you that release you've been craving. So let go, little thorn. That's it. Exactly like that."

"Oh god—oh god." Her body clenches, her mouth drops open, and she turns her head toward my chest as she comes.

It's the most beautiful sight as her eyes squeeze shut and pleasure washes through her limbs, the wave crashing with such intensity that her body jerks. I'm stroking her jeans and softly murmuring more words to her, telling her just how pretty she looks coming on her fingers. And when I instruct her to suck, she doesn't even hesitate. Dragging her hand out of her panties, her movements are heavy-limbed with the force of her orgasm.

"See how good you taste. How sweet your cum is, darlin'." I really don't want to do anything but hold this girl tight, to show her just how good I could really make her scream. Except, that dreaded moment has arrived all too soon. A moment when this game has to come to an end, because we're two people who aren't supposed to desire anything remotely close to what we've just gone and done while hidden in the deepest depths of this forest.

I allow her to stay slumped against my chest as I fix her jeans for her. Fighting every single screaming cell in my brain telling me to kiss her, to take her mouth and carry her to bed, and to confirm just how sweet I know she'll taste.

"Is it weird that I feel like I just wanna stay out here?" she rasps against my shirt.

"I know you do, but go inside and get into bed before you get cold, okay? I'll be in soon."

I swallow the lie.

Watching her slip out of the truck, with a tiny glance up at me through heavy lashes, she pauses. Her dark eyes gaze back at me through the thick glass of the passenger-side window, and then, with a sharp click, she closes the door.

I sit here, watching her make her way inside, surrounded by the heavy scent of her arousal and lust still filling the front seat of my truck. Punishing myself by not running straight after her, I stay in my seat with an impossibly hard cock I'm going to have to take care of. Alone.

Because I won't follow her tonight, even though every single part of me wants to.

CHAPTER 15

Briar

I'm supposed to be getting ready for a date.

There are three cute outfits laid out on the bed, and yet all I can think about—the obsession worming away in my brain—is the fact I made myself come while grinding in my uncle's lap last night. All I can focus on is the lingering imprint on my memory and the scent of him coiling around me. The way his mouth felt brushed up against my ear.

You look so pretty touching yourself in my truck.

Jesus, my thighs squeeze together at the replayed words in my mind, the ever-present echo of his gravelly voice.

Worst of all is that I lay awake hoping and praying that he would come and finish what we'd started. Even though a tiny part of me knew he wouldn't allow us to keep going with the dangerous game we'd entered into outside. As soon as my fingers closed over the handle of the door to his truck, when my eyes dared seek out his, I knew the spell was broken.

Along with the chill of the night air, the quiet thud of the truck door shutting sealed the moment and locked it away.

He didn't approach the bedroom at any point. I heard him eventually come inside, but he stayed on the couch. Leaving me alone, feeling like the mattress that had previously seemed far too small, now stretched out all around me like an ocean without a horizon.

By the time I got up this morning, he'd already left.

After the conversation we briefly had about not driving my car, I'm not entirely sure how to make my way down to Crimson Ridge. Maybe he'll come back soon? Somehow, I doubt it.

I don't imagine my dating life is particularly high on the agenda of my uncle, who growled in my ear, gripped my thighs, and told me he knows what my body craves. There is absolutely zero hope for me, absolutely no chance of me not turning into a puddle around that man now.

Might as well pack my carry-on and admit defeat. Horny Briar almost got what she wanted but has made things extremely awkward between us. Did I come onto him too strongly? Have I been the world's biggest cock tease?

Or did the man who held me and talked me through the most intense orgasm of my life actually want something *more* with me?

As I clutch my robe and try to gather together my brain cells, I hear gravel crunch beneath tires outside. This is it. This is the moment he's going to stride in here, he's going to fold his arms across that massive chest and tell me to get the fuck out of his life, I'm certain of it.

But instead, there's a knock against the doorframe, and I hear soft footsteps.

"Briar? Are you here? Are you decent?"

I poke my head out of the bedroom door and am met with the sight of a beaming Layla with two thermoses in hand. She looks stunning as ever, a horse-girl wet dream dressed in pale jeans, a turquoise sweater, and copper curls tossed into a messy bun.

As I gape at her unexpected arrival, it takes my brain an eternity to find words.

"Sorry, I'm kind of only half-dressed. I didn't know you were coming." Next to this girl, I feel like hot garbage.

"You can thank me later. I hear you need help getting ready for a date and that you could use a ride down the mountain." She breezes toward me, presents me with a divine aroma of coffee with creamer, and carries on into the bedroom. "Ooooooh, cute outfits. Which one are you thinking?" Layla plops down on the edge of the bed.

"Thanks for the coffee. But, how do you know I've got a date?" My eyes narrow on her. News can't travel that fast around Crimson Ridge, surely?

"Storm radioed up to the ranch earlier this morning. Said you needed a ride to town today . . . and might have mentioned something about bringing a gun with me in case a certain Hayes boy decides to get a little too handsy over lunch." Layla's green eyes dance as she takes a sip, winking at me.

"Oh god. He didn't?"

"I told him to stop being an overbearing uncle and let you live your best life."

I have to risk burning my mouth by taking the biggest gulp of coffee ever to hide the way my face wants to betray every dirty little secret from the events of his truck.

"So, are you going for cute hot or rail-me-cowboy hot for this date?

That makes me almost spit my coffee all over the place. "Layla," I scold.

"What? Wes is *fiiiiine* . . . Don't tell Colt I said that because he might bury him on the outskirts of the ranch next time he sees him, but I can appreciate a premium specimen of cowboy when I see one."

"I don't know. What do you think would be the best to wear? Suddenly, I'm really nervous." I rest the heel of my hand against my forehead. "Layla . . . I haven't been on a date in . . ." Forever. Never. I've never dated because my awful goddamn family didn't allow me to and shoved me straight into the arms of Antoine since it suited their schemes and power plays.

Bless the gorgeous woman seated in front of me. She takes my flustered attitude in her stride and doesn't make me feel anything but supported.

She's an angel living on Devil's Peak, I'm certain of it.

"It's okay. You're going to do amazing, and it's obviously meant to be that I'm here to be your one-woman hype squad. I've got you. Besides, I needed to go into town anyway, and you've got nothing to be worried about. From what I know, not only is Wes easy to look at, but he is also a really good guy."

"Aren't all the good ones supposed to be taken?" I scrunch my nose.

Layla chuckles. "Well, I didn't say he wouldn't be complicated . . ."

Nothing can be more complicated than the fact I would gladly get on my knees for my uncle, so I can only agree with her on that front.

"It's coffee and lunch. I should probably stick with cute hot . . . right?" Standing in front of the bed, I survey the options I've already laid out.

"To be honest, Briar, I think no matter what you wear, our boy Wes is going to be staring at you with big ol' cowboy-shaped hearts in his eyes . . . so wear something you feel good in. The rest of the magic will work by itself."

"Can I hire you to sit on my shoulder and flatter my ego all day?"

"Might have to get in line with the horses. Those needy things have my attention locked down." She reaches to pluck the coffee out of my hand. "Okay, let's do this. I vote for this adorable combo right here, city girl."

Her pick brings a smile creeping over my lips. It's the one I know will feel good when I wear it. A fitted jersey dress with long sleeves and a buttery-soft ribbed material that I can pair with my new boots and a coat. I'll probably be far too over-dressed for lunch at a tiny cafe in Crimson Ridge, but what do I care when there's only one man I intend to leave an impression upon today?

Rolling my lips together, I quietly shush the slutty little part of my brain that decides to pipe up and point out there is most definitely another cowboy I secretly hope will see me in this outfit.

"Let me get changed, and I'll be out soon. Make yourself comfy."

"You're going to make me fall in love with you, aren't you, Briar Lane?" Layla calls after me, giggling.

As I slip into the bathroom and finish getting ready, I hear her move through the cabin toward the warmth of the fire.

"Oh, by the way, I've already booked you for another date . . ." She calls out from down the hall. "My bestie Sage is going to be in town. She's flying in to come visit."

"What's the occasion?"

"She just launched her own PR and marketing brand . . . freelancing . . . generally being a badass and ruling the world."

Layla carries on telling me details of their friendship they've had since they were young, how long Sage is going to be here in town, generally making all of it sound so effortless. Completely normal and casual and the kind of thing that doesn't have any preconceived ulterior motives around business connections or potential clients to be wooed.

They're just girlfriends supporting one another, and my heart squeezes that this girl, who I barely know, is already inviting me to be part of that kind of celebration.

"So, I already call dibs on you and Storm joining us for dinner that night, alright? Maybe even Wes can come, too . . . if you guys hit it off today."

I stare at my reflection in the mirror over the vanity, allowing her words to sink in. There's a twist deep in my gut because even though Layla is absolutely right—if things go well today, there is every chance I might be going out to dinner with her and her friend, with him coming along as my date.

But as I tug the dress on and smooth out the fabric, my stomach flips. There's a voice that is far too loud inside me saying that I only want to have one man there for an evening out with friends.

And he's the man I shouldn't desire.

"You're sure I look okay?" I ask Layla for what feels like the tenth time since we left the cabin. She puts the truck in park and fishes her bag out of the back seat.

"If that man doesn't already have a plot of land and a house planned out for the two of you on his ranch by the time you've ordered a meal, I'll be shocked." My face must go pale because she shakes her head and laughs at me. "I'm joking, Briar."

"Not funny."

"I take it that's a *no* on 'seeking cowboy and marriage proposal' over lunch, then?"

"Layla." I shake my head and groan.

She laughs at me, green eyes sparkling. "Okay, so I've got plenty of jobs I need to get done. It'll take me a few hours at the least. You've got my number to text me if you need an 'SOS, get me out of here' emergency phone call."

That makes me bite back a smile. "Horse emergency?"

"I can be as creative as you like. Give me a number from one to ten if you need and that way I'll know how extreme of an emergency I need to conjure up. One is like you've got a sudden migraine; ten means the entire Peak is on fire."

"Why do I feel like my palms are sweating?" I shake my hands. Nerves fire through my bloodstream as I glance up at the cafe where I'm supposed to be in five minutes.

"You'll be fine." Layla toys with the keys and looks like she's trying to figure out something. "Just . . . remember this is a small town, okay? Local rumor and gossip . . . you know."

"What do you mean?"

"Wes knows your uncle, but don't believe everything you might hear about Storm from some of the locals here. Especially once they find out you're his niece."

I must have the world's most confused expression written all over my face. This was not what I expected for my predate pep talk. Is she talking about the fact my uncle obviously gets a fair bit of female attention? Is this about the waitress from last night and whatever might be going on between the two of them? Just thinking about that makes me cringe, because I certainly was quick to hop in his lap and grind all over him, and there was no effort on his part to stop things from going as far as they did between us.

"God, ignore me. It's just . . . Stôrmand Lane is kind of a local celebrity and not just for his rodeo achievements. I just didn't want you to get caught off guard by the kind of people in this town who don't know anything about his life yet seem to want to jump to conclusions without knowing the facts."

I'm trying to find words as we both start moving to get out of the truck. My phone is in my hand from when I checked the time and to confirm that Wes wasn't going to stand me up, and as I shut the door behind me, it starts ringing.

Un-fucking-believable. My stupid thumb hits the Answer button by accident.

Layla waves at me and hitches her thumb over her shoulder, mouthing that she'll see me soon and to wish me good luck before she disappears down the street.

"Briar? Don't hang up. Please, babe," the voice I never want to hear again pleads down the line.

Steeling myself and looking toward the cloudy sky above my head, I raise the phone to my ear.

"What do you want?" At least I am standing right outside the cafe where I'm supposed to meet an exceedingly handsome man for a date, and that gives me enough of a surge of confidence to feel like I can handle my douchebag ex for two minutes over the phone.

"Thank god you're okay." Antoine's fake concern sounds hollow down the line.

"You don't give a shit about whether I'm okay. We both know this, Antoine. Stop trying to contact me."

"Briar, please, you have to know how sorry I am."

"Really? You're sorry? That's bullshit I can smell even from here."

"What will it take for you to come home?"

That draws a cold laugh out of me, and I pull the phone away from my ear, staring at the screen in disbelief.

"Briar . . . babe . . . are you still there?" His voice sounds as tinny as his pathetic whining.

"No. I'm hanging up this phone and I don't want you to try to contact me anymore. We're done." My hands might be shaking, but I keep my voice firm and low. Even though there isn't anyone else around, I'm conscious all the same that this is a small town. It's not a big city where you overhear all kinds of random arguments over the phone between strangers in the middle of the day and on the center of the sidewalk—that kind of thing probably doesn't happen here.

Not without causing enough of a commotion for it to be news all over town.

"Crisp is worried sick, too. She's been trying to contact you."

"God—Antoine—can you just stop? Don't waste your breath. We both know that's a lie."

"We care about you."

"Yeah, so much caring. Were you thinking of me while you were balls deep in your secretary? Were you thinking of us when she sucked you off under your desk at the office?" I hiss into the phone. The rage of everything I discovered about his after-hours exploits burns hot and vicious up the back of my throat.

But I refuse to fucking cry over this asshole. I refuse to ruin my makeup and my day because of his lies and bullshit.

"Come on, babe. You know how it is." He shuffles something around in the background. Papers or files. Shoving his already-absent morals aside, perhaps. "You knew the deal between our families. You knew things weren't going to be like a fairy tale or some shit, but we can be good together. You're a Lane—I'm a Montgomery. There are different sets of expectations for people like us."

Oh, fuck him very much.

He and my sister could offer a PhD in gaslighting and manipulation.

"You know I've got PIs on retainer all over the country. If you continue to avoid my calls, I'll be forced to send out every bloodhound I've got looking for you. Do you really want to have to go through all that nonsense?"

"Are you done?" I suck in a deep inhale and close my eyes. The sounds of the quiet street fill my ears. Somewhere, there's faint music drifting on the breeze and I hear chatter as a group of women walk out of the cafe.

"Where are you? I'll fly to get you. Just come home, Briar."

Those words send a cold shudder down my spine. That place is not my home. Antoine and my sister are the worst type of people, and I have no intention of going back.

"Actually, I'm late for coffee. Gotta go."

With that, I hang up and turn my phone on silent.

I'm going on a date, and if I have my way, the names Antoine Montgomery and Crispin Lane will be dust in my rearview mirror.

CHAPTER 16

Storm

I wrench my jacket off and toss it on the bench seat beside me. Reaching up to fist my hat, I lift it off, and place it on the empty space next to me, scrubbing one hand through my hair.

Today has been a fucking day.

Half of it was spent on the phone video calling with Beau, figuring out what needs to be done to fix up his new ranch venture while he agonized over five different shades of white paint and the renovations that still need to be completed. The other half of my day has been spent convincing myself that Briar has been riding around in Westin Hayes's truck for hour upon hour.

Or, worse, that she's been riding him.

Jesus Christ.

As I sit, gathering up the energy to actually move my ass inside, the radio unit fitted in my truck goes off. Those of us who choose to live in the isolation of Devil's Peak all have a radio as a form of communication, and I could put money on this call being from either Colton Wilder or Sheriff Hayes.

"Stôrmand." The familiar grunt of Colt's voice fills my truck.

"Fuck you very much. When are you gonna give me a break with that?"

He chuckles. A noise I didn't think I'd ever hear as frequently out of that asshole as I do now that Layla is in his life.

"Well, when I know how much you love it . . . can you blame me?"

"Sounds like you've got too much time on your hands these days if you've got the opportunity to call me up and chitchat. Wanna gossip on the phone all night with me, Sunshine?"

"Christ." I can hear the shudder in his voice, and can't help smirking to myself.

"Well, then, spit it out, old fella."

"We're the same age."

"Last I checked, you've got at least a year or two on me. So, I'll take the win and the buckle, thank you."

The line crackles for a moment, and I can picture him scrubbing his hand over his face.

"As much as I feel like I'm going to regret asking, can you bring your ugly ass up here tomorrow and saddle up with us?" After a pause, the radio clicks on again. "Snow forecast is all clear."

Up on this mountain, we spend an awful lot of time planning around the weather, especially at this time of year when—while spring might be currently showing her pretty little face—conditions can still turn on a dime and get treacherous real fucking fast.

"The roads are looking good. Shouldn't be a problem." Along with snow and ice and every other goddamn complication that tends to come with a last flurry of winter is the risk of rockfall. While the sheriff runs a tight ship with his crew, who work their asses off to reopen the mountain as quickly as possible, there's always something that invariably goes south real fast.

You can't ever take it for granted out here. I suppose that's partly why I enjoy this place. It's a challenge living in the wilderness.

"That niece of yours coming along, too? Get Briar up on a horse and show her some real riding."

My throat tightens. I damn well know that Colt is beyond obsessed with his girl. Yet the mere mention of her name by another man?

Fuck, I've gotta get my shit together where she's concerned.

Tightening my fist around the radio handset, I pinch my brow. "Yep. She'll be there."

I hate the idea of leaving her alone more than the concept of her being around Kayce and his golden-boy charm all day. So, I guess seeing her on a horse and laughing at his dumb fucking jokes is just a reality I'm gonna have to endure.

"She's not confident enough to be around cattle," I tack on abruptly.

"Sure. Layla said she's a fast learner, though."

Jesus Christ, I'm instantly transported back to last night and all manner of *wrong* things occupying my mind on repeat where teaching my niece is concerned.

"You good?" Colt says. He must've said something that I completely missed because, I swear to god, I can detect the scent of her arousal again, and my dick has fucking well leapt to attention.

I'm on the radio with Colton Wilder, and my cock is thickening inside my jeans and, fuck my life, I need to end this conversation.

"Yeah, I gotta run." I bite out the words. "Be there in the morning."

"Got it."

I toss the handset back in its cradle so hard it nearly cracks.

Dropping my head back against the seat, I drag both hands through my hair.

Last night was a mistake. A really fucking good one at the time, but it was reckless of me, and I don't know what I was thinking other than that I wasn't thinking . . . and that I hated the idea of her being out on a date today.

So yeah, I might have indulged in a fantasy that shouldn't have happened between us because I was jealous of what a guy like Westin could openly have with Briar.

Maybe the sick part of me wanted to make sure she would be distracted and thinking about what we did last night instead of listening to his charming goddamn ranch stories.

Maybe I'm just a miserable old bastard who deserves all the shit I've had in my life. Who deserves to be alone.

But fuck, I haven't been able to scrub her from my mind all day, and I'm pissed off at myself for starting something that I can't finish.

Briar isn't mine.

She fucking should be, but it's impossible.

There's no way a girl as beautiful and clever as her would throw her future away for a man who, to the outside world, is her own uncle. No one cares about details like adoption or that we hardly know each other.

Headlines only love a scandal, and my name has already had too much bullshit attached to it once before. It took all of Erik's media connections to make that shitstorm disappear and vanish without a trace before anyone heard anything, not because he cared about his own adopted brother but all in an effort to safe-guard the Lane Enterprises name.

Yet, the rumors still flew around.

Small towns still talked.

One sniff of another family scandal featuring the last name Lane is all it would take for everything to end in disaster. I don't care about my reputation; I don't give a fuck what people say about Stôrmand Lane. They've already said and assumed the worst.

What I do care about is the girl with soft chestnut eyes, the kind that have the power to melt my entire fucking soul with just one glance.

I care about her too fucking much, and I can't seem to turn that off.

With fingers threaded through my hair, I stare down at the evidence presenting itself in my lap.

My cock is pressed hard against the front of my jeans, all from thinking about her. The breathiness in her voice last night when she admitted how she hadn't had much experience—we both knew she wasn't talking about learning to drive. Then, that moment when her teeth caught the fullness of her bottom lip, followed by her head dropping back against my shoulder.

That, right there, was the second I knew I was fucking done for.

As I glare at my cock, the asshole throbs, desperate to be relieved of that pressure building and building. I let out a heavy sigh, and with a guilt-laden glance around—even though I'm parked outside my own fucking place in the middle of nowhere—I lift my hips and unbuckle my belt. Shame and urgency collide as I flick the button, lower my zipper, and allow my length to bob against my stomach when I shove my briefs down just enough for what needs to happen. My filthy fucking brain demands that I deal with the obsession I have over this girl right this second.

This is an all-too-familiar scene. Only last night, I was hidden away while parked here in this very same spot, fisting my dick and jerking myself off. That clearly wasn't enough to satisfy the urge. There's a need I can't quench and I can't explain, and the more I try to stop thinking about my pretty little niece, the worse it gets.

With a growl, I spit in my palm. As my fingers wrap around my length and I start stroking from root to tip, my balls are already hot and tight, drawn up and ready for another round of fantasizing about someone I have absolutely no business looking twice at.

Straight to hell.

A flood of all the sensations from last night arrives at once, as if I'm right back there. Only this time, my hands explore freely. The beautiful girl grinding in my lap is panting and begging for me to touch her, to fuck her. And I'm sure as hell not a good enough man to say no.

Not when it would deny her what she needs.

In my sordid imagination, Briar writhes as I unbutton her jeans and slip my hand down the front, exploring just how soft and drenched her sweet little cunt is.

Please, Uncle Storm.

She begs me so politely in that raspy, sultry voice. And it takes nothing at all to slip a single finger inside her tight, wet heat. My fist tightens around my dick as I squeeze my eyes closed and tug harder. Curses tumble out of me, as the image is so vivid I can hear her moans and feel the way she squirms and submits to me. Her pussy flutters as I finger-fuck her right here in my truck.

Let me taste you.

She whimpers and asks so nicely. I let go, and the good girl Briar is, she's kneeling over me, swallowing me down, and the noise that escapes me is guttural.

Heat builds at the base of my spine. I feel the wetness and warmth of her mouth. The plush glide of her lips mimics every movement of my fist, and it's the moment I imagine her throat closing around my tip that my balls tighten and my stomach clenches.

Cum spurts out, coating my fist, as I feel every shameful pump of release. The pulse thundering in my ears comes in time with the rocking of my hips as I chase the sensation, wrestling with erratic breaths.

All the blood in my body is in my dick, and my every

thought is of her. I feel like I can even smell her, hear her whimpering with pleasure as she runs her tongue along my length to clean me up.

She's my perfect forbidden fantasy.

Holy fuck, I can hardly see straight.

I've just made a goddamn mess, and it takes me another few moments to get my shit together. I glare at my dick and the sticky mess I've made, and have to tug my T-shirt over my head in order to clean myself up.

The threat of being caught out here with a situation I absolutely cannot explain is enough to get me moving. Slamming the door behind me, I head straight inside to shower. As if running scalding hot water all over myself will absolve me of my sins.

After drying myself off and scrubbing the towel over my hair, my hearing is on edge, listening for any indication that Briar got back while I've been in here.

Do I want her to be back?

Do I want to walk out this door and find her safely returned, not looking like some asshole just felt her up in his truck? Or do I want to go out there and find everything quiet, back to the way it was with me all alone up on this mountain? Before Briar and her sweetness and spark that I'm so fucking addicted to turned up unexpectedly and flipped shit upside down.

I shove into a pair of sweats and a clean T-shirt, then head out to find the cabin empty.

My eyes immediately flick to the clock on the microwave. It's not late, but Christ, her date was at lunchtime and it's nearly seven p.m. Layla was supposed to be looking out for her, and I'm starting to feel like I need to revisit my plans to threaten everyone with a dick in Crimson Ridge to stay away from her.

Starting with Wes and his perfect goddamn charming smile.

He would look a whole lot less charming missing some teeth.

Right as I'm debating whether to pick up the radio unit and put out a call, the sweep of headlights plays across the cabin. A truck engine and crunching gravel announce the arrival of whoever just brought Briar back up the mountain.

That tightness banded across my chest eases as I glance out the window and see the familiar "Devil's Peak Ranch" logo on the door—Colt's truck pulls up beside my own, with Layla at the wheel.

I duck my head and busy myself with digging out some leftovers to heat up for dinner. I'm crouched down, rearranging the Tupperware stacked in the fridge, when the front door clicks shut behind me.

"Oh, hey." Briar sounds happy. There's a lightness in her voice. "How was your day?"

I straighten up and turn around, and the sight that greets me is the best and the worst fucking thing in the world. She stretches to reach up and hang her bag on the hook behind the door, and while her back is turned, that moment gives me the perfect opportunity to openly stare.

The dress she's wearing that hugs her thighs and ass is made of a material that looks so goddamn soft, a rich cocoa shade clinging tightly against her skin. She's got her dark hair piled up in a messy top knot. Fuck. My eyes bounce everywhere, down to the cowboy boots she bought that first day here, which reveal a small peek of smooth skin, a glimpse of her bare legs below the knee.

The worst part, or maybe the best part, is that she's wearing an outfit like that with my jacket slung around her shoulders.

She went on a date today wearing my jacket, and that triggers every feral, possessive sensation I've been trying my hardest to smother.

Briar turns, and the smile brightening her face says it all as she shrugs out of the coat. A move that shows off exactly how her dress molds to her curves. How it fits her body like a glove, and she looks so beautiful that there's no way Wes didn't fall for her within half a second.

Dropping the containers onto the kitchen counter, a rush of blood hits my ears. I'm pissed off at every single circumstance between us, and that's what turns my mind blank. Instead of trying to beat back this thing eating me alive, I give in to the surge of petty, rage-filled jealousy.

Shoving into my coat and boots, I've got my keys and my phone in my hand, the other on the door handle before I can blink. Without turning or properly looking her way—because I can't face having to take in another second of how stunning this girl is—I storm out of the cabin like a rampant whirlwind.

And because I'm desperately doing my best to make this girl despise me, the words as I slam out the door are a snarl, a bark, as she watches me leave, open-mouthed.

"Don't wait up, darlin'."

CHAPTER 17

Briar

So . . . tell me everything.

Layla's message pops up in my Instagram inbox. I'm lying on the couch, doom scrolling and stalking my uncle's old rodeo footage and, in general, feeling like a complete mess.

You were far too good at avoiding my questions on the way home earlier.

I'm well-versed in the art of deflecting conversation off myself.

So, your game of fifty questions about me and the ranch and the horses was cute and all . . .

Picked up on that, did you?

Now it's time to spill, city girl.

I'm sure you've got something better to do than talk about my date.

Uh oh.

That doesn't sound promising.

No wonder you wanted to grill me about saddles and leather care.

Sounds like there's a story to today's events.

He was nice.

But . . .

I guess the fact he wanted to talk about my uncle the whole time was a bit of a mood killer.

Ouch.

Westin, you fool.

He probably thought it was a way to break the ice.

It just felt like I should tell the two of them to get together if Wes'd rather grab a beer with Storm and talk 'rodeo.'

I bet the idiot was nervous as all hell.

Did he ask you out for a second date?

Do you think you'll give him another shot?

He did, but I said I'd have to let him know when I'm free.

I don't know . . . Maybe I could try again?

153

My nerves kind of took over and I feel like I was part of the problem too.

I've never been on a proper date before, and I feel like I got all up in my head.

Wasn't really on my best form, if I'm honest. He deserves better than my hot mess.

Let's just ignore the fact that I was completely out of sorts thanks to the phone call and threats from my ex that were ringing in my ears as I walked in to find us a table. Not to mention other entirely illicit thoughts drifting in that I most definitely should not have been thinking about in the first place . . .

Excuse me, none of that. You are a CATCH.

Besides, even if Wes might've had a better shot taking Storm out for coffee instead, I'm pretty sure he's got something like three brothers.

There's more to explore on the Hayes family ranch if you like the look of those jeans, so to speak *wink face*

We chat a bit more, and I try to steer the conversation back to horses and her life on top of Devil's Peak, rather than an off-limits tattooed bull rider, or any of his cowboy friends. Not too long after, Layla tells me she has to go.

I'm left to my own overthinking, as per usual, and the crackle of the fire. I haven't even attempted to turn on the TV to watch anything or find a movie—I just can't be bothered. Maybe if I wasn't so distracted, I would read.

Instead, I find myself guiltily rewatching clip after clip of a certain rodeo pro on my phone, scrolling through all his old posts on Instagram, feeling the winding tension inside my core build tighter every second I hover and bite my lip at the details I find on-screen.

There's one particular slow-motion montage someone has put together of him preparing for events in and around the arena. It shows him doing everything from warming up to applying strapping tape to his wrist and forearm, and I've watched it on loop an embarrassing number of times. The chaps. The hat. The vest covered in sponsor logos. The swagger. All unmistakably the man whose presence fills this cabin, even when he's not here.

As I sit here in my pit of wrong thinking, one thing I can't help but feel puzzled by is that he stopped competing abruptly, but there's no mention made as to why. No injuries or major issues reported from the competition circuit. One day, he was seemingly everywhere, and the next, he no longer took part in any events on the rodeo circuit. Maybe he suffered a career-ending injury and simply chose to quietly retire?

Although, from what I know of that man, he certainly commands attention wherever he goes.

God. I really fucking hate that I don't know where he is, what he's doing, or worst of all, *who* he might be doing.

How many other girls has he *taught* while they've been seated on his lap in the front seat of his truck? Is that how Luce misplaced her lip gloss?

Ugh. I let out a frustrated noise and decide that no good can come of sitting here with nothing but the fire, my misbehaving hormones, and my overactive imagination for company.

As I take myself to the bedroom, my stomach flips when a familiar sound comes from outside the cabin. The rumbling hum of an engine pulls up and cuts out, followed by the heavy thud of the door closing. This is the part that I don't know how we handle from here on out. He didn't sleep in this bed last night, and from the way he took one look at me, scowled, and then hurled himself out the door earlier, I doubt he's likely to tonight, either.

Even if things are awkward, I'm sick of him pretending that couch doesn't fuck up his body. If we can't be adults and share a bed, then I'll be the one who sleeps in the living room from now on.

I loiter aimlessly in the bedroom, listening to him come inside and bang around in the kitchen before his footsteps draw closer down the hall. He won't be coming in here. I can guarantee he's moving this way with the intention of using the bathroom, so I pick my moment in order to corner him.

Just as he's about to walk past, I step through the open door-frame, putting myself right in his path.

"You know, most of the time, regular conversations are a two-way thing, kind of like when I ask you about your day and you actually answer."

Piercing blue eyes stare down at me. God, he's so fucking nice to look at—it's entirely unfair. Every time we're close like this, I have to tilt my head back to take him all in, and it gives me a front-row seat to the ink up his neck.

Sinfully hot tattoos I'm now fully aware extend down his chest, along his arms, with more scattered over his back too. A tapestry of stories from his life I'm so curious about, yet I feel foolish if I were to dare ask.

"You really do seem to find your bite after dark, don't you, little thorn?" His gritty voice is far too appealing.

"Are you simply planning to avoid me now?"

He folds his arms and drags a thumb across his bottom lip, studying me with that cool gaze. "I had work to do, and besides, I figured you might need some space."

"Why? I thought I was supposed to be helping you out with the ranch job." At least he's talking to me, but there's a thick blanket of tension flowing between us in the gloom of the hallway.

"Guessed you would be too busy going on your *date* to work with me today." His lip curls in a sneer as he snarls over the word like it's personally offended him. Oh, this man can talk. Waltzing around in his slutty gray sweatpants and a white tee that hugs all his muscles. My neck prickles, thinking about where he's just been.

"Is that why you've ignored me all day? What about you? Was it Luce again tonight? Was she hunting for another lost lip gloss on the floor of your truck?"

That makes him chuckle, and not in a friendly way. It's a heartless, callous noise. He's being a total dick, and my hand tightens around the phone I'm still holding. I've got half a mind to smack him upside the head with it.

"What do you care? How was your little date anyway? Did he hold your hand, call you ma'am, and be the perfect, polite, small-town-cowboy wet dream?"

I'm fuming at his belittling words. How dare he act like last night was nothing, or that it didn't happen, and then simply avoid and ignore me today, because he's obviously got a problem with the fact I went out for coffee.

Even though he's the one who made arrangements for me to be able to get there and back safely. He's the one who contacted Layla in the first place. Without her help, I would have been stranded on this mountain. My mouth opens and shuts as I try to find the right words to argue back with.

That's when the man, taunting me and glaring at me, seems to spy something that snags his attention. His head cocks to one side, blue eyes narrowing in on the phone in my hand. Before I understand what is unfolding, his large, tattooed hand reaches out and rips it from my grasp.

My stomach plummets through the floor.

Oh god.

Oh no.

Please don't look at what is paused on that screen.

I try to claw at his arm to get my phone back, but this man is like a dog with a bone, and he pushes past me, making his way into the bedroom.

Steely eyes flick up to mine, glittering and more unsettling than I've ever experienced before now.

As he sinks down on the edge of the bed, with my phone in his big palm, he presses Play, and the sound blares through the room like a demonic roar as the announcer on the recording reveals my dirty little secret to the crowd . . . and also to the man giving me an entirely unreadable expression.

"Ladies and gents, give it up for Stôrmand 'Storm' Lane."

CHAPTER 18

Briar

I'm squirming in place.

Would this mountainside and cabin kindly open up a giant sinkhole and swallow me alive? Because my uncle is holding my phone in his impossibly large hands, seeing on screen the pathetic evidence of my crush, my obsession, my whatever the fuck you want to call this kind of unhealthy behavior.

It's impossible to tell what he's thinking. Is he angry? Pissed off? Fed up with my crap and ready to march my ass out the door and turf me onto the curb outside a motel in town?

"Give it back." I hold out a hand expectantly.

He gives me a raised eyebrow in return. Silently casting his eyes over my figure.

I valiantly ignore his roguish, disheveled hair and sexy goddamn nose ring. "That's private." Embarrassment crawls all over my skin like spiders with hot coals strapped to their legs. As much as my stomach swoops whenever I'm around him, I'm still pissed off at his taunting from barely a minute ago, infuriated with him more to the point. This man is older than me by a mile but gives me whiplash at how fast his mood can change.

He's sitting on the edge of the bed, looking like sex and temptation and wrongdoing . . . and the asshole has probably had some other woman—ugh, who knows, multiple women, even—rubbing over him all night.

The part I hate the most about that awful scenario is that's all I want to do to him myself.

"Fine. Whatever. Keep the phone. The bed is all yours. I'll take the couch from now on." Rolling my eyes and letting out a huff, I spin on my heel to put some much-needed distance between us as I attempt to rapidly vacate the room.

He strikes faster than it would seem possible for a man of his bulk and size.

Before I can take a step toward the door, a powerful arm bands around my waist, leaving heat pouring through my body from that point of contact. It's a much stronger sensation than I'd ever imagined I could feel from a simple act like that. I'm tossed unceremoniously face-first onto the bed. The mattress dips and bounces beneath me as I land, sprawled on my stomach, with a yelp.

"What the fuck?" I splutter, trying to push myself up, but it's impossible. There is a mountain of a man behind me, and he straddles the backs of my thighs, pinning me to the bed with his weight. With one hand, he snatches both my wrists and secures them in front of my face, seemingly effortlessly, inside his giant paw.

His rings, his cuff, his goddamn tattooed name that makes my blood sing with desire, all of it fills my line of vision.

"Don't play the brat with me, Briar."

Holy shit, the deep warning in his voice in my ear sends my pulse racing. I've never been handled like this. This is rougher than anything I've experienced before, yet I don't feel unsafe.

In fact . . .

My eyes slam shut as the familiar ache and warmth spread through my core, my pussy, my breasts. Why does this man barely have to say two words to me and toss me around and I'm ready to throw all caution to the wind, to gleefully shred the last remaining vestiges of all sanity and spread my legs.

What the fuck is wrong with me?

Turning my face to the side, I dare allow my eyes to open a crack, feeling and seeing just how close his bulk is hovering over my spine.

To add to my humiliation, I'm panting.

Panting.

For my uncle.

"What do you want from me?" My voice comes out breathy, sounding just as desperate as I really, truly am. Even though it was so wrong, last night unlocked something inside me. He cruelly opened that door, the one that was supposed to remain padlocked and bolted shut, and now I've had a glimpse of what lies on the other side.

Even though it's a darkened precipice that I shouldn't want to venture toward, I'm so unraveled that temptation has taken the driver's seat, steering straight toward the cliff barrier that's supposed to safeguard me from the sorts of untrustworthy, horny decision-making currently rampaging through my veins.

"I could ask you the same question, darlin'." With his free hand, he slides my phone around on the bed, directly into my line of sight, and props it up on the pillow so we can both see precisely what is on screen.

Exactly *who* fills the screen.

"I asked first." My words come out awfully close to sounding like a whimper. God, his weight feels so good on top of me. I can already feel my eyes threatening to roll into the back of my head. My muscles feel as though they've melted into puddles. Bliss and a sense of freedom rushes through me like a warm breeze, because this is something I can give myself over to.

I'll gladly give him this kind of power when it feels so good. So natural. So unbelievably right with him.

161

I hate the circumstances of what we are and the technicalities around that connection.

"Is that what you want, Briar?" He lowers down so his mouth is at my ear, brushing heated and wet against me just as he did to me last night when he melted my brain. "Is that *who* you want?"

As he says the words, I feel it.

The snaking glide of his hand finds its way between my body and the mattress. He's wrapped around me, just like those mornings I've woken up, with him blanketing my spine and one hand cupping my pussy.

The video on screen is silent; he's muted the audio but leaves it on a looping clip of videos showing different rides across his career. I've watched this one several times before. It goes on for at least ten minutes. A compilation of slow-motion footage showcasing every single powerful and breathtaking detail of the cowboy at my back.

"Tell me, darlin' . . . Is that what you're wanting? The famous bull rider? The star Stôrmand Lane to fuck you and be done with you like some nameless buckle bunny desperate for a chance to taste my cock?"

A gasp escapes me at the coarseness of his words, mixed with the tightness of his fingers pressed against my pussy, the heel of his palm cupping me in a possessive hold. It's the perfect position to add pressure to my clit, but he's teasing me with wicked words and refuses to move his hand.

"I—I don't know." My hips shift involuntarily, and another whimpering noise comes out of me.

"Watch that screen. I know you want to. Because you're in here at night watching these videos . . . So you'd better tell me, are you getting yourself off imagining what it would be like?"

I grind harder against his fingers. On my phone screen, he's all strength and agility and fearlessness. Leaner, thanks to his youth and peak athleticism, but no less impressive than he is now. Behind me, that same man, only older and more hardened by life, is even hotter, more desirable.

Pure temptation and forbidden fruit I so desperately wish could drip all over my tongue and run like nectar straight down my throat.

I feel like my brain and body are tearing apart, nothing more than a shredded piece of paper.

"We can't—This can't happen." Biting down on my lip hardly suppresses the moan as I hump his fingers and seek out that coiled, spiral winding tighter inside me.

"You think I don't fucking know that." His lips brush my ear before his nose drags over that same spot. The heat of his palm grips both my wrists tighter, and his body shifts over the top of mine. I catch another glimpse of those rings, of his leather cuff up close, and my pussy ripples with being so near to the edge of that release I've been chasing.

Oh god. Our bodies line up perfectly, and we're grinding, writhing together on the mattress, fully clothed.

"*Please.*" My body is crying out, aching with the need for release. "I don't want him." I don't want the man on the screen, or my date from earlier today. I want the gorgeous cowboy whose body drapes over mine from knees to hips, to his strong arms holding me, to his mouth at my ear.

"Fuck, darlin'," he grunts against my neck, and I let out an unholy noise. Did I just outright start pleading with him to slide my dress up and put us both out of our misery?

I try to turn my head away, to ignore the vision of him wrestling in an attempt to remain astride the massive bull on my phone screen until that buzzer sounds, but he won't allow it.

"Look at it, darlin'. You want to watch? Then watch, while you grind that pretty little pussy on my hand and take what you need. Watch me ride that bull and imagine how it would feel for me to ride you."

For how often I've imagined being at his mercy, it catches me entirely unprepared for the feel of this man actually being on top of me like this. The potent masculine scent, the heat, the rustle of sheets beneath us.

"Take what you need. Your sweet little cunt needs this, and fuck, I wish I could give you more, but you're gonna have to be the one to take it. Use my fingers, and let me see how gorgeous you look when you come."

The illicit fruit he dangles in front of me is too tempting, too ripe, too mouth-watering. The layers of material between us are so thin, it's almost like I can feel every inch and vein of his hard cock. My fingers claw at the blankets beside my head, still pinned in his hold. Each needy, rapid roll of my hips draws in my climax. The roaring of blood in my ears and the rub of my hard nipples against the inside of my bra, it all combines and races up the climb to reach that perfect peak.

"Goddamn. This dress should be illegal." He nips at my earlobe, teeth sharp and pinching, voice rough with arousal. "You want to know where I was tonight?"

A sobbing noise comes out of me, followed by incoherent pleading and nodding against the blanket.

"I was trying to find every way I could to stop myself from tearing your clothes off you." He lowers his mouth closer still, pressing his heated lips against me and filling my senses with gritty, coarse words.

"Believe me, I wasn't with anyone else, darlin' . . . so whether you want to imagine it's me helping you get there, or if you need to pretend it's that man you've been watching in those videos, I don't fucking care, but you're going to come for me right now."

As he says those final words, he grinds his hips harshly against my ass, the soft fabric of his sweats and his rigid cock flattening me to the bed. Driving me onto his fingers, again and again, and that's what tips me over the edge.

My orgasm floods my veins as my toes curl, and a low moan breaks out of me.

"Oh my god. Oh my god," I chant, and my entire body clenches, my channel left feeling empty and so desperate to be filled, because this liquid pleasure would be so much more intense, a thousand brilliant pinpricks of light brighter and more tantalizing with his thick length stretching me.

"Fuck. Goddamn it, Briar." Above me, I hear the unmistakable grunt of intense frustration before a final savage thrust of his hips against my own. So forceful it knocks the air from my lungs.

I'm floating higher and out of my head, knowing that he nearly lost it with me because of that.

Because of what I do to him.

Is it better, or punishingly worse, knowing that he's fighting this attraction that we absolutely cannot indulge and should never have allowed to spark between us?

We lie there together for a moment. My heart still thundering wildly, and like last night, I'm trying to be the version of Briar who can handle herself with dignity after engaging in something that shouldn't have even happened in the first place . . . but I don't know if I can go another night without being held after such an intense orgasm.

God, I'm so needy. So fucking clingy.

He eases up from covering me without a word.

I wince and decide I can't face anything more humiliating than yet another man who willingly leaves me cold and alone in a bed. There are far too many memories I don't want that threaten to burst through the dam I've erected inside my mind, so I give in to the pathetic need to hide away and bundle myself under the blankets.

I know I said I would sleep on the couch, but if he's already preparing to run off in order to get away and insert distance between us. After the intensity of what just happened, my limbs are heavy and droopy.

Except, as I try to curl on my side to tuck myself into a ball and try to figure out what the fuck I'm supposed to do about the fact I turn into a cat in heat, rubbing all over my uncle every time I'm near him, the mattress dips behind me.

Strong arms band around me.

"Come here. Sit up for me."

I'm caught in a state of disbelief, so much so that I lose the ability to respond. All I can do is follow his guiding touch and brief instructions.

Reaching behind his neck, he tugs his T-shirt off in one smooth motion, leaving a whirl of ink and muscles filling every inch of space, filling my vision.

Wordlessly, he nudges me to raise my arms up. As I do so, I dare glance at his face, and his expression is pinched, brows furrowed. His intense focus remains on the task at hand—sliding my dress up and over my shoulders and head.

The whole time, he keeps his eyes on a spot somewhere around the point of my shoulder. Not staring at my body but keeping his attention on what he's doing. Once my dress is removed, he quickly bunches up a T-shirt—the T-shirt he was just wearing—and pulls it over my head, covering me in his warmth and scent. He maintains the same careful, attentive manner as he guides each of my arms through to set it in place.

I'm entirely too stunned to speak.

After he's done that, he reaches under the fabric, and that's when I suck in a sharp breath as his fingers graze the back of my ribs and my spine.

The cowboy-dream kneeling beside me on this mattress unclasps my bra, leaving me fighting the urge to shiver as his rough fingers brush lightly over bare skin. With more care and attentiveness than I could ever have imagined, he methodically works to pull each of the straps through the arm holes in order to help me take it off.

It's a series of steps that could have so easily been sexualized. Especially considering where we had ended up only moments before.

Only, there is nothing but care and a sort of tenderness in the way he just helped me get undressed.

Still lingering in heavy silence, he holds the covers back and gestures for me to settle myself beneath them. I curl onto my side, as I had been trying to do moments before.

Then he rustles around a little behind me.

The lamp on the bedside table flicks off, plunging us into darkness.

I'm not sure what to expect, anticipating that I'll hear the telltale thud of retreating footsteps within the next few seconds.

However, I'm dragged back against a warm, bare chest.

His legs tangle with mine.

My heart flutters and gasps with excitement in a way that I should absolutely squash and stamp down, because there is no way I can allow myself to become attached.

We don't need to say anything. We both know there's nothing that can be said, because last night in his truck and tonight, both of those stolen, reckless moments have stepped far beyond the boundaries of what should separate us.

I guess I'll have to deal with reality come morning—that the man I feel so comfortable wrapped up in is the one man I absolutely cannot have.

CHAPTER 19

Storm

Twenty square feet suddenly feels like it has shrunk to barely two in the wake of yesterday. This cabin is like a glass case, where every attempt I've tried to make, every effort to tread carefully with the aim of avoiding Briar, well, I've failed.

Miserably.

Not because I want to avoid her—the opposite extreme is true. It's the fact I know her dirty little secret, and that calls to the side of me I shouldn't even be considering letting off his chain.

The smug, all-too-pleased-with-himself asshole, who wants nothing more than to throw this girl down and show her everything she's been missing.

To teach her all the ways her body and goddamn soul can respond to my touch.

Right now, these close confines are feeling like a hellfire punishment sent to torment me. That this girl is right under my feet everywhere I turn, and my brain is so scattered—so fucking hung up on everything that has happened between us so far— that I keep tripping over her.

Physically and metaphorically.

The harder I try, the clumsier I get.

I even managed to walk in on her getting out of the shower this morning because I was too lost in my own mind, replaying what she felt like beneath me . . . and, well, I didn't mean to bust in on her, but another opportunity to see her half-naked by accident has done absolutely nothing to calm this fucking situation.

Five seconds into making breakfast for us, I somehow managed to crush her against the benchtop. Unintentionally, of course, but the asshole inside me wanted to keep her there and reach out for her, and I had to damn well scold myself for continually being drawn toward her body.

The entire shit show of a morning has basically involved me apologizing while Briar tells me there's nothing to worry about. However, she won't meet my eyes, and her cheeks have been tinged pink.

It kills me that she won't look at me.

Even though I know what we did last night was consensual, it still fucking grates me that she's embarrassed or ashamed or whatever the fuck is going through her mind.

She's a damn gorgeous sight when she falls apart, and holy shit, I was so close to losing all control with her. The fact this girl had me grinding against her ass until I nearly blew in my pants tells me everything I need to know about how well and truly fucked in the head I am.

That girl has nothing to feel churned up about. I'm the sick bastard who won't, or can't, seem to keep my hands off her or my head on straight. I'm the one who snapped after seeing that she was watching old footage of me. I don't know how or why, but after being so messed up as I thought about her being on a date, then seeing her wearing my coat, then knowing that she was even moderately interested in something about my life . . . it fucking killed off any last glimpses of common sense that might have been floating around.

That moment smashed my already-busted moral compass, and now I don't know what the fuck to do.

I know her scent, her moans, her gasping breaths.

I also know that she's been keeping a secret, and that spurs something feral to buck around inside my chest.

She felt so damn good in my arms, in my shirt—sleeping beside her has been the best I've ever slept in my life. I don't think I ever before made it through the night, untroubled and uninterrupted, the way I have with her softness and quiet breathing on the pillow beside mine. I spent so many years trying to numb myself with booze or sex or just wiping my body out, and none of that ever worked. I'd still be awake or lying with restless limbs or up and pacing around in the darkness of the devil's hours. All while the rest of the world was deep in dreamland.

Yet, with Briar, I'm tugged into such a deep, restful sleep I don't even notice her getting up and leaving the bed. I only seem to stir once she's gone and feel that uncomfortable goddamn sensation inside my chest cavity like someone is trying to grip my heart inside a fist.

So, as we slide into the truck together in order to make our way up the mountain to Devil's Peak Ranch for the day, I crank the stereo and figure it's going to be a hell of a lot easier on both of us if we don't have to talk at all.

The buzzer sounds, and I hurl myself off the back of the snorting, violent beast. Guys rush in, bullfighters working to distract the animal as I get myself to safety and clear of the arena. Noise, heat, dirt, it all rushes into my senses.

Pulse racing, wrenching my glove off, I'm already certain that might have just been a championship-winning ride. Might even hit the nineties club.

The announcer calls my score: it's a 92.5.

Electric elation rockets through my blood, igniting my veins, and that combined with the adrenaline of the ride leaves me almost numb. Beau is right there, grabbing me, shaking me by the shoulders, and he's yelling in my face. Music blares and the arena lights dance off his eyes as he pulls me in for a hug and keeps on hollering.

My friend who already had one hell of a ride tonight himself, who could so easily be on top of the world right now, is celebrating right alongside me. My brain can't process this feeling. Beau could have easily won—his total scores came a close second behind mine. Yet it's my name they're screaming. It's my shirt clenched beneath his fist as he crashes our foreheads together, and the delight rolls off him at the sight of my official winning total lit up on the big screen.

I won.

I fucking won.

But I almost don't hear any of the excitement or joy coming my way.

Amongst it all, woven between the chaos of announcements, the media, the presentation, and the accolades from the crowd, that familiar pit lurks in my stomach. What does any of it fucking matter? Stôrmand Lane wins another title, and there are thousands of fans whistling and clamoring for my attention, yet no one is in those stands cheering me on. There's been no sign of my own brother—and I know for a fact he's in Las Vegas; he's in this very same city tonight and couldn't be bothered to show up.

The classic All-American rodeo star. Living the dream, without a single family member left alive who gives a shit. What a fucking joke.

As I'm finally released from the mayhem of being crowned a winner, finally freed to head out to the competitor's area, I hear my name. A couple of girls hang by the security, and as they call out their congratulations, hungry eyes rake down my body appreciatively. Girls who I'll never see again after tonight. One of them is blonde, leggy, a typical buckle bunny. Her friend looks much the

same. Both flash white smiles and bat their eyelashes in my direc-
tion as I draw nearer.

I might have a championship buckle, a prizewinner's check to
cash, but they look like a fucking excellent way to forget about the
emptiness inside my chest.

"Keep them there if you can, Storm. We'll work our way through the front of the herd," Colt calls out to me, dragging my mind back to the here and now on Devil's Peak Ranch.

Hell, I've been so lost in my own head that I've hardly been concentrating on what I *should* be doing. That's flanking the heifers we're moving, not getting lost in my shitty past, and not wishing I'd made a different goddamn choice that night.

Pinching my brow, I cast my eyes over the mass of black bodies, their rough coats, their tufted ears flicking as they bellow and rumble in front of me.

The last thing I need today is Colton Wilder finding a reason to lash me with that sharp tongue he has when he's in a mood. The grumpy fucker hardly trusts anyone else to do anything around here on a good day.

Seated on their horses, he and Layla are over the far side of the paddock, guiding the cattle from the front. They needed help today with bringing the herd in for vaccinations, and I'll always turn up when he needs a hand around this place.

However, it's the younger Wilder man who has had my teeth on edge since I arrived earlier.

Kayce is being the usual blond-haired, blue-eyed prick he is. All the memories of my younger years are reflected back at me when I look at him. Everything I used to be, before the tattoos, before embracing the role of the bad boy on the pro tour. I was the guy who played perfectly into the narrative sponsors, and the PR machine all fed off it.

They fucking loved Stôrmand Lane—until they didn't.

My bulletproof, charmed life. Right before I made the worst

decision I could have made one night on a whim while blind drunk and wasted out of my mind in Vegas.

A decision that flipped my world and my career on their head for good . . . leaving me chasing my own sanity while hidden away here on this mountain. Worst part in all that twisted fucking time in my life is that the girl is not even around to see the fallout of her actions.

At least today has been full, keeping me numbingly occupied and endlessly busy. The kind of daily ranching grind that doesn't leave much time for sitting around *thinking*. Kayce has had Briar up in the saddle from the moment we got to the ranch, and I've been helping Colt out with his head of cattle so he can check them over now that we're into spring.

Steam rises off their black coats as the low, drawn-out calls, grinding groans, and snorts fill the air. We're only rounding up a small group. Colt doesn't run a large herd, but he's been keen to vaccinate and keep a closer eye on them after being away traveling.

Much like Beau, Colt's about the only other person on this goddamn planet I'd drop anything to help, and I know he'd do the same for me.

Christ, the man spent a night up a ladder in the pitch black and freezing rain helping me fix a hole in my roof when a tree came down a few years back. Damn thing nearly took out half the cabin, and yet he was there for me within the hour of putting out a call on the radio. Colton Wilder is one of the good ones, and as I watch, a hint of softness spread across his features when he looks over at the woman in the saddle beside him, with her copper hair in two long braids. I couldn't be fucking happier to see him finally find his person in Layla.

Even if their circumstances of meeting weren't exactly conventional, and even if they haven't had an easy road to get to where they are now.

Reaching up, I readjust my hat and lean one arm down to

pat my horse's neck. His weight shifts around beneath me, and his ears twitch. He's clever; he knows exactly why we're here and what is required. As I murmur a few words, telling him just how good a job he's doing, we both keep one eye on the mob in case of any breakaways.

Across the other side of the herd, Kayce flanks to one side of Briar, both of them on their own horses. They're not exactly here to help with the roundup—even though Kayce could easily get the fuck over here and lend more of a hand if he chose to—but at least he's alongside Briar and helping her build more confidence riding out beyond the pens by the barn.

I hate to admit it, but Kayce Wilder is good at this whole teaching bullshit. Much better and miles more patient than I could ever be. So I'm happy Briar could learn with someone she's comfortable around. Not to mention that during our time spent up here, I'm also happy that Layla seems to have taken her under her wing.

They spent an awful lot of time together yesterday, and the insane part of me wonders if Briar mentioned anything about me. About us. Even though there can't be an *us*, so it's already a ludicrous thought and has no right to even be a question floating around my mind.

The darkest part of me that still wants to wrestle free half expects Wes to show up any minute to whisk her away on another date. That's the part that wants to help him lose a few teeth and maybe break a few fingers, you know, for good measure. Fortunately for my sanity, she hasn't said anything . . . other than last night when she more or less admitted she didn't want him.

Or, at least, I think she did.

In all honesty, I might have been too caught up on the cocky wave I was riding, knowing she's been watching clips of my rodeo years, and could have willfully misinterpreted those four simple words.

I don't want him.

As I lean forward in the saddle, my eyes are drawn back to Briar yet again. Like she's the source of all the damn daylight shining down on us, and I'm scraping for just one more ray, one tiny glimmer to shine in my direction. Only this time when I glance over, that smug fucker inside my chest beats a victory drum. A floaty, intoxicating feeling swells to a crescendo.

She's already looking at me.

Goddamn, all those details I can catalog from here—her dark hair and soulful brown eyes and pouty lips—if it all doesn't scream that she's mine.

Even if she can't ever be mine.

Even if no one can ever know that I'm thinking about my *niece* in a way that I have absolutely no right to.

The herd continues to slowly move forward, with snorts and rumbling noises, until they're finally all in the holding pen where Layla wants them secured so she can start working on their vaccinations. That brings my horse to draw level alongside Briar's, and much to my frustration, Kayce is right there, beaming at me.

My teeth grind, and I can feel the pulse in my jaw. He and I, we spent a lot of time together these past few months while I based myself here at the ranch through winter to help run the place with Colt being away. I've also been doing what I can to help him get ready for his next stint on the road competing. This kid has got the makings of hitting it big—if only he hadn't spent so much time the past few years doing his best to fuck all that up by getting day drunk and losing sponsors faster than he could blink.

"Yo, Storm. You're free this weekend?" Kayce pulls his horse into step with mine as we make our way back toward the barn.

I give him an exasperated look. "Depends."

There's no way I'm agreeing to anything until I know exactly whatever the fuck this is.

"We're all going down to Crimson Ridge since Layla's friend

is coming to town, and she wants us to meet her. You'd better bring your miserable attitude so you can keep my dad company, alright?"

My fists tighten around the reins, and I run my tongue over my teeth. It feels impossible not to steal a glance at Briar now that she's so close and looks so damn good in the saddle.

The girl who I'm fairly certain had never ever touched a horse before arriving on this mountain and turning my life on its head.

"City girl here is in. Surely even your antisocial ass can leave the Peak to put in an appearance for a few hours."

"What friend?" I shift my weight in the saddle. If Briar has already said yes to this fuckery, and if Colt is going, then against my better judgment, it looks like I'm going to have to agree to this.

"Sage . . . they've been friends forever."

"It sounds fun," Briar chimes in.

"Gonna bring your li'l man friend?" Kayce looks over her way with a shit-eating grin on his face that I'll gladly remove for him.

One little mention of Wes is enough to have my shoulders stiffening. It takes every ounce of self-control I've got to keep my eyes planted on the back of my horse's head.

"I guess I can ask Wes if he's free."

Wes. Jesus. Not Westin. She's already calling him by a nickname and sounding far too much like someone seriously considering seeing him again. Not if I've got anything to fucking do with it, but I don't get a say in who this girl spends her time with, so I have to bite down on my tongue hard enough to draw blood.

"Wes is a fucking good dude, you know. His family has been ranching out here a long time. Pretty sure he's taking things over at their property so his folks can retire. He's always offered if we need a hand with anything up here or if I need a place to train closer to Crimson Ridge; that's just the kind of guy he is."

Fuck off. Fuck right off right now.

Kayce is basically selling her this guy, making his best pitch to Briar about how goddamn perfect her cowboy date is. The worst part of all this is that it's all true. He *is* a good guy, with all his good-guy, salt-of-the-earth bullshit.

Westin Hayes is everything I'm not. He's got a ranch to his name, a family who all works the land together, and there certainly aren't rumors whispered behind hands—hushed tones and wide eyes as they ask each other how a person could possibly do something so awful and get away with it—every time he walks through the door.

What the hell do I have in comparison to a guy like that? I don't even own the property I live on.

Evidently, the girl in the saddle beside me does.

Black thoughts about perfect-cowboy Wes and how I'd rather chew off my own foot than have to sit through dinner with him and Briar *together* take precedence in my mind as I make sure the horses are away in their stalls. As I check in with Colt and Layla, who let me know they're able to handle things from here with the cattle. Through the endless chatter between her and Kayce as they talked about fuck knows what, because I'm not even listening. No, I'm too busy figuring out ways to break his jaw and make it look like an accident. Right up until the moment I'm driving back down the mountain with the pretty young thing perched in the passenger side of my truck.

"You never answered Kayce's question earlier, you know." Briar looks out the window, but her voice floats my way. "Whether you're planning on joining us for dinner this weekend."

"Didn't think you'd concern yourself with my being there or not." I shrug. Molars clenched. Fists strangling the steering wheel.

"They're your friends, too. Layla wants you to come. Besides, I assume Colt would quite appreciate having you to sit and be grumpy with him."

She's teasing me, attempting in her sweet way that she does to coax and prod and try to lighten the thunder-cloud mood I've brought along with me for the drive.

However, I'm a dick, and in return, all I've seemingly got to offer is a snarling, jealous hellhound.

"What about Wes? Planning on inviting him along? Planning on taking things further with him this time?" The words are out of me before I can do anything about it.

Briar's head whips in my direction, her dark eyes flash, and those enticing lips hang a little parted. A plush mouth I shouldn't be stealing glances at every five minutes like an addict. Yet, here I am doing just that.

She wets her lips, studying me for an agonizingly long stretch of time.

"Is this my uncle asking . . . or the guy who shows up after dark?" Her voice is soft. As if there's a risk of someone hearing her words that she knows neither of us are supposed to be entertaining.

I fix my eyes on the road. Fuck. This is dancing us closer to something we've been careful to avoid until now. "You're one to talk. Those thorns of yours are doing a good job of keeping everyone at arm's length." We've been experts at side-stepping any real conversation after the couple of nights when I've watched the most intimate sight of this girl falling apart in my arms. "Don't think I haven't noticed the way your pointed barbs prevent you from getting close to revealing the real reason why you're even here or what you're running from, Briar. My patience only goes so far."

Briar fiddles with the cuff of her jacket—my jacket—where her palms rest in her lap.

"I'm not sure, okay?" From the corner of my eye, I see her

examine a thread on the sleeve extremely closely. "I don't know if I want to meet up with him again, like that, for a date."

"He wasn't good to you?" My neck prickles. "If I find out he did anything, so help me—"

"No, no . . . he was fine. It was nothing like that." Briar is quick to respond, to cut me off from whatever dark place I was about to plunge into, sensing my rising tide of tension.

"Then what?"

Puffing out a breath, she lifts her gaze to stare out the window. "He talked about you . . . kinda a lot."

Those words act like a warm and welcome breeze, blowing in and instantly melting away all the fraught emotion and clenched muscles. A mere handful of words have gone and got me feeling about ten feet tall inside the cab of this truck.

"Did he now?" This is news to me, and all of a sudden, just like that, Westin motherfuckin' Hayes is off my shit list.

"Oh, you can put all of that away." Briar swivels to face me from the other end of the bench seat and waves a hand in the direction of my unconcealed smirk. "Don't look so goddamn pleased with yourself." Her disapproving glare is far too cute for her own good.

"What would you rather have happened then, darlin'? Would you have preferred he took you somewhere and didn't talk to you at all?"

She squirms. Doesn't say anything. Immediately flicks her gaze down to the place where her fingers curl around the jacket sleeve.

"Briar. Answer the question." As I touch my tongue to the front of my teeth and demand more from the beautiful girl, who is becoming increasingly more flushed each time I look over her way, we turn into the gravel track that winds through the tall pines leading to the cabin.

Pulling up outside the cabin, I put the truck in park and cut the engine. The silence wraps around us in the same lingering manner as the night she sat in my lap while parked in this very spot, and surely, to all that is morally correct and honorable, that should be my warning to leave.

That deafening stillness is the alert, the siren, the alarm bell going off. My signal to get the fuck out of this vehicle and not wait to hear her reply. To not corrupt this girl with my goddamn messed-up fantasies.

Yet, I wait, keeping my fingers wrapped around the steering wheel in every effort not to put them somewhere inappropriate.

To prevent myself from touching *her*.

"It's embarrassing, alright." Briar chews her lip, giving me a glimpse of those dark eyes as her lashes hang low over her gaze.

"You can tell me." My heart thuds a little harder at the prospect of what I think this girl is about to put into words. What I suspect the real reason is. Something that I have no right to be curious about, considering that I'm her uncle.

But fuck. Do I want to hear it.

"I already told you the other night. I don't have much *experience*, so I need to get some somewhere, don't I? Wouldn't you rather, if it had to be with anyone, that it was with Mr. Nice Guy Cowboy Country Manners?"

Briar's words tumble out in a hasty confession, immediately followed by her slamming her mouth shut as if she's said too much, but the words are out there now, and she can't reel them back in. Her painted fingernails hook the door handle, attempting to push her side open, to escape this front seat after her outburst. However, fate, or whatever you want to call this pivotal, unsanctioned moment between us, clearly has other intentions.

Her door jams.

The harder Briar tries, huffing and making a small noise of frustration, the more resolutely it gives her the middle finger and refuses to budge.

I open my side and unfold myself from the seat, letting my

boots hit the dirt as I chew over the prospect of what this sequence of unlikely, and endlessly enticing, events has brought to fruition. Resting both hands on the roof of the truck, I allow my body to drape across the open doorway, filling the space with my bulk as I duck my head and affix my sights on the girl staring back at me. We stay like that, gazes locked, and I run my tongue to wet my bottom lip. Briar focuses on the motion, watching my mouth with a piercing intensity—something akin to terror and interest in her dark eyes and, fuck, if that combination isn't a potent drug—while I allow my eyes to take in every gorgeous inch of her.

Because this feeling right here is the same as being in the bucking chute, preparing to be released into the arena.

We both feel it, but only she has the power over what happens next.

This is the moment when the air crackles, the adrenaline spikes. It's the act of voluntarily climbing into a situation I know is going to go from zero to one hundred in the stamp of a hoof, a bullwhip slicing the air with a crack, flipping unpredictably in the blink of an eye.

Readying yourself to either be bucked off and stomped all over or hear that sweetest roar of victory when the buzzer sounds.

Or maybe, in my case, ruination.

"From the looks of it, you're gonna have to slide out this side, darlin.'"

CHAPTER 20

Briar

My door is stuck. Every single rational part of me is screaming, begging on bended knee, pleading with that door to pop open. To give me the excuse I'm searching for.

I should *want* to escape this man.

No part of me is supposed to feel the call of that beckoning finger of fate, the tingling allure of sliding across that space between us, to willingly get any closer to my uncle.

A girl like me is meant to desire someone else, anyone else. Not the brooding, tattooed, sinfully hot cowboy with startling blue eyes.

Until now, we've avoided talking about things that have happened—neither of us has seemed to be at a juncture where we could muster up the courage to figure out what the fuck keeps swirling and developing in the ether. All I know is that my body has pleaded with me all day for this man, at every moment and every turn. Watching him on the ranch, working with the cattle, riding his horse with all the skill and ease of a cowboy who would undoubtedly know how to use those skills in other ways. All while being jostled around in my own saddle until my nerves were frayed to pieces.

I've barely held it together.

Now here we are, separated by four feet of bench seat, the very location where we've already crossed lines we shouldn't have once before.

Unfortunately, for the sake of my sanity, my moral fiber, my ability to think clearly about any of this, I can't bear to consider spending another night in that house, another night sharing a bed lying next to a man who I am agonizingly drawn to, a man I cannot touch, without my lungs bursting.

"Slide over." His eyes glitter. The way he says those two words makes my pussy clench in memory of what happened the last time I obeyed that same order.

There is a part of my brain that knows what I'm supposed to do in this scenario. That is implicitly aware of the *right* course of action to be taken in this moment.

I slam the door in that bitch's face.

The woman inside me who doesn't give a fuck, who is so sick of being denied what she wants, is a slut for this man.

She willingly does as he instructs.

"Fine." Trying to sound disaffected, I give in, shifting my weight, inching along to the driver's side, and get to the edge. He doesn't move.

The temperature outside may be dropping rapidly, but my entire body feels like it has gone up in flames. I'm trapped here, peering up at him, and my brain feels like it has gone blank.

"Would you have gone home with him yesterday? If he asked you?" The man before me looms large, filling every inch of the open door. He leisurely rests both hands on the roof, with arms extended above his head, consuming the only available exit, like a god.

Fuck. There's no way I can answer him honestly without giving him more fuel to taunt me about my *crush*, or whatever this fascination is. So, I settle for petulance by rolling my eyes. "I don't need to answer that."

"Briar. Humor me." He's gentling me. Giving me that husky voice, the one he uses when he coaxes the horses. Still. Not. Moving.

"No. I'm not playing that game."

I can't do this push and pull. I can't play this fucked-up version of truth or dare. I'm so messed up in the head that all I want is for this man to show me more than the couple of glimpses he's now given me of how naturally my body responds to his instruction.

Of course, I'm going to have to find a way to satisfy that craving elsewhere.

I swing my feet out the door, but our legs are entwined, my bent knees brush the front of his shins, and the only option left is to shove past him. All I have to do is duck beneath his arms, to try my best to avoid looking at the perfectly fitted jeans right at my eye level, but as I do so, my boots barely hit the ground.

My uncle—the man I've quickly become enamored with—circles my waist with his arms before I can run away, just like last night, and hauls me back. Spinning me around, slamming my front against the side of the truck, it happens so quickly that I flatten both palms in order to brace myself.

Trepidation, excitement, and delight rush through my veins, a heady concoction of feelings that shouldn't coexist.

I'm caged in and definitely, absolutely do not wish to be released.

"*Storm.*" My voice is breathy and needy. A white plume gusts past my lips, the air chilled now that the spring sun has set.

He makes a dark noise, sounding pleased and tortured that I've called him that for the first time since I arrived here.

"Truth time. If you were with him . . . letting *him* show you things . . . who would you be thinking about?"

My back presses against his broad chest. His warmth blankets me, as it did last night, and my fingers curl against the cold metal on the side of the truck. I see his tattooed hand placed just beside mine. *STORM* in black ink stares back at me, and right now, I would do incredibly slutty things to have that hand on me.

"Come on, little thorn. If he touched your sweet pussy, who would you think about?"

I swallow a whimper, and a swarm of butterflies explodes in my stomach.

"What does it matter?" All notions have flown out of my head, and my blood races through my body, responding to the acres of contact between us. His arm banded across my stomach, his tight hold on me, that connection running the length of my spine.

"Would you be lost in the moment with your only thoughts being of him? Would he have you panting and writhing and desperate for him and him alone?"

"I don't know why this matters to you." I want the fact that he's asking to mean something it doesn't, and short of admitting that there is no earthly possibility of me being with another man and *not* thinking about Stôrmand Lane, I don't know what to say.

His mouth finds my ear, leaving goosebumps flying across every inch of my skin when he rumbles out, "Wouldn't you prefer to learn with someone you can trust?"

"I'd say I can't trust anyone."

Storm's fingers glide down the front of my jacket. *His jacket.* The one I can't bring myself to stop wearing because I'm addicted to his scent.

With practiced efficiency, he unfastens the front, allowing the opening to hang freely.

"You liked what we did in the truck." It's a statement. A fact he knows to be true.

"Maybe." Fluttering wings have taken off, causing a riot in my stomach.

He chuckles. "It's ok to admit you did. I won't tell anyone . . . besides, you trusted me last night."

I pause, but my hips betray me. Giving away my immediate answer to that question when they follow his fingers softly tracing the waistband of my jeans.

God, this man is too skilled, too expert in this. He's got a bevy of women ready to throw themselves at his feet—or do whatever leads to losing their sanity and beauty products in his truck. Why the hell is he even looking twice in my direction?

"I liked it," I breathe out, feeling shaky but not wanting to break this spell.

He hums, a sexy, masculine noise, and that tattooed hand that's been dwarfing mine, pressed to the metal of the truck, lifts and snakes down my belly.

My stomach caves as he uses both hands, still wrapped around me, to deftly unbutton my jeans. There is every chance my heart may escape my throat, it's thundering so hard.

A gasp bubbles up. "Wh—what are you doing?"

"Tell me—if you'd gone on your little date . . . and afterward he took you somewhere nice and private, if he slid a hand inside like this and found you drenched, would it be his hand you wanted touching you or someone else's?"

As he murmurs those devious words, I lose focus far too easily. They trap me, enthrall me, and I can only pay attention to the place his fingers are on my body—the band of flesh where my underwear sits, directly above my aching pussy.

Somehow, I'm supposed to locate words, when the only thing preoccupying my brain is each searing, exploratory glide and brush of his fingertips. No matter how hard I seek, not a single adequate word is to be found.

Instead, my breathing hitches, and a tiny moan of pleasure comes out when the calloused fingers I've watched handle horses and metal and show so much skill make contact with my bare skin.

"Easy. Just breathe for me." His voice is like gravel and honey as he nudges his nose along my jaw. At the same time, one hand dips beneath the fabric, moving lower and lower, and despite him telling me to do the opposite, I forget how to use my lungs.

"Oh god." Another desperate little noise escapes my lips. My fingers curl, nails scraping against the faded paintwork. How am I still standing? I've never had anyone touch me like this before, taking their time, teasing my body, exploring me gently. He presses against my lower stomach, adding a firm, soothing pressure to the softness there, and makes a satisfied noise before reaching my pussy.

"Jesus," Storm exhales against my neck as his fingers discover the truth.

I'm soaking wet.

"We can't . . ." My protest is futile, dying on the night air when his thick fingers dip into me, exploring and finding my swollen clit. We're out in the open, surrounded by trees, the darkening sky, and a scattering of stars.

Even though logically, rationally, I know the nearest person is miles away, the illicit nature of this moment still sends a shiver running through me all the same.

My heartbeat thuds relentlessly between my legs.

"Feel how wet you are. I'll bet you're aching, aren't you, darlin'?"

He's absolutely right. At the sound of his voice, my pussy clenches, my blood floods with lust, and I'm so tightly wound it feels as if I'm ready to explode.

Storm rubs his fingers through my slickness, massaging and taking his time, driving me insane as he briefly circles over my clit, then moves away. Over and over. It's like he's got hours at his disposal. There's no hurrying at this moment, not like last night when he dry humped me into the mattress, with both of us seemingly out of our minds and swept up in some sort of frenzy.

This experience, right here, is like he's savoring the most

intimate part of me, and it alters my brain chemistry entirely with each firm stroke.

"You thinking about him right now?"

Holy shit. There's an edge to his voice that wasn't there before. If I didn't know better, I might think it sounded a lot like jealousy, or something possessive, something controlling at the very least. I don't hate it. In fact, that makes a part of me melt even more rapidly. As he presses his mouth against my ear, hot and wet, his touch intensifies, unraveling me faster and faster.

I swallow thickly. "No."

A rich, satisfied sound coats me from head to toe. "I need to know . . . If you did go with him and he put his mouth on you—"

A moan bursts out of me when he circles my clit, hard. I jolt beneath his touch, my nails scraping the side of his truck. It's all too much. He's too much. I'm so hopelessly and woefully in-experienced at any of this. My sweep of desire cuts him off as I blurt out my confession before he can finish his question. "I don't know—I don't know what that's like." My outburst flies in the night air with a loud whimper.

He stills his fingers.

"No one has ever had their mouth on you?"

Oh fuck, I didn't mean to tell him that, but my mind is scrambled, and my body is a mess of desire and wanting to come. I shake my head, suddenly feeling the scalding burn of shame hit my cheeks. Is he going to think less of me? How goddamn unwanted I've been that no man has ever desired me enough to reciprocate in that way.

"Fuck." Storm's mouth drags down the side of my neck, leaving a wet trail in his wake. "No one has taken care of you at all, have they, darlin'?"

He keeps toying with my body, gently edging me with clever circles and movements. Those strong fingers wedge lower, lower,

lower inside my jeans until he finds my entrance and presses inside. Playing and teasing and stroking deftly at my center. All I seem to be capable of is a series of whimpering noises, panting, desperate breaths on the crisp night air. Simply dissolving for this man.

"You're so fucking soft, so wet, so perfect. I shouldn't be allowed to do anything more with you. There's no way in hell I should be allowed to touch you like this, but I can't fight it." He nips my earlobe with his teeth and, holy shit, that feels so good.

"I know it does." His words are wicked and low.

Oh my god, I'm pretty certain I moaned all that out loud, even though I didn't intend to.

"You deserve to be taken care of . . . to have everything you want."

Storm begins to place kisses along my neck, my jaw, all while he fingers me so slowly and torturously. Playing my body so that I dangle on edge, leaving my hips chasing each motion—following after each glide through my drenched core—as he presses inside me, then drifts back up to my clit.

"Please." I don't really know what I'm begging for. To make me come? To fuck me? To let me go before I ruin everything?

With the hand not shoved down the front of my panties, he skates his palm up over the layers covering my body until he reaches my neck. Just like the first night in the bathroom, he wraps his hold, firmly cupping my jaw, except this time it's entirely different. Storm demands that I turn for him, and of course I do.

Of course, I allow him to tilt my head, positioning my neck just how he wants me.

"Tell me if you want me to stop." His murmur is so close, so unbelievably seductive.

At first, my lust-hazed mind doesn't understand why he said those words. Then I feel it. His lips, warm and tasting like the night air, the hint of spice and mint and masculinity that is him, all invade my awareness as he presses his mouth to mine.

He kisses me with the same determined, sinfully commanding strokes of his fingers.

I'm done. Disappeared high into the sky overlooking this mountain. My knees might buckle any second because this kiss, from a man who is so much older, who is so forbidden, who I'm not meant to feel the surge of intense heat and desire for . . . He takes something that is supposed to be *wrong* and transcends that into something heart-stopping.

Stôrmand Lane kisses me and it feels as if he just flipped my entire life on its head.

My whimpers flow into his mouth, and each drag of his lips against mine feels like we're losing control. His stubble rasps against my skin, and the sensation is utterly consuming, leaving me drugged and unable to want anything but *him*.

I don't want him to stop.

I can't stop.

With a groan that I drink down, I feel his tongue slide against mine, pressing past my lips and exploring my mouth. God, had I ever even been kissed before this man crashed into my life? Whatever I experienced prior to this moment doesn't bear mentioning, nothing but a weak imitation of what a kiss should feel like.

His mouth and tongue create a warmth like firelight that builds from my toes, sending shivers and sparks right through to my fingertips.

This man is giving me a perfect preview of what he can do with my body, if only I'd let him.

"Storm . . . please . . ." My moaning and begging into his mouth cause his fingers to slide from my jaw, resting against the column of my throat.

"Do you want to learn how good that will feel for your body?"

The sound that comes out of me is far too desperate, but it seems to please him. Calloused fingers press tighter against my neck, not restricting my breathing, but it does something to me having him hold me like that all the same. His other hand mirrors the movement with a firm, possessive, cupping hold beneath my panties.

"Let me teach you, darlin'. Let me teach you what it feels like to come with a man's tongue in your pussy."

CHAPTER 21

Storm

"Let me teach you . . . all the things you want to know. Let me give you that."

Fuck, what am I doing? What am I suggesting here?

I've never been one to hold back when it comes to sex, and I've never repeated women, but this girl, this beautiful creature, feels so delicate in my arms. She feels like a hundred goddamn prizewinning podiums and buckles rolled into one. Something precious. Something worth treasuring.

Like the softest glide of delicate silk, her cunt is warm and wet and unbelievably responsive beneath my touch. The insane need to have her and taste every inch of her is unfiltered gasoline funneled straight into my veins. Fueling the obsession for all things *Briar* that I can't keep denying, even though I'm supposed to. I'm not supposed to give into all the ways I want her over and over and over.

"Oh fuck. I can't think—you make it impossible to think," she pants against my mouth, but her hips keep moving, grinding into my palm cupping her sex.

"Then don't. Just say yes to this. Forget about anything else and let yourself be taken care of." My teeth catch her bottom lip, and I tug gently, drawing the sweetest little horny noise out of the girl trapped in my hold. I feel it in the vibration beneath my fingers wrapped around her slender throat. I feel it in the way her pussy gets wetter the longer we do this dance.

"You're crazy. This is insane."

That's not a no. I can work with that.

"We're going inside." Reluctantly, I drag my hand from her panties, but there's no way I'm moving from this spot until she realizes just how much her body wants and needs this.

"See how perfect and sexy and sweet you are." I bring my hand up and push the fingers coated in her arousal past those lips—I nearly fucking die at the plush sensation of her mouth— and with the way Briar moans softly, the sound heads straight to my aching cock.

I'm hard as steel. My dick straight-up demanding me to strip her naked and just fuck right here, hanging halfway out the open door of my truck. Wanting nothing more than to hear her cries ricocheting off the pine trees surrounding us.

Perhaps that's a fantasy to bring to life another time.

Right now, I'm eating up the tentative way her tongue works over me. Fucking hell, she roams the most gentle, exploratory laps, brushing over my fingertips, tasting herself there.

"Can you walk? Or do I need to throw you over my shoulder, little thorn?"

She makes a tiny noise of protest despite me pressing gently on her tongue.

"Well, you're leaning all over me like one of the horses. Thought I'd better check you've still got use of your legs." Pressing my mouth against her ear, I'm fully addicted to the little shivers of pleasure rolling through her.

I want to kiss her again, to seal our mouths together and soak up every last drop of those delicious simpering noises she makes. I want my mouth on her warm, soft cunt. Goddamn,

I just want to taste and lick and bite down on every inch of smooth, delicate flesh until it's impossible to ignore the fact she's been thoroughly marked as mine.

That sensual, heady noise is followed by a barely-there sound of protest when I slip my fingers from her mouth.

"I can walk," she breathes, sounding dreamy as fuck.

A feverish need washes through me as I untangle myself from Briar and usher her with a gentle touch against her lower back to walk ahead into the cabin. The whole time, my stare fixates on the curve and slope of her thighs below the place where my jacket skims over her ass, because, at least in this moment, I can openly stare at this girl. Before getting through the door, she peeks back at me over her shoulder, looking every inch a curvaceous package of temptation.

Crowding Briar inside, I assist her with the act of shedding jackets and boots and layers that I'm impatient to get rid of before I point in the direction of the couch. "Sit there." Briar seems to be in enough of a daze that she follows my instructions without any further protest. The last fucking thing I want to do right now is slow things down when my heart is thundering like a stampede inside my chest, but I have to light the fireplace, and while I do so, she eats up my every movement with an openness that feels electric beneath my skin.

Maybe she's been hiding just how much she's wanted to look my way without restraint, much as I've been trying, and failing, to do when it comes to her.

At least this way, it gives both of us a moment to get things straight, or at least for me to ask the sorts of questions I should be asking. All of it is most definitely the sort of shit an uncle shouldn't be daring to think, or breathe out loud, but fuck, there's no way I can resist Briar anymore. Seeing as I'm destined for hell, I'd rather pack my bags, knowing I've had her consent along the way.

Once the flames are dancing, casting shadows and flickering orange light around the room, I turn toward the sight of my undeniable obsession. The girl I potentially spell ruin for.

Briar has her feet tucked beneath her, jeans still unbuttoned, settled loose over her hips, and she looks my way from behind her thick curtain of dark lashes.

Staying crouched on my haunches in front of her, I rub a thumb over my jaw. The scent of her still lingers on my skin, and fuck, if that doesn't make it damn near impossible not to pounce on her. I want her cum on my tongue. I want her velvety cunt swallowing my cock. I want to feel her squeeze the life out of me when she comes and begs and moans my name.

"Tell me what you enjoy the most."

Her dark eyes widen. "I—I don't really know."

"Just think about it . . . You said it yourself: You're good at taking care of things on your own. So, when you're all alone, what do you use? A toy?"

Her flaming cheeks say it all.

My heart double bounces. The image of Briar spread out while I run a vibrator over her soaked pussy evaporates anything else from my mind real fast. "Have you got it here with you?" Goddamn. I nearly choke on my own words.

"I want to die of embarrassment right now." Her teeth sink into that lower lip I want to suck down on again and feel how it makes her tremble.

"We're just talking . . . I need to know."

"You really don't. We shouldn't even be having this conversation."

"What was all that outside about getting experience from someone you can trust?" I cock my head to one side, unashamedly looking my fill. This girl had better get it straight in her mind that I'm not going to give in.

She wants this; she's just too afraid of *something* or *someone* to admit it and reach out for what she desires.

Briar buries her face in her hands. "I can't believe I said that," she mutters into her fingers, voice muffled. "I can't believe I'm even considering this . . . that we're talking about this."

I use the opportunity while her face is hidden to make my move, shifting across the couple of feet separating us, and it's easy to position myself right in front of her. From here, kneeling on the floor at the edge of the couch, I can easily glide my palms over her, smoothing over her thighs. She jolts, breath hitching, hands flying away from her face as I make contact.

"So you enjoy using a toy, which you may or may not have stashed in that carry-on of yours. Any hard limits?" As I use my touch to guide her into position, Briar might be giving me a wary look through those eyes, but her body certainly knows what it wants. Good girl she is, her legs part, allowing me to settle between her knees. Exactly like having her perched on my lap in the truck, I can't help but keep touching her, maintaining a slow, rhythmic glide up and down the material hugging her thighs.

She gulps, watches me, and I give her time to catch her breath, not trying to rush things, because this girl is skittish enough as it is. Eventually, Briar finds an answer. "How do I know if I do have any, or what they even are?"

"What feels like an immediate *no* for you? And if you don't know, that's okay. You can always tell me when you come across one."

Briar makes a soft noise and her hips twitch, chasing the movement of my palms when they skate higher towards where her button hangs open. "You say all this like there's going to be more than one occasion where this happens."

She just pointed out the greatest irony of my life, because up until now, I've never wanted anyone more than once.

"Trust me—I already know that once I get the chance to taste you properly, one time won't be enough, darlin.'"

That seems to have the desired effect, because a shudder rolls through her frame and her breathing quickens.

"Tell me this . . ." I'm so fucking gone for this girl. If she stops things, of course, I'd respect her wishes, but I might actually die if she does. Or my dick might fall off. "How about you tell me what turns you on? If you don't know what your limits are, let's start with what you know you *want*."

Curling my fingers over the loosened waistband, I pause, giving her a heated look, a look filled with every filthy promise about how good this is going to feel, but a look that requests permission all the same.

Like the perfect fucking dream girl she is, Briar lifts her hips up so I can tug her jeans down.

"I like . . . I like the idea of you doing whatever you want. For you to use me . . . and show me." With a gasp, her words rush out, and her fingers claw the sofa.

She's nervous, but at least has the courage to ask for what she wants.

Keeping things slow, I carefully work the material down her thighs, my eyes fixated on her face the whole time.

"You like the idea of giving up control?" Jesus. My blood pumps around my body, or what's left of it that hasn't already flowed to my groin at least.

Briar nods. Her eyes glaze over a little as I hold her ankle and press that sensitive spot, tugging the leg of her jeans off one side, then the other.

Fuck, she's gorgeous. I drink all of Briar Lane in from this angle. From the pale pink socks extending up over her calves, to where her black underwear peeks out beneath the hem of her sweater, to the tangle of dark curls bundled on top of her head.

"I don't really know, but what I do know is that I like the way you are with me." The words are so quiet, such a soft admission. "I want more of that, and I want it with you, even though it's probably wrong to say that out loud. I don't care when or where. It feels good—safe—if you have control."

It's my turn to swallow hard now because my brain is going to extremely bad places, thinking of exactly how I'd like to use my niece and show her things and use her pretty little holes in ways that will get her off over and over.

Christ.

This beautiful girl just admitted she's got a free-use kink, and if I wasn't already desperate to get my mouth on her, I'd be feral for her sweetness and submission.

My brain must have stalled for too long, because she buries her face in her hands again, peering down my way through her fingers. "Oh god. That's weird, isn't it? Do people ask for that kind of thing? That's something too weird, right?"

"No." I shake my head and quickly place a kiss on the inside of her knee. "It's fucking sexy. You're the hottest goddamn thing, and here you go and hand me permission to make you come as many times as I want, whenever and wherever I want? You just reached inside my brain and brought all my fantasies to life."

Briar looks at me with her mouth hanging open. "You like that, too?"

"If it involves you coming . . ." My fingers curl to hook the waistband of her panties.

That's when Briar starts to squirm. Her hands push at my shoulders in protest. "Wait . . . I haven't showered, I . . . I haven't shaved . . ."

Those words do something to me. Drawing a deep, primal noise from my chest.

"You think I don't want all of you? I want all of that, exactly you as you are. If we're gonna do this, I need you to understand what it's like to have someone who wants you, no matter when, or where, or how."

Briar sucks in a sharp breath as I continue to inch her panties down, revealing the soft swell of her stomach, her curves, and her delicate skin that I want to spend an entire day mapping and learning.

"Darlin', if there's anything you ever need to know about the type of man I am . . . it's that I'm over here, goddamn desperate for you, without question. You're saying that you give me permission for your body to be *mine* anytime I want. Then believe me when I say that that comes without any sorts of conditions or bullshit excuses that pricks you've been with in the past might have used with you."

Fuck this. There's no way this girl is going to hide from me. Moving with purpose now, I work the fabric past her hips, and the shadow of her pussy starts to reveal itself. She's fucking perfect. Everything I've already had the pleasure of exploring with my fingers is now presented for me, and my mind is already three steps ahead, anticipating the first heated slide of my mouth over her.

"I'm not them, Briar, and when I tell you that, you best believe I'm gonna have you falling apart on my tongue anytime of the day or night."

"What if I'm not good at this?"

When I drag her damp panties off her legs completely, I shove them in my back pocket and glance up. Hovering my mouth over her, savoring every shaky breath and quiver this girl is giving me, I plant a slow kiss over her pussy. The whole time, I keep her trapped in my gaze.

"There's nothing you need to do but enjoy this, so put your hands on my head, and I want to hear how loud you can be for me."

Briar's little noise is part protest, part whimper, and it's so fucking sexy.

"I'm not supposed to feel this way . . . like I need to touch you, but I want to, all the time," she admits, hesitating for just a moment, before those tentative fingers of hers thread into my hair. She pushes the strands back off my forehead, and it damn near makes me groan.

I blow gently over her pussy, glistening and flushed with her arousal.

"Put your hands on me whenever you want, darlin'. Because I sure as hell won't be keeping mine to myself."

I'm done talking. The scent of Briar, turned on and drenched, is my undoing. My mouth closes over her, and she's sweeter than I ever imagined. Her hips shift upward as her back bows, pretty painted fingernails sink tighter into my hair, and she melts beneath me. Her immediate moan is music and fucking poetry to my ears.

Maybe another time, I'll tease her and edge her and show every inch of this perfect little cunt the sort of slow, sensual attention it deserves. But, for now, I'm desperate to have her coming apart, to know how she feels when she shatters on my tongue for the first time, and besides, there's a whole night stretching out ahead of us. Most of which I intend to spend wedged between her thighs.

"Oh god. *Storm.*"

Well, fuck. Hearing her whimper and gasp my name is the type of pleasurable torture I could only hope for. Stiffening my tongue, I work her clit and drag more and more and more out of her. She's panting, whining, damn near riding my face from below as her fingers tug on my hair. How responsive Briar is, well, that's gonna be the fucking end of me.

If I wasn't already far too hung up on this girl that isn't supposed to be mine, then her pleading words, her shaking thighs wrapped around my head, would have just sealed my fate.

There's absolutely no way I'm gonna be able to stop. She told me she wants me to have her anywhere and anytime I like. Perhaps I'll do my worst just to keep her.

Adding two fingers, I use them to pump in and out, curling up inside her channel until she's whining and gasping.

"Oh god, oh god, oh god," Briar chants, her hips moving in

time with the hard swirl of my tongue as she tenses up beneath me. "I'm—oh fuck—I'm—"

As she clamps down rhythmically, I pull my fingers back a little, and there's a flood of wetness that gushes over me as she falls apart. Briar can't stop shaking and clinging to my head. That addictive, sweet scent, her cum, her slickness, it all drowns me, and I can't help the dark groan that leaves my chest.

Holy fuck, this girl.

"What . . . sorry . . . oh my god . . . That's never . . . I've never . . . I'm so sorry." She's trying to get away from me and pulls my hair in an effort to escape my mouth coated in her release.

My palms clamp her hips in place, and I nip her wet inner thigh. Not a hard bite but enough to get her attention and stop the spiral she's disappearing on.

"You're a squirter, darlin'." I run my tongue over the sting. "That's so fucking hot—you have no idea. I can't wait to see how many times in a row I can make you scream my name and soak my face."

"I want this couch to swallow me up. I'm so sorry."

That draws a growl from somewhere deep in my gut. My cock is painfully hard, leaking in my pants, and I'm trying not to think of ways I can track down the pathetic limp dicks who made this girl feel like she doesn't deserve to enjoy unrestrained pleasure.

I loosen the top few buttons on my shirt, then drag it over my head, and swoop over her. Briar's dark eyes go wide as I shove one knee between her legs on the edge of the couch, plant one hand beside her head, and, with my other hand, wrap my fingers around the front of her throat.

I don't stop. I don't pause. I take her mouth and kiss the fuck out of her, thrusting my tongue past her lips, eating up every single tiny noise she makes for me as I do so.

My fingers squeeze a little tighter as I force her to fully taste herself on my lips and tongue, feeling the frantic beat of her pulse beneath my fingertips.

When I pull back, she's panting. Starry-eyed, with kiss-bitten lips, looking exactly how my girl needs to look all day long.

She runs her tongue over her bottom lip, and I know without a doubt she's tasting herself there. I see it in the way her pupils blow out, the way she's already flushed from her climax but is eager for more.

"See how good you taste. See how goddamn feral you make me. Now, tell me . . ." I put a little more pressure around her throat, admiring the way my name tattooed on my fingers sits so perfectly against her neck. "Does that make you want to fuck, darlin'?"

CHAPTER 22

Briar

*D*oes that make you want to fuck, darlin'?
I'm so horny for this man. I'm almost certain my blood has turned to flames.

Damn him for taking all of a few minutes to not only show me exactly how he can make my body do things I didn't even know it could do but then for being able to calm my panic and turn me on all in one knee-buckling kiss.

There is absolutely no way my legs work. Not after that orgasm. Not after the way he just claimed my mouth and made me taste myself. Especially not after how easily he just proved to me that I've gladly lost my sanity and have chosen to dive head-long into the deepest of waters.

"Please. Yes. I want to . . . I want you so badly." My fingers come up to rest over his wrist, the one still wrapped around my throat like a collar.

"Tell me what I need to know."

For a second, I'm so completely struck by him, his hard planes of muscle, his tattoos, his unruly hair I never want to stop sinking my fingers into, that I can't imagine what else he could possibly want to know.

Then, his meaning hits me.

Oh, right.

Sex.

The talk.

"I'm all clear, and I'm on birth control." I gulp. Please don't ask me when the last time was that I had sex with anything non-battery-operated. I've already died in an inferno of embarrassment in front of this man enough for one lifetime.

Yet, for some reason, he's not disgusted by the mess I just made.

I just gushed all over him like a fountain, which had never happened to me before. I've heard of squirting, but I didn't think my body would ever . . .

He flexes his fingers, watching my mouth with open hunger, and I straight-up whimper again. Each time he moves his fingers, every sinful little point of added pressure makes my clit throb in response.

"I'm clear, too." Storm's voice is rough. So beyond sexy that I'm afraid my pussy is never going to recover after my time here ends. But I quickly thrust that niggle in my brain to one side. We're not thinking about that right now.

We're also trying really, really hard to believe this man—this living, breathing sexual fantasy—when he says he's all clear. I want to believe and trust him so badly, I really do, but my mind drifts back to the bar . . .

His impossibly blue gaze tracks mine, flickering across my eyes. I see the moment he recognizes the hesitation in me. This man sees straight into my bruised and cheated-on heart and the instinctive distrust that lurks there like a parasite.

Before I know what's happening, his strong arms hoist me up and he crosses the distance to the edge of the kitchen counter. My bare ass is deposited straight on the cool surface, and his expanse of muscled, bare chest, an ocean of tattoos, fills my vision when Storm braces his palms on either side of my hips. Leaning down, he makes sure we're level. Eye to eye. "What's going on inside that head?"

I open my mouth to try to insist that it's nothing, that I'm too young, too insecure for a sex god like him, that he should by all rights just ignore me because I'm clearly an idiot . . . but his brows draw together, and a click of his tongue is all he needs to do to force me to come out with it.

My brain is still swimming in a sea of oxytocin and dopamine in the aftermath of how masterfully he just played my body, and I ineloquently blurt out words without thinking.

"What about the other women you're with? You know, the ones losing their things inside your truck."

Storm's face softens, and god, if that doesn't make my stupid little heart leap straight out of my chest. He lifts the hand tattooed with his name, the same one that has teased my pussy, collared my throat, and now allows those inked fingers to absently play with a loose curl framing my face.

The enormity of the contrasts present in this man are so striking, so arresting. I feel like I can hardly get enough air in my lungs when he treats me to such a delicate little gesture.

"I know you don't trust easily, but here it is all the same, Briar. Over winter, the weather here can turn to shit real fast." He rubs the strands of my hair between his fingertips. "A couple of months back, a snow front rolled in unexpectedly, and between me, Sheriff Hayes, and a few others, we offered transport home for anyone in Crimson Ridge who had gotten caught out by the conditions. I helped a group of the bar staff and patrons get home safely. That girl was nothing more than a moment in time when I helped a stranger amid a group of other strangers."

The blue in his eyes holds me so firm. There's only truth to his words, even though I've been so quick to assume he's no different from the people I've been surrounded by my whole life.

Using the backs of his fingers, he strokes my cheek, then

drops that same hand down to slip beneath the hem of my sweater. "I've got a reputation I'm well aware of, Briar. As much as I might wish it were possible, I can't change who I was in the past. Rumor is rumor, and I've learned the hard way there's no stopping that, but I haven't been with anyone for a long time."

As he speaks, so level, so sure, in a deep tone that leaves me a little breathless, those large palms roam up from my hips beneath my top, over my ribs, until they reach my aching breasts. With the deft kind of touch a gruff, surly cowboy like him shouldn't have, he begins thumbing the peaks of my nipples through my bra.

I nearly float off the kitchen counter. Forget this entire conversation—I need this man to play with my tits all day long. The throb in my clit has now spread, blooming into a pounding heartbeat between my thighs.

"Okay." Do I sound like I'm ready to start moaning for this man again? With the way he's managed to reignite my entire body, I'm about two seconds from grabbing hold of his belt.

"And just so we're understanding each other perfectly, while we're doing this, you so much as look at another man's hat, I'll stomp the fucker's chest better than any bull."

"His hat?" I trap my bottom lip between my teeth, mostly to stop the slutty noises threatening to escape with each passing motion of his thumbs stroking over my hardened nipples.

"You want a hat, you wear mine. All of this, you're giving to me, and I don't give a fuck if it's in secret or not . . . No one else comes near what belongs to me."

God, I want to climb this cowboy.

"Briar, this thing you want . . ." Storm tortures my nipples some more, because he seems really intent on having me entirely under his spell. "Even though you've given me control, it still has limits, you understand?"

"Limits?" I'm getting ready to pout when he shakes his head

with a wry smile. Already guessing the immediate protest dangling on my tongue.

"Let's call them boundaries. There will be moments, days, when you might not want it. There needs to be something in place so you can easily lay that line down, and it lets me respect that."

"Oh. Have you . . . have you done this kind of thing before?" My heart is thrumming in my neck.

"Not as any kind of agreement like this. But I'm familiar with the concept."

My head is trying to reconcile what he's saying, but as I watch, he does something entirely unexpected. His hands slip from beneath my top. With practiced movements, he removes his leather cuff and takes my wrist in his hold. Lifting my hand, he then proceeds to wrap the leather around my wrist. It feels warm and supple and sits loosely over the protruding bone, even though he's fastened it as tight as it will go. The deep brown hues are textured with a swirling pattern embossed into the surface, but it's been worn and faded with so much life lived.

Storm rubs his thumb over the cuff while holding my arm. "If you're wearing that, then it's on . . . whenever, wherever . . . But if you need to take a break or you're not feeling the mood, you can leave it off, and I promise I'll always respect that, okay?"

Well, shit. I'm very ready to be the perfect slut for this man because I think he just unlocked a new desire inside me. Having the possessive, subtle weight of that strip of leather fitted neatly around my wrist just turned me into the horniest devil alive.

"Storm," I breathe. Staring at him, utterly transfixed. "We can't tell anyone about this. I don't want to fuck your life up with more stupid rumors . . . It's too easy for people to misunderstand . . ."

He kisses my palm, taking every remaining shred of sanity with that point of contact between his wet mouth, plush lips, and scratching rasp of stubble against the fleshy part of my hand. "While I hate to say it, I agree . . . Not that I give a fuck what other people think or say—and there's no possible way I would allow anyone in this world to speak shit about you and still have their teeth left intact—but I'd rather we keep things between us. If that's what you want?"

My stomach flips, and a giddy rush pours through me at the way his voice rumbles and dips low. As he speaks against my palm, keeping me snared in his blue eyes, it's like he means every single word and fully intends to protect me from anything and anyone that might lurk beyond that door.

The subtle dip of my chin is all it takes. A silent *yes*.

I'm in desperate danger of falling for this man. My uncle. *My Storm.*

"So . . . is the cuff staying on or coming off for the rest of to-night, darlin'?" Hitting me with a look that could melt panties, if I had any on, he rubs an inquiring, tempting thumb back and forth over the leather strap.

I've been so neglected and unwanted for so long; this thing he's agreed to, it makes my head spin. To possibly feel desired for the first time? To give someone the permission and control to use me, to expose me to everything I've been missing, to feel like they can't go five minutes without touching me . . . I'm swept away by the idea that this cowboy can take whatever he wants.

"It stays on." My pulse thuds relentlessly. I'm so beyond ready to experience every single aspect of this man in every way possible.

Fuck me. Use me freely. Those words want to burst past my lips. I want to seal my mouth to his and tell him all that and more through another of those simply life-altering kisses.

I didn't know what I wanted until he charged into my life, and now here we are on the precipice of something that no one else would understand. But it feels so unbelievably right, so safe with him.

Storm blows out a heavy exhale and curses softly, reverently, under his breath. Then moves.

"Arms up." Those strong hands fist my sweater while his gruff command sends a fresh wave of arousal through my pussy. He tugs it up over my head, tossing it somewhere, before moving to my bra.

"These fucking tits have been driving me to distraction." His eyes drag across my bare skin as he takes no time to unhook the clasp, then slips the straps down my shoulders, ridding me of that, too. Goosebumps erupt along my arms. This man is so determined, so sensual, and so confident with each step I could almost get lost in the fantasy of imagining he might've already planned this in his head long before tonight.

Sliding a palm beneath my knee, he hooks my leg, and the movement tips me back slightly, forcing me to lean on my hands. This position arches my spine and shoves my tits forward, and as he peels my socks off one by one—an act that shouldn't feel like foreplay, yet he somehow uses those tattoos and muscles and makes the whole thing entirely erotic—I'm left with no doubt this was his devious intention all along.

My breasts ache, feeling heavy and full, with nipples so hard he could simply breathe on them and I might fall apart again.

I love the sheer hunger in his eyes, unrestrained and without hesitancy, as he looks me over. The tiniest, sexiest smirk plays on his lips. He's far too confident, far too self-assured in this.

Meanwhile, I'm panting and throbbing all over, ready to lay myself down right here on this countertop for him to do whatever he pleases.

"Goddamn . . . you know I might just have you walk around here being my perfect slut without a top on every chance I get, little thorn. That way, I can play with these perfect tits anytime I want."

As he speaks, he pinches one nipple, causing me to cry out and involuntarily produce a desperate noise, then he gets a real spark in his eyes. I watch on, spellbound, as he plucks his hat off the counter and places it on my head.

"My pussy." He runs his thumb along my jaw, tilting it up for him. "My hat." Blue eyes flick up appreciatively as his voice drops into a lower, even more seductive tone. "*My cuff.*"

Storm holds my eyes as he drops forward to take one of my nipples in his mouth, and I lose a little more of a grasp on reality as my entire body quakes with pleasure. The warm, wet glide of his tongue and lips sucking and licking the tight bud drives me insane. I'm a mess of desperate pleas and the kinds of noises that perhaps, come morning, I might be embarrassed or self-conscious about . . . but right now, I don't fucking care.

He lavishes attention over both of my breasts, roaming his lips across the swell of them, and flicks my hardened peaks with his tongue until I'm writhing for him.

"*Mmmfuck.* You're so responsive. I think you love that idea, don't you? Letting me do whatever I want to your tits. Would you like them covered in my cum?"

The horniest sound escapes me, unbidden.

Apparently I like that idea. A lot.

That makes him chuckle, dark and desirous, against my aching breasts. But he moves now, unbuckling his belt fast and pushing down the waistband of his briefs as he stands between my slick thighs—the evidence of just how much of a complete mess I am for this man before me.

"Please. Please, Storm." The sizable length of him makes my pussy clench and stomach swoop. My eyes fixate on his fist as he strokes himself leisurely, his hungry eyes watching me as I watch *him*. I'm struggling to remember if, beyond secretly watching porn, I've ever seen a man thick and erect and veined like this. He's bigger than anyone I've ever been with before, and I feel the urge that I want to taste him too. I want to feel the velvety weight of him on my tongue.

But more than that, I want him inside me.

Storm seems to match my urgency, fisting himself, he swipes his thumb over the head, where there's a bead of wetness, and a devilish glint catches fire behind his eyes.

Leaning closer, he raises that hand to my mouth, allowing the weight of his rigid cock to bob between us. That thumb, covered in a smear of him, is forced into my mouth, coating my taste buds in the salty, tangy hint of release leaking out of his tip. A tantalizing hint of what it would be like to suck him down, let him invade my mouth, how richly satisfying that would be. It feels hypnotic, powerfully so, to know that this is the effect someone as inexperienced as me could have on his body.

He guides the head of his cock to brush over my pussy for the first time, and I feel like my heart is in my throat. How can it feel so good already, and he's barely touched me?

"You're gonna watch everything. Watch the way your cunt stretches around me, see how eager you are to swallow everything, to draw me into you. Feel how you're making a mess, dripping, and eager to be filled, so fucking wet and perfect." As he speaks, he rubs himself through my slickness, nudging at my entrance when he dips down, encouraging my hips to chase his dick, to chase what I'm so hungry for, and he damn well knows it.

"Just the tip to start." Storm brackets one of my thighs and presses the head of him forward with the other, dragging a whimper out of me. "Need to feel you fit perfectly around me."

He lets out a dark, sexy-as-all-hell groan as the tip of him slips inside. My eyes are riveted to the spot where his dick presses and inches forward into my body perfectly. The stretch of him is like nothing I've ever experienced before, yet feels so insanely good.

I'm in complete and utterly devastating trouble. I already know it. I already feel it. Somewhere deep inside every cell, a little thing just clicked into place. I'm not sure I'll survive this man.

"Goddamn, you're so tight. This little pussy of yours has had nothing but a toy and your fingers to keep you satisfied, hasn't it? But that's not enough for someone as precious as you, darlin'. You deserve to be fucked properly. You deserve to be stretched around my cock all day long, taking my dick like you were fucking made for this."

Storm uses his free hand to hook my other leg, spreading my knees obscenely wide and shifting me into the perfect position for his needs, and starts to move. Pushing his way slowly forward, wedging inside me on a slick glide. The horny mess that he reduced me to has ensured I am absolutely drenched, my pussy unbelievably ready to welcome him into my body.

"Oh my god . . . It's so good . . . please . . . I need more." I'm panting, having to balance myself on my palms in order to keep watching, because I can't fucking stop watching. The sight is so erotic. So wicked. As much as I want to run my fingers all over him and dig my nails into those muscles, I also love that this position allows him so much control. It's sending me into a shivering mess of pleasure that he's using me like this, right here on the kitchen counter.

And yet, it somehow makes me feel powerful at the same time. He's spilling filthy words, staring at my pussy being stretched around his cock, and yet there's so much desire in his voice.

I've never had someone make me feel so wanted before.

"*Storm*. God. I need you."

Hearing me beg seems to please him, because he makes another one of those rumbling noises, and I feel it in every inch of my body, right down to my curled toes. "Watch how you try to suck me deeper. Every time I feed you a little more, your sweet little cunt is begging for everything, trying to pull me in. I can feel you squeezing, trying to milk my cock already. So greedy. But that's why we're going slow this time, because there's a whole night ahead when I plan to have you stuffed full of my cock. Watching you take me like this is fucking perfect."

That's the moment he sinks forward all the way to the hilt,

and I can't help the loud moan that bursts from me. I'm doing absolutely everything he said—my pussy *is* clamping down around him, squeezing, trying to encourage him deeper.

It's so full having him inside me like this. The stretch is beyond anything I could imagine as he pulls back right to the tip before pressing forward again.

We both make noises that echo how intense this moment is, how much this feels like the most perfect, terribly bad choice the two of us could ever make.

Then, he's pumping into me. Long, torturous glides where he withdraws almost to the tip and shoves all the way forward. Again and again. The slick, wet sounds of fucking fill the air, and I'm coiled so tight from how much he's teased my body already that my orgasm flies headlong toward me.

I desperately want this to draw out, to last longer, but I'm gone and being sucked under already.

"Fuck . . . oh god . . . I think . . . I'm gonna come again . . ." There's no stopping it. I don't know how he's managed to control my body and spin me out of my head so fast and so thoroughly, but it's right there.

"That's it. Come the fuck all over my cock, darlin'." He moves like a whirlwind. One hand collars the front of my throat in a firm hold that is absolutely my undoing, while the other snakes between us to find my clit, all while he sinks so deep I feel him invade every inch of my sanity.

I tumble head over heels. Moaning and clenching around him. Clinging to his forearms for balance—or maybe sanity. Gasping for air in between my whimpers and moans.

It's so powerful I must've blanked completely. When my brain comes back online, our mouths are fused together, and my pussy is still rippling and squeezing around him as my climax keeps on rolling through in languid waves.

Storm grunts against my mouth and scoops beneath my ass to lift me against his body.

"Fuck. You're going to give me so much more of that. You're going to be coming all night long. My perfect little slut who was made to take my cock like a dream." With those filthy words that don't feel like anything but being coated in praise, he carries me to the bedroom, his length still buried deep inside me.

And as he tumbles us both down onto the bed, his hat tipping off onto the floor, I have no doubt he's going to make good on that very promise.

CHAPTER 23

Storm

The perfect girl wrapped around my dick moans against my throat.

She's nearly out of her head with pleasure after two orgasms, and I can't wait to see how easily she trembles when I drag more from her tonight.

In my life of avoiding repeat hookups, I've never once felt this kind of compulsive need for someone. To constantly be fixated on her every thought, every breath, every flutter of her eyelashes as they graze my skin.

This girl is every delicious wrong decision I could ever make.

We hit the bed, and I splay her out beneath me. She's a god-damn dream. A divine creature I've somehow been gifted, when all I've ever thought I'd deserve is darkness.

Persephone ventured down into the depths with Hades, didn't she? She willingly stepped into his bullshit and doom. Is that what we're doing here? Me, dragging Briar into my own personal underworld. What the fuck this girl sees in me, or is willing to overlook, I can't begin to fathom.

"Storm. God. It's so good." She digs her nails into my shoulders and, fuck, I want to unravel Briar Lane so bad. I'm caught in a frenzy of needing to see more of this girl's wildness. It's gorgeous and addicting, and she's my very own prize I've some-how won.

"How sensitive are these perfect tits after you come, I wonder?" My teeth graze over one of the tight little buds, and she whines, overstimulated and limp with pleasure.

"It's—I can't. It's too much." Her voice is breathy, gasping as a shudder rolls through her body.

I keep going. Slowly but intently letting the sensation begin to creep up again. Swirling my tongue and gently running my teeth over the furled buds before tugging and watching the way her puffy lips hang open with a gasp.

"This time . . ." My mouth roams, exploring my way down the softness of her stomach, which caves as I drag a hot, wet line in the direction of her pussy. "This time, I want to see the way your tits bounce, to see your face when you shatter again. Let's see if I can have you soaking these sheets for me, hmm."

Pausing to take my time, I run a long lick through her seam, and that has Briar's spine bowing up off the bed. Her fingers bunch in the sheets, knuckles blanching. I'd rather have her hands all fucking over me, but I can teach her that. There's plenty of time to help her realize how to ask for what she needs even while giving over control.

"No more. *I can't*," she whimpers. Which sounds a lot like a goddamn invitation. An immediate challenge for me to erase that assumption about her body's limitations.

"Yes, you can darlin' . . ." With one hand, I hook her knee and bring that leg up over my shoulder. "You're gonna give me another."

Those dark eyes gaze back at me, hooded with desire. Briar's pupils are fully dilated, encompassing all the rich brown, hiding those few honeyed flecks that usually appear close to the inner-most circle.

As my dick nudges her entrance, it's too fucking good. She's so slick and slippery, yet I'm still having to wedge my way inside her channel because she's so damn tight.

"Fuck, darlin', you're gonna take all of me. You're gonna let me fill this tight little cunt anytime I want."

Her lashes flutter, eyes rolling back, panting breaths hitching into a whine as I slip further in. Continuing to claim every last inch of this girl, who I'm not supposed to want.

I'm not supposed to crave this feeling or get lost in the heady pleasure of how responsive she is to me. There's no denying that I'm without a map in this particular place, entirely fucking lost when it comes to this girl.

My cock throbs, and my balls tighten. She grips me so god-damn tight; there are stars flying behind my eyes and straight high octane flowing where my blood is supposed to be.

This time, when I sink to the hilt, I can't help the dark, primal grunt that bursts out of me.

"Oh god. You're so deep." Briar spasms around my length, and my jaw is locked, rigid. A feral instinct is screaming to let go of control and simply piledrive this sexy-as-fuck piece of ass. It's tempting to race after the intensity of how much I just want to pump into her over and over again.

But I also want this to last forever. I'm obsessed with the flush on Briar's cheeks, the deep kiss-bitten shade to her lips and nipples. I'm starving to see what happens when I show her how incredible it feels to fuck good and deep and slow.

As I slide out to the tip, I feel it. The way she clenches around me. "*Mmmfuckkkk.* Your greedy little cunt doesn't want to let go, even for one second." With a groan that ripples through both of us, I punch my hips forward, enough force behind my thrust to make her tits bounce, and a loud moan bursts out of my gorgeous girl.

"Look at how badly you try to keep me buried deep inside." I slide back out, leaving only the tip for her velvety glove to contract around and, fuck my entire life, it's heaven being inside her.

"How about I make you squirt for me again?" My eyes remain fixed on her face, soaking up every shiver of unrestrained desire and the way her features tighten and contort with pleasure.

"I—I don't know if—" Briar's back bows as her words stumble. "Not another time." What she's actually saying sounds much more like, *Yes, please make me fucking gush all over your massive cock.*

"Yes, you're going to." My voice dips low as I struggle to hang on. "You're gonna make a mess of me, darlin'." *Thrust.* "Then I'm gonna flip you over." *Thrust.* "So you can watch yourself and see how well you take me." *Thrust.* "You're gonna watch yourself in that mirror."

"Oh my god." Briar moans out, louder and more desperate. It's a goddamn beautiful sight the way she unravels for me.

"That's it, just like that. I know you can be a good girl for me."

"It's too—too much." Her lashes flutter. She's right on that edge, ready to fall into how good this feels.

"*Mmm*, but your cunt says otherwise. Keep squeezing me, baby. You're the tightest fucking thing."

Her head tips back, exposing her throat. As I keep pounding into her with a force that makes her perfect breasts bounce and quiver for me, she moans in a higher pitch, whimpers, convulses, and starts to break apart.

I add my thumb into the picture, finding her clit, roaming down to drag the slickness between us from where she's impaled by my cock, and rub over that swollen bundle of nerves.

Briar's soft little body tenses up, and then she shatters like a fucking dream. She lets out a long, low cry, followed by a gush of wetness when I withdraw a little.

Fuck yes.

"You're fucking perfect. Look at you soaking me, like you were made for this."

218

Briar's lost the ability to form words. She pants and whimpers and makes the sexiest goddamn sounds that I'm going to hear every time I close my eyes.

She ripples around me, her climax dragging on and on with a long, rolling tail. It's different than last time—this one is trying to suck the life out of me.

It's so slick between us, her sexy as-hell flood coats the length of my dick and drips down my balls, and I love the fact she's made an absolute mess of me again tonight. It's like I've unlocked some kind of cheat code, and now I'm going to be trying to find all the ways and positions to make her gush all over me like this.

I'm so fucking close; the pressure is already locked in at the base of my spine. My balls are tight, lifted up, ready to spend inside her.

But I want her to watch.

I want her to see exactly how fucking much she's worthy of being treated properly.

"Can you make it nice and loud, darlin' . . . Show me just how good you can be." It takes every ounce of my self-control to pull out, scooping her limp form and guiding our bodies to line up and face the mirror at the end of the bed. "Does that turn you on when I flip you around, hmm?" My lips find Briar's ear from my position behind her, our eyes seeking out each other's in the reflection. This angle shows off our figures bathed in a shard of warm light spilling from the hallway, contrasted against the deep shadows of the room.

"You're doing perfect." I shove a pillow beneath Briar's hips and brace myself on my palms, allowing my body to blanket her spine. Those eyes track my own, glazed with so much pleasure in such a short time, but fixated on each place I touch and guide and caress her soft skin. "My own perfect little toy to play with."

Lining myself up at her entrance is goddamn bliss. We fit

together in a way that can't be a fucking coincidence, because this girl nestles beneath me like she's always meant to be there, and I've just been a fool to never know *who* I was supposed to have wrapped in my arms this entire fucking time.

Briar's mouth hangs open, her eyes glittering with the way the light glides across her features.

"Yours," she breathes out.

That one word—Jesus—I think that's my entire undoing.

"My toy." I press forward, sinking into her velvet heat. "My property." My cock surges, throbs. "My own little slut."

The pretty thing wrapped around my dick moans softly, clenching, letting me know exactly how much she craves all that and more.

"You like that, darlin'?" I watch her in the mirror. Breasts pressed against the bed, arms stretched out in front of her heart-shaped face to fist the sheets with my cuff secured over her wrist. A possessive noise brews inside my chest as I see her head tilted back to watch us, spine arched, and ass perched in the air. "You like being my plaything in secret? My perfect, pretty little whore to take care of?"

My hips drive against hers over and over, and I see the wash of pleasure as each thrust hits that magic spot I doubt any asshole has ever taken the time to find to give this girl the kind of proper fucking she deserves.

"*Storm* . . ." Her eyes roll back. Watching her lose it at the dirty shit spilling out of my mouth, I'm done for.

My cock is ready to explode. Tingling builds, pressure zips up my spine, and my thrusts falter against her ass.

"*Mmmfuck.* See how fucking good you look, full of my cock, filled with my cum."

"Yes. *Yes,*" she chants, a soft series of whimpers.

I drive forward, and my dick jerks, and my release floods her cunt. The way her pussy ripples around me makes my mind go completely blank. Wave after wave of pleasure roll through me, and I grunt in relief while pulsing into her tight, slick channel from behind.

When I come to, my mouth is fastened onto her neck. Sucking and licking and kissing that delicate skin is my newest obsession, like I've forgotten how to goddamn breathe without having the taste of this girl on my tongue.

A warning ticks in the back of my mind. Something tells me that it might already be too late.

Both feet are in deep, and maybe, almost definitely, I already have.

CHAPTER 24

Briar

"Well, this is new . . ." Storm's voice is thick and drowsy right beside my ear as he stirs from yet another heavy sleep. I have no idea what time it is; the room is layered with shadows, but I've been content to lie still. Truth be told, I'm blissed out, simply enjoying listening to his soothing, steady breathing at my back. Soaking up the rhythm accompanying each rise and fall of his torso fitted against my spine.

A smile slides onto my lips, hearing his words, because he's about to discover the opposite is, in fact, true.

"So, about that." As I muse out loud, my fingers wander down, tracking the corded muscles of his forearm. Tracing the veins and shape of him that I'd been so afraid to allow myself to admit I wanted to touch until now.

His fingers tighten over the place where he cups my bare pussy.

"Got something you want to tell me?" He nudges the shell of my ear with his nose. Hitting me with a voice so desirous and sinfully appealing that I've got absolutely no chance of withstanding any command he might give.

Not that I have any intention to.

The cuff is still *on*.

"This is, uh . . . it's actually how you always hold me in the morning." I swallow thickly. "You know, the times we've shared a bed . . . before."

Before you turned my entire life inside out and upside down with one invitation, one kiss, one moment of temptation I couldn't find my sanity or a single reason to refuse.

"Why didn't you say something?" A note of curiosity colors his voice. His words glide over me as he continues to pin me beneath a firm hold. My spine sits flush against his chest. The weight of his arm snakes down my stomach, settled between my thighs.

Why didn't I?

His question sends me into an immediate fluster. My cheeks burst into flames, embarrassment flying to every corner of my body. How am I supposed to put any of this into words? That I craved him touching me, long before we reached the point of no return last night.

How pathetic I am that I was stealing his caresses when he didn't even intend to give them to me.

"Briar," he rumbles, kissing my neck, sending liquid heat pooling beneath his fingertips. The way this man can read me so effortlessly, he can tell when I'm caught in a spiral.

"I—I don't know. I didn't want to make things awkward for you, so I would get up before you noticed."

I'm expecting him to tease or to have something typically smart to say. Instead, he makes a low noise, one that I feel extending from my spine to my chest.

He seems thoughtful for a moment.

"You should have stayed."

Those words, they're unreasonably sexy when uttered in that early-morning voice of his, and it's like listening to honey dripping over my skin.

Except, then, his wickedness follows, hot and tempting. "Or did you like it a little too much when your *uncle* was wrapped around you every morning? Is that why you developed a taste for early-morning shower time?"

I whimper as he begins to fondle me, confirming that, once again, I am absolutely drenched between my thighs for this man.

Storm lets out a satisfied grunt—a self-assured triumphant sound. Followed by him gently hitching my leg up exactly how he wants, followed by the act of pressing forward to wedge the head of his thick cock inside me.

As he works his way in, with shallow pulses of his hips, he continues to strum his fingers over my clit, and I absolutely melt for him.

"Darlin', it's no mystery why you suddenly needed alone time. I've known exactly why you've been in that shower every morning." Holy shit, he fills me with a delicious, insistent press forward.

"Oh my god."

"Though, it's a shame you didn't tell me all that aching and tension were for me. I can think of a lot of ways that I would have helped you out. All the times I could have joined you in there." He settles himself all the way, filling me until I can't think straight, then stays still. Storm doesn't thrust, or move, just allows my pussy to stretch and form to wrap around him, and holy fuck, it ignites something wild inside me.

"What was I supposed to do?" I gasp. This is so filthy. He wants to wedge himself inside me and then stay there? The way he's cradling my body against his, lazily fondling over my clit, dragging my slickness up to pinch and caress my nipples, it's almost as if . . . as if he would be happy to stay like this, buried inside me for hours.

The notion of that—of being impaled on his cock and nothing more than a pussy wrapped around him because he wants to be inside me—nearly has me whining and moaning.

"Well, for a start, if you wake up horny and dripping, then use me." His big palm cups and squeezes my breast. "Or if you want to play with that pretty cunt, I don't mind being an audience for you. I'll watch you come all over your fingers anytime."

"God. Storm." He's wicked, and yet I can't get enough.

"Look how perfect you are. Every curve, every fucking inch of you." His dick is all the way deep, so fucking deep, as he lies there, still not attempting to thrust or move at all. It drives me out of my head with how unbelievable this feels.

"Go back to sleep if you want, darlin'." Storm's lips follow the slope of my neck, sending a flurry of goosebumps and shivers across my arms. "Let me teach you this. What I want right now is to enjoy playing with you, while you lie nice and still for me, squeezing me so goddamn tight."

He makes a groaning noise as I do exactly that.

"*Mmmffffuck.* I don't need you to stay awake for what I want, but if it means I get to have you gripping me that hard, then go right ahead and lie there while I have my fun using your sweet little hole."

This man.

This fucking man.

I know for certain, right then and there—as he strokes his rough touch over every part of my belly, my breasts, my thighs, dipping down into my pussy with each pass over my form, even while still filling me—that I'm in serious trouble.

How am I going to survive being treated like this?

How am I ever going to find someone else that can compare?

I'm the definition of ill-equipped to handle Stôrmand Lane.

Having to spend all day around him today while he finishes up the last of the horses on Devil's Peak Ranch is going to kill me—of that, I'm certain.

The man is so smooth—it would be unbearable if it didn't turn me into a panting, wanton mess at every turn.

Every single glance, with a secretive twitch playing on the corner of his mouth—a mouth that I know exactly how and what is capable of when he uses it as a damn weapon on my body—combined with the effortless way he's strolling around these stables using his deep, sexy voice to talk to the horses is enough to do me in.

Wearing his goddamn chaps that make me want to drop to my knees and stick out my tongue.

Has he turned me into a sex addict after just one night?

Because I sure as hell cannot stop thinking about his dick.

All I seem to be capable of is running replays in my mind's eye. Flashes and glimpses and erotic snippets of us together. Seeing myself, a version of me that I didn't even recognize, reflected in that mirror after Storm fucked every last brain cell out of my head.

What I saw as he prowled over me like a conqueror, all tattoos and muscles, was myself splayed out beneath him. Limp and flushed and fucked out of my damn mind.

In a state of pure, unadulterated bliss.

As I shift my weight, holding the horse's head while Storm works on their shoe fitting, I feel the band of leather on my wrist dig in slightly beneath the sleeve of my jacket.

I'm hyperaware of the cuff's smooth feel against my skin. How it warms to match my body temperature. How it belongs to him or, more accurately, denotes that I belong to him.

At least for the duration of time we play this game.

For however long I choose to stay here, I guess.

My eyes roam all over his shoulders, recalling exactly how that same broad expanse filled the reflection in the mirror last night when he commanded me to watch.

How he loomed behind me. Tattooed and muscled and so imposing, braced over my spine.

The look on his face . . . it's imprinted in my damn DNA, I'm sure of it.

He looked ravenous. *For me.*

I'm giddy for more of his gritty orders, for his calloused palms roaming across my skin. I want him to tell me what to do, exactly when to watch, to see how incredible we look, to see how much I enjoy being full of his cock and leaking his cum.

His possessive behavior unlocked something in me, something compelling. I didn't expect to find it comforting, but being told I'm nothing more than his toy and slut to use . . . holy shit.

I've never been more turned on or felt more secure in my life.

"You're one talented man, Storm." The familiar voice of Layla interrupts my silent reverie of drooling.

Bent double, he grunts something inaudible, driving a nail with precision into the horseshoe. With the kind of ten-thousand-hour practiced perfection that only someone as skilled as he could achieve. I, a mere mortal, would certainly have either broken my thumb with that hammer or ended up with the nail straight through my hand rather than the horse's hoof.

"They look fantastic." Layla comes up beside me and runs a hand over the horse's long, glossy neck. "Ready to put in a big shift this summer, aren't you, gorgeous boy?" Big dewy eyes blink at her, and I'm no better than the horse, staring at Layla like she's the green-eyed elfin queen of this barn and I'm her humble servant.

From all accounts, Devil's Peak Ranch has never been busier since Layla's social media posts took off last year. She started out by posting cute videos and photos as a fun way to share her days when she first took a job here during her veterinary training, then everything snowballed.

Now, the upcoming summer season is almost fully booked, with a waitlist stretching from here to Crimson Ridge, and these horses are the star attraction.

"Yeah, well, Colt's a fussy bastard. I'm sure he'll take one look and tell me he could do better himself." Storm clips the excess nail endings with a pair of metal snips so they don't stick out from the hoof, then wipes his forehead with the back of his arm.

I nearly buckle at the knees when he hits me with those piercing blue eyes in the act of straightening up. It's only a quick glance, but it does something fluttery to my insides, all the same, to discover his eyes seeking out mine immediately.

"Like he's got time for that." Layla chuckles.

"For giving me hell? You know the prick will always find time." Storm picks up the file and makes quick work of smoothing down any rough edges above the horseshoe. Long, smooth strokes that keep me entranced with the tattoos on his hands and popping veins.

"How about I put in a good word for you? He might even pick up your tab for dinner this weekend if I ask nicely?" Layla teases back. It's all so effortless being around these people. There's no agenda or hidden purpose. I love the way everyone is just *good-hearted* to each other. Not trying to play a game, score points, or squirrel away some detail of a weakness to be used against the person at a later point in time.

"Fuck that," Colt says, arriving in the barn, looking rugged and like he's been carved from the very landscape out here. "You owe me about a year's worth of hot dinners, Stôrmand Lane. After clearing out my entire deep freezer of meat while I was gone." As he approaches, his eyes are focused only on Layla, with an unspoken language flowing between them.

God, they're so perfectly in tune with each other. It makes my heart pitter-patter to see that kind of soul-deep bond between two people.

A flesh-and-blood reminder that a kind of love like *this* does exist.

For the lucky ones, at least.

Colt leads his horse behind him, pausing on his way past us to stop and brush some fine hairs off Layla's forehead with a little smirk playing at the corner of his mouth, before he leans down and kisses her neck. It's the most romantic fucking thing I've ever seen in the flesh, and if I wasn't holding the halter in front of me, there is every chance my entire soul might have melted onto the floor.

"For putting up with Prince Charming, feeding your goddamn cows, and being balls deep in ice all winter so you could go skinny-dipping in the Mediterranean? I'd say we're even, old man." Storm keeps working but shakes his head as he files off the remaining nail-ends.

The two of them keep bickering in their gruff way, and Layla takes over handling things like the horse's saddle and tack while chiming in to the conversation as she works.

Meanwhile, I stand here wondering if anyone could look at me and immediately know. Would they have any inkling of the fact I'm wearing *his* cuff beneath the sleeve of this jacket. *His jacket.*

Would anyone ever suspect a thing? Our little secret and all the forbidden intricacies our arrangement entails.

The more I chew the inside of my cheek and shift my weight, the more this naughty little hidden detail turns me the fuck on.

Storm finishes up with his final horse for the day, with me doing all I can to be his perfect assistant. Now that I'm somewhat more familiar with the routine of how he goes about things, I feel like I can actually be useful in packing up and getting ready to leave.

We've just finished loading the truck when Layla follows us outside. "So, we're all meeting at six o'clock on Saturday . . . I'm leaving this oaf in your capable hands, city girl, to make sure he at least makes an attempt at cleaning himself up."

Shutting the tailgate with a forceful shunt, Storm gives a wry smile in Layla's direction. His blue eyes swing my way, and there's no mistaking the trouble flickering there. It's boyish and devious and far too goddamn attractive for my health. "Don't worry Layla, I'll be the perfect uncle and listen to everything my niece tells me to do."

I nearly choke, one hand shooting out in an attempt to steady myself on the passenger's door.

"Perfect. Drive safely, guys. Can't wait for you to meet Sage." Layla waves as she heads toward the main house, the setting sun casting an orange glow in the reflection that bounces off the big planes of glass windows along the south-facing vista of the property.

As I yank my door open, I level my sternest glare across the distance between us. "You can't keep saying shit like that. You're a bad, bad man."

I'm greeted with a cocky smirk as he slides into the driver's side.

"Yup, and you're getting hornier every time I say it, so we're all winning here, little thorn."

CHAPTER 25

Storm

"I did some searching online. I looked up that thing you were talking about." Briar leans forward to turn the stereo down.

"What thing was that?" I say. Hooking one wrist on the wheel, I steer us down the mountain road.

At first glance, I wonder what this could be about. Then I notice that Briar is squirming. Oh, it's definitely a sex thing.

The cocky asshole inside my chest crows with smug satisfaction.

"When you asked me what I didn't want to have happen or what my dislikes were."

"Ahh. Your limits."

"Yup. Those." She shuffles around and shoots me a quick sideways peek through long eyelashes.

"And?" I fail at any attempt to wrestle the grin off my face. My grip flexes around the steering wheel as we head back down the mountain after our day at the ranch.

A day when Briar spent the entire time undressing me with her big doe eyes.

"No painful stuff." She ticks off a finger. "There were lots of things on the list I found online that were about causing pain or experiencing pain, and I definitely don't want that." She shudders with a grimace.

Fuck, she's cute.

I hum in acknowledgment. "Fair. Not everyone enjoys that."

"Do you?" Her eyes bounce over me. Curious energy bounds around the cab of my truck.

"Ahh, points for trying, but we're talking about *you*, remember." Goddamn, if I don't love that she's intrigued, though.

She nibbles the inside of her lip, and I see a little flush start to dust her cheekbones when I shoot a look her way.

"No peeing or anything like that." Her nose wrinkles as she ticks off another finger.

That makes me chuckle.

"No blindfolding or stuff along those lines either."

Shifting my hold on the wheel, I reach over until my hand finds her thigh, and she jumps a little.

"That's good," I say, trying to sound sane and level-headed, not like I want to explode with desire knowing that this girl has been searching for things she might or might not like me to do to her.

Fuck knows when she's had a chance to do any looking online, but my dick is very enthusiastic about this conversation.

"I'm proud of you for figuring some of that out for yourself. As a start, that's perfect." I continue.

Briar ducks her chin and wriggles a little more, hearing me say those words. Knowing the asshole my adopted brother was, I'm sure this girl has never had anyone tell her they're proud of her before. Bunch of dickwads, the entire lot of them.

"You like to watch, so no taking that away. Got it." I run my tongue over my teeth. As much as this is about letting her have more of what brings pleasure—letting the little voyeur hiding inside Briar out to play—I'm no therapist, but it doesn't take a genius to suspect there are some deeper trust issues if she's not interested in being blindfolded.

"What about being restrained?" I press for a little more since we're already on this path, allowing my fingers to sink into the softness of her thighs.

Her cheeks develop deeper spots of rouge.

"You're sitting there squirming, darlin'."

Briar makes a tiny noise, one that might be part protest, part agreement, and I'm not sure if she even knows which of the two she really means right now. Although, after the eyes she's insisted on giving me all day, I'm long beyond caring what her brain might be saying about all this.

"Want me to pull over and take care of that ache?" As my eyes stay focused on the road, I allow my fingers to wander up the inside of her leg, exploring a little higher.

Her weight shifts, the luscious swell of her thighs rubbing together, traps my hand in place, and I know the moment she gives up any last lingering doubts, if there were any still rolling around her mind. That mouth of hers hangs open, ever so slightly.

"You want to learn something, darlin'?" My voice dips low.

Briar nods, eyes bouncing all over me from her end of the bench seat.

"Well, how about you show me your wrist."

"Here," she breathes, a little shakily, sliding back the sleeve of my goddamn jacket to reveal that band of leather sitting neatly in place. Just where it should always be.

"Good girl." Yeah, she damn well loves those couple of words, judging by that heavy swallow and the way her chest rises and falls faster.

"Out here?" Her teeth sink into the curve of her lower lip.

"Right out here, darlin'. That cuff is on, and goddamn, I need you wrapped around my dick."

Her eyes dart around, as if there's even the slightest chance another soul might see us. Meanwhile, something thrums a heavy beat quietly through the speakers, forming a background soundtrack to this moment, but I couldn't even tell you what song is playing because all I can hear is my own blood rushing and hurtling around my body.

"You want to be full of my cock?" Inside my jeans, I'm lengthening and thickening at the thought of how this is gonna go.

"Please." She shifts and turns toward me.

"Then give me those pretty lips. You're gonna put that perfect little mouth to use. I wanna feel you suck me down while I enjoy using your throat." I shift my hand from her thigh to hook the front of her jacket and tug, leading her, or more accurately demanding her, to shift closer in my direction.

Briar sucks in a sharp breath, hearing my rough-coated words and feeling the weight of my command. "How . . ."

"Slide on over here and take me out."

My perfect girl pauses, sheds the jacket first, then does exactly as I ask, a little hesitantly, but there's no mistaking the spark of curiosity and lust in her dark eyes.

"That's it," I say, encouraging her as she nestles at my side and reaches for my waistband. Adjusting my hips, I allow her nimble fingers to make quick work of my belt buckle, button, and fly—and Jesus, I'm already insanely hard and leaking. All the ways I want to have this girl in my truck are downright depraved, but hell, she looks like a goddamn dream perched beside me on this worn, old bench seat.

"Don't crash." Briar sneaks me a flirty little glance as her tiny fist reaches out to push the waistband of my briefs down, allowing my cock to spring free.

With one hand, I slide my fingers into her silky hair, tightening my grip as I keep my eyes on the road. Hearing her gasp and let out a small moan, well, I'm already damn near feral as it is, and that just unleashed something even more wild.

"Ask nicely, baby, and I might even let you have a taste of us both afterward," I growl.

She hums and lets me guide her head down, bracing herself over my lap—and fucking hell. One fist wraps around my length, and her fingers dig into my thigh, and I have to fight to stay focused on not losing control of this truck as her perfect fucking mouth closes around my leaking tip.

"Christ, darlin' . . ." My fingers thread a firmer hold in her hair, but I let her take it at her own pace. This is the first time she's giving road head, and who knows, it might even be the first time she's properly sucking dick.

"Keep that throat nice and relaxed for me. Imagine it's your wet little cunt I'm pushing into. Think about how much you love feeling me stretch you and slide deeper each time you drop down."

The whimpering noises she's making with her lips wrapped around my length send shudders right through me. My balls are already tingling, tightening with each heated, plush slide of her mouth, coating me in saliva.

"So fucking perfect, sucking me like you were made for this. Is that all you were made for? To take my cock anytime I want? Maybe I'll just play with you like this, keep you in my lap like my dirty little secret while you choke on me."

Briar's grip on my leg tightens, and she makes a desperate noise, humming and slurping, getting messier the more I talk her through it.

"*Fffuckkk*. Give me that pretty little tongue. Let me feel you swallow all of me." As she continues to bob up and down, adjusting and sinking deeper, lapping and hollowing her cheeks around me, I feel her spit trickle down my length. Her tongue running along my shaft is like a trip into the heavens. She starts moaning softly as my cock swells to fill more and more of her hot little mouth.

A series of sweet little noises that tell me just how turned on my girl is right now. God, I bet she's absolutely dripping.

With my balls already drawing tight in anticipation of unloading and coating her tongue with my cum, it's tempting to see this through to the point where I fill her throat and spill right here right now. But I'm feral for the feeling of having her squeezing and coming all over my dick again.

I steer us off the roadside into a shingled pullover area, beyond giving a fuck about the tiny chance of someone driving past this remote part of the mountain. It's unlikely as shit that anyone would be venturing around here at this time of evening, and there's no way I'm waiting until we get back to the cabin for this.

Briar pops off with a wet, sloppy noise as the truck stops with a jolt, a glazed expression lingering in her lust-blown eyes as she looks around, a little confused. I pinch her chin, dragging her to my mouth, and devour every horny noise drifting past those swollen lips, every hint of the taste of *me* lingering on her tongue.

"Such a nasty little thing, aren't you?" Nipping her bottom lip between my teeth, I tug and draw another delicious sound that rockets straight to my dick. "Secretly turned on by being used. Loving having my cock in the back of your throat, hmm?"

"Why did we stop?" Briar gasps and pants wildly into my mouth. I love how damn responsive she is, how eager she is to enter the arena with all my depravity and match it round for round.

"Because your sweet cunt is calling my name, little thorn . . . and waiting isn't my style."

I quickly tuck myself back in my briefs, leaving my jeans unbuttoned, belt hanging loose, and then pop my door open. Those dark eyes widen, watching me exit the truck.

Her head whips around, craning to look one way and then the other at the empty gravel road winding around the corner above and below us before turning back to meet my expectant gaze. The tall pines make everything seem a lot darker, like the night has closed in with stealth and cunning wrapping around the tall timbers of dense forest coating this part of the mountain.

"We can't . . ." she gasps.

"That cuff staying on or coming off?" Reaching inside the truck, I hook a palm behind each knee and drag her ass along the seat to my open door.

For a long second, while blood rushes mad and wild in my ears, her eyes flicker down to the leather wrapped around her wrist. Fuck it, I don't want to push anything, but I'm also possibly gonna lose my damn mind if she unfastens that strap.

She swallows heavily, then leans forward to hook her arms around the back of my neck.

"Fuck, you're my kinda insanity, darlin'." I scoop her against my body, lift her out of the truck, and sink our mouths together as she melts into me.

This time, her fingers tangle in my hair, and she thrusts her tongue in time with mine, letting all the unrestrained sounds of pleasure burst into my mouth and dance on my taste buds.

Walking us to the hood of my truck, I seat her on the warm metal above the motor. I know exactly how I want to devour this girl and show her all the ways she deserves to be wanted. With the kind of immediacy and urgency that doesn't settle for waiting, or wondering, or the kind of timeline that involves boring, sensible things like *driving home.*

This beautiful thing needs to be shown that when it comes to wanting her, I'm always going to be starving for a taste, no matter where we are.

Reluctantly, I draw back from her mouth, pressing a palm over her chest to guide her to sink back onto the hood. As I do so, I greedily drink down how flushed and kiss-bitten her lips are. The darkened shade they've turned and exactly how lust-blown her pupils have become.

"Storm . . . stop . . . We can't . . . not out here . . . What if someone sees us?"

Her words might be half-hearted arguments, but her hips are lifting for me and allowing me to hurriedly unfasten the button and lower the zipper.

"I don't fucking care." My mouth is already kissing and nipping at her bared flesh. Her hips, the softness of the tops of her thighs, the curve of her stomach revealed below the shirt that's keeping her top half warm.

"Look at the state of you. Horny and desperate. Gushing for me and ready to soak my cock when I push these pretty thighs apart and shove inside. You're already gonna be dripping, aren't you?" As I let the filthy shit flooding my brain make itself known, I'm a man possessed, pulling and tugging at her jeans to get them down her thighs far enough so I can expose her cunt. But it's not enough. Nowhere near enough. I need so much more than just a band of denim stretched taut and digging into her soft flesh, restricting me from getting to the sweetest center of her.

As her pussy is revealed, as the offending material is tugged down over her hips and ass, my mouth is on her before I can even think. She's glistening and swollen, and my tongue swipes along her slit, lapping up every drop of how goddamn aroused she is.

Briar lets out a string of curses and wild noises as I push my tongue against her clit, massaging over the pouty bud where it sits, needy and ready. Waiting for me to tease and torture in just the way I want to. Sucking down hard and drawing the swollen mess of her into my mouth makes her back bow up and her fingers tangle with my hair.

"Fuck. Holy shit. Oh my god."

That's it, beautiful girl. Lose your fucking mind just the way I am.

I've managed to yank one boot along with one leg of her jeans off, stripping it clear of her ankle, and with a triumphant growl, I push her thighs wide. My mouth closes over her entrance, and I tongue fuck Briar's sweet, drenched pussy, shoving and spearing into her repeatedly until her thighs tremble around my head. She's whimpering and begging while spread out like a feast on the hood of my truck, and I don't know if I've got anything in my veins except a pure, driving, all-consuming need to fuck and fuck and fuck.

Holding her wide, digging my hold into her upper thigh, I push one finger inside and suck on her clit. She rips at my hair with a loud moan, and just as I know she's about to detonate, I add a second finger and apply the pressure she damn well needs.

Briar falls apart. Shatters in a flood all over my face and hand as I lap up every drop. This time, she's so out of her head. Maybe it hasn't dawned on her what just happened, or maybe my good girl has already learned that I fucking love getting to be the one and only person to ever drag this response from her body.

Whatever. She's riding my mouth from below unashamedly, and I can't get enough of roaming with my tongue, dropping kisses and long licks all over her sweet, swollen cunt.

Something about being with Briar unhinges me. More than something as torrid as the forbidden nature of us being together in the eyes of assholes who think they know shit about us. It's like she unlocked a part of me that never existed before. Somehow there was a Stôrmand Lane who used to exist before she came along, and then there's the guy left standing in the embers of the fire where all that other bullshit has been burnt away.

The part of me that used to simply get off during sex and that was all it was has disappeared—that motherfucker has been incinerated in the space of only a few short days. I never used to repeat a hookup, never wanted to see them again, and yet here I am, ready to keep drowning in this girl gladly over and over.

Savage want and need take control as my cock strains against the front of my briefs, leaking everywhere.

Hooking her knees, I drag her body down to meet mine. Perching her ass on the very edge of the hood, I shove my briefs out of the way and fist my cock, notching at her drenched entrance.

"God. I need you deep inside," Briar whines.

"I know. I know, baby." My eyes drop to watch my tip wedge into her center, forcing my way in because my girl might be messy and begging for my cock, but she's the tightest fucking thing.

"Oh, fuck." She throws her head back as I push forward. With every inch that I sink deeper, her walls ripple and adjust to my length, and holy hell, she's the hottest, velvety little fist, squeezing me relentlessly.

From this angle? Her pretty little cunt is on perfect display, and visually, seeing her stretched around me like a dream is gonna have me rapidly lose it. Except, with the way I'm currently drowning in the primal need to fuck her hard and filthy, we have to move.

She protests and gasps as I wrap her tight and maneuver us around the side of the vehicle so that she's half hanging out the door to my truck. Briar tips back onto her elbows, with her knees spread wide, and now I've got exactly the angle I need to drive forward and own her just like my goddamn cuff around her wrist says I do.

"Show me your tits while I fill you up so much you're gonna feel me running down your thighs."

My hips pump forward with the slick sound of how wet my girl is for this filling the front seat of my truck. She fumbles and drags the material of her shirt up over her bra, and the soft, squeezed valley of her breasts isn't enough. "Show me properly," I say through a clenched jaw. Jesus. My balls are already tight and ready to spend.

Briar moans as she hooks the soft cup and pulls it down on one side. She can't reach the other, and that's when her head drops between her shoulders, and her eyes hit me with a hypnotic mix of panic and lust and the overwhelming sensation that she's about to shatter for me again.

I can't help myself. She's too easy to read.

"Did you hear a car, my pretty girl?" As I hold her legs so

tightly she can't squirm away, Briar makes a whining noise and claws the seat. Not wanting to admit just how much that fucking turns her on. Not wanting to dare acknowledge that deep down inside, she's a slut for my cock being buried inside her, right out in the open, where someone could see us like this.

"Fuck yes. Grip me harder, just like that. You get more and more turned on at the idea of somebody knowing about us? You want someone to see you with your legs spread for your uncle?"

Those chestnut eyes are lust-blown, her plush mouth hanging open.

Each thrust intensifies, and I know she's about to tumble over the edge.

"Don't worry. Your secret's safe with me. I won't tell anyone how my dirty little niece likes it best when her uncle's fat cock is buried deep inside her cunt."

My girl's spine bows off the bench seat as she trembles and shatters on a low moan.

"Do you want someone to know you're my little fuck toy who gets wet just thinking about belonging to me?"

Briar lets out the sexiest noises, whimpering as her pussy spasms and contracts around me over and over. The heady sensation pulls me with her, dragging up all the feral praise I know she wants to hear.

How perfect she is. How I want to fuck her again the second we get home. How I spend all day thinking about her being my sweet plaything to have whenever and wherever I want.

It's that idea, of getting exactly that and more, that has me letting out a string of curses. Tension bursts at the base of my spine in a blinding rush, and before I know it, I'm shoving deep, spilling inside as she clutches the seat and gives me every single piece of her.

My thundering heart flies around and tries to escape my chest as I thrust lazily in and out, letting us both come down gradually, slowly. I don't know exactly what Briar is feeling right this second, but if it's anywhere approaching how I'm feeling right now, it's goddamn perfect.

This right here has surely got to be perfection.

A gorgeous girl who deserves the world and somehow thinks I'm worthy of just a fraction of her time.

Someone I'm not supposed to have.

So, I do what I do best. I shove those thoughts aside and cling to the here and now as tightly as I ever did with my rope hand while trying not to get thrown off in the arena before my brief moment in the spotlight came to an end.

I pull out with a hiss, holding her thighs wide in order to survey the sight of her, flushed and swollen and glistening with the evidence of being thoroughly owned.

She nibbles her bottom lip, staring at me. "Was I good enough to earn a taste?"

A wickedness settles at the corners of my mouth as I lower my head and hover just over the spot where my cum is starting to well at her entrance. Keeping my gaze on her the entire time.

"You sure were, darlin'. Let me clean you up first, then I'll give you a taste of exactly how well you did."

CHAPTER 26

Briar

"City girl . . . whatcha doin' down here?"

I've hardly opened the truck door after we pulled up at Rhodes Ranch, the new ranch we're working at, when Kayce's brilliant smile hits me from the stable doors. He's wearing chaps and carries a massive saddle that would probably crush me if I attempted to lift it.

For a moment, I blink at him, entirely surprised to see him here, then my brain catches up, and I remember that he comes down from the mountain to, presumably, this ranch and others for rodeo training—or so I've been informed.

"Apparently wherever there are horses in this town is where I hang out these days," I chirp back at him and jerk my head in the direction of the man extracting himself from the driver's side.

Storm doesn't run off this time. Instead, he joins us around my side of the vehicle.

I'm sure my cheeks immediately turn neon pink because there are all too many things we have done on the hood of this truck, in the very same spot where Kayce is now leaning up against the faded paintwork to talk to us.

Oh god.

The giant cowboy flanking my other side flicks his blue eyes over the hood and then back to me briefly. How the hell he's managing to keep a straight face right now, I don't know, but I'm damn squirming.

"Rhodes has got me taking a look at some of the new boarders arriving for spring." Storm is hovering so close that my skin prickles, the heat of his broad chest searing my nape, and I have to clear my throat because *surely* it must be obvious that there is so much more between us now than there was merely a few short days ago.

Now that we're being seen in public together, I can't help feeling like there's a giant sign hanging over my head with flashing lights and arrows pointing at me for the entire world to see.

Niece who worships her uncle's cock . . . right here, folks!

"Sweet . . . I wish I could stay and chat, man . . . but there are broncs calling my name who want to try to take a piece out of me." Kayce readjusts his grip on the saddle. "But I'll see you guys tonight for dinner?"

"Sure," the man at my side grunts.

"Rhodes is inside," Kayce calls over his shoulder as he takes his chaps and golden-cowboy charm off toward a group of other similarly attired people gathered at the fence.

"Come on, *city girl*." I'm nudged in the small of my back, with a devilish chuckle copying his words.

"What? He's been nothing but lovely to me since I got here."

"As long as he doesn't go getting any ideas."

I tuck some loose hair behind my ear. "Honestly, Kayce is a good friend."

Something skips around inside my chest at the thought that this impressive, gorgeous man might be a little jealous. Except, I don't dare bring that up.

There are far too many things this man needs to do today, and me teasing him about Kayce Wilder would just be silliness. I'm wearing Storm's damn cuff, after all. If that's not assurance that I absolutely, one thousand percent, only have eyes for him, I don't know what is.

"This isn't a cattle ranch then?" I ask, looking around at the seemingly endless rows of stalls and horses.

"Just horses here, ma'am." A rich voice greets us. "I'll leave the cattle to the cowboys who like running around ropin' stock all day."

The man who strides over holds his charcoal-colored hat in one hand and drags the other through his hair. He's got that look about him that says he'd prefer to be around these creatures all day, while somewhat tolerating people on the side.

As he sets his hat back in place, I catch sight of a flash of white extending through the front of his unruly dark curls. It's dashing and unusual, even though he's probably around the same age as Storm—or a little older even, now that I'm seeing his short, salt-and-pepper beard up close—but that prominent streak of white doesn't seem to be from natural graying—it looks like it has always been there.

"Briar, this is Lucas Rhodes."

"Pleased to meet you." He brushes off dirt against the side of his jeans, then extends a large hand to wrap my palm in his with a firm shake. "The newcomers are down this way." Just like that, he steps aside and indicates for us to follow him.

God, I could hug this man for not asking questions about me, who I am, or how I fit into this picture. Obviously this place is busy, and I'm guessing since he's got plenty of jobs on the go, that doesn't leave time for chitchatting.

Although, from the look of him, I suspect he's not exactly a *talker* either.

As the two figures ahead of me mutter between themselves in gruff tones about their horsey business, I go much slower. Taking my time to peek in on each of the horses and see their names written up next to their stalls filled with shavings and hay.

Some are happy to ignore me. Others swing their long necks my way with curious eyes. A couple hang right over as far as they can reach, showing me impressive rows of teeth as they contort their lips to try to get a good look at what might be hidden inside my coat pockets.

I know enough about Storm's routine when he's undertaking his farrier work now. If I tagged along with them, I would be in his way, plain and simple. He seems to be happiest having his space to work alone and get in his rhythm, then he usually calls me over if and when I'm needed.

So, for now, I enjoy being around and watching the animals. They fascinate me and calm me in a way I can't really put a finger on.

The next stall I get to, I pause in front of. An almost jet-black horse stands right at the back wall. Big liquid eyes bore into me from behind the longest set of eyelashes I've ever seen.

As I stand there, one hoof stamps on the ground. Almost as if I'm being told to move along.

Something makes me stay exactly where I am. It doesn't really make any sense why, seeing as there are so many horses here, yet I feel like I want to figure out why this boy is urging me not to look his way.

Shoving my phone in my pocket, I hold my palms up and reassure him I haven't got anything in my hands to be worried about, then I step closer to his door. He lets out a snort, stamps again, and bounces his head several times, still hanging as far back from where I stand as physically possible.

Fuck off.

His message is loud and clear.

"Hey, boy." I keep my voice low. Glancing up at the name tag beside his stall, I see that he's one of the temporary boarders. "Just here visiting, are ya, Teddy?"

His nostrils flare.

"Teddy," I say, speaking his name again with a little smile. "You don't seem like a teddy bear at all."

Another stamp. A swish of his tail.

"No way, there's too much feistiness in you . . . and you're very handsome."

This time, his ears twitch my way.

"I bet you've got a soft side under all that bravado, though."

He moves fast for such a small space, suddenly right up in my grill, and I can't help my reaction to jerk back a little. The asshole bats those oversized eyelashes at me and makes a noise that tells me he's pleased with himself.

"Oh, it's like that, is it? You're all talk, aren't you?" I cock my head to one side and step back to where I was a second ago, my arms folded.

Teddy doesn't shy away this time. Instead, we stand there watching each other for a moment. Eventually, he lowers his head, much slower this time, and nudges my elbow.

"Hmm. Full of bullshit and hot air, and now that you want something, you'll demand it, huh?"

I let my palm roam up the long, elegant line of his nose, feeling heat and short hairs beneath my touch.

His warm, humid breaths puff out, and when I get to the spot between his eyes and start scratching with my fingertips, he makes a rumbling, contented noise from deep inside that powerful chest.

As I keep scratching, I feel eyes on me.

Turning my attention, it's not my cowboy I'm met with the sight of but Lucas Rhodes. The man stands with a shoulder leaned up against one of the wooden partition walls, with arms crossed and an ankle hooked over the other. It's not exactly a smile on his face, but he's thoughtfully observing our interaction.

For a moment, I worry I've done something I shouldn't have.

Lifting my hand away, I'm just about to step back and apologize for standing here patting his horses without asking first when a big, black, whiskery muzzle bunts my hand.

Lucas starts chuckling.

"I'm sorry." A smile tugs at my lips. "It seems I've ended up being Teddy's personal scratching post after two seconds of being here."

"Stay there as long as you like." He shakes his head and pushes off the wall. When he turns to grab a shovel and pitchfork from the stall behind him, I feel Teddy flinch a little at the sharp sound of metal scraping against the ground.

But Teddy remains there, letting me continue stroking as my fingers drift higher toward his soft ears.

"How long is he staying here for?" I ask.

Lucas joins me. "Not sure. This boy's had a hard road before now."

"Oh, really?" My eyebrows scrunch, looking between the two of them.

"He was rescued a few years back. Bastards used to thrash him, and now his current folks are trying to find the best-fit home for him."

"God, people are awful." I want to cry. This beautiful horse didn't do anything, certainly not anything to deserve being abused.

"You're not wrong there."

"He's so lovely. Why would anyone do something so horrible?"

Lucas lets out a little puff of a breath, something like a laugh.

"Our boy here didn't deserve any of it . . . which is why he's such an asshole now. I'll forgive him for being such a sour bastard, but those bruises take a while to heal."

"Bruises?"

He clicks his tongue and squints at the horse I'm practically cuddling. "Your best friend over here has bitten every one of us repeatedly, and he even got a good kick on my son, Brad, when he was unloading him the day he arrived."

My mouth hangs open, eyes bouncing between Lucas and the face still nudging against my touch. "You're joking."

"Nothing funny about a horse bite. Trust me." He considers me for a second, then dips his chin toward a bucket sitting on the floor at my feet. "Hell, since you two are getting on so well, might as well give him a groom up and down the sides of his neck and if you can reach his shoulders. Stay on this side of the door, mind you, but if he'll let you keep handling him, might as well give his mane and coat a brush while you're there."

I nod. "I'd like to try. Seems like it'd be just as therapeutic for me as it might be for him."

"Horses provide some of the best therapy out there."

Lucas goes to walk away, then turns back.

"Though, don't ever own one, or you'll be horse-poor for the rest of your life." He whirls a finger in the air, gesturing at the stables we're standing in—what I'm sure consumes his life, considering all the work that goes into running a ranch like this.

While I've only really seen Devil's Peak Ranch up close, I already know how much work is involved in a ranch's day-to-day operations. This place has even more horses to look after than they do.

As I grab the brush from the bucket on the floor, Teddy watches me silently, following my movements with dips of his neck.

When I straighten up, I show him the grooming brush, and he gives it a thorough examination before huffing in approval out those big nostrils.

Before getting started, I pull my phone out, snap a quick photo, and send a message to Storm to let him know where I've been side-tracked to.

Made a new friend.

249

IMAGE ATTACHED.

He's very handsome.

Do I need to be concerned about having competition?

He asked if I could give him a brush.

Lucky asshole.

You don't mind if I hang out here for a little while?

Take all the time you want, darlin'.

CHAPTER 27

Briar

I'm somehow meant to sit through an entire evening with dinner and newfound friends and not stare at my uncle, who will most likely be seated directly across from me in one of the booths lining this bar with "please rail me senseless" eyes.

Today was the best feeling ever. I completely lost track of time, indulging Teddy in the world's longest grooming. Even though I wished I didn't have to stay on the other side of the door, it also seemed like it would be an incredibly foolish decision to jump into his stall after Lucas Rhodes had specifically said not to.

While we were at the ranch today, the entire experience felt almost like being weightless with how much I enjoyed myself. I mean, time spent up at Devil's Peak has the same effect on me, but having the chance to hang out on my own, chatting to Teddy, and brushing his coat, the whole day was special in a way I can't quite put my finger on.

Now, I have to turn my attention to a far more tricky scenario than a horse who might try to take a chunk out of my flesh, given half a chance.

Tonight, I'm supposed to have fun, relax, enjoy a meal, and pretend everything is perfectly normal. Not that I've barely come up for air or escaped the bubble of bliss and fucking Storm has indulged me with since we first crossed that invisible line.

If I ever doubted he was actually serious when he said if the cuff is on, it means *it's on*, then I've been well and truly educated otherwise.

Working together during the day is like a constant round of foreplay, only for him to make it a game by cornering me and eating me out in extremely compromising places and positions.

He knows my body so well by now that the riskier the moment, the harder I come, and he seems to have made it his personal mission to have me damn near lose my mind and my pussy to him again and again.

At night, well, we're all over each other, tangled up in whatever this addiction is. Sometimes, he literally won't stop, chasing me up the bed to the point where I'm shaking and gasping and pleading with him that I can't take any more.

Only, he knows by now that I'm a dirty rotten liar.

That cuff could be taken off at any time if I truly, genuinely wanted him to stop.

The insane truth is that I don't want him to. I don't care if I'm boneless and limp and can't feel my legs anymore. All I want is to be used and treated to more helpings of the uniquely filthy yet worshipful concoction of whatever potion this man has pumped into my veins.

He fucks me like some sort of cowboy fantasy, winds me into a frenzy by calling me his toy and his slut, and at the same time it feels like the tenderest thing he could ever say to me. Afterward, those tattooed hands are so gentle, so caring, so damn careful it makes my blood ache with longing.

I'm in a world of trouble.

Logically, I know it, even while my stupid heart insists on ignoring reality, but my head understands that I've strayed onto perilously thin ice.

I've lost sight of the shore, risking the chance I could fall and plunge beneath the frozen surface at any moment.

Coming here tonight, I've kept an eye out for she-who-lost-her-lip gloss, but our overly friendly server from that night when we came here and grabbed a meal doesn't appear to be working.

The Loaded Hog remains Crimson Ridge's one and only option for a meal after dark, and even though it's prominently set up as a bar, we all made the decision to stick with water or soda tonight. I discovered that Kayce has been completely sober for about a year. He filled me in on a few more pieces of his story while we were out riding up at Devil's Peak Ranch the other day, assuring me he finds it helpful to not avoid socializing.

That guy is absolutely the type of person who lives for being in the thick of a crowd, so I get it—he'd possibly struggle far more if he were to simply sit out an occasion like this.

Laughter drags my attention in the direction of the doors and the arrival of the other members of our party for this evening. Layla bumps shoulders with a girl beside her, who immediately fills the room with a certain energy I can't help but sit up and take notice of. The two friends wear broad smiles and share an ease with each other that makes them seem more like being sisters than besties—not that I'd know that feeling, considering my own she-devil of a sibling. They exude the energy of a sparkling sun-catcher.

It's fun and light, and of course, this is Layla's best friend, considering how incredible the woman in question is to spend time in the company of.

"Sorry we're late." Layla wraps me up tight in her arms straight away. "Sage, meet our city girl, Briar."

The beauty queen in question launches straight in for a hug. She's flawless, with dark brown skin, a dewy complexion, and silky raven hair that falls in loose waves around her shoulders.

Layla looks like she walked straight off a photo shoot for

horse girls to swoon over everywhere, in her tan cowboy boots and cute floral-print dress. Sage is dressed all in black. Jeans hug her thighs, a simple jersey molds to her curves, and the matching leather jacket shrugged over her shoulders completes a look that is effortless and chic all at the same time.

She's so cool I could melt.

"Okay, okay, put the city girl down. Let's go fucking eat, man." Kayce playfully inserts himself between me and the other two, steering me by the shoulders in the direction of the largest booth. As he does so, he gives Storm a slap on the back. "I've been clinging to a bronc all afternoon, and I'm starving. You can bet if I'm hungry, then this asshole here is ready to eat a damn horse."

"You should totally hit them up. This place will need all the help they can get rebranding." Kayce waves a fry in the direction of the bar.

Apparently, a few months ago, the Loaded Hog was taken over by new owners after some shit went down last winter, of which no one seems particularly interested in talking about but I suspect they all know more than they're letting on.

"Next time I see them, I can put in a good word with the Hayes boys for you," he adds, then gives me a shit-stirring grin. "Or, maybe, our girl here can set things up for you, since she's getting friendly with one particular *Hayes* and all."

I nearly swallow my tongue.

"I was chatting with the guys when I saw them last. Wes's younger brother—well, he's not actually a brother, more like an adopted kinda deal—but anyway, he's the one who bought the business, the premises, the whole kit, and caboodle . . ." Kayce pauses to dunk another fry in sauce before shoving it in his mouth.

Layla, bless her sweet little cowboy boots, clears her throat and takes control of the conversation before he can continue. "We're not here to talk about the Hayes boys." She shoots a look my way with a wink, and my pulse eases a little because she knows I'm not interested in any further dates with Wes. Not that she knows the real reasons why, but that's neither here nor there.

To my left is the man I am doing everything within my power not to pay too much attention to, although I can't help but stiffen in his presence as Westin Hayes's name gets dragged into the conversation.

It turns out I didn't have to worry about staring at Storm with moon eyes all night from across the table. No, in fact, I have a much more devious situation to contend with.

Storm seated himself beside me and insisted on pressing our bodies as close as possible. I can't breathe without feeling his muscles and strong body sandwiched against my waist, my hips, and the entire length of my thigh. The heat coming off him simply radiates straight through the soft material of my dress.

I'm struggling to maintain my composure when I feel the vibration of my phone.

Uncle Storm:
No, we're certainly not talking about other cowboys when you're sitting at this table looking innocent as fuck, yet you're wearing my cuff.

My eyes nearly fall out of my head. Firstly, oh my god, now being surrounded by other people, the realization hits me. I haven't altered his name in my phone since I first arrived and entered his contact when we exchanged details. Long before things progressed to the point of knowing my toes curl when he drags orgasm after shaking orgasm out of me. Secondly, he cannot be serious about playing this kind of game while we're surrounded on all sides by people who will surely notice we're texting each other.

While I'm still staring dumbstruck at the screen, another message pops up.

Haven't changed my contact name, I see.

The uncle thing really does it for you, darlin', doesn't it?

Swallowing down the choked noise that nearly bursts out of me, I quickly swipe out of the conversation and lock my phone.

"Everything okay, Briar?" Layla asks.

I wrestle a tight grin onto my face. "Yep." I drop my phone onto my lap. There is no way in hell I'm going to reply to that. Not while we're at dinner, and certainly *not* while he's seated right beside me.

The next second, I nearly climb the back of the booth like a monkey because though this man looks busy talking quietly with Colt, his hand sneaks beneath the table, a single fingertip grazing the bare skin just below the hem of my dress. My face must turn beetroot red instantly, probably only continuing to intensify in color as he continues to steal a teasing touch, carefully hooking the fabric higher on my thigh.

Shitshitshit. I grab my soda and focus intently on the clink of ice and bubbles tickling my nose while resisting the temptation to pluck a cube out and run it all over my burning cheeks.

Reaching beneath the table as slowly and discreetly as I can, I push at his hand, not wanting to draw attention to this upped level of depravity he seems intent on indulging.

He doesn't budge, and I try to shift slightly down the booth in order to put a fraction of distance between us. That only results in him wrapping his palm around the top of my leg, leveraging every ounce of commanding pressure. While attempting to ignore him, I can only bite my inner cheek and pray I don't cause a scene.

However, there is a situation between my thighs that I absolutely cannot overlook considering his hand is *right there*.

I prop my elbow on the table, cradling my chin, and do my damnedest to tune back in to the conversation going on all around me.

Layla is smiling brightly, mid-celebration of her bestie. "Tonight is one hundred percent all about Sarge, just the way she likes it."

The woman in question raises her glass and shimmies her shoulders.

"Sarge?" I know I've been out of it for the past few minutes, but I didn't think I missed that much of the conversation. Confusion knits my brows together as I look between Layla, Kayce, and *Sage*, who are seated at the same end of the booth as I am. Surely I'm hearing wrong?

"My lovely bestie here christened me Sergeant when we were little." Sage rolls her eyes, propping her chin on one hand, mirroring my position. "Apparently, my powers of persuasion were a little lacking in the tact department. I've been cruelly unappreciated in my time, I tell you." She grins broadly, and Layla nearly spits out her soda.

"Oh my god . . . did you forget to pack your humility in that giant carry-on you brought with you?"

Another buzzing sensation from the phone balanced in my lap intensifies the pulsing thud between my ears.

Uncle Storm:
Don't even think about denying me what's mine.

I swallow hard. There's no possible way he's serious. As I let my eyes fall to one side, trying to discreetly look his way, all that brings me is a view of him talking leisurely. He's got his phone on the table in front of him and looks every inch the most relaxed cowboy in this bar.

Probably because he's got his hand up my dress and is progressively inching his way higher and higher the longer I sit here bathed in shame for how aroused I'm feeling.

"Briar, are you sure you're alright . . . You look a little on edge?" Layla says.

Bury me right here.

"Mmmhm." I take another giant gulp of soda.

Sage is still midway through verbally sparring with Kayce, saying something about his lack of organization, threatening that if she does move here, her first task will be forcing him to learn how to use an electronic calendar. With a chuckle, Sage shrugs, looking around. "There's just something about these mountains, though. Even though I'm a total slut for my weekly planner, being here brings out the go-with-the-flow in me."

"Don't believe a word she says." Layla points at me and I can't help but smile at their playful way with one another. She then turns her attention to the man with the golden smile. "As much as I hate to admit it . . ."

Kayce puffs up immediately, beaming. "Told you."

"Yeah, yeah, you might just be onto something. Happy?"

"Extremely," he says.

"Do I not even get a say in this, or are you lot of mountain heathens just determined to convert me to rolling around in hillbilly overalls?" Sage steals a fry off Kayce's plate with a wink, considering hers have already been polished off. He shoves the remainder in her direction, and she blows him a kiss.

Meanwhile, I'm doing my best not to squeak out loud each time Storm's fingers continue to explore higher up my thigh.

Can they tell? Oh god. Why that thought torments me with an ever-more-insistent ache blooming in my core is a very good question to unpack at a future moment.

"Well, that's my not-so-secret plan. Admit it—you'd love living here, Sarge." Layla nods, and her green eyes glitter.

"Look, I know right now I'm on the lookout for clients, but one cowboy bar in Crimson Ridge is not going to be enough to have me moving here permanently."

"You'll have the ranch website and social media to work on, too, right?" Layla nudges Colt, who most definitely has *his* hand on her thigh beneath the table.

If it's so obvious how they're touching, surely the entire table can see what the man beside me is doing? My heart feels like it's stuck somewhere in the back of my throat as I feel another text arrive, and I can't bring myself to open it. Right now, my every ounce of concentration is firmly on my facial expression, along with the need to breathe through my nose.

Colt speaks up. "Of course, we need all the help you'll be happy to give us, Sage."

"I honestly appreciate it, but I could do it all working remotely for the most part."

"What if I had a contact for a job, a new business starting up that might be the kind of thing you're looking for, Sage?" The man beside me speaks up, and all eyes fall his way.

As they do so, it's as if my stomach drops through the floor. I'm a stone statue of terror and horniness, utterly convinced that *someone* is going to ask where my uncle's hand is and why it's halfway to fondling my pussy.

"Who?" Kayce asks the question hanging in the silence.

Can they really not see what's going on?

"A friend." Storm shrugs, and I have no idea how he's able to play this so cool when I'm about two seconds from imploding. "It would require a lot of discretion, but I'd be able to put you in touch with their business manager to set up a meeting and see if it's a good fit."

"That sounds incredible. I'll definitely take you up on that." Sage pulls out her phone and starts tapping away to pull up her digital planner.

Storm's firm hold on me doesn't relent the entire time they discuss a contact email and how best to get in touch.

"There's gonna be a whole ground-up marketing, PR, launch sort of bullshit needing to be done. Figured it might be up your street, and having someone they can trust is going to be the most important thing," he adds.

I brave opening the most recent text, while the table is absorbed with more chatter. The allure of this cowboy is too great, and I'm too much of a fool for him.

Uncle Storm:
Remember, darlin'.

My cuff. My hat. My pussy to play with whenever I damn well want.

CHAPTER 28

Briar

"Okay, this is perfect." Layla is just about wriggling in her seat with joy, obviously leaping over the moon, and has all but already packed her best friend's bags for her.

Meanwhile, I'm no longer beetroot red after digesting the line of text on my phone screen. No, I'm now a fire engine, with wailing sirens and flashing lights all pointing to how shamefully wet I am for the man with his heavy palm and wicked fingers stroking my soft flesh with such tiny motions that it's impossible to see what he's doing. Yet here I am experiencing every slow glide as if it were magnified in intensity.

"I mean, of course they're gonna hire you, Sarge. We know that already," Layla says, giving me a long look, and I try my best to smile and act like everything is completely normal beneath this table.

The woman in question lets out a groan. "If—and that's a big if—this works out, there will be no goddamn overalls."

"I'll talk to Hayes next time I see him and ask what they might need help with here on the Loaded Hog rebrand." Kayce pulls out his own phone and sends off a text.

As Sage chews another fry thoughtfully, she replies, and they start chatting more about the prospect of her imminent move to Crimson Ridge. I feel the distinct vibration of my phone.

At first, I'm certain it's going to be another sinful message from the man beside me. However, the buzzing keeps going, and that's when I realize it's a phone call demanding my attention.

Inwardly, I cringe.

This time of night? Out of the blue? It's only going to be one of two people trying to call me, and neither of them is anyone I have the slightest desire to speak with.

Antoine's threat from the last time we exchanged words echoes in my ears. As much as I really, really do not want to answer this call, it's easier to take it and not have to deal with the potential manhunt that might ensue if I decline his attempts to contact me.

"Hey, I've got to take this," I say quietly to the man at my side, ducking my head, not wanting to meet his interrogating stare. Nor do I wish to draw too much attention from the rest of the table, all talking animatedly amongst themselves.

The others glance briefly at me. I see Layla's brow furrow slightly, and I lift the phone and point at it while mouthing a silent apology, well underway with the process of making a hasty exit.

Fortunately, Storm has already slid out of the booth, allowing me to quickly check my dress is back in place before I escape without so much as a word.

Relief gushes from my lungs, entwined with a sinking feeling in my stomach as I scuttle in the direction of the bathrooms. All I want right now is to get this shit over with as quickly as possible and return to my friends.

My phone screen flashes with "Unknown number" displayed in bold letters, and I know the call belongs to only one particular asshole who will be demanding my cooperation. At least it's not my sister's tongue-lashing I'll have to deal with this time around.

"What?" I hiss beneath my breath as I bring the phone to my ear.

"Babe, it's so good to hear your voice."

All the hairs on the back of my neck stand on end. His voice sounds syrupy, heavy with alcohol, the kind of sickly sweetness that causes nothing but rot with everything it touches. In the hall, there are doors separating the bar area from the corridor containing individual bathroom stalls. At least I can lock myself in one at the far end to deal with whatever this bullshit is as quickly as possible.

"I told you to leave me alone." I walk straight past the empty bathrooms, and my palm pushes open the door at the farthest end, which, much to my relief, is unoccupied.

"You know I can't do that, Briar. You're far too important to me."

"Fuck you. The only thing that is important to you is my last name. We both know that."

I go to shove the door closed behind me, but before I manage to latch the damn thing, the door busts open. On reflex, I jump to avoid the solid wood swinging my way. Piercing blue eyes meet mine, and I'm backed up within a frantic heartbeat. My mouth falls open as those unmistakable broad shoulders and tattoos loom large to fill the space between me and the exit.

Storm locks the door behind him, enclosing us in this shitty little bathroom, and crosses his arms. His gaze flicks between the phone held at my ear and back to hold my eyes.

How much of that did he just hear me say?

"That's not true, babe. I love you. I miss you."

Antoine's voice fills the quiet and bounces off the tiles and the cracked mirror above the handbasin. I want to shrivel up and die. The man standing less than a foot from me can hear everything, can hear every pathetic untruth being spouted from the phone, and I feel like my stomach just dropped through the floor.

My throat bobs with a heavy swallow. I try to plead with my eyes, to tell him it's not what it sounds like, to explain that this—whatever this unexpectedly perfect, soul-consuming thing that we have between us—means so much more to me than any painful second I spent with the man on the other end of this call.

"Why don't you just tell me where you are, and we can put all of this behind us?"

I'm frozen. Words refuse to form. My mouth hangs open and there's no air reaching my squeezed and shriveled lungs.

"No" is all I can muster. My tongue runs across my bottom lip, and I realize that I've been inching back while Storm has been closing the space between us.

My shoulders collide with the tiled wall.

"You know I'm sorry for what happened. She meant nothing. I've apologized all the ways I know how . . ." Antoine's pathetic attempt at fixing us rings in the air.

Storm's eyes flash, thunderous and deadly. The blue I've become so enamored with turns an electric shade as he steps into me and captures every last molecule of air surrounding us.

He's so broad that all I see is his chest and his tattoos. His scent wraps a hold on me that somehow eases this insanity and yet simultaneously makes it impossible to think straight when he's looming tall and muscled like this.

"It doesn't matter." Do I sound shaky? Do I sound like I'm crawling out of my skin worrying about what this man is going to think, how he's going to react to what he can hear coming through the speaker of my phone?

"Briar, you know it does. This can't continue, I need you to come home so we can work on this together, so we can . . ."

Antoine launches into a lengthy explanation of all the ways I supposedly need to forgive him, that's when I feel it. Meanwhile, Storm hooks a finger beneath the long sleeve of my dress, on the wrist of the hand holding my phone to my ear, and he tugs the fabric, peeling it back ever so slightly.

Revealing his cuff.

It's there, just as he knew it would be, securely fastened beneath the soft stretch cotton of my dress, and as he looks between the band of leather and my face, I see the wheels turn rapidly in his mind.

My lips drop open with a silent gasp.

He sinks to his knees in front of me.

Antoine carries on, barely stopping for breath, detailing a lengthy list of reasons why I need to come back home. All while Storm rucks my dress up to my waist, sending goosebumps flying everywhere.

I don't try to stop him.

Maybe this will be the last time we ever get to have something like this together. Maybe after hearing this phone call, he'll end whatever this insane dance we've been doing together.

So I'm going to let him do whatever he wants to me right here, while pushed up against this wall, as my shitty ex pleads and tries to make a case for me to fly back to LA.

" . . . come home. I'll send you the jet. Just tell me where and I'll have the pilot and crew ready and waiting for you in the morning."

Storm runs his tongue up the inside of my thigh, tracing the spot where his hand was only moments before, as he wedges himself between my legs. He hooks my knee over his shoulder, forcing me to brace myself by sinking one hand into his hair.

His eyes flash, as if he's pleased by that.

"Briar?"

"I'm not coming back." Despite the hypnotic sight of the man I've fallen so hard and so fast for currently on his knees for me, I remember to say something in reply. Does Storm have any idea how much I don't ever want to leave? Now that I'm here, I've found so much more than I could ever have hoped for in this tiny dot on the map.

"At least let me come and see you."

Those words set something ablaze. Within an instant, the air sharpens. Storm narrows his eyes and turns into a man possessed. While, a second ago, he was slowly roaming his tongue higher while teasing me, he now launches forward.

A finger hooks under the damp strip of fabric with no doubt a giant wet spot covering my pussy, expertly towing it to one side before he covers me with his mouth.

"No," I gasp. I try to prevent a series of moans from bursting forth as the man who knows how to work me hard and fast swirls his tongue over my clit with wicked skill. My fingers yank on his hair in an effort to remain upright.

"I know you're still in the country." Antoine starts to sound pissy now. "Which means I can be there overnight. All you have to do is tell me where to collect you from."

I suck in a breath.

"Are you screwing someone else?" he spits at me down the line.

Looking down at the man between my legs, commanding my body, I don't know what to say. My pulse thuds an insane rhythm in my neck, and I feel like I'm floating out of my head.

"I'm not telling you anything," I say.

Those startling blue eyes lock me in, glittering with triumph.

Storm growls against my clit, sending white sparks of pleasure flying straight down to my toes. This time, I lose the battle against the noise trying to escape me, and I downright moan.

I stare down, open-jawed, watching, fascinated at the sight of his mouth covered in the sheen of my arousal, and I feel him smirk against my pussy. His fingers tighten against my hips, holding me in place for him to eat me with savage intent.

There's no outcome here other than for me to fall apart while I'm on the phone, and I'm assuming if Storm has his way, I'll do so while chanting his name. He seems entirely unbothered that we're in a public bathroom or that the rest of the table will be wondering where we both are.

Oh god.

Everyone we're here having dinner with.

Storm sees it written all over my face, sees the moment my brain tries to fight how turned on I am that we're doing this illicit, risky thing, and that's when he sucks on my clit so hard my back bows, and my climax roars through me.

It catches me off guard, and as I bite my bottom lip to the point I might draw blood, Antoine's voice repeats my name. "Briar, can you hear me? I said just send me an address. Is everything alright?"

My body jerks as the man working me holds my eyes in his fearsome stare, slowly massaging me with his tongue, lapping at my clit, before he carefully sets my leg on the ground. Except that's where the gentleness stops. He's on his feet in a rush, grabbing my phone out of my limp hand.

"She can hear you just fine," he snarls into the speaker. "By the way, that's what it sounds like when a woman comes so hard she soaks your face and forgets her own name. Fuck off and lose this number, asshole."

He jabs the red button, ending the call, as I nearly sink to the floor.

Oh god.

Storm shoves my phone in his back pocket, hiding it away, then braces one forearm on the wall above my head. As I stare up at him, all I can see is the way his lips and stubble around his mouth are still covered in the sheen of *me*.

He looks feral and wild and so goddamn sexy I could die.

With his other hand, he shoves roughly beneath the fabric of my panties, which are still wedged to one side. This time, he plunges two fingers into me, and I let out a loud whimper, feeling how wet and slick I am, with the afterglow of my orgasm still roaming through my veins and desperate for more.

"You gonna block his number?" he grunts at me, curling his fingers and sinking deeper. Fucking in and out with the filthy, wet sounds of my pussy filling the bathroom.

"Already have," I whimper, my hands fly up, clinging to the front of his shirt and forearm.

"You're gonna tell me if that fuck face tries to contact you again." It's not a question; it's a command. He sinks in me past his second knuckles, leaving me panting and writhing, impaled on his fingers.

"Yes. *Yes.*"

"And you're not going anywhere, that clear?" He presses his forehead to mine, working me with those wicked digits and rocking his palm over my swollen clit.

I nod my head, wanting so badly to drag him against my mouth, but I also know why he's holding back, even though his eyes keep straying to my lips. He knows we have to go back out there in a second, and while my pussy might have been entirely owned by him, I'm grateful he's not leaving me to walk out of here with ruined makeup looking like I've been fucked senseless in this bathroom.

"You're not leaving." *Thrust.* "You're not going back to an asshole like him." *Shove.* "You're mine."

As he fingers me mercilessly, he crouches down once more. For a moment, I think he's about to torture me and drive me out of my head with more of his mouth on me, except instead he watches me with hawklike intensity. Storm twists his wrist around so that the back of his hand faces upwards. I don't need to see to know exactly what that has revealed.

"*Mmmfuck.* Look how good you look." Of course, I follow his voice, his sultry low tone that drags my attention down to between my thighs. "You love seeing how you stretch around my ink, don't you?"

The tattooed letters of his name disappear inside me, and I clamp down on him at the depravity of it all.

"My precious little slut." He punctuates each word with a thrust forward.

There's so much possessive energy washing off him and

coating me, I can't even see straight. This time, the orgasm is fast and gritty, and the wave crashes over me, slamming into the harbor with the rolling force of a hurricane. I barely contain the whimpers and slutty sounds, all demanding more from him.

I'm pretty sure that amongst it all, I begged for his cock, which of course, results in a self-satisfied smirk on those gorgeous lips of his.

As he pulls his hand away, he stands up and raises the fingers he just had buried deep inside my pussy in front of our faces, covered in the sticky residue of my climax. He rubs it between his thumb and middle finger, drawing them apart and making a show of putting my cum on lewd display as it stretches out, then he looks at me with an arched eyebrow.

I dutifully stick out my tongue.

"My good fucking girl." He groans while pressing past my lips, and I carefully lap up the evidence of how hard I just came under his command, cleaning him up while treated to his watchful gaze. My brain is twirling in giddy circles somewhere amongst the starry night sky, I'm certain.

Whether or not I can actually walk out of here without stumbling is another question entirely.

As he pulls his fingers away and then sucks on them himself, he hums out a dark noise of satisfaction. Then he looks down and makes careful work of hooking my panties back into place and settling my dress to look completely normal.

Not like I just humped his face and shattered on his tongue and fingers.

"Ready?" He flashes me with a wicked glance.

I blink at him, taking a second to process what he's saying. That's when my brain comes back online. "Everyone saw you come in here. How the fuck are we supposed to just walk out and explain this?" I whisper-yell, my hand thumping his impossible, strong chest.

"I took care of that."

"Oh really? How are you going to explain disappearing into the bathroom two seconds after me?" My stomach clenches. We haven't discussed telling anyone about this thing between us, and I don't feel like tonight, of all nights, is the occasion I want to spring this revelation on the only group of friends I've made.

The infuriating, supremely handsome man towering over me looks implacable. He's a calm lake while I'm a churning ocean of anxiety.

"I told them we might be awhile."

"What?"

"Don't look so panicked, little thorn."

"But aren't they going to ask questions?" They are absolutely going to ask questions.

"No." His lips tip up at the corners.

"How can you be so certain? They're gonna suspect some-thing." I brush my hands over my dress, trying to smooth it down while regathering my brain cells that have all pooled in my pussy.

"No. They're not."

"Why do I not like that look on your face?"

"I told them to carry on, that we might be gone for quite some time."

He tugs on my elbow, guiding me toward the door, and as he unlocks it, the thud surely signaling the moment when our dirty little secret is going to be revealed, he bends to rumble in my ear.

"I told them it was a family emergency."

CHAPTER 29

Storm

Damn, I've never known this kind of peace before.

Of making my way into the heart of these mountains after a long fucking day's work, looking forward to the sweet smile waiting for me.

I've been down in Crimson Ridge this afternoon, sorting out some final details with Beau's realtor, and now I'm ready for the ultimate prize.

My girl has been playing games today. While left alone, she sent me a photo I've pulled up on my phone screen every two goddamn seconds.

In it, she's taken a photo of her reflection in the bedroom mirror, covering those perfect tits with one forearm, the one wrapped in my cuff, being a slutty little tease. But that's not the part that really had my dick standing to attention. No, the real fucking cherry perched on top is the sight of my hat covering her glossy, long head of hair and the constellation of fingerprints and hickeys left all over her thighs.

They've colored up beautifully since last night.

She sent the image because I instructed her to, and being the good girl she is for me, Briar's slutty little photo arrived less than five minutes later.

Have I spent most of my day imagining all the ways I'm gonna worship her when I get home? Or, more accurately, have I spent the better part of the day already thinking about a future with Briar?

I don't know what she wants from this or from us. I don't know if I can expect her to stay in these mountains, but holy shit, I'm busy calculating what the odds might be.

What are the chances a girl so perfect could ever consider falling for me the way I've undeniably fallen for her?

This isn't about a fantasy of white picket fences or wedding bells; this is about two people choosing a life together, something I've never been able to fathom before now. Briar Lane makes me want to believe in something deep and soul nourishing and powerful as fuck.

She makes me believe I could offer her happiness.

To try to be that person who she deserves to be cared for and wholly loved by.

As I pull up outside the front porch, warm light spills into the darkening evening air, the curl of chimney smoke winds into the faded tinge of inky blue peppered with a handful of early stars, and I'm drawn like a magnet to where I know she's waiting inside.

After jogging up to the front entrance, I'm halfway through kicking off my boots and already calling out as I shut the door behind me.

"It's fucking on." My voice carries across the room against the backdrop of the crackling fire. "That picture . . ."

The words are out of my mouth already when I realize.

I fucking see it too late to swallow down what has already come out, but at least I haven't said anything too incriminating for Briar.

Because there's someone else here, and it's the last fucking person on this planet I'd want my girl to have to suffer being left alone with.

"Stôrmand."

The clipped, nasal tone of Briar's asshole sister is about as welcome in my house as a bucket of pig shit. Actually I'd take the pig shit any day rather than this human turd sitting on my couch.

"Crispin." I tip my chin her way, my brain trying to make sense of what I'm seeing.

"Hey." Briar's voice sounds so soft and small as she emerges from the bedroom, eyes wide, features pinched and drawn. In her arms is a bundled assortment of what looks like a pillow and blankets.

It's like all the color and vibrancy has been sucked out of her. She's back to being a ghost of herself, and now that I see her in this light, I realize with startling clarity that this was the version of Briar who showed up unexpectedly on my doorstep.

My fists clench, and there's a rapid pulse in my jaw.

"What brings you to Crimson Ridge?" I flick my eyes back toward the blonde woman perched on the couch, who glares severely in the direction of her younger sister.

"Well, I can't tell you how relieved I am to have finally found Briar. Her little disappearing act from LA has had us all wrecked with worry."

God, I can smell the bullshit pouring off her. I'm readying myself to put some words together, something to the effect of kicking her out on that bony ass.

Except she opens her bitch mouth, and I watch Briar damn near crumble in front of my eyes.

"I've been wondering where my sister ran off to, after abandoning her husband."

CHAPTER 30

Briar

The man across the room from me is even more striking than normal. Heavy shadows and firelight lick over his rugged jaw and tattoos, and I want to scream until my lungs explode.

My fucking sister found me.

As she says the words that clatter to the floor like a smashed vase, I can't tear my eyes away from his face. Those features I've traced over and over in his sleep, the slight furrow of his brow, the tiny scar hidden by his left eyebrow, remain impassive. He's entirely unreadable, and that lack of emotion terrifies me.

We can't say or do anything at this moment, and if this is it for us, I'm forever going to be haunted by knowing I'm in love with this man, even though there's every chance he will never look at me again now he knows the truth.

An ugly misfortune that I foolishly, like a stupid little naive piece of shit, thought I could outrun.

Yet, my flesh and blood, my older sister, has arrived like a foul wind, and while she might not know the extent of whatever this is between me and Storm, she's determined to ruin my life.

Of that, I can be absolutely certain.

Cris believes with every cell in her rotten core that I stole her life, so it has become her mission to ensure I remain in misery for however many years I might continue to wander around this earth.

Husband.

The word hangs in the air, like the resounding toll of a bell long after the hammer has struck metal.

My chest aches, and I want to drop to my knees and beg him to ignore what my sister just said. That any piece of paper between Antoine and me, a formal contract binding me to him out of duty and obligation and power-hungry families, it's all bullshit. I've never cared or felt a single thing for that piece of scum.

I want Stôrmand Lane to know that I belong to him, that I'll willingly be *his* as long as he'll have me.

"Briar here tells me that you've been gracious enough to sleep on the couch." My sister's voice pierces the tension in the room. "This place really is far too small for the two of you to both be staying here." Her nose wrinkles as she looks around, picking at some invisible piece of dirt on the couch with a fingernail.

"I was just getting your bedding for you," I mumble, gesturing with the items I'm still clinging onto like some sort of life raft amongst the insanity of all of this.

"You eaten, Crispin?" Storm doesn't make a move to come any further inside, remaining stoically in place by the door.

"I found something on the drive here from the airport. God, there really is next to nothing out here, though." She makes a face. "I've got a room booked in town tomorrow, so Briar and I will be heading down there in the morning."

My head whips in her direction. "No," I blurt out.

Eyes narrow on me from the direction of the couch.

"No, I won't be going anywhere," I say, shifting my weight.

"Don't be difficult, Briar."

"Crispin." The man by the door says her name with a venom I haven't heard from him, not since that first night I arrived and he was a terrifying prospect looming over me. "I'm gonna extend you the courtesy of a bed for the night, but you will watch your tone with Briar. I don't care how you think it is acceptable to speak to your minions back in LA, but your own sister is not someone you can order around in my presence and get away with it."

Her eyes bounce between the two of us. The woman isn't used to having anyone speak to her that way, but even someone who is as much of a raging cunt face as she knows not to provoke our *uncle*.

"You can share with me tonight, then we'll get you back to Crimson Ridge tomorrow," I say. Crossing to the couch, I drop the bedding and pillow onto one end, avoiding looking Storm's way.

The unfairness of our circumstances idles in my blood.

Why should we have to pretend and hide away? It's not like we're actually related . . . but either way, the very first person to reveal anything to, if we ever were able, is certainly not going to be my sister.

In fact, I'd gladly never have to lay eyes on the woman, let alone speak to her or give her any glimpse of insight into my life ever again.

"I'll be chopping wood if you need anything," Storm grunts, collecting his boots, before slamming back out the door into the darkness surrounding the cabin.

My heart feels like it has gone into overdrive. I'd barely recovered from the pure, sickening shock of Cris turning up at the front door. Now I have to face the prospect of spending the night sharing a bed with her, and it turns my stomach.

"Bedroom and bathroom are just down here." My tongue feels numb as I wrap my arms around myself and gesture with my chin.

My sister huffs and gets up off the couch, surveying the room and looking down her nose. I can see the judgment and the disdain spinning away like a hamster on a wheel inside her mind. She takes everything in with a look on her face that amounts to stepping in dog shit with her stilettos.

"Chopping wood? At this time of night? God, that man is a basket case." Her eyes roll dramatically. "He always has been nuts. Guess that's what you get when you were insane enough to willingly ride bulls for a living."

"It's an important job out here." My hackles rise. "I'll bet you're going to be grateful for that wood supply and fire when the morning comes and you're not frozen half to death."

Spinning on my heel, I make my way to the bedroom. Fuck this. I'm done and just want to go crawl under the covers and do my best to pretend this is all a nightmare.

"What the hell are you playing at Briar?" she snaps from behind me, following after my footsteps. Her voice drops into a blunt whisper. "You cannot stay here . . . not with someone like *that*."

My jaw sets. I really, really don't want to get into this with her, but I also have no intention of allowing her to get away with behaving like this. "Like what, exactly? Please enlighten me as to what your problem is now."

"He's a manwhore—slept with half the women in every state, I'm sure. And don't tell me you don't know about the rumors that he pretty much caused the death of his wife."

I steady myself against the bed, pretending to fuss with the extra blanket. While I don't have any grounds to be feeling a certain way about the crap coming out of my sister's mouth, considering my own secrets about being married, it's a shock to hear such an accusation all the same.

How did I not know?

"She was pregnant, too." My sister clicks her tongue and shoves her suitcase open. "What kind of man does that to a woman? Abandons her with a child on the way, to the extent that she's driven beyond the point of no return. It might not have been his hand that poured those pills down her throat, but it had his fingerprints all over the mess."

Sliding into the far side of the bed, I don't even look her way. I don't reply. There is nothing I want to say to my sister right now except to scream at her to get out and leave.

She keeps spewing her vitriol. "How can you even consider being here? That man is unhinged, and he's completely unsafe to be around."

My silence only gives her a platform to keep spouting her bullshit from, but I'm reeling and can't seem to figure out a way to make her stop.

"My god. You don't know anything, do you? Happily staying in a vermin-infested dump with a psychopath. I always knew dad sheltered you too much. He always damn well pampered you, and look at what good has come of it—"

"Cris, I'm tired. Leave it alone, and let me go to sleep."

"He's unstable," she snaps. "He might be our uncle, but his own wife was driven to the point of no return, and the note she left behind only proves how much responsibility he had. It's foul."

The only *foul* thing is my sister.

"How can you even consider being here for two seconds with him? Look at this place—it's filthy. He's living in squalor, and you're probably going to end up with some sort of disease just being around him."

I don't believe her. I don't for one second think the toxic cloud she's spewing has any truth. She's manipulative and poisonous, and while I have no doubt the man I've fallen in love with has a past, he's not the person she's painting him to be.

That much is the truth I know in the marrow of my bones.

Rolling on my side, I face the wall, turning my back on the woman who insists on continuing her character assassination beneath her breath while poking around on the other side of the room.

At least this cabin is tiny. There's no obvious way to tell we've been sharing a bed, that we've been inseparable on so many levels. Storm doesn't exactly own *things*, and the assortment of clothes I have are still strewn half inside my own suitcase tucked beside the closet.

The other side of the mattress dips as my sister gets in, assuming the location where my tattooed giant should rightly be. Who I should be able to openly kiss and wrap myself around or be encircled in his strong arms as he snores softly against my hair.

"Lord knows why Dad left you this shit hole in his will," Crisp mutters, fussing with her pillow and moving around so much that my teeth are nearly fused together with how hard my jaw is clamped shut. "Why haven't you kicked him out? He's been freeloading, living here for years."

"Crispin. Jesus." I have to restrain myself from shouting. "You've been here two seconds, and you're already trying to throw our own uncle out?" As I say it, I cringe, but it's the best I can manage, all things considered. "Just go to sleep. We'll deal with getting you back to Crimson Ridge in the morning."

When I tuck myself into a ball and stare at the wall, watching the light flick off when my sister finally shuts off the lamp, I'm a mess of emotions.

I can't go back with her. I refuse to . . . no matter what she tries to do to persuade me otherwise.

However, I can't risk hurting Storm.

Maybe girls like me don't get a happily ever after, at all.

CHAPTER 31

Briar

Seeing the taillights of my sister's car disappear down the mountain brought a wave of relief that I could never have imagined.

I damn near had to clutch the edge of the counter to hold myself upright, staring at the contents of my coffee that up until the moment she disappeared from view, I wasn't able to stomach a single sip of. Throughout the entire agony of time she took to pack her bag, the awkward silence left me hovering with bated breath. Eventually, thankfully, Cris slammed her door to the driver's side and left.

It took a good ten minutes of pacing around the cabin before I could calm down enough to feel assured she wasn't going to reappear like a ghoul from beyond the grave.

I know I have to sort things out with Storm. He vanished while it was still dark out, with the truck engine rumbling to life at some ungodly hour of the morning.

No doubt he didn't sleep a single second either.

There are a million things I need to say to him, yet there are also no words willing to come forth when I wrack my brain trying to find a suitable explanation for all of this.

Sorry would feel like a paltry, anemic excuse for my lies by omission.

He knew I had a shitty ex and that I had run from something back at home in LA. What he didn't know—because no matter how many times he attempted to leave the door open for me to explain things, I still avoided the truth—was the full extent of the turmoil of events that led me to land here in this cabin with a heavy thud.

Fleeing and leaving behind three years of a miserable, near-sexless marriage. Where I left my wedding ring, sitting on top of a pristine white kitchen counter, next to five printed A4 pages with a litany of screenshots and all the texts between my asshole husband and his steady rotation of secretary whores throughout the duration of our time wedded and supposedly upholding the sanctity of that contract.

The foul, cheating bastard can keep his side bitches. I left without so much as a word of warning, and I have no intention of ever seeing the scummy piece of shit again.

At least with Cris offloaded to some little bed-and-breakfast accommodation somewhere in Crimson Ridge, I have time to think, a scrap of breathing space to plan how exactly I'll manage to figure this all out.

My phone lies on the counter, and I chew the inside of my cheek, picking it up, unlocking the screen, before slamming it back down on the surface again. God, I'm a dumpster fire of a human.

All I want is to run into my cowboy's massive arms. To inhale that hint of leather and citrus and light smoky tinge that clings to him after a day with the horses. What I would give for him to fill this cabin with his warmth and grounding presence as he tugs on the hem of my sweater and draws me between his knees.

Except Storm isn't here, and a sharp slice of panic reminds me that he might never look at me the same way again.

He's got far more important things to do than deal with my bullshit baggage I've traipsed all the way up this mountain like a breadcrumb trail of disastrous life choices.

Even if things largely weren't of my own choosing, I still stayed under Antoine's roof. I still wore his ring. That was the real kicker. I allowed myself to be manipulated into doing every single thing my family wanted me to, as a good little Lane-family-empire pawn they could shove around the chessboard as they saw fit.

Whatever way it lands, I need to try to explain myself. My stomach is twisted up like a damn pretzel at the mere notion he might want nothing further to do with me.

Letting out a heavy sigh, I figure that I'd rather know . . . I'd rather have the truth spelled out for me in letters on a screen if he wants me to be gone and to never set eyes on me again.

It's the *unknown* that I couldn't bear to live with.

I can't text from up here on the mountain, but I snatch up my phone and tap out the message to his Instagram DMs instead, before I can successfully overthink things. My fingers fly and I press send immediately without rereading what I've just written.

All I can hope is that he'll be somewhere in service to pick up the message. Otherwise, I'm going to spend today stuck in this cabin like a starving tiger, ready to gnaw off my own leg.

Can we talk?

Dots bounce on the screen immediately, and my heart leaps into my throat. There's a risk I might shatter this phone, considering how tightly it's clutched between my fingers.

Pick up the radio.

I stare at the four words, and my brain stalls like a spinning wheel on a laptop screen.

The radio?

From the corner of the room, there's a loud crackling noise followed by static and I jump about five feet at the unexpectedness of the intrusion.

Then I hear my name.

"Briar." Another long crackling sound. "Pick up the handset. Hold the button on the side when you want to talk."

Storm's voice drifts from the small speaker unit, which is covered in all sorts of antique knobs and buttons. Truth be told, I'd never even paid much attention to this thing sitting on the shelf—it simply blended into the background of the place.

Why have I got giddy butterflies going on in my stomach?

I scoop up the funny-looking handset connected by a spiraling cord, entirely unsure of what to do.

"Darlin', you gotta actually talk." His voice might be altered by the radio, but it sounds rich and deep over the line, and it sets my pulse racing.

It feels awkward, but I hold the button down and speak into the handset.

"Hi." I definitely sound breathless.

Letting the button go, I stare at the unfamiliar object in my hands and chew my lip.

"Hey."

Just that one syllable settles my nerves more than this man could ever know. He doesn't sound pissed or short with me, just a little more tired than usual.

"Are we allowed to talk . . . like this?" My damn sister has got me second-guessing everything.

A chuckling noise comes from the receiver in response. "Why wouldn't we be?"

Pinching my brow with one hand, I huff at him. "You know exactly what I mean."

"Aren't uncles and nieces allowed to call each other?" Even through the radio, I can hear his smirk.

"Oh my god. Don't even start."

"I'm just playing, little thorn." Yup, there goes my heart, flying out the window to flutter off and land wherever it is this man happens to be right at this moment. "Besides, I would have thought talking over the radio would be preferable to sending messages, hmm?"

"Yes. Okay. You win."

"I like to win."

Well, shit. My thighs squeeze together, hearing that unmistakable tone in his voice.

"We need to talk. Is that okay with you?"

There's a pause; only static greets me, and just as I'm worried he's decided to abruptly end this call, I hear him speak again. "You got rid of Crispin?"

"I did. She's staying in town."

He pauses again, and I can imagine him rubbing his jaw, can picture his tattooed hand flexing as he scrubs over his mouth in the way he tends to do while thinking.

"The roads are good enough. You can bring that shitty little car of yours. I'm gonna read the address out for you. We can stay out here on the job I've gotta work on for the night."

"Is it somewhere nearby?"

"A ranch just out of town. I'm not risking staying at the cabin while your sister is poking her nose around, and you're not gonna stay there where she can get to you either." He says it so resolutely. So calmly. Like it's the most natural thing in the world that he would protect me from the family I've been burdened with.

"There's a pen on top of the radio, darlin'."

My eyes flick up to where, sure enough, a ballpoint and a faded notepad sit, and I note down the instructions he gives me on how to make my way to the ranch.

From what he's described, the location is remote but isn't perched on top of a mountain at least. With his steady, secure voice, he reassures me that I'll be fine driving there alone. The notion of getting behind the wheel and driving back down that winding road doesn't exactly settle my scurrying anxiety, but I'm motivated enough to get to him that I can't stop and think too long. I just have to do this.

"Pack an overnight bag." His deep tone cuts through my thoughts, and if I had any doubts about whether things were going to be alright between us, in spite of last night's revelations about my secrets, he sweeps all that to one side with his next words.

"Oh, and make sure to bring your favorite toy, little thorn."

CHAPTER 32

Storm

Fixing up Beau's ranch on his behalf is a whole lot more appealing when there's a sexy-as-fuck girl helping me out.

Briar arrived—that heap of junk rental car might be a death trap, but at least it served a useful purpose considering these circumstances—and I immediately put her to work.

She's nervous as shit after what went down last night, and I don't blame her. It took me a minute to get my head around what her sister was spewing, and while I don't care about any of it, I'm more determined than ever to plan my course of action right.

Wooing Briar Lane is like getting a skittish horse to finally trust me enough in order to take a look at its hoof. She's had it rough her whole life, not in terms of lacking money or materialistic crap—but emotionally and mentally, the girl has been through the wringer. Damned if I'm going to do anything to make her feel like she can't trust me.

Because one thing I knew as soon as I walked into that cabin last night is that I'll fight anyone and anything that tries to come between me and my girl.

She's a glimpse of something spectacular, the dance of fireflies on the night breeze, the roll of aurora clouds through the skies, the gentle wash of the ocean glowing and glittering like it's full of stars. All the kind of awe-inspiring sights that your brain can't quite believe actually exist until you see them for the first time with your own eyes.

So, I did with Briar what I do with the horses. I put her to work to run out the tension and stress lurking in her veins. Which is why she's standing with a bemused expression, holding a paintbrush in one hand and a roller in another, staring wide-eyed at Beau's new ranch.

"Painting? I don't know how to paint." Her lips twist.

"It's easy enough. I'll show you the basics. Just don't load the brush or the roller too heavily to start with." I beckon her over to where I laid out the paint trays and drop cloths, having already sanded and prepped everything earlier.

"This is your rodeo buddy's place?" She narrows her eyes at the wall, as if it might jump out and bite her or some shit.

"I owe him a favor or ten for being a good friend when most didn't want to know who I was anymore." Shrugging, I crouch down beside one of the cans of paint and pop the lid with a screwdriver.

Briar hovers beside me.

"So . . . he's not here?" She chews her lip, glancing around, taking in the open-plan living space. The rooms are empty and echoey right now, but there's an expanse of timber flooring and stone features around the large fireplace, with big windows looking out over the rolling country, the trees, and the mountains in the distance beyond the glass.

Once the ranch is properly running, those empty fields will have cattle and horses, but right now, the place is quiet. It's just the two of us here, with no one and nothing stretching for miles in all directions.

"Nope. The place still needs a lot of work, as you can see, and until that's all done, he's got a lot to take care of out of state."

"Will you work here?" She looks down at me, her big, dark eyes filled with curiosity. "Like you do for Devil's Peak Ranch?"

Still crouched on my haunches, I rub my jaw with a thumb. "Maybe. We haven't exactly hashed out the details, but Beau knows my shit, knows what I can do."

"He'd be an idiot not to have you." That's the first time a little smile creeps onto her gorgeous features since arriving, and it makes something squeeze inside my chest to see her relax a little.

"I'll tip some paint in here and get you started on that wall behind you." I point past Briar with the screwdriver, making her whirl around to see where I'm indicating. It's a fucking hideous pea-green color at present, with faded yellow outlines where whoever owned this property prior to Beau hung artwork and crap on the walls for decades.

Briar turns back to face me, looking slightly put out. Her eyes bounce over my chest, ever so quickly down to my jeans, and back up to my mouth.

That draws a laugh out of me, so I hook the front of her jacket—my jacket—and drag her forward so that her hips are exactly level with my gaze.

"Come on . . . did you think I was luring you out here just so I could get in your pants?"

"I hoped you would." She pushes the fingers of one hand into my hair, the front of her teeth dragging over that curve to her bottom lip I swear I could trace in my sleep.

I'm hopelessly in love with this girl.

"Darlin', if you wanna fool around, you gotta make sure I'm not falling behind on my jobs first."

Briar straightens up, standing to survey her handiwork. In doing so, she brushes some loose hairs off her forehead with the back of one hand and rolls her shoulders. She's made perfect work of the large wall, giving it two coats of paint, the off-white eggshell color a vast improvement.

I come to stand beside her, looking at the same blank wall.

"So, husband, huh? I'm guessing he's who was on the other end of the phone when I made you scream for me?"

Briar makes a rough noise and elbows me in the side. Her voice goes soft. "I'm sorry you had to find out that way."

"It's over between the two of you?"

"Honestly? It was never anything to begin with. I didn't have a spine and stupidly allowed myself to get talked into a business arrangement."

"Sounds pretty typical for Erik." My jaw tics as I think of all the bullshit he's clearly put Briar through over the years.

"So, wife, huh?" She leans her head against my side. As I draw her into me on instinct, I blow out a long breath. This is where the rubber really fucking hits the road, isn't it?

All the skeletons are primed and ready to tumble out of that particular closet.

"I think I need a drink for this conversation." My palm brushes over her hair, and she tilts her chin up to meet my gaze.

"You can tell me." That look, that assurance, that trust written all over her expression is something I don't fucking deserve, but I'm going to hold tight to it anyway.

"Come on, I've got some beers." I grab hold of her palm, threading our fingers together, and lead her through the sprawling ranch floor plan to where the entertainer's dream kitchen stands. All the appliances here have already been upgraded, so it's a fully kitted-out showpiece of stainless steel and perfectly polished wood countertops.

Fuck knows what Beau's intending to do in here, but the guy obviously plans on cooking . . . a lot.

"Sit your pretty little ass up there." Lifting Briar with both hands around her waist, she makes a tiny squeak of protest as

I set her on the counter, then swipe a couple of beers from the cooler.

Opening and handing over one bottle, I settle myself, leaning up against the length of bench directly opposite where she's sitting. Crossing my ankles, I enjoy simply looking at her for a moment. This position puts us eye to eye, and this just feels so fucking easy, so natural, even if what I'm about to try to talk about is like scratching nails down a chalkboard.

Tipping my drink back, I let a long gulp go down as I collect my thoughts in some sort of coherent fashion. Trying to make sense of the hornet's nest of memories that I most certainly do not want to kick. This is a box I've had locked and shut away for so long now; it's always a little rusty trying to open the hinges and rediscover the mess hastily shoved inside.

"One night in Vegas, I'd just had a massive win, one of my best rides, won the entire fucking circus, and walked away with my big fancy check and all that bullshit." Bringing the bottle back to my lips, I drink down another long draw while Briar watches me with those soulful goddamn eyes. "When I woke up the next day, I not only had a raging hangover to contend with and no memory of whatever the hell happened after the first few rounds of shots, but I had a fucking ring on my finger . . . one hell of a way to realize I'd fucked up so badly that not even the great Erik Lane could get my ass out of the legal mess."

Running my tongue over my teeth, I inhale through my nose. Here comes the really shitty part of this whole terrible tale.

"She overdosed ten years ago. We had legally remained married, but I hadn't seen the woman—Tegan was her name—since that night in Vegas, and truth be told, hearing of her death was like hearing about a stranger passing. Yet, I had to show up to her funeral and play the role of the widower and all the shit that came with legally being attached to one another."

Ten years... Ten years since I discovered exactly what my own goddamn brother had done.

"It's kind of a lot to take in," Briar says. "I remember being told you'd been married. I vaguely remember hearing about the funeral, but I didn't know much more than that. Of course, we were kept so far away from things. I feel like an idiot for not knowing or at least asking." She sips her beer thoughtfully.

"Probably same as how I didn't know they'd married you off to some asshole."

Briar sucks in a breath through her nose. "The Lanes are pretty good at keeping secrets, aren't they?"

She doesn't even know the half of what her father was capable of.

"My only real relief, if you could call it that, was that I'd been in an accident when I was a kid—the kind that meant I knew without a doubt I couldn't get a chick like her accidentally knocked up from a stupid, meaningless, drunken one-night stand."

"You can't have kids?" Briar's eyes widen over the top of her beer, she pauses with her bottle halfway to her mouth.

"Nope." Jesus, I didn't even think about whether revealing that special little gem might have this girl running for the hills rather than sticking around with the likes of me. God. I hadn't thought for a second about whether Briar might want kids of her own one day.

Fuck. It feels like someone just put my chest inside a vise and started tightening the screws.

But she doesn't seem to react to that piece of information, just carries on matter-of-factly. "So why didn't you get a divorce? Why'd you let her hang around?"

"Well, for starters, she didn't exactly hang around. We never actually lived or spent any time together. It was all just a piece of paper tying us to one another in a legal sense, but that was it. At the end of the day, I was permanently on the road competing, and I had zero interest in having a *wife*. But your dear old dad persuaded me it would be 'good for my image' if we stayed married, ticked that box, you know . . ."

"More like good for the Lane family brand."

"Precisely." I set my beer down. "So, Tegan lived in LA while I carried on with my life, and we occasionally exchanged details through my agent and lawyer. It sounds fucking weird to say it now, but ten years went so fast when all my attention was on the rodeo. Seemed like it was over in a blink."

"Couldn't you have fought my dad on it?"

Shaking my head, I try to pick my next words carefully. "Look, Erik was jealous as fuck of the attention I got while I was still in my competing days, and he hated even more that at that time in my life, I fed off the spotlight. I'm not proud of who I was if it didn't involve being on the back of a bull, but getting wasted and chasing women . . . it was my best attempt at filling a void." I flex my hands against the lip of the benchtop and chuckle to myself. "Probably a whole lot of shit to do with being dumped at an orphanage as a kid. Someone really shoulda shoved me into therapy for that at some point, but that's a part of me I've gotta make peace with."

We both sip our drinks, letting the dust settle on everything I just shared.

Briar clears her throat. "I have this recurring nightmare. It's from the day of my wedding. I'm in this stupid couture gown, walking down the aisle of some billionaire's country club, and I'm just sobbing. I remember my entire body was convulsing, and no one cared. They all sipped their champagne and clapped politely when the deal was done and hid their laughter at my expense behind their hands."

Her eyes get that faraway kind of look that I hate, but I'm also relieved she's telling me this and I don't want to stop things.

"Antoine reeked of smoke and cheap perfume, and I think they'd jetted straight in from his bachelor's party. I nearly threw up in my mouth when I had to kiss him at the altar."

"Did he ever lay a hand on you?" My grip tightens on my bottle. Forget digging Erik up out of his grave—I'm ready to board a flight to LA and smash this guy's face in with a sledgehammer.

Briar shakes her head.

"Other than occasionally having sex, no. It was only what probably amounted to a few times, like it was some sort of annual obligation over the course of three years, give or take." Now, it's Briar's turn to ruefully laugh. "I suppose I should be grateful, right? That my husband never wanted to touch me."

"I fucking hate that he even got that much. The asshole didn't deserve any piece of you, Briar." I tell her with so much force that she gapes at me a little. As if no person has ever told this woman she deserves to be treated like she's the most precious, important thing.

Not some kind of contract or deal.

"There's stuff I have to sort out with Cris." Her lips roll together. "I didn't have a plan before coming here except for running away. I still don't have a plan. Other than starting a new life, minus a shitty ex-husband, of course." Briar puffs out a small chuckle.

"Darlin' . . ." I cross the space between us and set my bottle down, cupping her face in both palms. "You've got me now. Forget all of it, fuck all of them. I'm not going anywhere, and I'll protect you with every last breath I've got."

CHAPTER 33

Briar

"What is this?" I pant against Storm's mouth as he carries me wrapped around him through the house. Somehow, we always seem to go from zero to a hundred in the blink of an eye. "What are we even doing?"

He sets me down, then roughly tugs my sweater over my head.

I allow him to do so, making no effort to stop where things are headed, even though the rational part of my brain is still protesting. As the material pulls free of my hair, my eyes bounce around rapidly, taking in our surroundings.

We're now in a very fancy, fully tiled, modern bathroom.

"What am I to you?" My gaze fixes on his handsomeness, filling the space in front of where he's seated me beside the handbasin. Is there any chance this man feels as deeply for me as I do for him?

"Does it matter?"

"After everything we just shared? I think it does now." I'm in so fucking deep, and this is the moment I've been dreading. The part where he realizes being with me is not worth the hassle it will undoubtedly bring to his life.

His business. His livelihood. What would revealing our true

connection do to all of that? I'd undoubtedly ruin it all, just like I always do for anyone who has the misfortune of getting close to me. And then this man is going to hate me just as deeply as everyone else in my life does.

Storm fists my hair, yanking my head back. "You're mine. You belong to me, darlin.'"

That sharp tug sends a straight line to my pussy.

"Is that enough assurance for you?" His voice is low and gritty, churning my body into a fiery need for him.

"Where have you been hiding this sparkling art of conversation?" I toss him an exaggerated roll of my eyes. Absolutely being a brat because, right now, this scalding tension between us feels like it's about to boil over. "All those years of dating, and those are the best sentiments you can come up with?"

The man in front of me makes a rough noise, his eyes flashing with something entirely dangerous for my health. He's sinfully hot, ruggedly so.

I want this man to do very, very bad things to me.

"Women don't want to date me, darlin.'" He shoves my knees wide, wedging himself in between my legs.

"I'm the guy they rebound with after their ex dumped them." Calloused fingers swoop around my rib cage, deftly unhooking my bra before dragging it off me.

"I'm the one-night stand, revenge sex." As he leans closer still and hovers over me, my nipples tighten and beg him to make contact, our noses nearly touching.

"I'm the bad decision at one a.m. that your parents warned you about."

"Lucky my parents don't give a shit. Both are dead."

"All the more reason for your *uncle* to warn you then."

"But you're not that . . . are you?"

Those two blue pools, lined with streaks of silver and the faintest hints of copper, stare down at me with sanity-stealing intensity.

"No. No, I'm not." One hand returns to my hair, and the other slides over my chest until he collars my throat. Wrapping me in a firm hold, his name stamped in ink settling over the column of my neck in the way I crave so much, a move that leaves me sucking in a ragged breath.

I love having his hand there.

I love the possessive weight of his cuff on my wrist.

I love him.

"Darlin', I'm the man who is dreaming about you when I finally snatch a moment of sleep." He licks a line of wetness across his bottom lip. "The rest of the time, I'm thinking about you every goddamn waking hour of my day."

He squeezes and tenses his fingers ever so slightly, with corresponding unfurling petals of desire blooming within my core in response to his touch. Liquid heat pools and gathers to the point that I'm dangerously close to begging.

"I can't tell you what this is, Briar, because I've never felt this way with anyone. What I can tell you is that I don't want to let you slip through my fingers all because of some bullshit like worrying about what other fucking people might think. There's been so much of my life already wasted because of that, but then again, maybe I was just waiting for you to come along and turn my entire world on its axis."

His words hang in the air between us. My throat struggles to work down a swallow beneath his palm, and his pupils swell, feeling the movement under his fingers.

"That's quite some speech you had tucked away there," I whisper.

"We done talking?"

Biting down on my lip, I study him for a moment. Then nod. "Thought so."

His strong finger traces a line straight down my chest, between the valley of my breasts, down the softness of my stomach, until he reaches the high waistband of my leggings.

There's so much dangerous heat behind the fixation he has on the path he's just carved along my body that I feel hollowed out and entirely at his mercy. He's staring at the thin fabric as if it might simply combust beneath the weight of his stare, until he roughly shoves his fingers beneath the top, and my stomach caves.

"That first night . . ." With the tip of his tongue pressed against the front of his teeth, he blows out a long breath. That deep voice is rough, thrilling me and enthralling me as he digs his hold further down, inserting his tattooed knuckles between my overheated skin and the stretched fabric. "You took these off and fucking ruined me."

This man sounds like he's bound up in some sort of torturous trance, and I'm responsible for the hell he's been enduring. His tone is coarse. Harsh.

The way those words hit me sends goosebumps flying in all directions, and a wicked desire winds tighter low in my belly.

Storm chooses that moment to strike. His grip is demanding; the rapid-fire punishing movements are just as ragged and desperate as my breathing when he damn near rips the leggings off me. My body rocks from side to side, and I swear I hear stitching tear at the seams as he pulls and shoves and manhandles me like his only purpose is to have me naked within seconds.

To use me.

Holy shit, that feeling is liquid and drugging. Being at the mercy of this man is a position I hope to hell and back that I'm able to remain in, gladly so.

The moment I'm revealed to him, left flushed and naked and on display, he balls the material up and throws it somewhere.

"You want to learn something, darlin'?" As always, when those words that I'm addicted to hearing descend to a lower octave, my stomach swoops.

My tongue runs over my lips, and I make a soft noise of agreement in the back of my throat.

"Go and get your phone." His blue eyes flare as he looks my naked figure up and down, then reaches out to rub one thumb over my mouth. "Got something to paint these pretty lips with?"

Well, shit.

I practically whimper as a bolt of desire hits my clit and my heartbeat pulses between my thighs. Somewhere amid everything, my head moves in the semblance of a nod, and I slip off the counter to go in search of my bag. Perhaps my sanity while I'm at it.

This is how much of a perfect, obedient plaything I want to be for my cowboy, I'm butt naked and fully prepared to roam through this ranch in nothing but his leather cuff as I go in search of my belongings.

Except, this man. This. Fucking. Man. He's already one step ahead of any game I might have been playing because I emerge from the freshly remodeled bathroom and see not only is the attached bedroom perfectly made up with sheets and pillows and a fluffy comforter, but my bag sits on the bench positioned at the foot of the bed.

A smile dances on my lips as I ransack through the contents, seeing exactly what he requested, and it couldn't be more perfect for this moment.

Turns out the tube of bright crimson lipstick I purchased on a whim on a random Tuesday months ago—lipstick I've never actually worn, instead leaving it to roll around the bottom of my handbag because I felt insecure as soon as I walked away from the cashier—is going to make her debut in the most deliciously wicked manner.

My heart is hammering with excitement and nerves and a little trepidation as I reenter the bathroom. In the time I've been gone, Storm has ditched his shirt and is slowly working on loosening his belt.

I nearly stumble, my knees pretty much giving out, as my

eyes race all over his naked chest, his tattoos, his V leading below the waistband of his jeans.

"Paint those lips for me." The look he hits me with is pure sex. Occasionally, in brief moments like this one right here, I'm reminded just how much more experienced this man is compared to me. Before now, it might have faltered my belief that this cowboy actually wants me.

Tonight, I have no such lingering question marks hanging over my head.

Feeling the caress of his cuff and his gaze, I walk over to the mirror and set my phone on the surface. Within a second, his muscled shoulders fill the reflection, looming prominently at my back.

I'm preening on the inside as my fingers tug the glossy black casing apart and twist the lipstick to reveal the untouched, perfectly crisp slant of the tip.

My eyes flick up to snag on his own in the mirror, and the pulse that was already hammering in my neck doubles in intensity. He's watching everything like a starving man presented with a feast after weeks lost in the desert.

In the mirrored surface, my breasts are full and heavy, with tightly furled nipples; his leather cuff is the only item adorning my body, and fuck, if it doesn't look so sinfully good.

Bracing one hand on the marble, I lean toward the mirror, giving every bit of me that I know he wants to see on display, for him alone.

As I start to drag the brilliant rouge over my bottom lip, the arch of my spine sticks my ass out, and allows my tits to spill forward. They hang, rounded and aching and squeezed together in an act that I hope screams from the rooftops how desperately I want him to suck and lick and pinch the sensitive peaks until I can't see straight.

When I move to glide the red over my top lip, highlighting

that cupid's bow, I hear it. The clank of metal signals the moment my cowboy is done with watching and waiting.

"On your knees." He lets his eyes drop to the floor, where a cloudlike plush mat cushions my toes. Indicating exactly where he wants me.

I turn, then sink down in front of him and wait, eager and nervous all in the same measure.

Storm grabs my phone and the lipstick I left on the counter, and just as I'm unsure why he needs the second item, he turns the camera on my bared breasts. Each nipple tightens immediately. My breathing hitches.

With one hand he begins filming, while with the other, he marks across the center of my chest in bold, crimson strokes.

Mine.

A dark noise of satisfaction fills the echoing space, and he tosses the capped tube in the washbasin at my back.

"Look at you." Strong fingers pinch my jaw as he examines my mouth. "Stick out your tongue."

As I hastily let my jaw drop wide and present my tongue for him, I can see he's being careful with the camera. It's trained down my body, more than up; whether or not my face is in the frame, I'm unable to tell, but it seems as if he's purposely trying to avoid it. Not that I care if my face is shown, but it's something that makes me fall even harder, tumbling wildly into deeper depths, because he cares enough to at least ensure if someone saw this video, my identity wouldn't be obvious.

"You take my dick so well, did you know that?" he murmurs, and the inherent praise in those few words all but guarantees I'll do anything he asks of me.

With his free hand, he pushes his briefs down, letting his cock bob free, long and veined, tempting me into sluttier waters when I catch sight of his leaking tip.

The fact that he's already this turned on by me, for me . . . I simply can't wait to show him how much that means.

"Flatten your tongue, hold it there for me."

Of course, I do just that.

Then he fists himself and glides across my waiting, gaping mouth. Allowing the velvety, musky heat of him to coat my senses and drive me insane because all I want to do is start sucking him, but he lets the weight of his cock rest there as he continues to thicken and lengthen and rub on me as if I'm nothing more than a hole for him to play with. It's that image that unravels me real quick. I can't help but make desperate little pleading noises.

"Goddamn. Your mouth was made for this. That's it—wrap those perfect lips around me so I can make a mess of you." As he speaks, he positions the camera to focus on the place where his thick length enters me, and I allow myself to form a ring with my mouth, closing around him as he lets out a groan. Now, I've got permission to blow him properly, and I'm determined to drive him out of his mind with pleasure.

I'm determined to put on a show.

My hands seek out his waistband, and I tug to drag his jeans over the slope of his firm ass, which allows me to peel his briefs lower.

Tilting my eyes up, I slide off his length and note, with a warm, glowing explosion of sparks inside my chest, that there's a red ring left behind from where my mouth was.

"Fuck, that looks so hot." His words echo my thoughts.

I lean forward and suck one of his balls gently, drawing it past my lips, and his entire body jerks as he draws in a sharp breath. I let go before using my tongue to sloppily trace the veined underside of his shaft, then dipping down to repeat the process on the other side.

"Put me back in your mouth." He sounds more desperate now, like he's unraveling, too. Even though my knees and thighs are already starting to burn a little, I'm nothing but determined.

With one hand curled around his waistband, now slung low

on his pelvis, I wrap my fingers around him and guide him to my mouth. Taking my time to swirl my tongue over the leaking head and roam my painted lips along the base before swallowing him down.

The noise he makes is filthy and delicious and I want to hear it so many more times.

"Your hot little tongue feels like heaven."

As I hollow out my cheeks and set to work, I feel his fingers slip into my hair.

Fuck, yes.

He must hear my sound of relief humming around his length, because at that moment he takes over.

Now it's all about him thrusting past my lips and pushing into my mouth as his fingers tense, stinging my scalp a little as he pulls on the strands.

"Keep those pretty eyes on me."

I do as he says without hesitation.

His face is half in shadow. He might have looked severe if I didn't know how much this act is the way he shows he adores me, even while I'm on my knees worshiping him. Before Storm, before any of this, I didn't know what it was like to feel this way.

"Such a good girl." His grip is ruthlessly tight in my hair, and I melt beneath that firm, possessive hold. "That face might look innocent, but you know how to be dirty, don't you?"

This time, he plunges further into my mouth, filling me, hitting the back of my throat as I gag around him. Spit starts to collect at the corners of my mouth, and oh my god, my pussy is a throbbing mess of desire.

My cowboy keeps praising me, talking me through all the ways I look like his perfect little toy, how good I am at taking his cock, and how I'm so sexy just like this. All while continuing to fist my hair and fuck my throat until my eyes are watering and drool runs down my chin.

"Look at how your tits bounce for me, how those pupils blow out every time you choke around me. I can see how much you love being owned like this."

I moan around his length, feeling him swell and pulse at the sensation.

"You always look sexy, but this might just be my favorite sight, darlin'. Puffy lips and smeared lipstick and tears just for me."

With my eyes fixed on him, fingers clutching the base of him, and my other hand clinging to the fly of his jeans, I try to plead for relief. Everything is so tightly coiled inside me, it feels like I'm going to fly out of my head any second now.

"You're wet, aren't you?" His words roughen as he's getting close. "*Mmm*, I bet you want permission to finger yourself?"

CHAPTER 34

Briar

Wetness coats my cheeks and my chin, providing the undeniable truth that I'm absolutely the mess he tells me I am.

"I bet you want to touch yourself so bad, knowing you haven't got anything on . . . It would be so easy for you just to slip a finger in and get yourself off . . . You're already slick and soaking. Bet you can feel it dripping down."

The porny sound I make around his cock doesn't even sound like me, as all I can do is swallow around his tip and continue to beg with my eyes.

"Go on then. Make yourself come. You've already got a wet cunt, desperate for me to fill you up." My relief is palpable as I lap with my tongue and hollow my cheeks while one hand dives between my thighs.

"Rub your clit while you suck my cock. That's it, darlin' . . . Shatter for me." Storm drives me out of my mind, with each word scalding me, coating me in a wicked blanket of attention and praise. "Fuck, you look so gorgeous on your knees, red lips wrapped around my dick."

His filthy words and the heady delight of finally getting

to touch myself all combine to toss me over the edge almost instantly.

As I whimper and convulse, Storm drags me off his length by my hair, openly devouring the way I look an absolute mess, all for him. I stare back, enraptured, with my mouth hanging wide, panting. Through glazed eyes, I struggle to focus, but I don't want to miss a single second of the way he watches my fingers, an urgent, desperate touch that keeps massaging my clit as I hunger for both my comedown and *more*.

Storm devours every circling movement, giving me the kind of look that makes me feel as though I'm wearing a beautiful gown and we're dancing together under the moonlight somewhere.

Not like I'm naked, kneeling on the floor, sloppy, and panting for his dick.

"*Fuck*, you're so perfect." He lets go of my hair and uses a thumb to swipe at my damp cheeks, then over my messy lips and chin, thoughtfully pausing a long second to drag my bottom lip down. I'm not sure what will come next, but he stops filming and pockets my phone. "You're gonna let me fuck you in front of that mirror, just like I've wanted and craved and gone nearly damn insane for ever since I first laid eyes on you."

With the sound that just burst out of me, I just confirmed exactly how much that idea is my kind of heaven, too.

Strong palms lift me off my knees, and his mouth covers mine in a branding kiss that steals the last remaining pieces of sanity I have left. Somewhere in my mind, once upon a time, I thought guys would never want to kiss me after I had them in my mouth. I'd been led to believe so many untruths about my body and myself, and one by one, Storm keeps dismantling those falsehoods, tossing them into the flames, allowing me to watch on as they burn to ash.

His fingers collar the front of my neck as his tongue slides against mine, and I simply melt. My hands run everywhere: over his chest, over his arms, along his powerful shoulders and sides. I'm so hungry for this man—I just want to be *his* and let him take everything he wants, again and again.

He draws away from my mouth with an anguished noise, spinning my body with such force I'm left stumbling against his chest. He positions us both so that we're standing in front of the mirror, taking in our joint reflections. Behind me, Storm looks absolutely feral, and I'm starry-eyed, with mussed hair and a mouth that looks downright sinful. All my lipstick has worn off, but my lips are swollen and flushed to match my cheeks.

As we pause there, chests heaving, he snakes both hands around me to cup my breasts, pinching and plucking at my nipples in that way he does so expertly. They're sensitive and agonizingly in need of his attention. So when he tortures them and squeezes my flesh, I simply sag against his torso with whimpering relief.

"Watch," he orders, then fastens his mouth over my neck and damn near devours me all along that sensitive curve of flesh. The movement is a forceful pulse of need and savage wanting, leaving my body bowing and almost buckling beneath the weight of his mouth. Storm bites and sucks on my pulse point, the point where my shoulder and throat meet, then back up to just below my ear.

The entire time, his blue eyes drill into mine, fearsome and potent and so sexy I can hardly breathe.

"I want to fill all your holes." His lips find my ear as his skilled touch continues to lavish my nipples with attention and tug on my breasts. "You'd look so good stretched out for me, wouldn't you?"

The question is downright wicked, leading me forward with an assurance as to what I'd like and what my body might enjoy when I truly have no idea. I'd barely gotten my head around someone truly desiring me enough to want to have sex with me.

Now, he's offering the kinds of pleasures I've only ever wondered about.

Yet, with him, I don't even have to think twice.

I trust him.

Humming in agreement, I tilt my head further, giving greater access because this is, without a doubt, the only thing I need. Oxygen is irrelevant when the only sustenance I require is Stôrmand Lane's mouth on my body.

One of those searing hot palms finds the back of my neck, and he guides me to bend forward for him, bracing myself on my elbows—so close to the mirror my breath starts to fog the glass—then he glides that heated touch along the curvature of my spine until he reaches my ass.

"Wait right there. Don't move." He's only gone for a brief moment, and even though my body is limp and heavy with pleasure, my mind sprints in frantic laps around this entire ranch in the space of time it takes him to leave this bathroom and return.

When he comes back, he's fully naked.

He also has something in his fist, the sight of which makes my core clench.

My vibrator.

For a moment, before this man reenters the room and closes the gap between us, he stands there, seemingly transfixed. Staring at the sight of me, bent over and all too eagerly exposed for him.

The scrutiny and intimacy of it all leaves me squirming.

"Storm—I—"

He's left me feeling nothing but confident in my body the entire time we've tumbled into whatever this thing is between us, but right now, I'm very aware that my ass has stretch marks, my hips have silver lines streaking over them, and my thighs are wobbly and dimpled. And he's standing right there looking like he's been carved from marble and should be displayed on a pedestal erected in the memory of the world's most handsome cowboy to ever exist.

"Shhh, darlin' . . ." He grabs a handful of my ass and drops down behind me. "Fuck, I've wanted to replay this moment. Do you know how messed up you had me?" His nose nudges along that track of soft flesh leading up from the back of my thigh. I feel the warmth of his breath, the slightest touch of metal from his nose ring. "Do you have any idea the filthy goddamn things I wanted to do to you from the second I saw you? This body has been the only thing I could think about, even when I shouldn't have. Even when there wasn't supposed to ever be anything between us, you had control over me." Those words are chased by a wet glide of an exploring tongue and harsh scrape of stubble roaming up that most delicate, tender part of the inside of my thigh.

His hot exhale gusts over my skin as I shudder and whimper each time that beard scratches the sensitive spot so close to my pussy.

"So let me enjoy teasing you." *Lick*. "Keep that cuff on so I can play with you anytime I like." *Kiss*. "Give me every inch of your body to explore a thousand times, and it won't ever be enough."

Storm's mouth closes over my pussy from behind, and I'm a mess of noises as sensations ripple through my bloodstream. He dives into me, turning my entire world on its head as he does so.

"Oh god."

The control this man emits tugs me into a place where I can only succumb to sensation. The glass in front of my nose and mouth repeatedly fogs as my sharp exhales and whimpers react to his teasing.

As that familiar quiet buzzing noise starts up, he runs the wand up my inner thigh until he finds my clit.

I'm so gone that I don't know whether I'm going to dissolve or evaporate. My body isn't even mine any longer; it's all his, and he knows it.

"This speed, hmmm?" he says against my core as I writhe and chase the way he drags the toy over me, then slips it inside my entrance, fucking me with it slowly. "You like that one, don't you."

It's not even a question. He just *knows*.

Shudders roam through me, and sparks fly everywhere, as my toes curl against the floor and my fingers claw at the smooth, cool counter.

"Storm. Fuck. *Please*."

He's wicked, teasing me, building me higher and higher, but never quite allowing the pleasurable sensations to remain attentive in one place long enough to let me come.

Then his mouth moves at the same time as he roams the vibe back over to position it against my clit.

His tongue glides a hot, wet trail up my ass, and I let out a gasp mixed with a deep groan.

"*Fuckohgodfuck*." All I can do is babble out a string of whimpers as he spreads me with one hand, swirling and licking and pressing his mouth against my hole, lighting up my body as those sensitive nerve endings come to life. I've never experienced anything approaching this, and he knows exactly how to keep me out of my head and from tensing up, because the rippling vibration against my clit is spinning me entirely out of orbit.

With the firm but gentle press of his tongue into my ass, and the rhythm against my aching bud of nerves, he ensures I disintegrate for him. My climax rolls up from my toes, leaving me shaking and coming apart on a long wail.

I haven't yet returned back down from wherever that orgasm just took me when I see he's right there behind me. His cock slides forward, pushing inside my pussy while I'm still clenching and rippling, and holy fuck, it feels so good to finally be full.

As he groans out the most delicious, rumbling noise I could repeatedly drink down, his heat and powerful body take over, shifting me and encouraging me with a firm hand to move up so that I'm on my elbows and my toes barely touch the floor, a position that leaves my spine perfectly arched to let him drive in deep. One of his hands runs the vibrator across my tits, and I'm a whining, boneless mess of pleasure.

God, the deep, primal cursing grunt of satisfaction he lets out is a sound I'm never going to forget.

"These fucking tits." He tortures my nipples over and over as he slowly thrusts in and out. "I've wanted to fuck them since that first night."

"*Please.*" I want that, I want him, I want anything if it means more of this.

He moves the buzzing sensation away, back down to the wetness between my thighs, but instead of homing back in on my clit like I'm expecting him to, he shifts his weight back. With his free hand, he grips my ass cheek and spreads me wide once more.

I pulse around his length as he withdraws right to the tip and moves the vibe over my ass. The feeling back there, while his cock is inside me, is unreal. My body shudders and shivers beneath him.

"That's it, darlin' . . . . Enjoy the way it feels with your favorite toy teasing your sweet little ass. I just know you'd take me perfectly there. You'd love the full-body orgasm, and you'd look so beautiful, shattering for me with my cock filling your tight little hole," he murmurs hotly while thrusting in and out of my channel, driving me insane with the vibrations rolling over my ring of sensitive nerve endings. Storm doesn't try to press inside; he's just resting himself there, letting the unfamiliar sensation feel so damn good that I'm entirely lost. "It's nothing to feel worried about, baby, and we'd go as slow as you want."

I'm pretty certain that I start pleading for him to just do it right here and now.

There's no doubt in my mind I want everything with him. It's not just sex; it's being with him, trusting him, and being cared for by him.

A groan leaves his chest as we both feel the surge of this climax bearing down on us. My pussy squeezes, and I'm whimpering, begging.

"Jesus. Fuck. I can't stop with you. I can't ever fucking stop." He tosses the toy, still buzzing, into the handbasin and wraps his big palms beneath my body. Storm drives into me so hard my hips bruise against the ledge of the counter, and my orgasm bursts, leaving me slumped as he holds me in position and pumps deep, his cock surging and unloading with a hot release buried inside my pussy.

He drapes himself over me, both our chests heaving, and fumbles to turn off the vibrator while covering my shoulders with wet kisses.

Can I still feel my legs? I'm not even sure.

I'm so blissed out, drowsy, and drifting somewhere far, far out of my body. Storm hums with delicious, rich noise.

"You've done so well . . . You can go to sleep, and I'll stay inside you just like this." He's tempting me with such wickedness, yet he knows exactly how that lures me to succumb to his devious plans.

"I don't think I could, with you playing with my nipples like that," I mumble on a soft little breath as he groans and keeps shifting his hips, sounding so unbelievably sexy. Everything is hot, and our skin runs damp with sweat. His cum starts to drip out between us as Storm keeps on shifting at my back. Of course, he melts my brain even further when he reaches down to swipe up that slickness and rubs it over my nipples.

Our gazes lock in the mirror, and that filthy move leaves my eyes glazed over as a gentle moan drops past my lips. The smeared evidence of his mark across my chest still lingers in red lipstick, and my heart crawls to curl up in his hands.

His.

CHAPTER 35

Storm

Sending Briar back in the morning after the kind of night we just shared wasn't exactly my plan. Every part of me insisted she stay—I damn well planned on threatening bloody murder in order to keep her right here, to park her shitty little rental car up, and tuck her by my side.

Except the whip-smart thing she is, my girl knew she needed to be at the cabin. That on the off chance her "fuck face of a sister"—Briar's own words—decided to turn up, uninvited and unannounced, trying to explain our absences would be much worse for all of us.

So I was left pacing and making my best effort to wear holes in Beau's perfectly finished floorboards of his ranch, in a futile attempt to carry on with all the shit I need to do today.

All the while, my mind has been, and is, firmly with her.

Every aspect of the past forty-eight hours has upended things. Tipped the scales to make it clear what does and doesn't fucking matter to me.

I nearly damn well told her everything last night as she curled up against my chest, nearly confessed how fucking brutally gone I am for her. The only thing that stopped me was knowing that Briar has more important shit to deal with than me blurting out that I'm in love with her.

She's had enough thrown her way; my stupid little sentiments can wait. Briar Lane deserves to be told she's loved and adored and has me damn well wrapped around her little finger when we're someplace special.

Not in the middle of a half-furnished ranch with paint cans and dust cloths draped around us like shrouds.

There's also the matter of timing.

What I would give to be able to freely tell her everything, without the conversation from the kitchen hanging over our heads. Not two seconds after revealing all my bullshit past, all my crappy decisions, and not when I just told her about the worst damn time in my life.

Briar deserves so much more than someone like me, but damn, there's absolutely no way I'm going to give her up.

I'm a selfish asshole like that.

The ghosts of my past came racing out of that hidden box last night, and at least she didn't run from me once she found out. It's hard enough coming to terms with the stranger who I don't even remember, wearing a ring I presumably gave her while blind drunk, signing on the bottom line to hitch herself to my life when I wanted nothing to do with her.

That sort of clusterfuck is especially tough to reconcile when that so-called estranged wife decides to overdose in the tub and leave a note insinuating that it was my fault.

As if she wasn't busy chasing another man who only wanted to keep her as a dirty secret, a hole to fuck on the side. As if I wasn't already so long shot of her, we hadn't spoken other than through lawyers in years before she ended things.

Her one decision tanked my entire career, taking the only thing I had, the only thing I was good at, and tearing it apart the moment she made that fateful choice that she didn't want to carry on any longer.

The worst part of it all, other than being a needless, senseless death of an impressionable young woman, was that she wasn't trying to hurt *me* by ending things.

I just happened to be the unlucky asshole who the hammer of public judgment fell upon.

As I shove my hat on my head and toss the few tools I prefer to keep with me in the back of my truck, the sun sets behind the pink mountains in the distance. The evening air is cool and crisp in my lungs as I blow out a breath that turns white before me. Crimson Ridge herself glows more burnt umber than red at this time of night, with spring on its way. High in the faded light, the crescent moon reveals itself as a thin silver line. It's one of those clear-skied evenings where the stars begin to pop out and wink one by one the longer I gaze up at them.

I want to be able to show this to Briar.

I want to lie here, in the flatbed of my truck, with her wrapped in my arms, and count the stars as they show up.

She's my person. The girl that all these sorts of meaningless, simple moments are meant to be shared with. Not experienced on my own like I've done for so long now, but with her tucked against my chest, where she'll no doubt tell me the names of the stars appearing before us because she's smart as hell and knows so many things like that. Even if she shrugs off her knowledge and pretends it's no big deal.

Maybe tomorrow, I'll lay it all out.

I can cook her breakfast, make her coffee with the almond creamer she prefers, and sit her ass down at the table that I only ever want to sit at when directly across from her, and I'll tell her.

Or maybe I'll just outright burst through that door and blurt the words. Simply beg her to stay with me. To put it all on the line. I've got absolutely fuck all to give her, but she might take a chance on a broken old asshole and choose not to leave.

My chest squeezes as I settle inside my truck, readjust my hat, and then start the ignition.

314

It's only ever her that I see in these brief, quiet inhales. Thoughts of our time together over the past weeks fly in, consuming everything.

The second my hand finds the slope of her waist from behind, my pulse begins to thunder. Briar stands in the kitchen, another assortment of twigs in hand, as she fills a water glass from the faucet. The same one that has doubled as her vase and has sat on the table beside the window since she arrived.

"Flowers," she hums, tilting her head to one side as I fit myself against her spine. That small movement allows my lips to brush up the curve of her neck with ease.

I stand at her back, like the lovesick fool I am, watching her fuss with the handful of branches. Just like she's done so many times since first arriving here. A little ritual she carries out seemingly every few days. These flowers have small buds on them, but since it's still early spring and snow's still on the ground, they're nowhere near close to blooming yet.

"Flowers?" One of my hands braces against the counter as I curl around her from behind. "Even though it's technically spring out there, it's practically winter still, darlin'."

She makes a point of grumbling, and I can't help the smile that forms against her neck. "They might not look like it right now, but eventually, one day, these will be spring flowers."

"Right now . . . they still look like twigs in a cup," I tease.

Briar huffs in the way she does; it's a cute little frustrated noise I love hearing her make whenever she's inwardly rolling her eyes at me.

"Back in LA, everything was fake. The smiles, the flowers, the supposed antiques. Nothing was ever real." She starts to carefully arrange a dozen lengths that look to be cut from a shrub she found outside.

"To me . . . it feels like home when there are fresh flowers. It means someone cares enough to make a place beautiful with something that isn't practical."

"You want this place to feel like home." It's not really a question, more of an observation, as I rest my chin on her shoulder and watch her fingers move the angles and positioning of everything around until she seems satisfied before adding a little more water.

"I want this place to feel special."

I've been lost inside my thoughts for the entire drive back up the mountain. When I pull up outside the cabin, I see the light spilling from the interior, and to my relief, it's just my girl there. On hearing my truck arrive, Briar's right there in an instant, opening the door to greet me, a smile brightening her features.

This right here is it.

This is how I want to feel every time I pull up and crank that hand brake, and it's a sensation that settles in my chest, warm and secure.

Coming home to be with her is the fucking prize.

Knowing that Briar's goodness and sweetness fill every inch of space inside that cabin—yeah, that shit swells inside my chest, like a firelight glowing, too.

CHAPTER 36

Briar

"*Mmmfuck*. Grab my hair, darlin.'"

That deep voice I'm addicted to breaks through my dream. Half-asleep, my body rides wave after wave of pleasure before I find myself nudged away from slumber and dragged into a waking state.

Under the command of Storm's tongue.

He hums against my clit, and of course, I do exactly as he instructs me to. My hands find a sleepy path to settle in his hair, threading my fingers, while my hips shift and lift beneath his mouth.

"Good girl." He licks and sucks and speaks into me as my legs start shaking. Proving just how long this man has been between my thighs while I've been asleep.

My cowboy doesn't let up on his assault, groaning and running the wet glide of his tongue up the inner swell of my thigh before he climbs up the bed to spoon my languid figure from behind, hitches one leg, and slides into me.

I'm soaked and swollen, and my body is so ready to welcome him inside already.

The way he uses me so perfectly is insanely hot.

"God, it's too much." My voice is raspy, and I absolutely don't mean a word I'm saying. The fact this man has been eating my pussy while I've been sleeping is filthy, and I'm more than hopeful he'll treat me to this special kind of depravity every morning.

"Too much? You didn't seem to think so when I had you riding my face at three a.m."

The moans coming out of me are borderline pornographic.

"*Mmmm.* That's exactly what you sounded like, too. Except much, much louder."

"You're going to kill me."

"That tight little pussy of yours disagrees. The way you keep clamping down harder says you don't want me to stop."

Storm keeps thrusting his hips against mine, stretching me, filling me, leaving me clutching the sheets, helplessly spun out of my mind with pleasure. The sounds of filthy, wet fucking are the soundtrack to this moment, along with skin slapping against skin, and the scent of sex wraps around us.

I'm oh so close to losing it when a sharp noise, a jarring bang—oh god, a car door slamming—bursts in on our private moment.

"Briar?" Hardly a few seconds later, there's an insistent rapping of knuckles against wood to accompany the muffled sound of my name, followed by the thud of the door swinging shut.

My sister's voice carries through the house, louder this time, as I hear her dumping her coat and bag. Of course she let herself in.

"You didn't lock the door earlier?" I let out something between a whisper and a gasp.

"Didn't exactly think we'd get interrupted at this time of the morning," Storm whispers back. I scrunch my eyes, because bless him for getting up at the crack of dawn to stoke the fire, but damn him for forgetting to lock the door after fetching more wood.

"Briar, I swear to god, if you're still in bed . . ."

My entire body clenches up. Meanwhile, the man at my back remains buried inside me, still slowly pumping his hips, fucking me from behind, seemingly without any intention of stopping.

"Tell her to go away, or I'm going to walk out there butt naked and tell her myself." He nips my ear and tightens his hold on my upper thigh, making it impossible for me to do anything but remain pinned in place.

"I just got out of the shower, Cris. Give me a few minutes to get dressed." My pussy ripples and pulses, giving away just how my body reacts to exactly this kind of risky moment.

Storm makes a wicked noise, a quiet laugh, feeling everything.

"Fine," Cris grumbles. "Hurry up. It's medieval that there's no cell phone reception here. I had to drive all this way just to find you moping around."

At my ear, there's another delicious noise. I can only imagine what the man owning my body is thinking right at this moment.

"Where's Uncle Stôrmand?"

Shit. *Shit.*

This time I really do begin to panic. It sounds like she's walking closer. All the while, I can feel the crest of another orgasm coming up to claim me.

This is so messed up.

"You gonna tell her where I am?" he whispers, lips fastened against my neck. "That I'm balls deep inside your pretty little cunt?"

I'm unable to stop tightening around him on reflex. Goosebumps fly across my arms.

"Uhh, I don't know where he is," I say to Crispin. The door to the bedroom hangs wide open, and I can't drag my eyes away from the gaping wooden frame. "He didn't come back here last night."

"Then why is his truck parked outside?" Her icy tone floats through the few feet separating us from where she stands in the lounge.

Fuck, right now, this right here is the moment I completely freak out.

Storm slows his movements, but only just. His warm, hot mouth stays pressed against my ear. One giant palm slides up to my tits, plucking and strumming my nipples as if he's got all the time in the world, not like my sister is about two seconds away from bursting in, as she could so easily decide to walk in here at any moment.

"Tell her I was out with friends, Briar," he instructs, all the while torturing me and pleasuring me to the point I can't see straight.

"He . . . he went out with friends, I think. They came and picked him up. Maybe he crashed there." My teeth sink into my bottom lip to catch the whimpering noise threatening to climb up my throat because as I stumble my way through the lie, he starts tugging on my nipples, hard.

Just the way he knows I love them to be handled.

"Jesus." His rich, rumbling sound leaves a shudder roaming straight down my spine. "Feel how close you are . . . Bet you wanna milk me fucking dry, to get every last drop, the way you're gripping me like a fist."

"Oh my god," I silently chant the words over and over.

"Bet he was with one of his whores." My sister makes an ugly sound in the back of her throat.

He hums, not sounding pissed off—in fact, he sounds extremely self-satisfied.

"If only she knew. I've got my own pretty little slut right here." Teeth scrape my neck, and his palm slips down between my thighs. "My perfect, beautiful thing who wears my cuff, my hat, and was made to take my cock." He sucks on my earlobe and rubs my slickness all over my clit, and I nearly forget everything about why I have to be quiet, barely hanging on by a fraying thread, instead of straight-up moaning out loud.

My sister continues to loiter. The sound of pacing footsteps on the wooden floor and the sound of cupboards opening and closing as she pokes around tells me exactly where she is in the kitchenette.

Storm is intentionally dragging this out; he knows how unbelievably close I am, and there's no chance he's going to let me come until my sister leaves.

Letting out a frustrated noise, Crispin stamps her foot. "For pity's sake, Briar, I'm not waiting around while you take all day. I'll meet you at that awful cafe in town for breakfast, and we're talking about you coming home."

She starts moving away. For the love of god, I hope the sound of the door shutting and her car engine is going to come any second now.

Except, the door opens, and there's no familiar thud to indicate that she finally left.

"Oh my god, will she ever leave?" I gasp, fists balling up in the sheets when he picks up the pace, seemingly unconcerned that our intruder hasn't yet departed. My mouth turns into his arm beneath my head, and my teeth connect with his skin. There's no other way I can stop myself from whining or crying out.

"His boots are here," she calls out.

There's too much suspicion in her voice.

I can't hold on much longer, but I somehow spit out a reply. One that hopefully tells her to fuck right off. "Pretty sure he's got more than one pair of boots, you know."

Storm curses something rich and approving, then starts pumping into me, sinking as deep as he can go.

Stars form behind my eyes.

"Fine, whatever. God, you need to sort your shit out and get out of bed earlier in the day. I always knew you were lazy, but this is next level, Briar."

The door slams.

Behind me, there's a growl, a deep noise that rumbles straight from his chest that's pressed against my back.

He flips us so that I'm on my hands and knees and drives into me ruthlessly.

Sweet relief floods my veins when I hear the car start and pull away.

Storm fucks me so hard, so powerfully, I'm drooling and biting down on the pillow as he tells me all the filthy things he knows I want to hear right now. That I'm his. I belong to him. I've got his cuff on, and that means he gets to own my body whenever and however he wants, his perfect little fuck toy.

"Come right fucking now. I want you to come harder than you've ever fucking come in your life."

As he fists my hair and snakes a hand round to find my clit, everything consumes me.

"That's it, my beautiful whore."

My toes curl, and a low moan rips out of me as I blank completely. White spots take over my vision and I'm pretty sure my hearing, along with my sanity, disappears.

With a groan, his hips stutter, then he buries himself as far as he can go. His cock pulses into me, throbbing inside my pussy as my climax feels like it never ends.

It's so intense that I'm left in a daze. Simply melting against the man who wraps me up in his arms. My Storm, who pulls me into his chest with murmured words and wet kisses that coat me from head to toe in nothing but the sweetest, kindest, softest embrace.

Right then and there, the words hang on my lips, and desperate need aches behind my ribs. I want to tell him how much I love him.

Yet, the familiar, awful, gnawing feeling holds me back, insipidly reminding me of a poison spreading from its source.

Uttering those words might be the truth, but it would be the worst thing I could possibly curse him with.

CHAPTER 37

Briar

I'm like a fawn on ice skates with wobbly legs as I pull up and park outside the only cafe in Crimson Ridge. The place where my sister lurks in wait for me.

My unsteadiness isn't due to trepidation, but from being so thoroughly blissed out after Storm took it upon himself to torture me in the best way possible this morning.

He knew I needed to be given the perfect kind of distraction to settle my mind and my nerves before descending into the viper pit.

My pussy is definitely a little sore. Meanwhile, I'm floating along the sidewalk on a serene ocean of contentment, no doubt with a goofy, lovesick grin on my face, as I shove my keys in my handbag.

The "death-trap rental," as my cowboy likes to call my car, came in useful once more. As much as he might want me to drive his truck, we both know I'd be a hundred times more of a crash liability if I attempted to navigate a stick shift until I've had a *lot* more practice.

What I would give for all of that and more under his steady, guiding hand.

I'm instantly drawn to thoughts of future summer evenings, lazy weekends in the sunshine, driving with the windows rolled down, and building my confidence up behind the wheel with him by my side.

He makes me feel like I could damn well sprout wings and fly to the moon if I wanted to, and I've never encountered that kind of unwavering faith in me before.

There's a glowing, glorious sensation that spreads through my chest as I imagine what a future with Storm could possibly hold.

How much I so desperately want to be with him.

In all honesty, I feel like a new woman. Before leaving the cabin, I caught a glimpse of myself in the mirror, and as I took in the sight I realized the girl looking back at me was finally the person I've always known was there on the inside.

The version of Briar Lane who is free to be herself.

This rugged, beautiful life, these mountains, they've awakened something that feels secure, settled, like warm spring rain caressing my skin. It makes all the noise that used to relentlessly buzz around in my brain ebb away, making the decision to stay here even easier.

I knew there was no way in hell I'd return to where I ran from—there was no going back.

Now, it's clear and sparkling that this life is the one I choose, the one that allows me to feel more comfortable in my skin than ever before.

As I reach the cafe door, with its cute, covered porch and jasmine vine climbing over the latticework, I pause outside so I can send a quick message to Storm, letting him know I made it safely.

Hiiii. *heart eyes*

I didn't crash.

Reporting safely from the bustling metropolis of Crimson Ridge.

I'll come meet you at the ranch as soon as I'm done here.

Wish me luck.

As I type and delete a series of kiss-face emojis—instead, opting to simply hit Send rather than terrify this gruff man by acting like a total boy-obsessed lunatic—I'm tempted to swipe over to the forbidden little secret hiding in plain sight. Thoughts of the video and all the insanely hot memories conjured whenever I let my mind drift back to that moment. I still can't hardly believe it's on my phone. That girl in the video is me, and the entire, wicked scenario, our illicit night that nobody knows about, keeps burning a hole in my pocket.

What if someone saw? Would they know who he is to me? The man's hand that distinctly shows his name, with his fingers tangled rough and brutally commanding in my hair.

At the time, I suspected, but didn't fully realize, the care he took not to show too much of my face so it would be almost impossible to tell it's me he's owning.

The only secret giveaway is my tattoo beside my breast.

Though there's next to no one in the world who knows that I have it, not even my sister.

Quickly shaking off the flood of memories, I shove my phone away in my bag and suck in a deep inhale, preparing myself to deliver the speech I've partially prepared during the drive into town.

I've got the first part down, rehearsed that shit out loud, and I'm primed to cut off whatever unhinged rampage Cris might go on.

After I inform my sister that I'm staying here and never wish to see her ever again in my life, adding the details of my lawyer she can communicate through, what I'll say might be a little less finessed, but I'm sure I'll manage.

As I push through the door, there's a tinkling bell, and my eyes flicker to the table where, what feels like a lifetime ago, I had coffee on my disastrous date with Westin Hayes.

Today, there are two guys around my age having brunch together—one has his arm affectionately draped around the back of the other's chair, and the two are laughing over a video pulled up on one of their phones. Something tugs on my heart a little, pointing at them, saying, *Hey, that could be you and the man you're head over heels for.*

Does Stôrmand Lane go for coffee? Or indulge in any kind of activity that doesn't involve chopping wood, rounding up cattle, or fitting horseshoes? You know, the kinds of mundane, trivial things that might pass for a date? Could I convince him to do something like that, with me?

There are rows of tables to my left, and the place is more or less fully occupied, with the hum and clatter of the cafe taking over my senses.

My sister's blonde hair, pulled back into a severely tight ballerina bun, is easy to spot. But, as I draw nearer to the table where she sits facing me, I want to freeze and turn around, to bolt for the door.

My eyes widen, and my throat seizes up.

However, forward momentum keeps propelling me closer even though my stomach is churning and queasiness rises within me like a putrid tide.

A man turns in his seat, designer glasses perched on his nose, dark hair perfectly styled into the look he's always favored—one that screams "Fortune 500 CEO"—a maroon cashmere sweater fitted to his lean frame.

My rat-bastard, cheating husband.

Antoine still has the audacity to wear his wedding

band—that eighteen-karat gold ring gleams at me as he gets to his feet and pulls out a chair.

I fight the urge to vomit all over his thousand-dollar loafers.

"You bitch." Ignoring the man standing before me, I want to reach across the table and claw my sister's eyes out.

"Aren't you glad to see your husband?" She empties a sachet of sweetener into her coffee before stirring the contents I so dearly wish contained arsenic.

"Briar, don't make a scene. Just take a seat." Antoine smiles at me with his unnervingly white rows of veneers. The man I am legally chained to until I handle paperwork and lawyers and all sorts of shit I haven't even begun to fathom.

Or should I say fangs.

"Why are you both here?" I carefully put as much distance between myself and Antoine as possible. My skin crawls even being this close—that sickly perfumed fragrance of his aftershave gets stuck to the back of my throat.

"Like I told you on the phone, this is not a negotiation, Briar." Cris rolls her eyes. "You're coming home with us, and it looks like we've gotten here just in time. I can't imagine the state we might have discovered you in if we'd left you squatting in that filthy hovel with *him* any longer."

If I were a Doberman, my hackles would be on end, and my razor-sharp teeth would be bared.

"I'm not going anywhere. This is home for me now. I want a divorce, and I want nothing more to do with Lane Enterprises, and—"

"That's cute and all . . ." Antoine cuts me off, his finger tapping on a Manila folder lying on the table. "But I think you'll find yourself a little more compliant in a minute or so."

My eyes shuffle between the folder and its mysterious contents, up to Antoine's poker face, and over to my sister, who sips her coffee and watches me with beady eyes.

"Anything been going on that we should know about?" Cris says. "You know, the media does love a good scandal to feast on."

"Your insinuations are boring, Crispin. Fly back to LA and focus on making someone else's life miserable for a change."

"Briar." My shitty husband tries to make himself sound important, like I'm supposed to fall in line as he's always expected me to, but I'm not in the mood for his threats.

"What are you going to do, Antoine? Pull out a series of photos your stupid PI has been running around snapping of me?" I jerk my chin at the folder, knowing there's no way anyone could have taken anything incriminating of me and Storm together.

The places we've been are far too remote, too isolated. It's not like we've been rolling around Crimson Ridge wrapped up in each other in a way that would be easy to spot.

Antoine gets a look on his face that says he's already won, and the nauseous sensation in my stomach really starts to build to a rolling boil.

He pulls out his phone from a pocket and lays it on the table in front of me. With a couple of taps of the screen, he brings up a video and my vision blurs at the edges, forming a tiny, dark tunnel. Sound distorts and fades into a faint buzzing in my ears as the recording starts to play.

"Your hot little mouth feels like heaven."

As that familiar husky voice speaks, and his name in inked lettering fills the camera frame—his fingers burying into my hair, tugging roughly, and commanding me to his bidding—I see my tattoo come into focus for the briefest second.

"You think I'd waste my time with PIs?" Antoine leans close and sneers. "It's called spyware, you dumb cunt. I've had access to everything on that phone of yours for years."

Years. Not months. Not weeks.

This man who has been fucking around behind my back our

entire sham of a marriage had me monitored. While he was busy cheating, the asshole invaded my privacy on my own cell phone.

"How do you think Crispin knew where to find your sorry ass? We've known all this time, and I gave you a chance to do this the easy way. I gave you the opportunity to make a sensible choice, but you threw all that away."

As I sit like a statue, growing more numb with every word, I see it all laid out. All the years of my life I gave up for these people. Guilted into trying to make amends for the fact my birth tore away our mother. A woman I never got to meet because the day I arrived was the day she was taken. My father begrudged me for destroying his whole world, and my sister allowed her grief to fester until she lost any semblance of humanity toward me.

So, I agreed to their business arrangements. I said yes and obliged their demands for subservience and shoved aside my own life—because I didn't deserve to live, did I?

When I'd taken away the person they loved so dearly.

It's all your fault. It would have been her birthday if it weren't for what you did.

"The jet is booked to depart at seven this evening." Antoine's voice is cold, hard, and calculating when he interrupts my desolate thoughts. He makes a disapproving noise as he stops the video, leaving me feeling entirely violated, with my head spinning, that he's had access to my phone this entire time.

"I'm not leaving." My voice barely manages to come out in a shaky whisper.

"Briar, you've always been so pathetic, when are you going to get it through your head that there are more important things than what you want?" Cris skewers me right through the heart, as always.

"No, I'm not going anywhere with you."

"Yes, you are." Antoine gets up and braces himself on the back of the chair to lean over me; he drops his mouth close to my ear, which puts his cloying fragrance over me like a gag. "I guarantee you I've already got a lineup of your father's old maids and cleaners prepared to give statements that they saw your uncle going into your bedroom when you were a minor. They'll go on record to say they found pregnancy tests in your bathroom trash while you were still underage. I'll have doctors who will say they helped you two cover up the fact he committed assault."

I'm shaking as the man carries on, eerily calm and deathly assured of his success.

"You think the negative publicity was bad when rumors flew that he played a hand in his wife's death? Just wait till I leak it to every news outlet that former pro rodeo star Stôrmand Lane was fucking his teenage niece."

Antoine taps his phone screen, bringing up the still frame from when he paused the video a moment ago, the shot clearly showing inked fingers in my hair, *STORM* tattooed on his knuckles, and the side of my breast.

"Welcome to the patriarchy, you little whore. Something you should remember is that Montgomerys will always win."

I don't know if I can think, or speak, or feel my extremities. Every part of me has become numb and hopelessly broken. I came in here with a plan, and these two lecherous creatures torpedoed that within a second.

How did I ever think I could escape their bullying, cruel existence?

"You've got until the time we're due to take off. Go pack your shit and say goodbye to your stupid horsey friends . . . And don't forget, if you even think about not getting on that jet tonight, everything I need to destroy that man is right here, ready to send with one click."

He shoves the phone under my nose once more, and while it's almost impossible to focus on the blur of text on the screen, I see enough.

Flashes of words and phrases of his prepared media release. Gross violations of Storm's personal life, none of which matters because Antoine's not interested in the truth. This man's interested in a character assassination, and he sits in control of the media narrative like a spoiled emperor child.

All of the evil untruths are there, along with screenshots from the video, ready to be distributed with one tap.

Just like he's got me pinned beneath that bony, pale thumb of his once more.

CHAPTER 38

Storm

Over the sharp, repetitive banging of nails being driven into wood, I hear a car pull up outside the barn. If I'm not nailing horseshoes into place, then I'm busy doing the kind of work that always seems to be in high demand around the various ranches that populate Crimson Ridge. Either way, for someone who spent half his life flung around on the back of a bull and thought that would be my entire career, I now spend a lot of my time with a hammer in my fist.

A smile tugs at my lips, where I've tucked the three final nails to finish securing this plank. The sharp tang of metal coats my tongue, and the faint scent of stored hay fills the air.

My eyes drift up to the open doorway of the empty space as I pluck one nail out and pinch my lips together to hold the others in place. Briar knows I'm working out here, or at least she'll pretty quickly figure it out by following the sound of hammering.

I set to work driving these last nails home, and by the time I've secured the third in place, her footsteps scuff and catch my attention.

Without fail, she always steals my attention.

Even in the short amount of time since this morning that I

haven't had her with me, nearly every thought has been full of Briar. How much I've fallen for her, how best to convince this girl to stay with me. They've rolled around on repeat inside my brain.

Does Briar want to be with me? Does she want *this* life?

Putting all bullshit complications about what others might perceive of us being together to one side—because absolutely none of that matters to me in the slightest—does this girl have any idea how badly I want her to stay?

Our lives are already entangled, just like our clothes in the bedroom we share, the same way our bodies find the ability to be at any given opportunity, and all I can think is that she belongs in my life.

I've never had a reason to grow attached to anyone, and now I can't imagine my days without her laughter, her sharp quips, her soft palm finding its home wrapped up in mine when it's just the two of us.

All of that chaos crumbles into insignificance as she draws nearer.

My eyes devour what she's wearing, openly staring because, holy fuck, Briar Lane could make angels weep with how beautiful she is.

Her hair is pulled up into a high ponytail, with a silky-looking, champagne-colored dress swishing around her knees. Cowboy boots hug her calves, making this girl look like she could be every rancher's wet dream.

Wearing my goddamn jacket.

"A dress? Don't want you getting too cold, little thorn." Fisting the hammer in one hand, I drag the back of my other across my forehead. I've been out here fixing up the stalls for the past few hours and managed to work up a sweat even though a spring chill still lingers in the air beyond those doors.

Briar reaches where I'm standing and eyes me from head to toe with a hidden little smile. "Seemed more practical for what I had in mind." Her coy shrug is cute and all, but it's an act. I fucking love that she's become so much more confident in herself and knows how to ask for what she wants.

"Doesn't look like you're interested in getting your hands dirty." I toss the hammer into my toolbox. "Maybe just your knees instead?"

Briar bites her lip. Those dark eyes glimmer at me and are once again my absolute undoing.

She hums, a gentle noise, something sensual and wonderful, and it makes me fucking ravenous for her. "Thought you might like to see what's underneath . . ."

"Oh, you thought, did you?" Resting my ass on the edge of the wooden workbench I've set up out here, I drag my girl to stand between my knees.

I tuck one hand into the small of her back beneath the loose jacket slung around her shoulders, and I use the other to hook a strand of her hair behind one ear. My girl looks up at me with a soft expression, and I'm so fucking done for. All I can do is steal the opportunity to kiss her pillowy lips because I damn well can and should be able to, any time and any place.

Briar deserves that and so much more. Sliding our tongues together and drinking down her faint, gorgeous noises of pleasure, I want her to understand this is so much more than just sex.

While that side of our connection—my cuff, the trust she's put in me—all of that is undeniable, I also need her to be assured that it doesn't just begin and end there in my mind.

As I kiss and nip and lose myself against her mouth, my hands move of their own accord. The sight of this girl wrapped up in my clothes is indelibly grooved into my brain, but right now, I'm in pursuit of what lies beneath that outer shell. Once I've unfastened the jacket—the one I've worn out riding, in the wilderness, on dirt trails, and through a thousand memories of life in these mountains—I take a moment for my palms to roam over the contrast of Briar's softness revealed beneath that heavy material.

How she's wrapped up in a piece of *me,* but beneath that lies buttery-smooth fabric I'm pawing without stopping because she feels amazing, every curve and dip of her hips, her stomach, her navel, I can trace it all with my fingers.

It's an expensive, wafer-thin material. The kind I'm so unaccustomed to actually feeling beneath my calloused, work-worn fingers. Two minutes ago, I was avoiding splinters and feeling the jarring thud of metal driving into wood, and now I've got *her,* soft and pliant and feeling like a delicate feather I want to stroke and caress. I want to inhale that unfamiliar yet wonderful sensation all day long.

One last tug of my teeth, pinching her bottom lip until she whimpers for me, that'll have to satisfy my craving for the moment. I want to look my fill of her. Slipping my palms over her shoulders to lift the jacket, I peel it down her arms till she's standing between my knees without anything in the way of me enjoying the effort she's gone to. The wrap dress tied around her waist—the style of this particular garment—puts her cleavage on tempting display.

Her stiffened nipples peek out at me.

Wrapping my palms around her ribs, I bring my thumbs up to those hard little buds and tease her tits through the fabric.

"No bra? Wonder what else you forgot to wear beneath this dress, hmm?"

My girl came here with a plan. She gives me a flirty little look, sinking her teeth into that kiss-bitten lower lip.

"Damn, woman, you're tempting me into leaving everything and tossing you over my shoulder. I'm about two seconds from taking you home and not coming up for air for a couple of days."

A strange expression washes over her face as I exhale heavily, gravel coating my words.

"Though . . . as much as I want to do that, Beau needs to talk to me in about twenty minutes or so, and if you let me get inside that pussy, I'm gonna want to fuck and fuck and fuck."

I keep thumbing her nipples and watch as her pupils blow. Her whimpers grow louder the harder I rub and slide my touch over her tits.

"Storm," she moans softly.

"Darlin', I lose control around you . . . I lose time, my morals vanish, every damn thing just ups and disappears because none of it fucking matters."

Only *you* matter, I want to add.

"Use me then . . . in other ways." Her voice is husky with desire.

My hands go still, pausing, as I take in the sight of her.

Taking in what I think her meaning is, I *think* I understand, but can't quite be sure.

Before me, Briar moves with surprising decisiveness. She quickly grabs the jacket I set carelessly beside my hip, then folds it so she can sink to her knees and give herself something more comfortable to rest on than the hard ground.

"You said something the other night." Her gaze rests on my mouth, and she runs her tongue over her bottom lip. "Something that I haven't been able to get out of my mind."

Her sensual touch roams up my jeans and up my thighs, coming to rest on my belt, nudging just below the cotton of my T-shirt.

"Might have to remind me." I thread my fingers into her hair, and my dick is painfully hard at the prospect of what she's offering.

"That you liked the idea of marking me." Her elbows squeeze together, and from this angle, looking down, that tiny action puts her flesh on display, rounded and full and threatening to spill over. Seeing how confident my girl is in her body now is the sexiest damn thing.

Then she gives me her hooded, lust-filled eyes.

Jesus.

This girl is out here in the middle of the day, kneeling at my boots in a barn, telling me she wants my cum all over her breasts? Holy fuck, I've done a lot of wrong things in my life, so I'm not sure what has given me the opportunity of this particular gift to play with.

"You want me to fuck those perfect tits?"

She nods, gnawing on the swell of her bottom lip.

"Then you're gonna have to get it nice and wet. Be extra sloppy for me." I tug on her hair, drawing a gasp. "Undo my belt, darlin'."

Briar fumbles a little, trying to hold my gaze, as she squirms and squeezes her thighs together. I shift my ass lower, spreading my boots a little wider to give her a better angle.

"That's it," I murmur. Watching her intensely as she frees my painfully hard cock and wraps her tiny fist around me. A couple of strokes is all it takes for me to swell and grow thicker beneath her touch.

"Well, you know what to do," My growl drops out. "Spit on it."

Her breathing shallows as she leans forward and drops a line of spit before wrapping her lips around the swollen tip. That angle, with her mouth teasing the head of me—goddamn—gives me the perfect sight of her tits and lips and dark eyelashes fluttering my way. A look that asks me if I like it. What I think. If she's pleasing me.

Of course, she fucking is. Every time, it's perfect with her, and I'm about two seconds from confessing it all when she sucks me in deeper. Hollowing her cheeks, she swirls her tongue and whimpers around my length.

"*Mmm.* Made to swallow me like the good girl you are." She's more and more turned on the longer she's suckling on me, gradually dipping a little lower. As she does so, I feel her tongue running along the underside, tracing the veins and tasting my skin.

"You can do better than that. Don't just lick. Spit properly."

The moan Briar makes tells me everything. She draws back off me with a filthy, wet pop, a long line of spit hanging between my tip and her mouth. Swallowing for a second, her beautiful brown gaze darts between my face and my cock, before she leans forward and, this time, lets loose a trail of saliva, coating me.

"Use me. *Please.*" Her voice is hoarse with desire.

Briar shifts her weight, keeping her eyes on mine without wavering, as she hooks her fingers into the fabric, concealing her cleavage. Then tugs.

Her breasts hang free, and she presses them together, rubbing along the underside of me. I have to suppress a groan, because her soft flesh, now slick with spit, is being dragged up and down my dick as she moves and arches and then dips her mouth to wet my tip again. Holy shit.

That's when I lose whatever thread was holding me back from just outright using her.

She asked me to.

As I slide my thick length back and forth and cradle the heavy weight of her breasts to wrap around me, breathy gasps and moans fill the air. My fingers knead the softness and roundness, and I can't help the feral need for my girl that surges up from the deepest recesses of me.

"You want me to own you? Use you?" I grunt out as I fuck her tits and squeeze them together, holding her tighter around my length. "This spot right here where I wrote the word in red letters. Do I need to give you another reminder of exactly who you belong to?"

She nods and begs for exactly what I'm promising. "I do. I want that."

"You get off on being owned, don't you, darlin'?"

Briar's so gone with lust that her mouth hangs open, panting and whimpering.

The tingling builds, and pressure coils, and I can feel the moment racing through my blood like a stallion in full flight.

"Stick out your tongue." It takes everything in me to not just throw her to the ground and shove my cock inside.

I'm so close. My deep groan fills the air as she dutifully does exactly as I say, and I fist my dick. Aiming the head at her chin, on the next firm stroke, that's when my balls draw up. With a deafening rush of blood in my ears, I come so fucking hard. My cum shoots forward, surging across her presented tongue, her lips, perfect little chin, and drips forward onto her chest as my cock throbs and spills.

"*Ffuck.*"

Every panting breath, each thump of my heart inside my chest, it's hers.

Dragging Briar up to standing, I hold her steady in one arm, then swipe my fingers through the evidence of me painted across her skin. Then shove my hand below her dress, seeking out her slick center.

"How about you let me keep you forever." I press two fingers inside, because just as I thought, Briar is bare beneath that flimsy fabric. "How about I leave that cuff on your wrist permanently, so I can bend you over and see just how wet you are for this all day long."

My girl's eyes glaze over as she swipes her tongue out to taste where I've painted her flushed skin.

"You'd let me, wouldn't you? I know how much you love having me inside your sweet little body. It doesn't even matter where for you, does it? You'd beg me to fill all your holes at the same time if I could." Curling my fingers, I plunge in and out, fucking my cum into her and pressing my thumb hard against her clit.

Briar gulps and shakes as her climax starts to build. She's panting, begging.

I don't even know what I'm saying. It's filthy. Desperate.

Just like I am for her.

"Take whatever. Please. *Please.*"

"Maybe I will. Maybe I'll shove a toy in your ass and stuff your mouth with my fingers while I bury my dick so far in your pussy you'll be ruined for life. You'd be marked so fucking deep when I fill you with cum that you'll never want to leave."

She squeezes my fingers so damn tight. Convulsing around me as she falls apart.

"That's it. My pretty little cum slut," I murmur as she sags against me, a whimpering mess, looking gorgeous as hell.

It takes a while for us to both come down, as I draw my fingers out and give them to her to wrap her lips around. Briar does exactly that, cleaning off the evidence of both of us with soft, little pleasured noises. I repeat the process a couple of times, gathering up the residue of my cum, letting her lick off the taste of me . . . and her.

"Goddamn. You're the most perfect thing, darlin.'" My throat bobs with a heavy swallow as I turn my attention to helping put her dress back in place and then tucking myself away.

Briar watches me do so, a softness in her expression, but doesn't say anything.

As I reach for my belt, my girl makes a sweet little sound, then takes over. "Let me do it." Her voice is quiet, but those gorgeous lips curve up, and her eyes crinkle a little as she gazes up at me.

I lean back and watch, soaking up every second her fingers thread the leather on itself.

"Thank you," she breathes.

Hooking my finger beneath her chin, I bend forward and press a soft kiss against her plush lips. Briar tastes like us, and I love that we're both mingled just like this.

My damn phone starts buzzing, tucked somewhere in my own jacket pocket on the other end of the workbench.

"Go. You've gotta take that." Her lips move against mine.

"Beau can fucking wait," I grunt.

With a playful shove, she pushes against my stomach, and that smile brightens. "I'll see you at home later."

With that, Briar leaves me so I can try to focus on things like work and whatever crap Beau is ranting on about on the other end of the line after I answer the phone in a daze.

As I walk to the barn doors and watch her taillights drive off, all I can think about is how goddamn good it feels to hear my girl say that word.

Home.

CHAPTER 39

Briar

Antoine and Cris have made it their business to reinforce just how important it is that I play their game. This house echoes with nothing but soulless wealth and the footsteps of vapid, power-hungry people who occasionally drift in and out with my husband, but for the most part, I'm back to my meaningless existence.

The only solace I can find is that I'm protecting Storm, even if doing so is tearing my heart into a thousand fragmented pieces.

If misery had a face, she would be painted in my likeness.

Missing him is my constant companion. It lingers on my heels like a morose shadow, clinging to me as I randomly find tears rolling down my cheeks while pouring a coffee into the white bone china mug I want to smash against the matching polished white countertop.

I wake up with damp cheeks and have to bury my face in the pillow as I scream until my throat gives way and my body turns limp.

There has to be a way out of this nightmare, but right at this moment, my well of inspiration has run dry. I'm defeated and the only course of action I can take for the foreseeable future is to rot in this place.

Appeasing my sister and my insipid husband while protecting the man I love with every fiber of my soul. That's what the seconds, minutes, and hours of being Briar Lane amount to.

Somewhere, somehow, a spark still glows inside my chest, reminding me that there must be a way out of this. The only problem is that the longer I spend suffocating and slowly drowning in this fishbowl, the fainter that glow becomes.

I worry about the day I wake up and it's been extinguished completely.

What then?

What happens when that tidal wave of inky black comes to claim me and drag me to that place where I just give up?

As I curl my knees against my chest, sitting on the ground beside my bed, I hear his rumbling chuckle. I feel his fingers graze the side of my face, touching me with a tenderness I never experienced before. He's not touching me for any particular reason, just reaching out to grace me with an affectionate brush of his skin. Just because he wants to.

I glance down to my hand when my phone's soft vibration nudges me like a dog seeking out a pat.

Another message has arrived.

The sight of which sends the faintest, tenderest flutter of a delicate wing hidden away inside my stomach.

Antoine allowed me to keep my phone; I'm sure he knows that if I have access to it—or, more accurately, still have access to Storm—the one-sided contact would be more painful than any punishment my own husband could inflict on me.

These messages are both the only thing keeping me sane and the worst kind of torture rolled into one. Each new arrival has me scrambling to open it, inhaling each word like those miniature characters on screen are my own personal oxygen mask, and staring at the steadily increasing string of unanswered texts that I could practically recite line by line, word for word.

He checks on me.

Talks to me as if I'm sitting right there on the bench seat of his truck as he drives with one wrist hooked lazily over the wheel.

Not like I'm the heartless bitch who vanished, leaving only a note on the kitchen bench. Two words that broke me to sign indelibly onto paper through streams of tears.

I'm sorry.

He deserved so much more than that, yet it was all my torn, fractured heart had to give in that moment. The only way I knew to prevent him from attempting to follow me.

The wonderful man he is, Storm sends me photos of the cabin, the horses, and all the simplicities of life in the mountains that I miss with a cavernous ache inside my chest.

Last night's messages almost cracked my determination to be strong and not give Antoine any reason to go public with his bullshit and twisted untruths. My resolve almost shattered as I lay in bed watching the dots bouncing on the screen, waiting as he took an infuriatingly long time to write his thoughts. They'd stop, pausing, while my heart sank, believing that this time he'd finally given up trying to communicate mid-message.

Except, when the vibration finally came through and the bubble popped up on screen, fat tears rolled freely as I read over his sweet words.

Storm:
I don't know why you left, but I'm right here.

Whenever you're ready to come back, this home is yours.

As I lay there last night, sinking into the gloom and fending off the dark thoughts threatening to come back to take over, he kept talking to me. Almost as if he could sense I was floundering there, curled on my side, my sanity splintering, losing my damn mind with loneliness and hopeless heartbreak.

You want to learn something, darlin'?

Well, here it is . . .

I'm in our bed, with a pillow that still hangs onto your sweetness. All I want to do is wake up tomorrow morning and, by some miracle, hear that shower running. Even though I'd much rather have you by my side, at least if you're in that bathroom, it would mean you're here and not a thousand fucking miles away.

I miss the little humming noise you make when you take that first sip of coffee in the morning.

I miss the way you twitch a little in your sleep just as you're dozing off. It's cute as fuck.

Biting back the surge of emotion, I turn my attention to the newest messages that arrived while I've been huddled here on the floor.

You took my cuff.

So, even though I don't know if you're ever coming back, you're still mine, unless you return it to me in the mail or some shit.

I might not have your sweet little body here to hold on to, to use you however I want, but I can still tell you all the things I want you to hear.

All the things my girl deserves to hear.

I'll keep on checking on you, little thorn, even if you never reply or want to see me again.

That's the problem, you see. I've got all the time in the world for you. My life used to be counted by the tiniest of margins, by seconds instead of minutes or hours, and I'd spend every single one of however many seconds I've got left trying to make you happy.

Blowing out a long, unsteady breath, with fat tears brimming over, I swipe out of the message thread before I throw all caution to the wind and break down and beg him to come rescue me.

This isn't Storm's mess to fix.

I don't doubt for a second he'd come if I asked him to. What I couldn't live with is the knowledge that I'd knowingly put him back in the worst, sickening kind of spotlight. Antoine might look like he's polished and refined, but he's brutally calculating. The man would ensure not only that there was fresh clickbait fodder spread to the media like a virus every week, but he'd pay the most immoral, unscrupulous vultures to camp outside our little slice of paradise in the mountains.

He would hound Storm until life became unbearable, and it would be all because of me.

So, I do what any self-respecting woman with heartbreak roaming through her veins would do. I spend time poring over his videos, his rodeo montages, and I give myself the opportunity to be with him, even if it's just a glimpse of a frenzied eight-second bull ride.

After drinking my fill, I quickly visit the Devil's Peak Farriers Instagram page, fully expecting there to be nothing new on the page, and I brace myself to ignore the litany of thirsty comments left on any photo or video Storm makes an appearance in.

However, there's a brand-new post, and my heart immediately triples its rhythm upon first glance.

The sight I recognize is a close-up photo of the kitchen. No one would know where Storm's taken this photo unless they had been to the cabin, and my eyes bounce around the image, noting the tiniest details.

The cupboard door that always hung crooked has been fixed, now proudly sitting straight on its hinges, and on the front panel are three brush strokes of paint in different shades of charcoal.

I'm utterly confused as to why he's posted this photo and immediately tap into the caption. Hope is determinedly flapping its wings, yet I'm biting the inside of my cheek almost raw with nervous anticipation that it might be left forlorn if I discover through a fucking post on Instagram that he's playing house with someone new.

My eyes snag on the simple words paired with the photo of paint samples and the cabin's kitchenette I wish I was standing in right now.

"Painted with the color on the right because they all look the same to me, but I'm guessing it's what you would pick. I stood in the middle of the hardware store today with a different color in my hand, and then all I could hear was your voice telling me it'd look stupid, and that it would clash with the art you bought that day. So . . . hopefully you don't hate it?"

The caption reads like a diary entry, but I know it's for me.

Not only is this man taking care of me by talking to me, checking on me, but he's also taking care of our cabin.

I'm so fucking in love with him, it aches.

My hands shake and my cheeks are damp from where my eyes won't stop leaking, and I very nearly don't notice another photo to swipe through to, sitting hidden behind one showing the kitchen cupboards.

That picture punches a hole in my damn chest and captures the residue of my soul. Stealing it straight back to Crimson Ridge.

There's no additional caption, just the image.

A water glass sits on the wooden table, in the center of frame in front of the window overlooking the forest outside.

It's filled with a small bunch of freshly cut spring blooms.

With that one photo, my Storm just reached through the phone screen and helped me drag myself out of the spiraling depths.

I'm going to find a way to get back to him, even if I have no idea how to do so—there is no way I can give up now.

I've got to figure this out on my own and hope to god he's still waiting for me by the time I escape this hell.

CHAPTER 40

Storm

"**W**hat were my grandparents like?" *My girl looks at me from across the small table, her coffee cradled in both hands and breakfast half-finished. She's wearing my shirt, and even though it drowns her, I swear to god I'd go to my grave a happy man if that was all she ever wore.*

"Ma and Pop? What do you wanna know?"

"Anything, really." *She sips her coffee and then clears her throat, all cute and disapproving when she catches me staring at her tits instead of concentrating on the question.*

I scrub a hand over the back of my neck and chuckle. "Shit, I forget you never even knew them."

"My dad never talked about them." *It's not sad, her tone, more wistful than anything. There's a certain type of lingering curiosity there. Briar tilts her head to one side and flutters those eyelashes of hers with enough power to bowl me over with just one sweep against her soft cheeks.*

She kills me with those eyes every damn morning, I swear.

"Good people. They brought that hard-grafting European mindset with them when they migrated here. Honest to a fault but firm. Mind you, they needed to be, with my wild ass nearly setting shit on fire at every turn."

"*You would have been a nightmare, I bet.*"

"*Hey.*" I raise my eyebrows, which allows me the pleasure of seeing her grin in a way that seems so much more natural and carefree than the smile of the timid little thing who first turned up here. "*I was a perfect angel.*"

Briar nearly spits her coffee across the table.

"*Come on.*" Her big eyes roll dramatically.

"*Sainthood levels of perfection.*" I fake the sign of the cross over my chest.

"*The poor things. Did they ask if they could return you? Exchange you for store credit?*"

I'm laughing as I shake my head and drag a hand through my hair. God, this girl makes me feel so much younger, so much lighter. We can talk about stuff I haven't even thought about for years, and it just feels natural.

"*Yeah, I kinda put them through it, but they were already pretty elderly when they fostered, then formally adopted your dad and me. Mom wasn't in good health, but she always made sure we were taken care of and knew we were loved and safe, because she'd seen enough kids come from crappy situations that she understood what we needed was stability when they adopted us at the same time. Then, Pop was just a rock. Always there no matter what, you know.*"

I swallow hard, thinking about the man who would have adored this girl to pieces. Pop wouldn't have said much, but I know he would have been wrapped around her little finger.

"*We weren't good at talking, but he could see I needed something to tame my demons, so he got me into rodeo. Put me on a horse and gave me every opportunity he could. Drove me miles to compete, always with his terrible hillbilly music playing and saying about two words the whole time. And if I came off during a ride, he'd look me over and chew his dip and say something like, 'You dead, boy?' which for some stupid reason would make me laugh, and then he'd shrug and suggest we head on home. The old bugger knew I was stubborn enough that I wouldn't leave, that I'd get straight back up there just to prove him wrong."*

An incoming call bursts through my haze of memories. I've never moved so fast to check my notifications as I have these past few weeks since she's been gone.

Except, the message is not from her.

It never is.

Beau's name peers back at me, and I have to fight the urge to swipe out of everything and just fucking hide out, allowing my soul to wither all day.

Instead, I decline the video call but stab the green button with my thumb to answer the voice call and grunt.

It's not even a *hello*.

"You ghosting me, wild one?" Beau's voice rumbles down the line.

Running my free hand through my hair, I blow out a breath. "Nah, sorry, just had a rough patch."

Beau knows my shit. He knows exactly what it's like when I get low.

Hell, I've seen him at his worst after a bad loss in the arena, too.

"Thought as much."

"Things are going okay at the ranch, though. Nothing you need to worry your pretty little head about."

He chuckles, and in the background, I hear cars going past. "I saw the photos you texted. Looks awesome, man." The line jostles a bit, and the sound of a truck door shutting drowns out the noise of suburbia I know he's itching to leave behind.

Silence stretches out.

I lean forward on the wooden chair, elbows on my thighs, staring at my boots. My brain is awash with memories of sitting right here, of seeing *her* only a few feet across this table.

"Gonna tell me, or do I gotta get on my knees and treat you real sweet to get your secrets?"

That brings a ghost of a smile to my face. "You'd fall in love with me too quick." I scrub my hand over my mouth. "Wouldn't want to go breaking your heart, boy."

Beau takes his time. Fucking forever, it feels like, to get it out. "That what all this is about?" he muses. "Something crawled inside your chest and jump-started that lump of coal to life?"

"Fuck you very much."

He blows out a whistle to himself. "She got a name?"

"None of your business."

"Oh, so you're in deep-deep, huh?"

Being around Beau, living a breathing rodeo in each other's back pockets for enough years that we did, I know the exact expression on his face right now. Smug fucker.

"*Shitttt.*" He sounds far too pleased with himself. This man has been waiting for goddamn years, threatening me that one day it'll happen, that I'd finally know what it's like to be left feeling this hollow and broken. "She got you real good, then?"

I mull over things, not exactly knowing how to explain anything, or if I even want to. "You ever thought you had it all, then woke up, and it was like the dream version of your life vanished?"

Beau shifts, and the speaker rustles as he readjusts himself. "Can't say I've been lucky enough to know how that feels."

Poor bastard is married, and yet I can hear everything I need to know in the way he says those words with such finality. Weighed down by years of being stuck in something that looked perfect on the outside but had a decaying core right from day one.

"She must have been something," he adds.

"You have no idea."

"Did you fuck it up?"

"Hey. Low fucking blow, Heartford."

The asshole is smiling. I can hear it through the phone. "Well . . . you're in Crimson Ridge, crying into your pillow. This

chick has obviously gone, so I'm just trying to put the pieces together here."

She's not some *chick* or some meaningless hookup. Briar is
everything I never knew I needed, and now she's gone, and it's
slicing away at me, day by day.

Except, I don't say any of that.

"I don't know. I don't fucking know, alright?" My fingers tug
at my hair. "Your smug fucking mustache happy now?" I grunt.

"Not if you're hurting, man." Beau clears his throat. "You love
someone, and it cuts something extra savage when they're not
around."

My chest aches just hearing him say it out loud. Because it's
the goddamn truth.

"What the fuck am I supposed to do if I've already lost her
before I ever truly had her?"

He makes a wry-sounding noise from the other end of the
line. "As much as it kills me to admit this . . . because I know
you get off on being a clever prick and all, but I don't know. I've
never had someone like that, and whatever it is, it sounds fucking brutal."

It's my turn to chuckle now. "It really is."

"You want me to come out there?"

What I've done to deserve a friendship like Beau's, I'll never
understand. The guy has got an imploding marriage, legal shit
up to his eyeballs as he tries to work out a drawn-out, messy
separation, and a new business he's starting up. Yet, here he is,
offering to fly to the back of nowhere just to sit and drink a beer
or two and make sure I'm doing okay.

"Nah, man. Besides, it's only a few more weeks till you're here
anyway."

"I'm fucking counting the minutes to get outta this circus, I
tell you."

"We can catch up for a cold one, or maybe an entire

goddamn bottle. Who knows how much I'll be needing to numb myself by then?"

"Jesus. Maybe I do need to fly out there sooner."

"Take a joke, Heartford. You'd think with that slug on your face, you'd be able to know a joke when you see it."

"Whatever, you love it. Bet you wanna know what it feels like tickling your pussy." It's damn good to hear him like this, and I'm grateful for the brief opportunity to lighten the weight yoked around my shoulders. "Dream of me. I'll be in Crimson Ridge before you know it, and you won't have time for anything except drooling over my good looks."

"Fuck off."

"Love you, too, Stôrmand. See you in a couple of weeks."

CHAPTER 41

Briar

Sitting across from the attorney dressed in a peacock-blue blazer and skirt, I brace my head in my hands. Clara is patient and seems sympathetic to my predicament—or at the very least, she's paid enough that she puts on a good performance.

We've been going through the contents of my father's estate, his will, and all the papers I have privy to as one of his designated Lane Enterprises heirs. It's been weeks now of sitting amongst the sea of documents looking for *something*, but I'm not sure exactly what we're looking for.

All I know is that when I find it, I'll know.

"Briar, why don't you head home . . . take a break?" Her heels clack as she gets up from the office chair on the other side of the conference table we've covered with stacks of folders and box files.

There's also what seems to be an endless supply of electronic documents to go through if this search proves to be unfruitful, but I've got a gut feeling we need to begin with the reams of printed paperwork. If there is anything worth my while, it's going to be buried inside files like these rather than in an easily searchable digital filing system.

My father was intelligent like that.

"Clara, be real. You know I'd rather sleep here than go back there."

She grimaces. "God, I wish I could hit that son of a bitch with some sort of legal punch to the balls for you."

"Pity he's got more connections and media strings to pull than we've had hot dinners combined."

"Ain't that the truth . . . but please know I wouldn't hesitate to spread some grotesque rumors about him and a weekend with a cheap hooker and a confirmed case of syphilis."

I snort and shake my head. "Does it make it better or worse that I'm almost certain that kind of thing isn't actually a rumor where Antoine is concerned?"

As I reach for my glass of water, my phone starts vibrating on the table.

While every cell in my body perks up in hope the name on the screen will be my cowboy, I'm greeted by the sour taste of "Crispin" flashing across the display instead.

"Go ahead, get some fresh air, and touch some grass while you deal with that." Clara nods in the direction of my phone. "Unless you want me to bear witness to her bullshit?"

I hit the green button and wave her off, pushing out of my seat as I bring the phone to my ear.

"Where are you?" my sister demands.

"Hi, Cris."

"Cut the shit, Briar."

"You know where I am, or is the tracking on my phone not performing adequately this evening?" I hope she can hear the extra helping of sugar dumped into my words.

"I know what you're doing."

"Oh, I don't doubt that for a second." After hitting the elevator button, I watch the light begin to climb to meet me here on the tenth floor.

"You create shit and be prepared to lose it all." Her voice shakes. "You won't get a cent of Lane Enterprises . . . none of the shares, none of the property portfolio . . . I will make sure you are left with nothing."

"Do your worst, Cris. I really don't care."

It's the truth. I have no interest in my father's business or inheriting a dime from his empire.

What I care about is the man I love and protecting him from these venomous creatures.

"It's pathetic . . . Whatever you're trying to look for . . . you won't find anything. Keep looking, I dare you. You'll wake up one day and realize that all you've done is waste years of your life sitting on your ass in a lawyer's office."

Stepping onto the elevator, I pinch the bridge of my nose. At least the offices are quiet at this time of evening, and I've got a smooth trip to the ground floor all to myself.

"What would you rather I do? Sit on my ass in that house listening to Antoine fuck his latest bimbo just down the hall? Wait for him to force himself on me one night when he's coked up and drunk as hell?"

My jaw clenches. Cris is miserable and bitter, and I don't need to contend with her anger.

"You deserve it," she bites at me from down the line. "It would serve you right if he did."

Oh. She. Did. Not.

"What the hell is your problem?" It takes everything to stop myself from outright yelling as the elevator dings, doors swishing open, and the empty lobby greets me.

My entire body trembles with rage.

I quickly cross the marble floor, making a dash for what might not exactly be fresh air here in this godforsaken city, but I at least can suck in a deep lungful of warm, evening air.

"*You.* You have always been the fucking problem." That's when I hear it. A hurt, tearful little child in her voice. While I might be speaking to my psychopath of a sibling, the truth behind her foul temper peeks out.

"Crispin, I was only a baby. They tried their hardest to stop the hemorrhaging." There is a spacious courtyard out here, surrounded by glass and polished marble, with an ornamental fountain in the center. Lights glow at me through the bubbling water.

"You took her away. It was your fault."

We've been here what feels like a thousand times over the years, yet she's always refused to take responsibility for her own trauma caused by the simultaneous events of my birth and the subsequent loss of our mother.

The woman I never met.

"I've told you so many times, I wish there was a way to undo what happened, but holding me responsible is shitty behavior, not to mention unhealthy."

"Fuck you, Briar."

Blowing out a breath, I dip my fingers into the tumbling water. "Get yourself a therapist, babe. Better yet, go and get yourself laid. That's probably ten times more useful—might dislodge that pole up your ass."

With that, I hang up and shake the water off my other hand. I won't continue to put myself in the firing line to receive more of her venom. It's been her default setting for twenty-six years, and I'm done being her emotional punching bag. She's an adult, and screw her; I'm not going to be held responsible for whatever toxic cloud my sister is determined to carry around, and willingly allow to poison herself over and over.

Some people just don't *want* to see things differently, no matter how many opportunities you extend them to get help or find a way out, and Crispin Lane is absolutely one of those kinds of people.

"Briar?"

I spin around at the sound of the breathless voice calling my name.

Clara looks as if she just sprinted down the stairs, her eyes wide and cheeks pink.

"What's the matter?" My grip tightens around my phone. God, I hope this isn't going to be another kick to the shins, because after suffering the sting of that verbal slap from Crispin, I don't know how much more I can take tonight.

"I think you'll want to come and see this."

I triple-check the address on my phone before finally gathering the courage to ring the doorbell to the suburban bungalow with butterfly ornaments scattered through the front garden. I press it and step back, waiting.

My heart hasn't stopped pounding during the entire drive over here.

I lay awake all night rehearsing what to say.

What if no one is home?

What if they moved house? Or cities?

This could all be for nothing, and I'll be back to having nothing but hope and desperate prayers to carry me through however long I end up stuck here for.

This has been the longest stretch of torture, and my fingers feel like they're numb from clinging to the edge all these weeks upon weeks.

Just as I consider ringing the bell again, I hear movement inside.

The door cracks open on a security chain, and a woman with a gray bobbed haircut and pale blue eyes hidden behind reading glasses peers at me.

"Are you Mrs. Mitchell?"

"Who's asking?" She looks me up and down cautiously.

"My name is Briar. I'm so sorry to turn up unannounced, but I was hoping you might have a few minutes?" My palms are sweating.

"What's this about?"

"I'm here to talk about your daughter, Tegan." I watch her features soften as I say her youngest's name. "I also believe you know my father, Erik Lane."

The woman standing before me goes still, and for a moment, it seems like she might slam the door in my face before she relents.

"Graham, we've got company," she calls over her shoulder as she closes the door just enough, and the metallic scrape of the chain sliding free announces my entrance.

"Thank you. I'm so sorry to put you out like this."

"Briar, was it?"

I nod as I step inside, instantly catching sight of the high school senior portrait of a young girl with bouncing blonde curls, a brilliant smile, and a distinctive beauty mark on her upper lip.

"If you had to endure a man like Erik Lane as a father, then it seems the least we can do is offer you a soda . . . unless you want something stronger?" Mrs. Mitchell leads me down the hall to the quaint kitchen. As we pass the living room, a man gets to his feet out of a recliner.

"This here is Erik Lane's kid." She calls over her shoulder.

The man with a full head of white hair studies me quizzically, as if I've got a tail, or horns. Pretty sure he considers me devil spawn.

"Our condolences. We read about Erik's passing in the news." His voice is cautious, and I don't blame him. If the papers burning a hole in my handbag are true, there would be no prize for guessing that Mr. Mitchell wouldn't exactly be over the moon to have someone bearing the last name of Lane under his roof.

"You want a cookie, honey?" God, this woman seems so lovely, and it breaks my heart knowing what they've been through.

"Just the soda is fine, thank you." I take the offered glass and follow to where she pulls out a chair at their round dining table.

"If this is about the NDA, I can assure you we have kept our mouths shut all these years. No different now that your father has passed." Mr. Mitchell sits beside his wife on the opposite side of the table from me.

A flash of worry catches in her eyes as she hastily meets my gaze and then turns to scold her husband, her mouth opening with words poised.

"It's fine, Mrs. Mitchell," I interrupt and reach a hand in their direction. "Please, I'm not here about that—well, I sort of am, but not in the way you might think."

They both look back at me with furrowed brows.

"Can you tell me, is this your bank account?" I pull out the highlighted papers from my bag and slide them across the wood.

Mrs. Mitchell pushes her glasses up her nose and barely glances at the paper before looking back at me.

"Well, of course it is. That's the agreed-upon sum your father offered us and where it's always been directly deposited into."

"Erik Lane?" I press.

"Yes, of course, Erik Lane, who sat in that very same seat as you're in now, and gave us his whole spiel about nondisclosure and the consequences for Lane Enterprises if anything about this was to get out, and then offered us an annual lump sum . . . as if it would bring Tegan back." The voice of the man across from me shakes a fraction as he speaks his daughter's name.

"We give most of it away each year." His wife offers me a tight smile. "Try to make sure it gets to agencies who help other girls who need the kind of support Tegan might have benefited from."

Swallowing heavily, I feel the prick of heat behind my eyes. It's so unfair that the selfishness of my father has wreaked such devastation on good people.

"I can't imagine what you've been through." My words seem pathetic, a measly gesture.

"Honey, it's been a long time. We made our peace with her decisions. While we didn't support the way she behaved in the years she was with your father, she was our daughter all the same."

My clammy palms rub up and down the fabric of my jeans.

"Must have been quite a shock to you and your sister." Her kind eyes hold mine.

This woman has no idea how true that statement is right now for me—evidently not for my sister, but that's my next bridge to cross after this one.

"That's actually part of the reason I'm here." My mouth feels like it has been stuffed with cotton. "Now that our father has passed on, my sister and I want to make right some of his less-than-ideal actions."

The couple sitting across from me exchange a quick glance.

"We would like to formally acknowledge Tegan's child, our brother, but in order to do so, you can appreciate the delicate nature of us being directly in contact with the adoptive parents. I know all about the lies my father spread to make it seem as if she was still pregnant when . . . when . . ." I trail off, unable to say the words or put a voice to how despicable his actions were.

Mrs. Mitchell's eyes glaze over, and her husband conjures a tissue to hand to her within a second from out of thin air.

"We write to them. They send us photos. He just turned eleven and is madly obsessed with baseball. He plays Little League like it's his only job on this earth."

Another magical tissue appears and is slid across the table to me because I'm also leaking tears now.

"Your father never wanted the paperwork." The man shrugs and takes his wife's hand, rubbing circles over her palm with his thumb.

"I'm hoping it's not too much to ask or to presume that you might have kept it?"

"Probably could have landed us in a lot of shit with your father if it ever got found, but I had a secure spot for it all."

Beside him, his wife sniffles and tuts disapprovingly. "Graham, a shoebox on top of the closet is *not* a secure location. Don't go trying to lead this girl down the garden path."

"Would you mind if I took some photos of whatever

documents you have, just so I've got a copy I can take with me back to our lawyers? You'll keep the originals here, of course," I hastily tack on.

Mr. Mitchell hoists himself to his feet, then stops to look at me with a decade's worth of distrust.

"How do we know you really are Erik's daughter? You could be a journalist for all we know, and in that case, I've already told you more than I'm supposed to say out loud."

Tucking a strand of hair behind my ear, I quickly grab my wallet and pull out my driver's license and hand it over. As he quietly takes it, studies it, eyes flitting between the photo and my face, I use my phone to bring up an internet search. Within a couple of clicks, I find a photo online that shows my sister, me, and my father from a few years ago, attending some corporate schmooze fest.

"Here." I slide the phone his way. "There are a million reasons for you not to trust anyone or anything to do with Lane Enterprises, and I completely understand your hesitation. I can only hope this will go some small way toward rectifying things."

Mr. Mitchell grunts, and hands the phone to his wife, who readjusts her glasses as she dabs the damp corners of her eyes.

"Thank you for coming today, Briar," he says.

I reach across the dining table, and as Mrs. Mitchell returns my phone, I take the opportunity to give her hand a squeeze. "I'm sorry it took so long for me to get here."

"Don't be sorry, kiddo. Your father went to a lot of effort to keep things quiet, so I can't imagine you would have had a hope in hell of coming to visit us while he was still alive." Mr. Mitchell gives me a tight smile before placing a kiss on the top of his wife's head. "Now let me get you that paternity test . . . and I'm guessing you might be interested in the letter she left behind for us, too?"

CHAPTER 42

Briar

"**I**s there anything you miss most from your competing days? You know, being the champion rodeo starlet and all."

"I don't miss the injuries." My cowboy grimaces. "Luckily, I never truly got smashed up like some of the other guys. A couple of broken ribs here and there, a few torn muscles, but there were some nights when one of the others entered the arena expecting to win a buckle and, instead of going home after the show, ended up in intensive care."

"Honestly, I don't know how you did it." Resting my head on his broad chest, the steady thud of his heartbeat beneath my ear is so damn reassuring.

"You don't wish I was still that guy?" His fingers play with my hair while I lie curled into his side, and there's a hint of something faint and soft in that question, a tiny light cast on the complexities of Stôrmand Lane. "The guy you're busy drooling over on those video clips you keep watching on repeat like an addict." The teasing in his voice doesn't disguise the way he asks with more than a touch of sincerity.

"No way." Tilting my head so that our eyes can lock, I reach out and brush my fingers over his lips. "I like this guy."

Storm rubs a strand of my hair as if deep in thought, and gently kisses the pads of my fingertips.

My entire body melts into a puddle.

I love him beyond anything I ever thought possible.

"I miss the sense of family on the tour . . . We were a pretty tight-knit bunch. Traveling and supporting each other on the road. I'd never really had that before, and then it was all taken away virtually overnight after Tegan passed."

As he speaks, I watch his throat move and feel the rumble of his morning voice, and I would happily stay right here forever if I could. Despite all our past hurts, we've somehow managed to both still be left standing even though there might have been days when it felt impossible to do so, thanks to the circumstances we found ourselves in.

"I don't blame them," Storm adds. "Probably the pressure from their sponsors, managers, and just the day-to-day bullshit of a pro career. I didn't need to be dragging them down with me when the pro tour decided I no longer fit in their comfortable little box, so it was easier to vanish, fall off the map, you know?"

My heart hurts for him that the actions of someone else, someone he hardly knew, took away his career.

"I wish someone had been there for you."

"Beau was, even when I was a dick and didn't deserve his time. That's why I'd do anything for him. He was one of the only ones who kept in contact, even though he had the biggest public profile out of all of us on the pro tour, and it could have all blown up in his face. Beau came to visit and slept on that god-awful couch and made sure I wasn't sitting out here with a loaded gun and a bottle and a head full of black thoughts."

We lie there in silence together for a while as I trace the lines of ink down the side of his neck, and he keeps playing with my hair.

"I bought pills once," I whisper the confession I've never shared with anyone. "About six months after the wedding, I sat in my

bathtub at three a.m. and drank half a bottle of vodka . . . but couldn't go through with it. I think I swallowed like two pills, then ended up bawling and passing out."

Storm makes a low, velvety noise that travels through my entire body. It's comforting and warming, and as the ripple of that humming sound extends everywhere like a soft glow, he wraps me tighter. Hugging me to his chest, encased securely within his powerful arms, the man who owns my heart takes a deep inhale through his nose.

"I'm happy you're still here, darlin'."

"You're certain the property in Crimson Ridge is untouchable?" My steps have nearly worn through the tiles of this ostentatious kitchen while I've been pacing up and down, speaking with Clara on the other end of the phone line.

I don't give a fuck that Antoine or Crispin might record or listen in on this entire conversation; in fact, I'm perfectly happy if they hear what my lawyer has to say. It just adds weight to the fact that even though they might threaten to scrub my name from anything relating to Lane Enterprises—not that I want a rotten cent to come my way from now on—I have an assurance that they cannot touch my home.

"No, Briar. You're entirely safe. That property has, in fact, always been in your name. It was never legally your father's. I can see from the documents here in front of me that the trust was set up not long before your birth, by Jan and Ingrid Lane."

"My grandparents," I breathe out a little shakily.

"Yes, they left the Crimson Ridge property registered to a trust under your name; legally, you own it. However, until you reached the age of eighteen, your father was considered the party responsible . . . you know, before you were an adult kind of deal."

"So, what you're saying is that my father hid it from me."

"I wouldn't like to make assumptions . . ."

"He hid it from me." I nod to myself while taking in the ghost of my reflection in the glass overlooking the swimming pool.

"It does appear like he wasn't interested in allowing you to know it existed."

"That's fancy lawyer speak that I shall choose to interpret as, 'Your dad was a first-class asshole.'"

Clara chuckles and doesn't say anything.

"Well, we know he was busy hiding a lot of things, so here we are."

"How are you feeling about all of this? Remember, I will be right here if you need to deflect any questions my way."

As she says the words, I hear the front door open, and voices echo off the polished tiles.

Chewing the inside of my lip, I drop my voice a little lower. "Okay, they're here. We're really doing this. You've got the car waiting for me?"

"The driver is already parked outside. If they try anything, I've got my contact at the local station doing a routine patrol of your street, and they can be at your house within minutes if needed."

"Just make sure it's not *me* who's the one getting arrested if they do get called in."

"Don't actually bite them, and you should be good," Clara deadpans. "You know what? On second thought, do what you want. I'm sure I can make it seem like you tripped and fell teeth-first."

Blowing out a low breath, I put the phone on speaker and lay it flat on the gleaming white bench. In the exact same spot where I left the evidence of Antoine's rampant infidelity a couple of months ago.

As I watch both my soon-to-be ex-husband and my sister arrive, I plaster on the fakest smile I can muster, considering the circumstances.

"Briar, this needs to be quick. I've got meetings on my calendar all afternoon." Antoine doesn't even look up from his phone. My sister trails behind him, evidently still with that stick firmly wedged up her bony ass.

"Oh, don't worry, it won't take long at all. In fact, I have to meet my own lawyer shortly, so it'll be worth all of our while if we handle this promptly."

I glance quickly at the phone, seeing Clara's name still illuminated on the screen as she listens in.

Cris rolls her eyes. "Typical, Briar. Making this all about you and being hysterical. Did we really need to come all the way out here for whatever this is?" She dumps her handbag on the countertop and adjusts her high ponytail. My sister sports her requisite matching, cream-colored designer yoga bra and leggings, looking every inch the LA native.

Ignoring her snipe, I gather up one of the piles of paperwork already lain out before me.

"Antoine, I need your signature on these documents, please." I push the tabbed and annotated divorce papers toward him with a pen. "Crispin, I don't want, or need, anything from you, but this should make it nice and easy for us to never have to cross paths again, as this is my statement and legal filing already submitted to the Lane Enterprises board."

Scooping up the second set of papers, I shove them in her direction.

In my head, I start counting down.

Five.

Four.

Antoine screws his nose up and lifts a couple of the pages with a forefinger, before letting them drop, then sneers back at me.

Three.

Crispin skim reads the first couple of paragraphs on her page and starts laughing.

Two . . .

"Are you fucking for real?" Antoine snaps. "I've already told you, this arrangement isn't going to be anything but the business deal your father promised me. I'm not signing these."

"You're the dumbest bitch alive." My sister shakes her head. "What's your plan? To run back to the mountains, shack up with our uncle, and have his babies like some hillbilly whore? You'd never outrun those headlines."

She gives me an ugly smile, and Antoine does the same. His face already contorting into an expression that tells me he's got the threats ready to fly, his way of attempting to drag me obediently back into line.

Not this time, douchebag.

"Here's a headline for you." Spinning around the first of the pages from my third stack of documents, I hand them each a duplicate copy. "How about something catchy like, 'Lane Enterprises founder groomed a minor, impregnated her, and then refused to acknowledge either her, or the baby'?"

They both hardly look at the printout before them, eyes bouncing up to glare at me.

"Oh, yes, let's just clarify that little detail, shall we, Cris? Seeing as you happily followed Dad's lead in spouting the bullshit rumors that Tegan Mitchell was pregnant. Even though her healthy baby boy was actually born prior to her death."

I take their continued silence as my opportunity to keep pressing forward.

This time, I pluck the duplicate copies of the photo showing my father with his arm around the bare waist of a *very* young teenage cheerleader. She beams at the camera, all of fourteen, complete with her blonde curls, red lipstick, and a distinctive beauty mark on her upper lip.

"Or, what about, 'Underage statutory assault by Erik Lane revealed: the man who covered up his depravity by planting a girl in front of his brother while blackout drunk, just so he could use the excuse that she was Stôrmand Lane's wife as a way to keep her in secret at his apartment'?"

Cris turns bright red.

From the look of him, I think Antoine might burst a blood vessel.

"Do either of you need to sit down? Want a glass of water?" I smile and cock my head to one side.

My sister finally rediscovers her forked tongue. "What is this shit, Briar? I didn't think you'd stoop as low as making up outrageous lies. I should have you fucking committed."

"No. What I'm doing here is providing an opportunity for both of you to not end up in jail for aiding and abetting a man who was a predator."

I take a deep breath and smooth down my hair.

"Tegan Mitchell didn't specify who she referred to in the note she left, and the convenient assumption that played into the hands of our father was that it was her husband—even if they were only married on paper—who drove her to take her own life."

Tapping the papers in front of me, I fix my sister with an unflinching stare.

"As it turns out, she meant our father all along. No wonder he was so eager to cover every little sordid detail. Maybe she wasn't thinking straight when she wrote something nonspecific. Maybe she was scared right till the end, and that's why she didn't outright name him. Or maybe she was simply trying to protect her newborn son from his own biological parent. Either way, she left it all detailed for her own parents. An attempt to give them closure, knowing how much pain they would be in."

The air in here is so thick I could slice it in two.

"I doubt you'll want to look through all of these documents right now, but I have had my attorney copy you into the files via email, so you can enjoy perusing them at a later, more convenient time. Although, Cris, you're familiar with all these details, aren't you? You're more than familiar with all the details of Tegan Mitchell's child being born prior to her passing. While I don't want to make assumptions, since you were well aware of our father's efforts to make sure the story that she was still pregnant at the time stick, I doubt you'll need to take a look over things."

"This doesn't win you a divorce, Briar," Antoine says. "You can trash your fortune if you want, but I'm still owed the connections to Lane Enterprises your rotten fucking last name gives me on our marriage certificate."

Antoine leans on the counter, narrowing his eyes on me.

I straighten my spine and glare right back.

"Actually, it does. Because Montgomery Media arranged for corporate entertainment that, for some strange reason, always seemed to include a performance by a certain high school cheer squad. Not only was my father grooming Tegan Mitchell while she was still underage, but your very own family and business were the agents ensuring he could get away with it right in the public eye."

He sneers my way. "That's bullshit. You can't prove anything."

"Would payments made directly from Montgomery Media into the bank account of a fourteen-year-old do? What about transcripts of text messages and emails? Tegan might have been young, but she was intelligent enough to keep records."

Antoine curses beneath his breath, knuckles going white against the countertop. "You're a foul little cunt."

"And you're a filthy fucking cheater who is going to give me that divorce right now. You're going to sign those papers; otherwise, my attorney is going to press send on her own media release . . ." I check the time on my phone screen. "Oh, in about the next ten minutes, give or take. If I've calculated my time zones correctly, it should land just in time for a breaking-news headline on the evening bulletins across the UK and Europe, embroiling Montgomery Media in a child prostitution ring and the subsequent death of Tegan Mitchell."

Shouldering my handbag, I gather up the remaining copies of evidence that I don't even need to bother showing them. "But what would I know? I'm just a dumb bitch, right?"

"Dad regretted you being born." My sister spits out her last jab of poison, and I don't even care. I'm so fucking done.

"Considering that he drove a young woman to end her own life, coerced his own brother to marry his hidden secret while under the influence, and refused to claim a child that was his . . . I don't really give a shit what he thought about me."

"The Mitchells signed an NDA. I'll make sure they get dragged through the most painful, expensive lawsuit I can come up with if they breathe a word." Cris has almost gone purple as she sees her precious Lane Enterprises potentially collapsing around her ears.

"Oh, they're not going to say anything. However, the company's board has been fully briefed and made aware of my final act as a primary shareholder. They have signed off on a new trust fund that all the shares I had previously been entitled to as a result of Dad's estate shall be paid into immediately. I've also instructed the company that Dad personally informed me of his insistence to go ahead with back-paying them share profits for the past ten years . . . you know, his lasting contribution to recognizing the important work of adoption agencies around the country. It's all detailed on page five."

Cris quickly flicks through to the part of the document where the annual multiple-seven-figure donation is listed, along with the total sum of back pay covering the past ten years.

"Our brother might have been screwed over by you and Dad, but I'll gladly ensure he benefits financially, and I'm sure that boy will live a much healthier and more peaceful life having absolutely no knowledge of his connection to the Lanes."

As I talk, I watch Antoine hover over the documents, pen in

hand but yet to actually connect with the tabbed lines requiring his signature.

"Look, Antoine . . . We can do this right now, just a few quick signatures, or we can fight this out in a war of dirty secrets in the public eye. Think of it this way, give my freedom to me, and you're free to go rub your tiny dick over as many Hamptons socialites as you want and schmooze up to all their Ivy League club papas to bag yourself a rich ornament who will happily sit around this place playing LA housewife."

He looks as though he's about to start arguing with me, then checks his watch. "Fine. Run back to your little game of incest by proxy."

Laughing now, I cross my arms. "I don't expect you to understand any of this because you've never cared about anything or anyone other than your own overinflated ego. So no, what I'm going to do is go live my life. I'm going to do something good in this world, and I'm going to do it all with a man who stands by my side and understands me better after a matter of weeks than the likes of you people have done in twenty-six years."

I rip the papers away from him as I see that he's signed the final location and quickly double-check to confirm I've gotten everything I need from him.

My sister has remained suspiciously quiet while watching on, and when I take a glance at her, there's so much rage flowing through her veins that in just a second, she launches at me, quickly rounding the kitchen bench, and slaps me square across the face.

"Get the fuck out of my life, Briar. You're the worst thing that ever happened to me." Her voice trembles, high-pitched and screeching.

The hit blooms into a rash of heat under the force of her assault. It stings like a bitch and leaves my head spinning.

You could hear a pin drop in this marble and glass-clad mausoleum.

"Are you okay, Briar?" The concern in Clara's voice cuts through the silence over the speakerphone, only punctuated by my sister's heavy breathing.

"I'm fine, thanks, Clara. I'm ready for the driver now." Rubbing my jaw with my free hand, I look at my sister with nothing even remotely like anger. All I feel is sorry for the misery she's chosen to let fester inside her all this time. "Crispin, I hope to never see you again as long as I live, but do me a favor and go to therapy . . . or better yet, take up woodchopping."

Turning on my heel, with quick strides toward the front door, I feel the weight of the past years of my life melt away as each foot brings me closer to the sparkling midday sun dancing outside.

For the first time in my life, I'm officially free.

With trembling trepidation deep inside my chest, as I rub one hand over the leather cuff still secured around my wrist, all I can hope is that the man I left behind might have been willing to wait all this time for me.

CHAPTER 43

Storm

Running the faucet, I carefully set the glass beneath the flow of water and hold the stems of the flowers to one side so the delicate petals don't wilt.

The kitchen still has a faint essence of new-paint smell to it when I stand in this spot beside the basin. The countertops are no longer cracked, shitty surfaces. I replaced them with new polished wood that looks a million times better than it ever did before.

I even replaced the awful couch.

The bathroom is on my list to work on next, but with the summer season approaching and Beau arriving in town any day to look over things at his ranch, the amount of hours I've had to work on the cabin have been steadily diminishing.

Turning off the faucet, I cross back to the wooden table—which is now freshly sanded and oiled and looking equally as smartened up as the countertops—and set the flowers in the spot where she always used to put them.

Spring blooms have popped up and seem to form a cheerful carpet everywhere I look, yet all it does is jab at my stomach each time I see their brightly colored faces, reminding me that it's been weeks upon weeks since that day she left.

In all that time, I haven't heard from her.

The reality is starting to settle in my gut, heavy and oppressive, that Briar may never come back.

We didn't make any promises to one another. For all I know, or can even hope, she's ditched her shitty ex and maybe left the country. She deserves to live a life and have her freedom beyond living beneath my brother's thumb, and sometimes when I lie in bed at night sending her messages, ones that she opens and reads straight away but never replies to, I think that maybe she's wandering around art galleries in Paris or driving herself on a scooter around Rome or some shit.

Then I tend to spiral into dark thoughts about the array of pretty boys lined up to play tour guide with her, and that makes me seriously consider booking a ticket to LA just to try to find out where she might have gone.

I've never been tempted to go back to that fucking city, but for Briar, I'd jump on a direct flight in a heartbeat.

Dragging my hands through my hair, I wander aimlessly across the few feet to the kitchen and rest my ass against the counter. I've got a fuckload of work to do. I've got messages from Beau to respond to. Then I need to drag my ass to go see Lucas Rhodes about the horses on his ranch.

Except, instead of making a start on any of those things, my eyes catch on the couch. It's a much more comfortable replacement for the piece of shit that used to sit in that spot, but all it does is remind me.

Seeing it brings back memories of her.

I'm stroking myself while she's rubbing her sweet pussy against my thigh, grinding herself down while we're slowly, leisurely making out.

The band of my cuff strapped to her wrist brushes against my collarbone as her fingers tug on my hair.

I tell her how beautiful she looks being the perfect little fuck toy for me to use, how she's not allowed to come like that, but I want her right on edge.

The words sit right there on the edge of my consciousness, resting on the cusp just like her climax is—that I want to confess how much I love her.

Instead, I suck on her tongue and growl. "Ride me, darlin'."

Briar rewards me with a smile and a delicious moan, and it's the most precious thing in the entire world. Sinking forward against my mouth at the same time as she slides down over my cock, my girl straddles my lap, and this is exactly how I want every fucking day to be for the rest of my life.

It's tortuous how every corner of this cabin reminds me of what it was like to have her in my arms. I swear to god her scent is still imprinted in the wooden beams and fixtures because I'll catch a hit of *her* every now and then, and it stops me dead in my tracks.

On those bitter, foul-tasting, low days, when I've contemplated throwing all caution to the wind and going after her, the only thing that stopped me is knowing that if I did, it would fuck things up even more.

If she didn't say goodbye other than in a two-word note, doesn't reply to anything I send her, and doesn't want to come back . . . then the message is pretty damn transparent she doesn't want me to go after her.

I'm not going to force anything. That girl deserves the right to make her own decisions, and while it goddamn makes my heart bleed to think that she might move on, I'm also painfully aware that she can do better than a guy like me.

Yet, I'm a creature with a sickness, one that remains in some tiny part hopeful, because at least Briar reads my messages.

She opens them.

That has to mean something . . . right?

"Storm?" The sharp crackle and static of the radio slices right through my maze of thoughts I've been lost in.

"Storm, are you there?" Layla's voice fills the room.

I only takes a few paces before I'm swiping up the handset to respond in all of a couple of seconds. "Go ahead, Layla."

"Thank fuck. We need you up here at the ranch."

"Someone injured?" Shit, I run my hand over the back of my neck. It wouldn't be the first time I've worried about Colt getting hurt or some fresh hell like that, and with how isolated they are, medical help is always going to be a long way away.

"No—but one of the horses. They've thrown a shoe."

I blow out a breath. At least it's not a call for help with Colton Wilder half bleeding to death on my hands. "Don't fucking scare me like that, Layla."

"Well, in my world, this is an emergency. Winnie looks to be in pain, and I'm asking, politely, for you to get your ass up here right now."

The radio crackles.

"Please, Storm? For Winnie?"

"I'm on my way. Just keep her in the barn, stop her from moving around too much, and wrap the hoof if you need to until I get there."

"Thank you. I know you'll take excellent care of her for me."

"Be there soon."

Hanging the radio up, I don't have time to keep thinking about the girl I'm missing, like my fucking heart has vacated my chest and crawled after her. There is too much shit I gotta do, and this visit to Devil's Peak Ranch is likely to take me the rest of the day.

Grabbing my jacket and hat and shoving into my boots, I pause with one hand on the door handle.

Before leaving, I tug my phone out of my pocket and snap a quick photo of the vase of flowers. There's no opportunity to linger or agonize over typing a caption, so I just post it to my Instagram and add it to the collection of daily photos, trying to at least show Briar that even if she's not here to see it, this place is always going to be her home.

I shift the truck into park and hop out onto the gravel of the deserted yard. Just as I slam the door shut behind me, ready to make my way straight toward the barn where I know Layla will be waiting with Winnie, I hear a throat clear roughly.

"Stôrmand."

Leaning on the rail to the porch of his fancy fucking mountain property, looking out over the ranch and Devil's Peak, Colton Wilder gives me a look I can't interpret. Or, more to the point, I can't be bothered to.

"Get your ass up here." He beckons me with a wave to join him, and as he stands straight, I see he's got two beers dangling from one hand.

"Bit unlike you to be taking an afternoon off, old man."

He hits me with a grunt and a shake of his head. "Just come sit with me for a minute, would ya."

"Take it your horses are all fucking fine, then," I grumble as I climb the short flight of steps flanked by stonework and cedar-wood, joining him in one of the ridiculous oversized outdoor chairs he's got on this porch.

"How else was I supposed to get you up here, *hmm*?" He hands me one of the drinks and then settles back with a sigh and readjusts his cap, tugging it back down over his dark hair.

"Preying on my weakness. You know I'd run up here on two legs through snow if those damn horses were injured. Thought only your asshole son was the one to stoop low enough for bull-shit pranks around here."

"Quit your bitching and drink your damn beer."

I stretch my boots out in front of me and drop my hat onto the seat beside mine, so I can sink right back into the plush cushions.

We both sit there in silence, listening to the creak of the pine trees in the wind, as a long sip of my beer goes down on a smooth glide.

Colt eventually clears his throat again.

Turning to face him, I narrow my eyes. "If this isn't about a problem with your horses, and you seem to have something wedged in your windpipe over there, wanna spit it out?"

"Look, I'm no expert . . . but speaking as someone who almost fucked everything up because I didn't go after the girl . . ."

Heat races up the back of my neck. "You don't know shit, sweetheart." I tip my beer back and nearly fucking drain the entire contents. My throat works as my mind scrambles to figure out what Colt thinks he knows.

"Well, I can sure as hell tell you how fucking miserable it feels when you wake up one morning and realize you let someone special slip through your fingers."

I let the air rush out of my lungs, scrubbing one hand over my face. "That obvious, huh?"

His eyes drift to my knuckles for a second.

"Storm, you and I have known each other a long-ass time. In all those years, aside from these bloody horses, I've never seen you take care of anything, or anyone, including yourself."

An elephant sits itself on my chest, and I struggle down another swallow of my beer.

"It hurts like a bitch, and I don't know much, but I can tell you love is a motherfucker." He leans forward with elbows resting on his knees.

"Yeah, well, that motherfucker certainly knows how to play dirty."

"She coming back?"

I shove my hand into my hair. "Dunno."

"You heard from her?"

"What is this? Fifty fucking questions?" I grunt.

Colt scratches his beard and studies me quietly. "I'm not gonna let you waste away by yourself on this mountain and nearly make the same mistake I did."

"Yeah, well, shit was simple for you."

That makes him bark out a laugh. "Yeah. Real goddamn simple."

Considering that I watched him mope around this ranch for nearly half a year before he finally went and found his girl, I know he understands this feeling, this sensation of being hollowed out and having your heart squeezed so damn tight it might implode.

Even if I don't want to admit to him that I've been struggling to know how to even fucking breathe without her.

"As someone who nearly screwed up the best thing that ever happened to me, I'm telling you now, if you even have the faintest idea of where she is, go get her." Colt turns his bottle around and around in his hands as he speaks softly.

Tugging on my hair, I shift my weight around. "This is shit I don't know, Colt. Put me on the back of a bull; I can hang on and try not to get myself killed. Give me horses; I can hammer nails and fit shoes all day. Want me to herd cattle? I can fucking do it with one arm tied behind my back and a lame horse."

I set my nearly empty bottle down and crack my knuckles, leaning forward now. Feeling like my gut is churning as I admit out loud what I've kept swallowing down for weeks on end. "What if she doesn't fucking want what I have to offer? What if the reason she left is because I screwed it up."

He continues to study his beer, as if reliving his own version of this fresh hell I've found myself incapable of climbing out of.

"Do you think you did something?" Colt finally speaks.

I hate that I can't answer that question. My time with Briar was so intense and intertwined with her learning things about herself and exploring her own identity . . . I've wondered the same thing too many times while tossing and turning through sleepless nights. I've woken up with drenched sheets after nightmares that she was hurt by my hand in some way. That I was too rough with her, too demanding, too desperate.

Coughing into my fist, I finally dredge up a response. "I don't know, but shit, maybe I'm just cursed to be alone . . . Either way, how am I supposed to know what to do?"

Colt just shrugs like an unhelpful bastard. "You don't know until you at least try."

"You boys hungry?" A gentle voice interrupts us. Layla appears, looking every inch the dirty little liar she is.

Scowling in her direction, I shake my head. "Don't expect me to pick up the radio next time if there's a real emergency."

"Sorry?" She hits me with green eyes that are anything but apologetic. Her gaze, filled with curiosity, bounces quick-fire between me and Colt, trying to work out how much we've discussed so far. If Colt knows about Briar, then of course she does, too.

"Winnie girl deserves better than to be dragged into your web of lies, Layla." I scowl and receive an unrepentant, beaming smile in return.

She settles herself on the armrest of Colt's chair and immediately swipes his beer to steal a sip.

"Let me feed you dinner and make it up to you?"

I try to think of an excuse to leave. The last thing I feel like doing is sitting around watching these two be a pair of lovebirds all night.

"Don't pretend you're not hungry. I know how you eat. Stick around for a bit. There's even a bed if you want to crash here for the night," Colt says.

"Bit cozy, isn't it? How does that work anyway, you and Kayce all under one roof? Isn't that too weird for him?" I raise an eyebrow.

Layla immediately flushes.

I'll take that as a yes.

As I know how these two can't seem to keep their hands to themselves for five seconds, that doesn't surprise me in the slightest.

"We're actually living up in the cabin on the ridge, but on nights like tonight, we'll stay down here at the main house." Colt gets to his feet. "Kayce is overnighting in Crimson Ridge for a couple of days and training over at Rhodes Ranch."

"Good. He needs a few bronc rides that'll try to chew him up and spit him out before the season starts."

"Come on, let's figure out what we're gonna feed you." Layla pats my shoulder as she stops beside my chair. "Wanna make yourself useful and chop some potatoes for me?"

"As long as you promise not to ask me shit about fuck, I'm happy."

"Okay." Layla twists her lips, and her expression softens slightly. "Although, just saying, if you need help booking the next available flight out of here, I'm your gal. Hell, just give me the signal, and I'll drive you to the airport like our tails are on fire."

My default scowl is met with a smile that says she knows all my secrets.

As Colt and Layla head inside, I pause before following them. Their Wi-Fi might be patchy, but it sometimes works out here, and today it seems that I'm in luck to be able to check my messages.

I scroll straight past all the notifications from Beau, other business inquiries, and stupid, brainless comments left on my social media posts.

There's only one name I'm looking for.

There's only one message thread I open, confirming for myself what I already knew would be the case.

No reply.

I've already fucked up so much in this life. I'm not going to dare ruin Briar's by being selfish. Except, she read my latest message, and if she's seen that, then surely she's seen my daily photos showing her the cabin, the flowers, all the things I'd do for her, if only she'd let me take care of her forever.

Jesus. Maybe Colt was right, and I *do* need to go find out the facts for myself. How much longer am I gonna be content to sit here alone, not knowing?

As I lock my phone screen, tucking it away in my back pocket, and kick my boots off at the door, I'm already hollering.

"*Layla.*"

She pops her head around the corner from the kitchen, a grin taking over her face as she recognizes my furrowed brow and determined expression. "We're getting your city girl back?" Excitement lights her green eyes.

"Let that man of yours take over the cooking . . ." I grab her by the shoulders and steer us in the direction of where I know Colt's office and computer live. "I'm gonna need you to help me book a flight."

CHAPTER 44

Storm

The gravel scrapes beneath my tires as I pull up in front of the cabin with a skid. If there's any chance in hell of making it to the airport to catch this fucking plane, I'm gonna need to haul ass.

I don't bother removing the keys. I just hurl myself out the door and refuse to pause, not even for the extra second it might take to shut it behind me. All I gotta find is a clean set of clothes and I'll figure everything else out later.

Except, as I jump down, a flicker of flames visible through the window catches my eye. Smoke fills the air, hanging low and heavy with the cold dragging it down to ground level.

Fuck.

The cabin.

Instinct drives me as I race up the couple of steps, my heart in my mouth. Did I leave something on? Could the electrics have sparked?

Jesus. Please, no. I can't lose this cabin. This is *her home*. What the fuck am I going to do if I lose this place, with all the best parts of my goddamn life all contained within these walls?

I can't handle losing Briar and all the memories of being with her.

As I get closer to the door, I don't even think twice about barging in blind to try to put it out myself. Waiting while I get on the radio and send a call out for the fucking mountain rescue, all the while watching this place go up in flames like a tinder box, would be be a living nightmare I have no interest in enduring.

Busting through the door, I'm already halfway to the kitchen to start running the faucet and finding something to smother the flames with, when my brain catches up with the scene in front of me.

Brown eyes meet mine from across the room.

She's crouched in front of the fire, with a couple of pieces of kindling ready to add to the building flicker of orange painting her skin in a soft glow.

Holy fuck.

Right there, that moment is when I nearly hit my goddamn knees.

I don't know which one of us moves first. We collide somewhere in the middle of the room, and as Briar launches forward, I catch her mid-leap, wrapping her arms and legs around me.

"I thought you'd left—that you gave up on waiting. You weren't here, and the place felt so cold." Her voice and body shake, interspersed with sniffled sobs, as dampness and flowing tears meet my neck.

I'm left speechless, holding her so tight there is every chance my girl can't even breathe, because I don't think I fucking can.

"Darlin' . . ." My voice cracks. My mind is spinning. "That's no way to go about begging for my cock . . . creepin' in here after dark." The words croak out of me.

Briar's sweet little body goes still for a second, her face still buried in the crook of my neck, before she starts shaking . . . this time with silent laughter.

"God, I've missed you." Her lips are plush and warm, tucked against my racing pulse. "So much." I feel her warmth and scent wrap around me tighter, to match the way her fingers curl into the hair at my nape beneath the brim of my hat is the best fucking gift I could ever receive in this life.

"You're back." I breathe the words into her hair. Part of me doesn't want that to be a question. Every part of me, in fact. I'm saying it like a prayer, hoping the fact she's here in my arms, in our home, means that she's here for good and that I don't have to face the prospect of figuring out how the hell I'm supposed to do life without her.

"I never really left. This whole time, I've been dreaming of being here with you," she whispers, the words setting something bright and hopeful alive inside my chest.

Turning us around, I gently set her down on the kitchen counter. As much as I want to march straight into that bedroom and not resurface for an entire month—to make up for every single soul-destroying day she's been gone—I've got too many words flying around my brain. They're horribly jumbled and tangled and ineloquent, but I'm hoping like hell they'll form something worthy of telling her all the things she deserves to hear from me.

"I'm sor—" She starts speaking as I pull back, and I immediately cut her off, cupping her jaw and resting my thumb over her lips.

"Just give me a second." I stay there, between her knees, seeing brief flashes and glimpses of the memories of us here in this very spot together—fragments and shards of little scenes that I've replayed in my mind's eye thousands of times over the past few weeks.

Her cheeks are tinged with pink, damp with all those tears I felt a moment ago, and her eyes glisten with a little redness to them from that outpouring of emotion. I have to swallow back the lump forming in my own throat as I bring my other hand up to her face.

Using both hands now, I glide the pads of my thumbs over

her cheeks to wipe away any remaining wetness there, inhaling the way she softens and starts to breathe slower beneath my touch.

Briar's lashes flutter a little as I flex my fingers against the side of her neck, taking my time exploring the elegant curve of her cheeks and brush some of the loose strands of hair off her forehead.

I reach up to drag my hat off and toss it onto the counter, then lean forward to let my lips meet her forehead. As I do so, she exhales a shaky breath, the puff of air gusting against my Adam's apple.

"In case it wasn't obvious." With voice dropping low, I pull back and fix her with a look that I hope to god conveys how much this moment means to me. "Doing life without you is miserable." I brush my lips over her cheek, and Briar makes a soft noise.

"Please stay with me." *Kiss.* "Let me be part of your life." *Kiss.* "I love you so fucking much, and I'll be in love with you forever, darlin.'"

This time, I let my lips finally touch hers. She's as soft as I remember, as delicate as one of those flower petals sitting in the vase by the window, sweet as the scent that gently fills this cabin each day, and against all hope, Briar kisses me back.

Her fingers close around my arms, holding on with the same kind of reassuring touch that lets my chest expand fully.

Our mouths move together in a slow, exploring connection, and right here feels like the type of first kiss we maybe should have had. The kind of romantic, gentle glide of wet, pillowy, soft lips of two lovers who finally get to close that distance and feel the electricity crackle in the space between their bodies. Except, I wouldn't change any of the opportunities I've been blessed with to taste this girl's sweetness before now.

She hums against my mouth, and I drink down the utter miracle that this moment feels like.

Now that I've had the chance to kiss her, to properly *show* her what this moment means to me, it's like the words finally slot into place, and they're right there, ready to tumble out.

Drawing back a fraction, I let our eyes reconnect and tilt her chin ever so slightly with my forefinger. The rich brown of her irises has cleared from the weight of emotion moments ago. Now they're shining and brilliant, and her pupils dilate a little more as my thumb brushes over her lips again. Because I'm fucking addicted to touching her, feeling her warmth, having that sensation of Briar Lane back in my arms.

"This is the first time I've fallen, truly fallen," I murmur. "I've been thrown from the back of a bull and tossed into the dirt countless times, but this right here is where I've crash-landed. This will be the only time I'll ever fall in love, darlin'. *It's you.* You're it for me. Most likely, it has always been you, and I never truly knew who I was looking for in the stands all that time."

Her chest rises and falls as her lips hang parted, staring back at me.

"Can I say something now?" Her whisper is matched with the tiniest curve of a smile, and that look fucking seals my fate. If I didn't already want to give her the entire world, I'd do anything to have her smile like that at me every single day for eternity.

"Depends." I'm grumbling but not really at her, more at the agony of not knowing how these next few moments are going to go. "Maybe, but then again, I'm just an idiot who's standing here terrified you're gonna break my heart, little thorn. So be gentle with me, okay?"

I slide my hand down to take hers, tucking it against my chest beneath my palm.

"Storm . . ." Her face softens as she meets my gaze, and just before she says whatever she has planned, I see it.

There's a flicker of her eyes down to where I'm clutching her fist inside mine, clinging to her like I'm about to drown at sea. Briar does a double-take, and her eyebrows scrunch together.

"Wait—what is this?" Her hand wrestles free from my own, despite my grunt of protest, and she twists her head to one side, reading the evidence laid out for the world to see.

"It's you, darlin'." The words rumble out of me as her eyes dart across my knuckles, back and forth with disbelief at what she's seeing inked there.

The letters that I've had set there on each finger, indelibly so, just for her, to keep her close.

Even if my girl never came back to me.

BRIAR

"When did you do this?" Her wide eyes flick back up to mine, and she twists my hand back around to face me so that I can see the tattooed letters that I know fully well are there.

"About five minutes after you left." Shrugging, I steal her hand back so that I can clasp it to my chest again, the one enclosed beneath her name that now rests right above my thudding heart. "Little did I know why I'd always kept that space free. I didn't know it was meant to bear your name, but now I know the exact reason there was never anything that felt right to be permanently marked there. I'd do anything you ask me to, darlin' . . . I'd give you the entire fucking world if I could . . . and even if you never came back to me, at least I'd always be able to keep you close." My other hand, the one tattooed with my own name, comes up to cup her jaw.

"I love you." Briar lets the words drift between us, words that she can't possibly know how much they mean, coming from her.

"This right here . . . this cabin, this life, it's all I've got to give you, Briar." My throat works as I focus on detecting any flicker of indication she might regret any of this. "You know I can't offer you a family of your own if that's what you were wanting . . ."

Her lips curve and she's already shaking her head before I finish speaking. "None of that matters. I'd never wanted anything but happiness, and *this right here* is exactly that for me. It's so much more than I ever dreamed might be possible."

Lifting her hand to my mouth, I kiss her fingertips. "No one's ever said those words to me before," I admit.

"Good. Wait—" Her eyes widen a little as if she's startled herself with the force of her own admission. "Sorry, is that messed up? Is that weird for me to say out loud? I fucking love you, so much, and I don't know if I could handle knowing there had been someone who got that part of your heart before I did." The brightest damn smile eases across her face like a beam of early morning sunlight.

"Be selfish all you like . . . We both know I am when it comes to you." My mouth twitches at the corners as I watch her tongue poke out and wet her bottom lip.

We both linger there, staring at each other as the crackle of the fire and my thudding pulse punctuate the quiet. I know, for me, this certainly feels like a dream that I hope like hell isn't going to disappear in a cloud of smoke.

"The cuff is on," she says it so quietly, almost hesitantly, while biting down on that plump curve. Those beautiful dark eyes stray to my own mouth. It's as if she doesn't think I've been about two seconds from losing the battle with my self-restraint this entire time.

"You look beautiful in anything, Briar," I hum, letting my hand slip down to sit over her throat. "But you look especially gorgeous wearing my cuff and my ink."

"Can we add the hat?" Her eyes flash as I squeeze ever so gently.

"You want to wear my hat?"

She nods quickly. "Your hat, your cuff, it's all yours, baby."

My pulse triples.

"Holy fuck. You got it straight in that pretty head of yours that I love you, right?" My voice is practically a growl.

Briar nods again, pupils blooming. "You like hearing me call you baby?"

If I wasn't already feral for this girl, she just sealed our fate. "I love you . . . Remember that for about the next twenty minutes or so, okay?"

"Please. *Yes.*" Her breath hitches, and she's already squirming.

Reaching over, I grab my hat off the bench and set it over her glossy curls, and this right here is *everything*. I take a moment to let it all settle in my veins, rich and nourishing, as I drink her in from head to toe.

My girl, who I'm never fucking letting go as long as there's breath in my lungs. Scooping her up, it feels like I could float across this damn cabin with how good it is to have her curled into my body.

My lips find her ear, and the shudder roaming through her beneath my hold sets the spark blazing that has been waiting to ignite this whole time.

"Ready to learn something, darlin'?"

EPILOGUE

Briar

Nothing feels as good as being back on this mountain, back in my cowboy's arms, and returning to Devil's Peak Ranch.

It's as if my lungs are able to fully expand once more, and my heart feels lighter than ever in my entire life.

This feels like a brand-new beginning in so many ways, and I couldn't wipe the grin off my face as we drove beneath the hanging steer skull and sign welcoming us back to the top of Devil's Peak.

Within a heartbeat, I was waylaid by Layla for coffee, who insisted that I join her while Storm got started on the horses he'd be working with today. After whisking me inside the house—complete with warm, lengthy hugs and more than a few tears on my part at the relief of being back surrounded by good, caring, kind people—she also let slip details of her little plan she had set in motion.

Turns out Layla Birch is a girl's girl, a locked vault of epic proportions, and had been keeping our secret for quite some time—since that night when we all went out for dinner, in fact—and had I not been at the cabin waiting for him the other night, she'd have enacted a plan to make sure Storm was about to get on a plane in order to come and find me.

"City girl," she said. "I spent a winter stuck on this mountain with a man I wasn't supposed to be looking twice at . . . Trust me, I know the signs."

We spent hours talking, and Layla filled me in on what I missed, with her excitement in full flight at the news that Sage would return to Crimson Ridge any day now for some final meetings with her new clients before she relocated at the start of summer.

I can hardly believe I've been sitting at the kitchen island of a beautiful ranch homestead making plans for the warmer weather, able to breathe easily knowing that my life is my own to do with as I please.

I've got a future to plan for, and it looks fucking incredible.

Now, Layla is heading on horseback to her and Colt's cabin, which is on a more isolated part of the ranch, looking every inch a cowgirl dreamboat. Kayce is around here somewhere, and I'm assuming Colt is, too. However, I haven't seen either of the Wilder men since arriving today.

Although, I am certainly not complaining about having a private moment to appreciate Storm while he's hard at work.

Damn, the sight of him in a pair of chaps does something to me I can't explain.

Am I a chap slut? A chap whore? Either way, I would do very questionable things to ensure those make it into the bedroom at some point in time.

"Do you always get this wet watching your uncle work?" Storm is bent over, with a hammer in one hand, holding the hoof of the horse he's currently attending to in the other. As he speaks, he tilts his head up just enough to flash me bright blue eyes and a devilish smirk.

"Shhh. Oh my god, you can't say stuff like that here." My eyes dart around the barn.

"Oh, can't I?"

"*No*," I hiss, still craning my neck to ensure no one is nearby to hear his wickedness.

He quickly snips off the remaining pieces of nail sticking out of the hoof, then rhythmically files the points down to a smooth surface.

The man is wearing a white T-shirt, stretched tight over his broad shoulders, and with each practiced glide back and forth of his tools, I'm treated to a show of straight-up forearm porn.

Corded muscles flex and roll, with veins and tattoos popping all the way down to the backs of his hands.

My mouth goes dry as I stand there, openly watching him, because it feels incredible to be able to. Yet, the sensation that I *shouldn't* still lingers . . . and well, shit, apparently, it still turns me the fuck on.

Storm sets the horse's hoof and brand-new shoe back down, then fixes me with a heated look. I'm captured in that piercing blue gaze as he picks up a new horseshoe and a hammer, all the while maintaining eye contact.

I shiver, and Storm advances on me straight away, still with tools in his hands.

"Show me your wrist," he says, not touching but looking at my body with raw desire, and that sets alight whatever embers were merely glowing just before.

My hands tremble a little with nervous excitement. Pulling back the sleeve of my sweater, the leather strap—the evidence of how much this man entirely owns my heart and goddamn soul—sits around my wrist.

The cuff is on.

"*Hmm.* Thought so." His lips tip up at the corner.

"We can't. Not here. What if someone sees?" I'm backpedaling fast as Storm continues to crowd my space, and before I know it, we're inside the tack room. A rich scent of leather fills the air, and my pulse flutters frantically.

"This will only take a minute."

Confusion and arousal are waging a battle inside me, yet I already know that this man could ask for anything and I would trust him with every fiber of my being to take care of me. Even within these risky moments he likes to indulge us in.

"Show me your pussy."

My gaze flicks to the wide-open doorway behind him, and I shake my head. "Storm, no."

"The cuff's on, isn't it? I want to see exactly how wet you are. So you're going to pull those jeans down and tug those panties with them. Just enough so I can see."

"God, you're going to get us into so much trouble." There's absolutely no disguising the way I'm panting for him.

"Says my pretty toy, who's drenched right now." His big hands flex around the tools he's still holding on to as he gestures to a point just behind me. "Now, sit your ass on that saddle stand and show me. I want to see my sweet little cunt."

I have to swallow quickly before wetting my lips. He's serious. With trembling hands, I undo my fly, unzipping and tugging everything down exactly as he instructed. As the material gathers around my thighs, a shudder runs through me when the cool air brushes up against my overheated skin, followed by the hard surface as I rest backward against the wooden stand in the position he wants me to. My heart is pounding with anticipation and eagerness for every scrap of his attention. Loving it when his intensity is so firmly fixated on me.

Storm crouches down on his haunches, still refusing to touch any part of my body. Instead, he sets about inspecting me up close.

Well, shit. That builds the arousal in my core from a simmering heat into a raging blaze. Yet, I can't help but keep on checking the empty space beyond that open door every two seconds.

"Show me properly, darlin'." His voice is dangerously low.

When I drag my gaze back to watch him, those blue eyes have darkened, with his pupils starting to blow out.

I can feel it. The slippery sensation. Why this is turning me on feels insane, but the fact this man has to *see* me, no matter the time or place, leaves me glowing.

"Two hands. Show me just how wet you are."

A whimper falls out of me as I do exactly as he tells me to.

"Oh, darlin', look at how messy you are. Look how ready you are. God, you're just gagging to be squirting all over my tongue and my cock while bent over this saddle stand right now, aren't you?"

"*Please.*" This is driving me into a frenzy, and he damn well knows it.

He hits me with another of those looks that leave me at risk of melting right here on the barn floor, then leans forward. Keeping those eyes firmly locked on mine, Storm tortures me with one lick straight up through my parted pussy lips, humming as he coats his tongue with the taste of me.

I'm absolutely ready to combust. Ready to beg for him to eat me out right here and now and fuck the risk of someone else walking in.

Except he reads all of that in the way I'm damn near writhing to chase his tongue as he settles back on his haunches, and he gives me a devious expression.

"Good girl. Now, back to work."

"Oh my god. Why?" No. He surely cannot be intending to leave me hanging like this. I'm shaking and desperate, and the temptation to finish what he started right here and now is overwhelming.

Standing up, his grin is downright sinful as he takes in the sight of me perched here, completely gone for him. "That's for making us both have to be in agony all day long."

"Come here, darlin.'" Storm's voice is thick with desire. "Full weight. No hovering. Ride my tongue and drown me in that sweetness."

He holds my hips and drags me down onto his mouth as I lose my goddamn mind.

We barely made it through the door. I could see he was about two seconds from pulling the truck over and re-creating our roadside escapades as we made our way down the mountain this evening. Except, something tells me this man had a reason for making sure we got home and locked the door.

By this point, I'm seriously hoping we can hide away from the rest of the world for at least a few days.

We've got a lot of missed time to make up for. Or at least, orgasms to make up for if Storm's intentions are anything to go by.

As his tongue presses forward and roams through my slit, his fingers swipe through my center from beneath, gathering up the slippery wetness there. Only, he doesn't push inside like I expect him to. This time, he drags all that slickness around to my ass and starts to play with me back there. Drawing slow circles at the same time as he mirrors the motion with his clever tongue.

"Oh god." I moan much louder than intended and feel a surge of heat flood my veins.

I look down to a filthy sight, watching him lick me while at the same time studying me closely for my reaction. While that leather cuff around my wrist bone is his permission to use me any way he desires, my cowboy doesn't ever push it too far beyond my realm of experience all in one go.

To be honest, we've been working our way closer to this since I've been back, and while there's no denying I'm nervous, I also haven't been able to stop imagining what it would feel like with him.

I might have done some online research one night after waking up from a particularly intense dream where he'd been buried deep inside my ass, and oh my god, the way my body woke up ready to detonate was something else entirely.

"I want that. I want you. *Please.*" With one hand, I brace myself against the headboard, and with the other, I sink my fingers into his hair, allow my head to drop, and simply let go.

His mouth works miracles on my pussy and reduces me to a quivering mess in no time at all.

Sucking and nipping my flesh in time with the press of his finger, he rubs harder over those sensitive nerve endings, producing a feral noise when I give him exactly what he wants as he sucks down on my clit—making my back bow and dragging out a flood coating his face that I've since learned not to feel so embarrassed by. Especially not when he actively sets about making me squirt for him at any given opportunity.

This man apparently hasn't lost his competitive edge, despite being out of the rodeo arena for so long.

"Stay right there," Storm says in that way he always does, sliding out from beneath my thighs. As if I had the ability to do anything but. I'm sure it's his own private little joke, feeling more than pleased with his efforts to reduce me to a boneless puddle.

The mattress dips behind me as his giant frame moves around, then he's positioned at my back. Reaching around, he hands me my vibrator, already on the setting he knows I like best, and drags a sloppy kiss up the side of my neck.

"You want me to take this sweet little ass while the taste of your pussy is all over my mouth?"

I somehow manage a nod.

"All you gotta do is follow what I tell you, alright? Trust me to know what your body needs."

God, I love this man so much. He's not rushing me, yet he somehow manages to guide me into new states of pleasure time and time again. Pretty sure I murmur something to the effect of how much I missed him and how badly I need him and tell him he can have whatever he wants.

"Rub that all over your clit for me. Slow circles around that tight bud until you fall apart." Of course, I'm already doing that even as he says those words, which draws a deep chuckle out of him.

While I get lost in the way the vibrations roll through my body, he drizzles lube over my ass, causing me to jolt with the unexpectedly cold sensation. He quickly sets to work carrying on the teasing he gave me a glimpse of just before.

It's too good, too addictive, and on reflex, I start pushing back against his hand within the space of a few minutes.

"Baby, I need more," I whine. Everything about this moment is perfect, and right here, right now, I want him to go faster, even though a tiny part of my brain understands why he's not.

"*Shhh.* Just breathe for me. Stay nice and loose." As he rubs and presses against my hole, my body gives way and allows him to slip a finger inside.

The more he gradually works me, those ripples of pleasure keep flowing in every direction, and I'm not going to survive much more of this before my next climax threatens to sweep in.

As the stimulation on my clit tips me over the edge, Storm keeps praising me, telling me the filthy things he knows I want to hear. When I come back to my senses, I can feel the added stretch and pressure now that he's slowly started working another finger inside.

"Goddamn, you're doing so well. Look at you, every part of you fits perfectly, stretched around my ink."

My fingers clench in the sheets as a loud moan falls past my lips.

"Want me to film this for you next time, hmm? Show you how good you look taking me like this?"

He already knows the muffled noises I'm making are an agreement.

Yes. Please. More. Own my entire soul forever.

"Put that toy inside your pussy for me. As far as you can go."

His voice is thick with arousal, and as I do just that, his fingers pull out gently before more gel coats down my seam.

Then, the broad head of him is there, replacing his hand, slowly pressing forward.

Everything turns into bright sparks behind my eyelids. There's a little burn as I keep on yielding to his slow, careful attention to my body. The more he nudges his way forward, the more I get lost in the way he continues talking to me. That deep, velvety tone flows and caresses my skin and makes sure I stay safely with him, even though I might be floating on wave after wave of desire threatening to spirit me away any moment now.

"Breathe, darlin' . . . just like that for me. Keep breathing. We're only gonna go nice and slow." We both let out a groan as his tip slips inside. "Fuck, you're the tightest thing. Relax and let that toy take care of your perfect cunt while I fill this sweet little ass like I know you want me to."

Storm commands my body with precision and the utmost care, and I'm sobbing with pleasure as he pushes deeper, working his way inside me until I can't think straight.

The vibrations extending through my pussy must be driving him insane, too, because each grunt comes louder, and his grip tightens against my hips as we both succumb to the moment.

"Fuck. *Fuck*. It's too good . . . Your hot little ass is squeezing me to death. Fuck yourself with that toy nice and fast now. I need you to come because I'm not gonna last with how good this feels. You have no idea how good this feels." He says the words through gritted teeth, while my whimpering sounds come thick and fast.

I tumble, headlong into a full-body climax that extends through every cell, every muscle, leaving me a shuddering mess in his arms as he wraps me tight with one powerful arm and bands my back against his chest.

There's nothing but pure pleasure and desire and so much love flowing between us as I feel him throb and swell, his length burying deep inside me as he comes and lets out a primal groan in my ear.

We're only hearts thundering and pulses racing and sweat-slicked skin as he tumbles us forward onto the bed. I hardly even register as he helps me pull the vibrator out and turn it off before roaming his hot palms everywhere, kneading my softness and murmuring how much he loves me.

Lying there connected like this feels so undeniably special. As he tilts my face toward his, fusing our mouths together, kissing me long and deep, I can feel every single one of those words.

Fragments of scenes of all of our other stolen moments together fly into my head, back from a time when there wasn't supposed to be anything between us, that night outside his truck when he kissed me for the first time—it all swoops in and cradles me so sweetly.

This man, our life together, it's so much more than anything I could have dared imagine.

I'm ready for an eternity more of learning exactly how this kind of love is supposed to be.

BONUS EPILOGUE

Storm

Anticipation crackles in my veins, lighting a trail right down to the soles of my boots. The hum of my truck's engine intermingles with that bonfire feeling popping and sparking in my bloodstream. That all-too-familiar sense of anticipation brought about whenever days like today transpire. The hours on end when I've had to go without seeing my girl.

Look, I want more than anything for Briar to have a life of her own. Being with her, getting to be part of her orbit, isn't about always being glued at the hip. As much as I love the way we get to work together, I'm the first one to insist she nurtures her passions, sees her dreams brought to reality, and doesn't restrict those ideas from shining.

But I'm also selfish as fuck and hate the days when she's gone. Even if it's for a good cause, like the assortment of rescue horses she's busy accumulating.

The truth of it all is that any day spent without Briar reminds me too much of a time when I didn't know if she was going to come back.

As I pull up, the cabin glows, illuminated by the late summer evening. A twinkling spot amongst these trees and mountains that for a long time in my life always sat lifeless and cold. A bleak sort of existence that used to be nothing more than days spent with only the sound of a hammer against metal for company. Another way that my girl has brought color to my world.

Briar has been away for the day with Layla. They've been visiting some potential sponsors and working on plans for the equine therapy program they're building together. As much as I'm insanely proud of everything she's managing to achieve with the horses and the people she's helping when they come to sessions . . . I'm itching to see her.

As I park my truck and head inside, I pull up the video already loaded up on my phone so I'm ready to show her. I just know she's going to lose it over the clip. One where her boy Teddy politely accepted a cut-up apple from Beau earlier this morning, leaving the guy looking like the smuggest prick on the planet behind that goddamn mustache of his, only for Teddy to damn near take a chunk out of Beau's hat straight after.

Best part of it all was that, in his scramble to save his hat, Beau ended up on his ass in the water trough. A full dunking. And Sage was right there to get the entire thing in high-resolution, on camera.

The grin grows wider on my face as I pause the video on the still frame that shows his expression, ready to show her . . . and yet, as I close the front door behind me, something even more appealing than the sight of his 'stache disappearing into a horse trough catches my attention.

Singing.

Immediately, all thoughts of my phone and watching Beau Heartford take an unexpected bath go out the window. Quickly setting everything aside, I make my way through the cabin as quietly as possible, following the sound of her voice. Briar, in the bathroom singing to herself, brings me straight back to memories of that fateful night. In the here and now, it's warm and an orange sunset streaks above the mountains, coloring the sky in pastel shades overhead. Yet, I can't help but compare it to a time when all that was here was goddamn snow and this place resembled a pitch-black ice box.

Further evidence of just how much everything has changed since I've had Briar in my world. How much I've changed for the better, too.

As I draw closer, I can't help but smirk thinking of that occasion that feels like a hundred years ago, that first meeting that was not too dissimilar to this moment.

Now, creeping to where the door stands wide open, I lean one shoulder up against the doorframe and soak her in for a long, greedy moment where I can enjoy watching her before she notices I'm here. My girl is a fucking goddess, hair spilling in long waves over her smooth skin, wrapped in a towel . . . with only my cuff wrapped securely around her wrist.

She has her back turned, and she hums to herself while scooping that silky mane of dark hair up into a bun.

"Oh, you made my job too easy for me, darlin.'" Reaching behind my neck, I tug my T-shirt over my head in one motion.

Briar squeaks with surprise, jerking around to see me shedding my clothes at record speed. She laughs as I throw the bunched-up fabric on the floor and immediately start undoing my belt.

"Let me teach you this important lesson . . ." My lips curve as I watch her eyes track the movement of my fingers. Openly staring at the fly of my jeans. "A lesson on how to conserve water while taking a shower."

She's adorable, blushing as usual, and yet she has that same hunger in her eyes that I feel at all times where my girl is concerned. There's no getting enough of Briar.

Reaching out, I catch the edge of her towel, but instead of letting me rip it from her, she shrieks and giggles and shakes her head before trying to push me away.

"Uh, uh. You can shower alone, cowboy." Her fingers cling tight to the towel, refusing to let it fall. "Don't pout at me. You're a big boy." She huffs, something slightly nervous in her smile.

And yes, I'm absolutely fucking pouting.

I stand over her, allowing my thumb to run back and forth across her slender wrist, nudging at the edge of the leather band. This is new territory. We haven't come up against a situation where Briar hasn't been clear with me, and I've only ever respected her wishes if she's taken the cuff *off*.

My girl studies my expression, then rolls her eyes. "It's just . . ." She swallows and darts her tongue out to wet her bottom lip before glancing at the shower curtain. "I just don't want to get *wet* is all."

That has me swooping on that single statement like a hawk. "Why does it feel like you're hiding something?" Tugging her body closer, one of my hands swoops around her rib cage, and she winces as soon as my grip tightens on her figure.

Her face screws up and my stomach plummets through the floor. "What's wrong? Are you hurt? What happened to you today?" Within a split second, I gather her body, scooping her up so that she's sitting on the vanity. Another of those pained looks tightens her features when I bracket both sides of her ribs in order to lift her.

Briar puffs out a little whine, a slight hitch in her breathing, and squeezes my forearms, holding on tightly to me. "I wanted to *surprise* you."

"Well, right now you're about to surprise me with a fucking heart attack, darlin' . . . so for the love of all things unholy, just put me outta my misery."

Those dark eyes of hers dance between my own as she nibbles her bottom lip. My pulse is goddamn racing for the sky the longer she weighs telling me whatever the fuck is going on right now. Finally, fucking finally, she lets go of her vise grip on the towel. "Go on then. I should've known you'd be impossible to keep this from."

Swallowing thickly, I reach forward to pinch the edge of the towel. Yet I stall. As much as I damn well need to know, I'm stuck, immobile. On the inside, I'm damn well reeling at the thought of Briar being hurt. This takes me straight back to the day I found her lying on ice when she'd slipped over and knocked herself out with that fall. This is every moment I don't hear back from her straight away when I text and convince myself something bad has happened and I haven't been there to protect her. This is all the times she's had to drive somewhere on her own during winter and I've spent the entire time stressing until I hear that she made it safely to where she needs to be.

She cups my face. "Don't go pale on me. It's nothing bad, baby. *Promise.*"

"You're freaking me out," I admit quietly, thumbing the towel.

"I just wanted to pick a moment to surprise you with something . . . looks like you're too quick for me, as always." Her fingers play across my jaw and brush my stubble. "Forever my headstrong bull rider who knows no limits."

That has me picking up her wrist, the one with the cuff, eyeing her with a narrowed expression. "No limits? I think that might be a little rich, coming from you, darlin'."

"Complaining?" Her lips tug up at the corners.

Leaning forward to dust my lips against the side of her neck, I run my mouth across her fluttering pulse, slowly feathering kisses until I find the shell of her ear. "I'd be six feet under and still trying to find ways to make you scream my name. I could have no pulse and still crave your moans. You wouldn't hear a complaint out of me even if I was dead and buried, because I'd still find a way to explore your *limits.*"

As a shudder takes hold of her body, this time I yank the towel away.

The sight that's revealed leaves the air rushing from my lungs like it did any of the times I ever hit the dirt in the arena.

All I can do is stare.

Curving below the text already there—the permanent reminder to *flourish* written just below her breast years before I ever came along—is a new tattooed line.

"Stôrmand Lane."

Scrubbing a hand over my mouth, I'm not sure if I remember words anymore. Pretty sure my mind has melted.

"Do you like it?" My girl's voice is soft, a little hesitant, and I'm certain that I've lost all sensation in my limbs. Every ounce of blood coursing through my veins pounds harder than ever as I see my name freshly inked there.

"Oh . . . I'll just—" She tries to cover it up, sounding apologetic.

I cut her off.

Taking her face in both hands, cupping her cheeks, I seal our mouths together. A hard, desperate press of my lips against that perfect mouth. As I do so, a ragged noise breathes from my lungs, straight into hers. It's all I can do not to straight up maul her. I focus instead on dropping kisses everywhere, tracing her brow, her nose, her cheeks.

"Fuck, darlin' . . ." *Kiss.* "You're stunning . . ." *Kiss.* "The most beautiful fucking thing . . ." *Kiss.* "What did I ever do to deserve you?"

She hums with a tiny giggle, her relief evident now as she tries to catch my mouth with her own. "I thought you didn't like it for a second." Her exhale is filled with a little more levity now that my brain has come back online.

"Like it?" I pull back, one hand still caressing her soft cheek, as I crane my neck to look at the tattoo again. Brushing the edge of the clear protective wrap with my fingertips, I examine it closer this time.

My tattooed fingers bearing her name run over the

see-through bandage. Her name on my skin, my name now on hers.

The weight of something so special, this gift she's given me, has my heart damn well ready to explode.

"It's perfect." My throat feels raw as I barely get a whisper out. "You're perfect."

"My cowboy needed his home . . . marked permanently," she whispers back.

Something roars deep inside my chest, pride and the deepest, most soul-stealing love for this girl. Beyond anything I could ever try to put into words or explain. And it's also in that moment that all that fiercely possessive worry about her rises to the surface.

Taking her face in both hands, I pin her gaze beneath my own. "Where did you get it done? Who did the work? Why didn't you tell me? I should have been there. Did they give you numbing cream for it? Did you eat before—"

Briar shakes her head, a bright smile widening despite my grilling her for details. "I went to your guy." She lightly taps the space on my knuckles adorned with her name.

"Good." My teeth clench. That's acceptable, I guess.

"Linda was able to fit me in." His wife. She's got an excellent hand. Another positive.

"Me and Layla went for ice cream afterward . . . Does that make you happy?"

"Partly. But I still should have been there to make sure they took care of you properly." I can't help grumbling about it. As much as I'm so in awe of her for wanting to do this for me as a surprise, the worry about her not being treated well during a tattoo or it not being cleaned properly after . . .

Briar laughs at me, watching the way my mind so obviously races behind my eyes. She strokes my stubble, then presses her fingers to my lips. "*I love you.* Thank you for being so concerned . . . How about you come with me for my next one?"

"You want more?"

She nods, a shimmer hitting her eyes. "I was thinking we could get something matching?"

"Done." I kiss her delicate fingertips.

"You don't even want to know what I was thin—"

"Don't need to. Whatever you want. I'm in."

"Okay, Mr. Romantic." She grins at me, then tilts her head to one side, teeth catching her bottom lip. "Are horseshoes too cliché?"

Leaning down to rest my hands either side of her hips on the vanity, I drop our foreheads together, inhaling every sweet scent of my girl.

"You could tattoo anything you like on me, anywhere you like, and I'd only ever say thank you."

It's the entire truth. She's already inked indelibly on my heart that belongs to her.

"You know I'll never stop finding ways to tell you how much I love you. I'll only ever say thank you for letting me love you, darlin'."

ACKNOWLEDGMENTS

Crimson Ridge holds my heart, and this series has completely changed my life as an author. I'm incredibly grateful to every single reader who has taken a chance on my cowboys and their swoony, forbidden love stories set among the mountains.

When I think of Crimson Ridge and the journey it has taken to bring these books to life, there is no one I need to thank more than Mr. Rose. No one is more supportive, patient, and forever by my side throughout this journey. Thank you for being there when I need to talk endlessly about fictional characters, for embracing the chaos that comes along with having an author on a deadline in your life (who may or may not need to be lovingly reminded to eat a meal, drink water, and get some sleep), and for being the first person to always tell me to pursue my creative dreams. I love you with everything I have. This one is for you.

Thank you to Kensington Books for taking such great care of our cowboys. We know they can handle a little rough ridin' (and most definitely enjoy it too) however, when it comes to books, there is a whole lot of careful attention and gentle handling needed. I'm so thankful for all the hard work and collaborations behind the scenes to bring these stories to readers everywhere.

To my agent, Nikki Groom, your boy Uncle Storm is HERE and looking more gorgeous than ever. Thank you for all your tireless work to champion Crimson Ridge and help this series soar to new heights.

Sandra, your talent for creating beautiful book covers never ceases to amaze me. I truly am in awe of your gift for taking my ramblings and turning them into a swoonworthy work of art.

Of course, much like a rodeo, bringing a book like this to life takes an entire village behind the scenes. To my team helping keep the wheels turning and all the plates spinning—particularly when I have to disappear for deadlines—you are absolute angels. I'm so endlessly grateful for everything you do. Thank you to my editors, alpha, beta, and early readers; you are absolute magic. The love you have poured into these two is so deeply appreciated.

To everyone who has shared about this book, hyped, ever so gently insisted on a bestie reading it (or crashed into their inbox holding Uncle Storm aloft), you are just so damn special. Crimson Ridge wouldn't be here without your excitement and enthusiasm.

From the bottom of my heart, and from Uncle Zaddy Storm and our girl Briar . . . we send you all our love.

xo

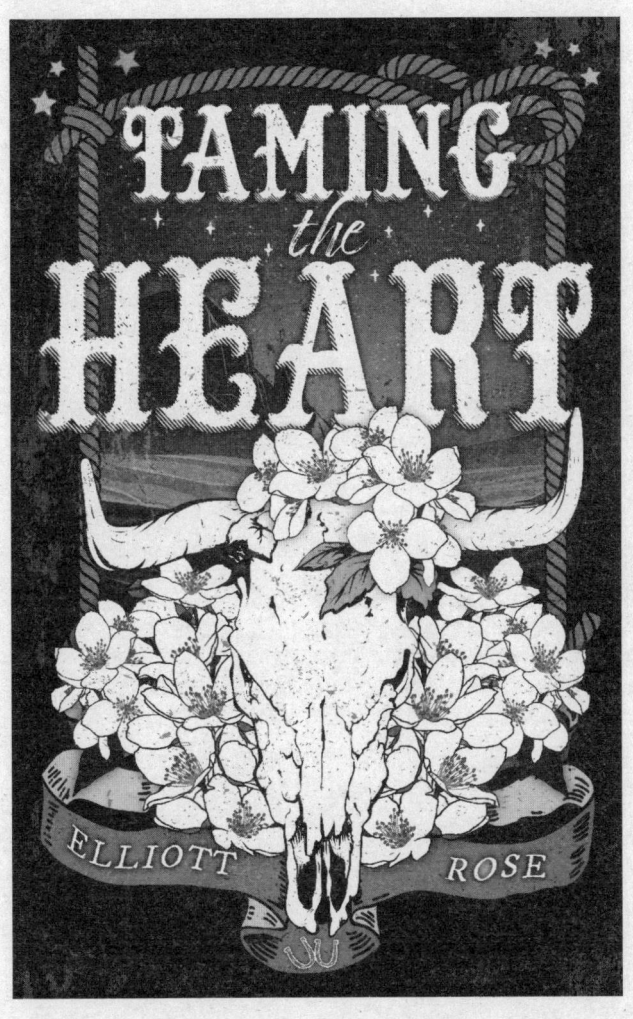

TAMING
the
HEART

ELLIOTT   ROSE

Ready for a sneak peek at the next book
in the Crimson Ridge series?

KEEP READING . . .

CHAPTER 1

"**C**ome here, you cocksucking little slut."

My head whips up from mindlessly scrolling on my phone, jerking on reflex at the sound of the female voice yelling from opposite me on the sidewalk.

Goddamn. I'm in my biggest hoodie, even though it's seventy-eight out, with my cap pulled as low as possible. The last thing I need is some crazed fan thinking they know anything about me or my life to launch a tirade of obscenities in my face.

I'm in the process of moving back to Crimson Ridge to get *away* from the city psychos. Not having them running at me yelling weird shit in public just to try and get me reacting a certain way on camera.

My hackles raise, and my teeth clench to match the way my fist wraps around my phone. I cast a furtive glance around to see what the hell is taking Tessa so long.

"*Aghhh.* Fuck you. Don't you dare."

The voice gets louder, and a series of thudding noises helps me pinpoint where the source of the commotion is originating from.

I'm standing with my ass resting on the hood of my truck. It would be an easy escape to hop in the driver's side and lock the door, which I'm about two seconds from doing when a waterfall of crap spills down the steps of the art gallery storefront a few paces directly in front of me.

"You motherfucking, cheap whore, piece of shit."

A whirlwind of long black hair, black jeans, and black boots to match comes into sight, clattering down the flight of stairs while chasing after an explosion of belongings. Whoever this is has their hands full with a to-go coffee in one, a cell phone in the other, as the contents of their handbag—which seems large enough to comfortably contain a small dog—are busy forming a tsunami of personal items down the flight of steps.

The bottom of the world's largest purse has busted apart, leaving everything inside to imitate a tumbling bag of marbles pouring down the staircase, with her shit busy flying in all directions.

Shoving my phone in my back pocket, I take a couple of steps forward. The least I can do is stop this lady's stuff from rolling straight out into the street.

"This is what you do to me? After everything? Little bitch." She's bent double, trying to trap notebooks and pens and highlighters from skittering down the steps using only her feet. While the useless bag with no ass hangs limply at her side.

I have to bite my tongue not to laugh. She hasn't even noticed I'm here gathering up as many bits and pieces as I can in an effort to help.

Another quick glance up and down the sidewalk confirms that Crimson Ridge is just as sleepy and unpopulated as ever, so at least there's no one lurking or watching this all unfold.

Surely, even if someone passed by, they wouldn't recognize me with my hat pulled low. Or, at the very least, they'd have to get right up close before they made a connection as to why I look vaguely familiar.

Still crouched down, I start gathering up shit like her water bottle, more pens—Jesus, how many pens does one woman need—fluttering receipts that threaten to disappear into the gutter. I quietly tuck as much as I can under one arm.

Darting a glance up, I see that she's set the coffee down and is busy scooping up items off the stairs, hidden behind a curtain of shiny, dark hair.

I can't see her face. What I can see, however, is a fantastic ass. Curvy thighs and figure-hugging charcoal denim that makes sexy-as-hell creases just below her waist. A simple black tank skims the high waistband, and holy shit, that's when I realize my eyes have drifted up. The side profile of an incredible pair of breasts hidden beneath silky fabric leaves my mouth dry and the back of my neck heating instantly.

Fuck.

This is not the time or the place to get busted gaping like a horny teenager at a pretty girl on the main street of Crimson Ridge.

Dropping my eyes, I do a final sweep of the sidewalk, and it seems like I've mindlessly gathered up just about everything while down on my haunches. I clear my throat in order to grab her attention, since she's still muttering obscenities at her handbag beneath her breath and doesn't seem to have noticed that I'm right here.

I'm preparing to thrust everything into her arms and beat a hasty retreat to hop in my truck, when she seems to finally notice my boots where I'm standing before her. One hand whips up, flicking her loose waves out of the way, and fucking hell… honeyed, dark eyes meet mine.

There's a flash to them. A spark catches me entirely off guard.

"Oh, Jesus. You saw all of that? What a clusterfuck." She stands up and dusts her palms on the front of her jeans in the process. There's no double take, no lingering curiosity. This girl just matter-of-factly tucks her hair behind one ear and huffs out a frustrated breath.

"You ok?" I suddenly remember how to form words.

"Me? I'm fine. This bag, however, is going to be sacrificed on a ritual bonfire at the soonest possible opportunity." She nudges at it with the pointed toe of her black cowboy boot. They're cute and suit the all-black look she's got going on, but aren't overly girly either. It certainly looks like the couple of inches of heel she's sporting could stomp on hearts without a second thought.

"Here." One syllable is about all I can offer. Why am I suddenly tongue-tied?

She meets my eyes again, then drops her gaze down to where I'm still clutching a bundle of items rescued from the exploding handbag situation.

As I hold out my fist, her eyes widen, drawing my gaze to see what she's reacting to. Immediately, my gut clenches because my first instinct is to consider that maybe she's recognized me after all . . .

"Oh, well, aren't you a real gentleman cowboy."

My brows scrunch together, a little confused, trying to figure out her meaning.

Clutched in my palm is a small drawstring bag. It's gold, velvety fabric, and something juts from the top where the strings haven't been pulled tight. A purple silicone curve peeks out.

"Huh?" Confusion must be etched all over my face. As she arches one eyebrow at me, followed by that pretty mouth of hers tipping into a wicked smirk, my slow-ass fucking brain catches up with the play.

I'm standing on the sidewalk, waving this girl's vibrator around like a hot dog vendor at a ballpark.

Her *wearable* vibrator.

The tips of my ears start to singe. What the fuck am I supposed to do? Tuck it neatly back inside the pouch before handing it over like it's a goddamn credit card to settle the tab while out for dinner?

"Do they not have toys to play with in this little part of the mountains?" Bright flecks of amber glow in amongst the rich ochre of her eyes, which in turn match the deeper, sun-bronzed brown of her skin.

"Cat got your tongue, hot stuff? You know, it's got ten different speeds and customizable settings. It also does this awesome pattern if you set the mode just right where it really makes your eyes roll back."

Her head cocks to one side, almost as if she's daring me to touch it, or not touch it. I don't fucking know. What I do know is that there is a place beyond the tenth level of hell awaiting me if I get snapped in a compromising position like this.

"Shame really." Mystery girl makes the decision for me, reaching out to pluck the bag and its contents from my hand. "As much as I'd love to give you a Ted talk about finding a woman's clit before I've even had a drop of caffeine, alas, I've got places to be."

With no more than a shrug and a wink, she tucks the toy away and pulls the side strings to seal up the bag. Not a hint of embarrassment or shame or annoyance at this situation. We could be standing here discussing horse feed for how casual this girl is. She's entirely unbothered, and I'm rendered speechless. Officially incapable of forming a coherent string of words in her presence.

No hysterical behavior to contend with. No toddler-like tantrums, threats, stomping around, or insisting on calling a publicist on speed dial at the first sign of a minor inconvenience. At the prospect of a *public* scene that doesn't fit the carefully crafted persona.

It's . . . refreshing. Like settling down in the cool grass, finding relief in the shade after a long afternoon spent in the saddle beneath the baking sun.

"Wow. Really melted your brain there, didn't I, cowboy?"

I clear my throat. "I don't need the Ted talk."

A devastating curl touches her lips as she looks me up and down.

"Sure about that?"

"You betcha." My skin prickles, and the words come out sounding a whole lot like a grown man growling, even to my own ears.

Mystery girl looks mighty pleased with herself for continuing to get under my skin. Meanwhile, I'm still clutching half her crap, minus the wearable fucking vibrator I'm not gonna be able to stop wondering about now.

Why does she have it in her purse?

Does she use it often?

What does it look like nestled inside her soft pussy?

Christ. Stop. This is not a drill, I need to exit through the emergency doors right this instant.

"Well, since you're standing there stumped by a vibrator, can you at the very least do a gal a solid and point me in the direction of where I might find myself something to shove all this crap in? Better yet, could you be a country gentleman and duck into the gallery upstairs and see if they've maybe got a cardboard box or something?"

She clamps the velvet bag between her teeth, freeing up both hands and proceeds to relieve me of all the things I'm still holding onto. As she steps closer, her scent drips into my awareness, hitting my senses like a dropper from a vial. It doesn't just gently breeze in, no, the fragrance of wild orange and honeysuckle demands my attention and floods my veins. Just like everything about this girl, it's not a performance. It's purely magnetic and sexy, and holy fucking shit, I absolutely cannot be looking at this girl with that bag tucked between her plush lips and its sinfully hot package inside, thinking these thoughts.

Even if I wanted to, I can't.

Even though I *want* to.

Clearing my throat like it's full of rust, I readjust my cap, squeezing the brim. "Wait there."

Turning on my heel, I duck and look around on reflex. Town

is still deserted. There are a couple of older ladies on the opposite side of the street, but they're busy chatting amongst themselves as they walk. From the other direction, a vehicle draws closer, and I dip my chin. Better to be on the safe side.

My grip wrenches open the back door to my truck, and I fist the duffel sitting on the floor. Upending it without so much as a second look, I let my own things tumble out, then proceed to head back to the far-too-beautiful girl who I am absolutely not looking at in any way.

I'm helping a stranger. This is just me doing a good deed.

Not like I'm desperate to ask her name or find out if she works in town or something insane like that.

"Lovely." Her eyes roll as I shove the faded canvas into her hands. "Do I get to keep your sweaty gym socks, too?"

"Best I could do. Left my spare designer purse back at the ranch."

She's crouched down now, shoving everything in the bag. As I stand there grumbling and trying not to stare at the patch of skin on her spine between the waistband of her jeans and the hem of her top, she hits me with a quirked little smile, plush lips twitching, and my asshole cock gets far too interested in this scene.

A pretty girl with fire in her eyes kneeling in front of me.

I have to cough into my fist and think about the last time I had my nuts nearly crushed during a gnarly ride.

"I'm not gonna find a dirty jockstrap you've stuffed in here as a memento, am I?" Her nose scrunches as she efficiently shoves everything in and zips up my duffel. I guess her duffel now.

"No. Maybe just a cock ring, if you're lucky." The retort is out of me before I can do anything to stop it. Fuck it, I want this girl to know I'm not boring, I'm not usually so tongue-tied, and I certainly don't want her thinking I'm a stuffy old country bumpkin.

"Well, if the wearable fits…" Laughing a little, she stands up then slings the strap over her shoulder. With one hand now reacquainted with her coffee, the other shoves her phone into a back pocket, and then she sticks out her palm.

This is the moment, right here, when I could take her hand and shake it and feel how soft her touch might be in contrast to that sharp tongue.

It's tempting, hovering right there. Urging me on and recklessly goading me into doing the thing I shouldn't do—the thing I can't do considering my life and my circumstances—to ask for her name, her phone number.

Her eyes hold mine, flickering for just a second as if a force is tugging her gaze; she's fighting it as we stand in the middle of the sidewalk with only an arm's length between us.

Just as I lift my hand, reaching out to take her extended palm, just as I see the split second when her gaze falls to my mouth, another arm snakes through the crook of my elbow.

My fingers curl into a clenched fist, dropping back to my side like a stone.

"Hi, babe. Sorry I took so long."

I watch as my mystery girl's eyes bounce rapid-fire taking in the woman glued to my side, flicking down to where her arm threads through, interlinking with mine, before landing with a thud on the spectacular diamond adorning her left ring finger.

Before I can say a word, she plasters on a polite veneer. "Right. Well… thanks for the help. You guys have a good one." Her smile flashes with a tightness to it, a glance that avoids my eyes, and she whips around on her heel.

All I see is a last flutter of her dark mane and smooth brown skin as she rounds the corner and disappears out of sight with my bag slung over her shoulder.

"Jesus, Tessa. Did you fucking have to?" I wrench my arm away. "Babe? Really?"

"Oh, excuse me, Beau Heartford, for doing my job."

My goddamn sister flutters her eyelashes at me, thinly

disguising an eye roll. The extensions I pay for, along with her fabulous salary for being the best damn manager I could have ever hoped for.

Doesn't change the fact that she's my baby sister and gets on my every last nerve.

"You don't have to do that every time, you know." I hiss, well aware there's a black cloud forming over my head.

"Oh, shit…" Tessa's blue-gray eyes, the ones that match my own, widen. "Were you into her? I can go get her number if you want?"

"No. It's fine. Leave it be." Shaking my head, I hurl myself into the driver's seat of my truck. My sister has been running interference for me for just about my entire pro career. Keeping the buckle bunnies and overzealous fans away with her well-oiled routine of flashing that damn rock on her finger and clinging to my arm like an octopus.

"You sure?" She slides into the passenger side, studying the side of my face like she always does.

My teeth grind, and I white-knuckle the steering wheel. Nope. That girl is too young. A PR nightmare waiting to happen. I'm not interested in looking for anything but some peace by finally moving out here, and if that means being on my own, then so be it.

"You done all the shit you need to do?"

"Jeez. Let's make a stop to get you a coffee or something on our way outta town, because I sure ain't paid enough to put up with your grumpy ass."

Tessa's phone rings, and as she takes the call, I can feel her give the side of my head a glare before cheerily greeting her husband on the other end of the line.

As I pull out into the quiet main street lined with lush trees and flanked by all the quaint goddamn store frontages that make up Crimson Ridge, my head pounds.

Fuck the circumstances I've found myself in. Fuck the world and their opinions and their incessant need to demand I be someone I'm not.

I'm going to put all that just happened clear out of my mind. I have to.

I'm not going to cheat on my wife.

On a station platform, with nothing to read,
and a four-hour train journey stretching ahead of him...

That's where the story began for Penguin founder Allen Lane.
With only 'shabby reprints of shoddy novels' on offer,
he resolved to make better books for readers everywhere.

By the time his train pulled into London, the idea was formed.
He would bring the best writing, in stylish and affordable
formats, to everyone. His books would be sold in bookstores,
stationers and tobacconists, for no more than the price
of a ten-pack of cigarettes.

And on every book would be a Penguin, a bird with a certain
'dignified flippancy', and a friendly invitation to anyone who
wished to spend their time reading.

In 1935, the first ten Penguin paperbacks were published.
Just a year later, three million Penguins had made their
way onto our shelves.

Reading was changed forever.

—

A lot has changed since 1935, including Penguin, but in the
most important ways we're still the same. We still believe that
books and reading are for everyone. And we still believe that
whether you're seeking an afternoon's escape, a vigorous debate
or a soothing bedtime story, all possibilities open with a book.

Whoever you are, whatever you're looking for,
you can find it with Penguin.